T0384329

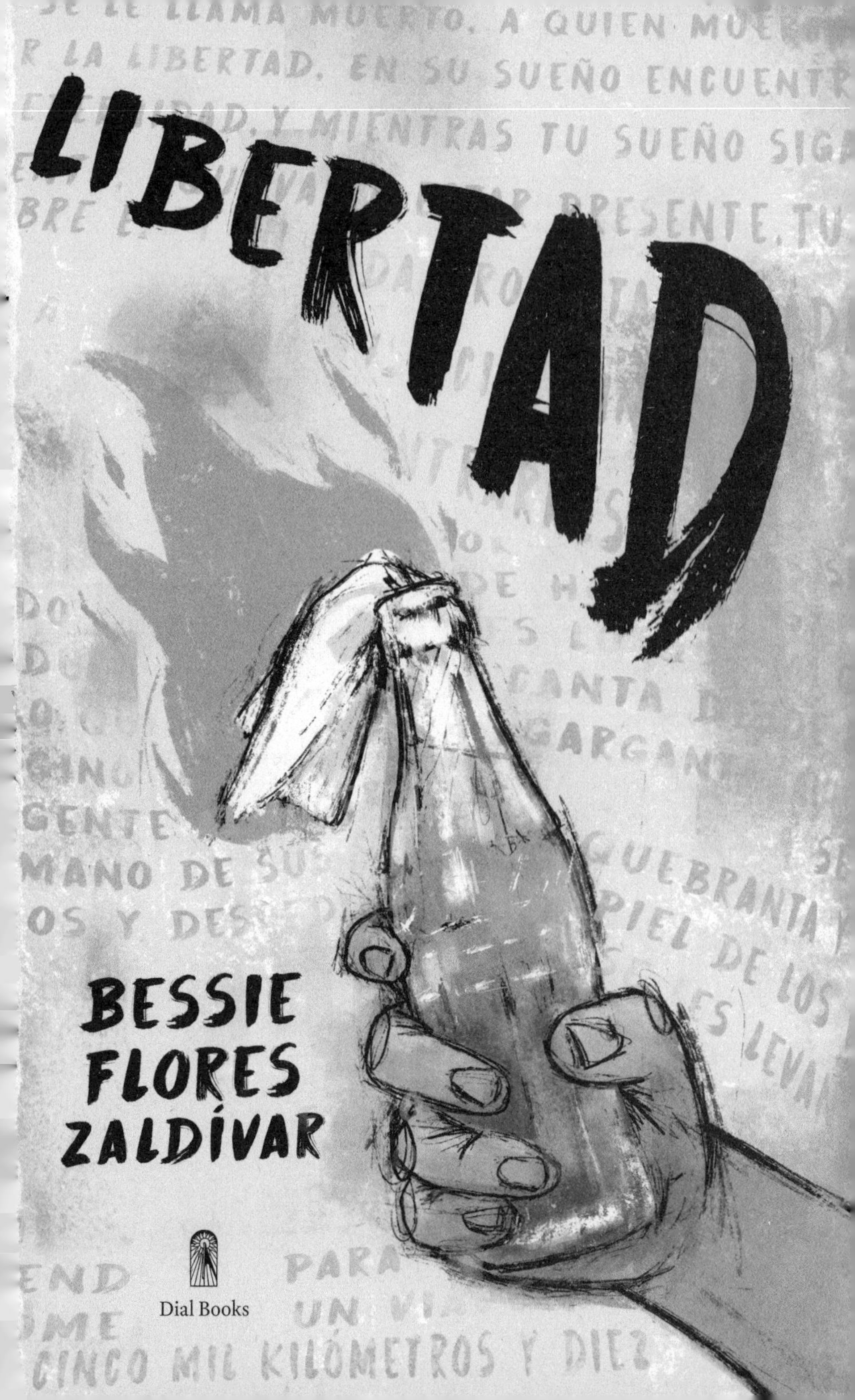
LIBERTAD
BESSIE
FLORES
ZALDÍVAR
Dial Books

Dɪᴀʟ Bᴏᴏᴋs
An imprint of Penguin Random House LLC
1745 Broadway, New York, New York 10019

First published in the United States of America by Dial Books, an imprint of Penguin
Random House LLC, 2024
Copyright © 2024 by Bessie Flores Zaldívar

Visit us online at PenguinRandomHouse.com.

Library of Congress Cataloging-in-Publication Data is available.
Printed in the United States of America

ISBN 9780593696125

10 9 8 7 6 5 4 3 2 1

BVG

Design by Maya Tatsukawa
Text set in Laurentian Pro

This book is a work of fiction. Any references to historical events, real people, or real
places are used fictitiously. Other names, characters, places, and events are products
of the author's imagination, and any resemblance to actual events or places or
persons, living or dead, is entirely coincidental.

The publisher does not have any control over and does not assume any responsibility
for author or third-party websites or their content.

Para mi mamá, María: mi primer amor

Y para Emo y Fer: ser su hermana mayor
es lo más bonito que me dio la vida

Please know that *Libertad* depicts and engages with subject matter that may be distressing and triggering for some readers. A list of these subjects can be found on the next page.

This story includes mentions and descriptions of state-sanctioned police brutality and intimidation, gun violence, murder, homophobia, domestic violence, misogyny, death of a close family member, possible sexual assault, and illegal/unwanted distribution of intimate photos.

Tegucigalpa de noche y día
Como me dueles toda
—Juana Pavón

When does a war end? When can I say your name
and have it mean only your name and not
what you left behind?
—Ocean Vuong

PROLOGUE

FEBRUARY 2017

"This fucking city," Camila breathed, rolling her eyes that way she did, fast and loud—like this fucking city.

She shifted, trying to turn to look behind us. The end of her spine dug into my thigh at a painful angle. "Sorry, Libertad," she said, squeezing my wrist. I could taste the vanilla in her perfume, sweet but sharp in my mouth.

I followed her line of vision. We watched the cop walk back to the police car, Miguel's student ID in hand. There was something measured in the way he moved his body. An evident relishing in the flow of his stroll.

My older brother, Maynor, often said Tegucigalpa was best understood by a single rule: la ley del más fuerte, *the law of the strongest*. The refrain came to him often while driving—when it was clear that stoplights and traffic regulations were not the dominant language in the streets of la capital. Rather, it was the driver with the biggest car—or least scared of a wreck—who set the pace.

In the driver's seat, Miguel also turned his whole body around to look at Carla and Valeria in the back seat. Valeria was trying her best to keep it together—lips pursed and long, thoughtful blinks, like she was finding a way out of this behind her eyes. Her parents, like my mother, would kill her if we ended up having to call them.

Miguel shrugged. "I told y'all I didn't have a license."

The streetlight caught the upper half of his face, emphasizing the sharp bridge of his nose.

"Why don't you just call your dad and put him on speaker? He can tell the cop he let you borrow the car. And that you turn eighteen in, like, three weeks," Carla suggested. The mascara she had applied minutes before brought out the desperation in her eyes.

"I'm driving at night without a license, in a car not registered to my name, with four underage girls. *And* just look at y'all." Miguel ran his fingers through his still-damp hair. His eyes swept the car. "I can't even tell him we're driving home. We clearly look ready for pijín. Oh, and Camila's sitting on Libertad's lap in the passenger's seat—neither of them wearing a seat belt. That's, like, at least four violations."

"Okay, okay," Valeria said, turning around to look at the police car. The cop stood next to la patrulla, leaning against the driver's door, plugging Miguel's student ID into some system in his car. "Just give him what he wants."

"I don't have that much money on me." Miguel sighed. "So unless all of you help me come up with at least two thousand Lempiras— we're fucked."

"Fine." Valeria shoved at the boxes pressed against her hip. She and Carla barely fit in the back seat around all the junk, hence the seating arrangement with Cami in my lap. "It's better than the alternative."

El chepo strolled back to the car and knocked on Miguel's window. Miguel rolled it down so quick the squeaking of the handle barely registered. The breeze of the night hit Camila's bare thighs. She rubbed her arms—up and down. Behind the cop, the city lights of Tegucigalpa blinked its hundred eyes.

"Bueno," the officer said, handing Miguel his student ID. "You're not supposed to be driving without a license, and I don't believe you're eighteen. I don't believe *any* of you are. Also, what these two señoritas are doing"—he gestured toward Cami and me in the passenger's seat—"is dangerous. I'll need to impound the vehicle and detain all of you until your legal guardians can claim you."

Miguel took a deep breath. I wondered, then, if he wished there was another guy in the car—someone who might help him do the talking. The police officer's eyes moved between us girls, a glint of hunger in his gaze. Miguel swallowed.

"I understand, Officer Ortiz," he said, glancing at the silver name tag clipped to his left pectoral. "But that's a lot of paperwork for you. And we're just kids, you know?" Miguel stopped for a second to scratch the back of his neck. "We're not up to nada malo. The girls and I were talking, and maybe we can fix this another way. We know how poorly the government pays hard-working police officers . . ."

Ortiz's eyes lit up. Bingo.

"¿Qué proponen?" Ortiz leaned in, pressing his left arm against the top of the window frame. His breath reeked of stale cigarette smoke and onions.

Miguel pulled back a little. "How about . . . two thousand Lempiras, for your trouble? And I promise I'll get my license sorted out soon. We're not going far. My friend here"—he gestured to Camila—"just didn't fit in the back. But it won't happen again."

Ortiz stared into the car for what felt like a minute but couldn't have been more than a few seconds. He licked his lips. There was a frogginess to his features.

I dug my nails into my palm. If he didn't go for it, we were screwed. Add attempted bribery to the list.

Ortiz heaved a sigh and pulled away from the car. "Bueno," he said, throwing his hands up in surrender. "If that's what you can offer . . . I'll take it."

There was a defeated annoyance to his tone, like we had swindled him, made him waste his time.

I wondered what Maynor would say about the law of the strongest right now. Was money the exception to the rule? Or did money determine who the strongest was, who held all the power in any given situation?

Miguel reached for the wallet in his back pocket. He had to lift his body from the seat to get it, bending his head to avoid hitting the roof.

"Come on." He turned to the rest of us. "It's four hundred each."

My shoulders dropped. Yes, this left me with less than a hundred crumpled Lempiras for the rest of the night—but still, better than the alternative. The four of us handed Miguel the purple and yellow bills, wrinkled from being shoved in pockets or pressed against waistbands.

The cop grabbed the cash and shoved it into his front pocket, not bothering to count any of it.

"Buenas noches," he said, slapping the roof of the car twice before turning back. Miguel started the engine. As he moved away from the curb, Camila turned the radio's volume back up. Reggaeton filled the car, pierced by Carla's and Valeria's exploding laughter. Warmth rushed through my veins.

"This fucking city," Cami repeated, laughing this time.

"Guess I'm not drinking tonight," I said. "'Cause that was all my money."

"Same," Valeria echoed.

"We'll figure something out." Carla shrugged. "Además . . . una aventura es más divertida si huele a peligro, right?" She loved quoting that Romeo Santos song.

Maybe it was the tamarind Quetzalteca shot we all had before getting in Miguel's car. Or Camila's weight and exposed skin on mine. Or Carla's laughter soaring out the windows. I found myself saying, "Right. Ahuevos, maje."

We rolled the windows down. The night was a hot blanket over us. Miguel drove up Lomas del Guijarro, right hand on the wheel, left elbow resting on the window's ledge. Cool night breeze on our faces, strands of hair stuck to our lip-glossed mouths.

I'd heard Tegus described as a hole my whole life. Climbing up Las Lomas, the dentation was visible. Mountains devoured the horizon in all directions, and at their feet began the snaking roads and concrete bridges, which had multiplied by a dozen in the past few years. Gray had overtaken much of the green—but still, trees'

5

canopies stuck out between structures. Fuchsia bougainvillea burst over walls. Air plants grew on cables. Cables: Those were everywhere. Looped from post to post, around houses, between trees, and sometimes clumped together in a black winding ball that weighed down whatever it clung to.

At the base of Las Lomas was el Bulevar Morazán. The black pavement glimmered from afar. The stretch was lined with gas stations and pharmacies and American chain restaurants: TGI Fridays, Popeyes, KFC, Wendy's, Pizza Hut, Burger King. Cars and motorcycles moved through it like zooming lights.

I caught Camila's reflection in the sideview mirror. The yellow streetlights made her light brown skin glow. We locked eyes and the corner of her mouth pulled to a smirk. It was only a second, almost missable, and then she looked out again.

Outside, it smelled like nightlife: fried food and gasoline. The car's cheap stereo system threatened to collapse under the beat of a Bad Bunny song, and the speaker right by my calf tickled me with its vibration.

I adjusted to move away from it, and Camila shifted with me. Something about our synchronized motion made my whole body throb, a pressure between my legs. I felt hyperaware of everything, like the weight of the car resettling from one end to the other as we went up and down the hills. No such thing as a straight road in Tegus—it's all winding curves and sharp turns. As we reached the top of the final climb in Las Lomas, the whole city came into view.

The mountains that enclosed Tegucigalpa shimmered white and yellow lights. The blinking eyes had grown exponentially in the past few years, as people from all over the country moved to the capital in hopes of jobs and opportunities that didn't exist. Makeshift houses of aluminum sheet roofs, walls of wood and adobe, doors of empty space amassed in the outskirts, stacked on top of each other. On the north end stood el Cristo del Picacho, a concrete, thirty-foot tall sculpture of the Messiah, illuminated by lights at its base. Christ looked over the city with his arms stretched out; it was unclear whether he was trying to hold or contain us.

Carla lit a cigarette, blowing smoke out the window.

"My parents better not be able to smell that." Miguel glared at her in in the rearview mirror.

"Relax." Carla rolled her eyes. The smoke didn't mix well with the sugary perfumes circling the car, nor Miguel's citrusy cologne. But it wasn't more than a few minutes before we reached La Esquina.

A short but fast-moving line stretched from the bar's front gate. As its name implies, La Esquina is on a corner. It had once been a house, repurposed a few years ago into a two-story bar. It still almost looked like a house—brick walls painted white, small black-iron gate entrance crowned with a modest wooden sign that reads *La Esquina* in bold, black letters. But the second floor was now a big wraparound wooden balcony with high tables and chairs. From outside, I could see the people smoking and drinking up there. I could even catch loose scraps of conversations underneath the loud salsa music.

Miguel found street parking at the end of the block, and all four of us girls were waved in without being asked for our IDs, per usual.

Miguel knew he had to hand the bouncer a hundred-Lempira bill for the lack of his. Fifteen minutes later, we sat at one of the tall wooden tables set against the rail of the balcony with a kamikaze fishbowl in the middle to share. Carla's older brother was close friends with the owner of La Esquina, who was always at the bar. He gave her the pitcher on the house. The blue liquid splashed around the container as we moved the table with our bouncing knees and shifting bodies. Sour green gummies glinted at the bottom and four straws bobbed on top. Miguel got himself a Coke and rum that he downed too quickly for a designated driver.

Under the table, Camila's knee bumped mine.

"Who else is coming?" Valeria asked without looking up from her phone.

"Aura says she just left her house," Miguel responded, also on his phone. "I think Andrea and Lia are with her."

"Is Pablo coming?" Carla asked, her tone too transparent in its attempt to pass off as casual, like we might not notice who did the asking if she was quick enough.

"Why?" Miguel teased, grinning. "Do you want him to? Should we call him?"

Carla blushed and reached for a cigarette. "I was just asking."

"Did you hear about Daniel and that girl from San Pedro?" Camila interrupted.

"Eso es paja." Miguel shook his head. "He told me she made all that shit up 'cause she got embarrassed."

"Of course he'd say that." Valeria's tone was even, but her body stilled.

"Wait, what happened?" I asked, pulling my gaze away from the street below.

Just then, Cami put her hand on my thigh under the table. Her hand was warm, hot even. I put mine over hers and squeezed her fingers, softly. Warmth rushed up my stomach, through my chest, and all the way up to my throat. I leaned forward to sip more of the blue drink, careful not to move my body too much, or rather, careful not to risk disturbing the parts of us that touched.

"There was this party last weekend at someone's house, I think some guy from another school. Anyways, Daniel hooked up with a girl from San Pedro. Who has a boyfriend. Who was *also* at the party. This girl was very, very drunk, right, and she goes and tells her boyfriend that Daniel basically forced her. So *he* goes to beat the shit out of Daniel . . ."

An hour passed us like this: Carla got another fishbowl, which we pooled our remaining money to pay for, and Miguel got another drink for himself. Several people from school arrived and hovered around the table for a few minutes to chat. Valeria and I counted the rest of our money to see if we could get a round of tequila shots. We couldn't. Then the music switched abruptly from an old bachata to reggaeton.

Someone whistled. Around us, people got up to dance, moving toward the roofed section of the second floor. The four of us followed, pulling Miguel along.

"There's *way* too many people in here," Miguel shouted over the music. Never a big dancer, his shoulders and hips went stiff whenever he was put in this situation.

"¿Qué?" Carla yelled back.

It was hard to do any actual dancing without bumping into someone's extremities or stepping on feet. The first song hadn't ended, and sweat already pooled under my shirt and the back of my neck. Heat radiated from the bodies and steamed the air—perfumed tangy sweet. The floor was a mix of adhesive and wet. Moving my body now, I could feel the alcohol ripping away my senses.

My friends held a dance circle for a few songs, until Pablo appeared behind Carla. He wore tight jeans and a polo shirt, like Miguel. Like most guys. His hair was slicked to the side, and he must've come to find her as soon as he got here, because he wasn't as sweaty as everyone else. He whispered something in Carla's ear—she nodded and followed him without a word.

Miguel pulled Valeria to him, and they paired off, dancing on their own. Camila and I stayed next to them, close to each other but not quite touching. It was a Maluma song about a girl who drank too much to remember him from the night before. The beat, the alcohol, the heat, the smoke. I drew sweaty strands of hair away from my face and then time turned liquid. The seconds spilled fast, but a lifetime contained in each one.

Two men approached us. They looked older, patchy facial hair and the wet, shiny look of people who have been drinking for hours. I thought I recognized one of them but couldn't place how. Maybe one of Maynor's friends?

"Do you want a drink?" the taller one asked Cami.

She shook her head and mouthed *gracias*.

"What about you?" the other one yelled my way.

I wondered how they made this decision—who talked to whom and why. I declined by shaking my finger, my throat already sore from trying to talk over music the entire night. My hand gesture felt harsh, for some reason, so I smiled at him to make up for it. He smiled back. They asked for our names, leaning in for a response. They got close to us the way boys and men do. One or both of them carried the overpowering scent of cheap cologne. An overly sweet synthetic fragrance that failed to blend seamlessly with the smoke and alcohol on their breath. The dull weight of a headache welled at the back of my head.

"I'm Edgar," the taller one yelled, stretching his hand. The way he moved his body allowed me to place where I'd seen him before. He had gone to the same school as us, many years ago. He must've been a senior when we were in sixth or seventh grade. I shook his hand. His palm was moist and warm. The other guy said his name, but it was too loud to make out and I didn't ask again. They danced next to us, gradually moving closer, thrusting their hips in our direction.

Something rolled in my stomach. Where had Miguel and Valeria gone? I was about to ask Camila when I felt her hand on my arm, her mouth by my ear.

"Come with me to the bathroom." Her breath was warm against my neck.

I nodded. We excused ourselves to the men. They leaned in for a kiss on the cheek, pulled out their phones to ask for our Snapchats. Camila pulled away, yelled that we'd be right back; this wasn't goodbye. I felt grateful for the easy lie, for her clear thinking. I took her hand and let her guide me to the bathroom.

There are two bathrooms in La Esquina. The one upstairs had a line that didn't seem to be moving. "What's going on?" I asked the girl in front of me, pointing to the bathroom door with my lips.

"Some guy and a girl locked themselves inside," she said, crossing her arms. "They won't come out."

"Let's try downstairs," I said to Camila over my shoulder.

Getting down the stairs was difficult—it seemed like everyone on the first floor was trying to go upstairs at the same time. We squeezed by a group of men laughing and yelling about a missing watch. A girl whose mascara had smeared from crying slid between me and the wall, tipping to the side as she stumbled up the steps.

I had always hated these stairs. Wooden planks with absurd, unkind gaps between them. Falling through felt like a real possibility.

Downstairs, we elbowed our way around the people trying to order at the bar. There wasn't a line for this bathroom, tucked around a dark corner as it was. Before I could knock, Cami turned the doorknob. It was empty. We hurried inside, locking the door behind us. I flicked the light switch. Nothing happened. I tried a couple more times. Camila turned on her phone flashlight. I copied her. Torn, wet toilet paper fragments spread over the black vinyl floor. The *untz-untz-untz* of the music outside shook the room.

Cami kicked the toilet seat down with her foot, and sat, which I found bizarre. Usually, she tried to hover over public toilet seats.

How drunk was she? We'd drank the same amount, so at least as drunk as I was, right?

I set my phone face-up on the sink. The movement of my reflection startled me. I'd forgotten there was a mirror.

My hair looked wet, patted down around my temples. My face was red. My mascara wasn't quite smeared, but small flicks of it dotted the corners of my eyes. Before I could begin to come up with a solution for any of this, Camila's reflection behind mine pulled my attention. Her pee stream hit the toilet bowl. She scrolled through her phone, flashlight still on, pointed at the floor in front of her. I opened the faucet. My hands felt sticky and moist after shaking Edgar's and friend's hands.

"I'm gonna text Valeria and see where they went," she said.

I nodded. "I think Carla ditched us for Pablo."

Cami snorted. "I don't know what she sees in him." She stood and pulled her skirt up. I tried to keep my eyes on my hands and the stream of water but couldn't.

For a second, I peeked. Then I forced my eyes back as I pressed down on the liquid-soap dispenser. The scent of grapes swamped the bathroom. Something about it summoned a wave of nausea. Camila tried to flush the toilet. It expulsed water but stopped short of flushing. She tried again—nothing. She shrugged and slapped the lid back down with her foot.

As I flicked my hands in the air to dry, a few drops sprinkled my face. There wasn't a towel, and even if there had been, I wouldn't have touched it. I settled for wiping my hands off on my pants. Then I moved aside so Camila could wash her hands. I checked the time on my phone. It was a quarter after eleven. The phone's screen was wet from the sink or my hands, and I rubbed it against my shirt. The music was getting louder.

I checked the time again before remembering I had just a second ago: eleven-something. I wanted to text Valeria or Carla, but when I found their chats, it turned out I'd already texted them a moment before. Camila was still washing her hands—had she been washing her hands a long time?

I was drunk. I was very, very drunk.

I looked at Cami looking at herself in the mirror. She'd also placed her phone face-up on the sink, the flashlight bouncing off the ceiling and onto the mirror. She pulled her hair up with one hand and used the other to fan air onto her exposed neck. She was wearing a nude lipstick that matched her skin tone. I couldn't remember noticing that before.

My friend. *Best* friend. With the sharp cheekbones and curled eyelashes. My best friend that I didn't really treat like any of my other friends. And none of my other friends treated me like she did. But aren't all friendships different? Many girls who are friends must be exactly like me and her. They *must* hold hands under tables and stay on their phones with each other until they fall asleep each night and plan hangouts for just the two of them without calling them that, and, and, and.

All the thinking made me dizzy. Time was moving slower. I leaned my forehead against the door and closed my eyes. I heard Camila shut off the faucet, and waited for her to nudge me aside, to tell me it was time to round up our friends.

I waited. And waited. Had it been three seconds or five minutes? I was about to turn around when I felt her hand on my shoulder. A *what's up* was on the tip of my tongue, but I stopped short of saying it. Somehow, I knew. Knew to turn around slowly to face her. Knew to draw my face close to hers. To let our foreheads touch. Our mouths found each other. And we kissed.

We kissed. She tasted like everything—toothpaste and spit and tamarind and the blue color of the fishbowl. She dropped her phone. The noise was startling, but we didn't stop. Not immediately. Then her mouth was on my neck and I could feel my heartbeat in my ears, louder than the music even, and—

BANG. BANG. BANG.

My heartbeat was louder than the music because the music had stopped. Time hit play, and everything that had spun in slow motion a second ago rushed back to regular speed around us.

BANG. BANG. The knock shook my backbone. Why had the music stopped?

"Fuck," Camila mumbled, grabbing her phone from the floor.

I turned, opened the door. The light outside was blinding. I was too drunk on my best friend's mouth to process that the overhead lights of La Esquina shouldn't have been on. But I was just sober enough to recognize the person in front of me.

"Maynor?"

"Let's go." My brother's mouth was tight. "The police are here. We gotta go. *Now.*"

"What—why?"

For a second, I wondered if what he was saying and what I had just done was related. I felt dizzy, disoriented. I knew Camila was right behind me and I wanted to turn back around to see her face but couldn't. Wouldn't.

"What do you mean why? You're both underage. Hurry the fuck up."

Maynor had always been good at in-the-moment reactions. He knew how to keep moving, how to propel everyone around him toward safety. I was always more the paralyzed-by-fear type.

I remember getting out. I remember the sirens and the red and blue lights and feeling cold and getting in a car with Maynor and Camila and somehow there was Valeria too, but no Miguel and Carla. And there was someone else I didn't recognize, but I couldn't make my eyes focus.

I remember making stops to drop people off. A house I didn't know and then Carla's, where Valeria and Camila were spending the night. I remember all of this in flashes—a still image of a memory here and there, but all of it disembodied, no time in between to glue the pieces together. Random, floating moments with no clear sequence.

"Whose car is this?" I asked. I'd been in the back seat at some point, but now was in the passenger's. I pressed my face against the window—the glass was cool. It felt good.

"A friend's," Maynor said. "I'll drop you off at home and then go to hers. To return the car."

"How are you getting home then?"

My voice sounded thin, young. I thought maybe I'd spoken in my head, because he didn't reply. I was just about to say it again, but he cut me off.

"The cops were hungry tonight," he said. "Bunch of places got shut down."

"Is that . . . normal?" I was the kind of drunk that makes it hard to say what's normal and what isn't.

Maynor took a minute to respond, again. "No," he said. "It's not. They were looking."

I still didn't understand. But I also didn't feel like trying that hard.

"I didn't know you were coming to La Esquina," I said. I hadn't seen him at all. How long had he been there?

"I wasn't. But my friend . . . she got a message about the cops shutting places down. I figured you and your friends would be there."

"Oh," I heard myself said. "Thank you."

He didn't say anything. I turned to look at him—it felt like I was still missing something.

Maynor's eyes were on the road. He was dressed as always—jeans and some fútbol jersey. His hair looked the way it does when he's been putting his fingers through it.

Was he upset with me? That didn't seem possible. Maynor was never upset with me, not really.

"What's that thing you always say?" I said, making a futile attempt to stop each of my words from sliding into the next. "¿Tegucigalpa es . . . la ley del . . . más fuerte?"

The corner of Maynor's mouth ticked up, but his expression remained stern. "Yeah," he said. "La ley del más fuerte."

"Yeah," I repeated.

Why was he so quiet? We were almost home. I couldn't wait to fall asleep. To stop pretending that I had any understanding of what was going on.

"That's a nice shade," Maynor said.

I looked out onto the road, trying to figure out what he meant.

"Camila's lipstick." His eyes slid to mine, and he nodded his head in the direction of my neck, pointing with his lips.

My hand shot up to my neck instinctively. When I brought it back down, there it was—a nude smear across my fingertips. The street-lights were just bright enough to make out the contrast between her skin tone and mine.

ONE

Mami honks for the third time, and I know it's not going to be a good day. Her right hand stays, pressed down on the steering wheel for a prolonged, unbearable beat. A buzz lingers in my ears even after she stops.

"*Puta*," Mami curses. "Every single morning with you three. Where is your brother? I'm going to be late again."

I want to point out there's only one person missing, so technically, it's not "us three": Alberto and I have been sitting in the car for the past fifteen minutes, enduring this. But silence is the only move with our mother at six a.m.

Also, I'm all for ditching Maynor. He's made us late every single day for the last two weeks.

"Puta, puta, puta. I'm leaving him. Every morning, the same fight con este cipote."

But she doesn't start the car. Her hand drops from the steering wheel, and she reaches for her phone, tucked in the cup holder with centavos and hair clips. She dials Maynor for what must be the fourth time now.

As the back tone beeps, Mami does her eyeliner in the rearview mirror with her left hand. From the back seat I see the frame of her dark eyes and full eyebrows. It takes her less than a few seconds to draw the line from below the inside of her eye to the outside. She does it all in one swift motion—no halts, no second guesses.

I've always been fascinated by my mom's hands. She can drive while doing her makeup and answering a call at the same time. When I was a child, her hands seemed eternal to me. There was always one more thing she could pick up, even with everything else.

Like the three calls before, Maynor doesn't answer. Mami hangs up before it goes to voicemail. She holds my eyes for a second in the mirror, then honks again.

"I'm gonna get fired. Is that what you all want? If it was one of his stupid fútbol games, he would be the first one in the car. Pero como es mi trabajo a nadie le importa. Libertad, go look for your brother. Incredible, a grown-ass man who can't get ready on time."

I sigh getting out of the car, careful not to slam the door. If Mami thinks que estamos siendo malcriados, her anger spills over. Hot.

I walk up the stairs past Abuela's room to Maynor's, hoping he's, at least, dressed.

He sits shirtless on the edge of his unmade bed. His black hair is wet and water droplets run down his neck and back, tiny mirrors all over his skin. But the room doesn't smell like shampoo or deodorant—none of those ready-for-the-day scents. It's the seamless merge of dirty laundry and sunlessness that hangs around him. He's not even on his phone or putting on shoes, just staring at his hands.

"Maynor, the fuck? You want Mami to kill us all?"

For a second, it's like he didn't hear me. Like he's watching a movie play out on the back of his hands. He looks up at me confused, eyebrows scrunched together, eyes void of recognition.

I feel like I pulled him out of a dream. But before I can say anything, his face breaks into a smile.

"Tranquila, Libi. You know how she gets. I'm coming."

His last sentence is drowned out by another ten-second honk. I swear the whole block hates us.

As he looks for a shirt in the pile of clothes on his bed, I'm taken aback by how skinny he is. I don't think I've looked at him recently. Not with enough care to notice.

The bones in his back are delineable. His jeans would fall to his knees if it wasn't for the belt buckled around his waist so tightly the denim folds on itself near the zipper. A few bruises spread over his lower back and left arm, near his bumpy half-moon elbow mole— shapeless purple spots ringed with yellow and green.

This isn't uncommon for Maynor. Nor for any good goalie, really. He's been beaten up by a soccer ball ever since I can remember—a sign that not much gets past him. Growing up, I believed him when he said he would go pro. Everyone did.

He finally picks a shirt and puts it on. Of course, it's a fútbol jersey. Today's is actually my favorite—a vintage Olimpia, the current champion of the Liga Nacional de Fútbol. Red and blue stripes with a white lion's head embroidered on the heart. I remember Maynor begging Mami to buy it for him years ago.

Another honk.

"Apúrate, maje," I say. "No time for you to comb your hair, just wear a hat or something."

A couple minutes and honks later, Maynor climbs in the back seat next to Alberto, leaving me with no option but the passenger's. Maynor usually calls shotgun (older sibling right and all), but I have a feeling he doesn't want to be too close to Mami right now. She starts speeding away before I can close the door.

"How is it that your twelve-year-old brother and seventeen-year-old sister can wake up early and be ready on time, but you, a twenty-five-year-old man, can't?"

Maynor stays quiet, which is what I would do too. Daddy Yankee's new song plays on the radio. Just as Alberto starts to hum along, Mami cuts the volume.

"I'm asking you a question, Maynor José. What are you gonna do when you have your own patients, huh? Show up late to your appointments? What if there's an emergency? Let them die?"

"I'm—no, of course not, Mami. I just overslept. I had to stay up until three, reading like five hundred pages for my radiology class," he says.

This placates Mami for a minute. He's good at that, using the career Abuela and Mami are forcing him into—medicina—as an excuse. *Los sueños no pagan las cuentas,* Abuela said when Maynor insisted he had what it took to be a professional fútbol player.

Of course, Mami must not have heard him sneaking in at two

a.m. And come to think of it, I've never seen him study for anything. Which isn't surprising, really. He hates the career they've chosen for him.

"Bueno, hijo. But this can't keep happening—if you're late tomorrow, I'm leaving you. None of you care about my job. I'm up on time to take all of you to school *every day* but you can't do the same for me. I've been taking you to soccer practices for fifteen years, Maynor, and not once have you been late. Not once! You wouldn't do this to your abuela, would you? Malagradecido."

Again, it's not *all* of us. But when Maynor screws up, we all go down.

I catch Maynor's gaze in the sun visor's mirror I'm using to put mascara on. He winks at me. I shake my head, which is a big mistake, because my hands are nowhere near as steady as my mother's.

It doesn't help that there's more potholes than paved concrete in this city. I lick my finger and try to rub off the black mascara smeared under my eye. The sun visor's mirror is too dirty and speckled to tell if the hint of black I can still see is from my own eyebags or actual dye. I reach for my phone to use the front-facing camera instead, but of course, there's nothing in my pocket.

Fuck. That's right—I need to remind Mami to pick up my phone at Texicell, the place where they'll keep resurrecting your phone even though it's clearly time to get a new one.

My phone, otherwise known as the biggest piece of crap in the world, otherwise known as my whole world, has been in and out of Texicell ever since Maynor handed it down to me. And even though its visit to the doctor this time is sort of my fault, Maynor had already made it nearly unusable before passing it on. But I know Mami won't buy me a new one until the self-taught technicians from Texicell declare it irreparably dead.

Reminding Mami about my phone right after her rant about us being ungrateful is tricky. Usually, though, our forty-minute drive through the city allows for as many changes in mood as songs. Mami turns up the volume again and switches stations—she can't stand reggaeton this early.

Hardly 6:30 a.m. and the streets are already living. Sun is all out, and I swear I can feel the heat radiating from the pavement. Cars honk, and when that's not enough, people yell at each other: *Cabrón ¿No sabes manejar, pendejo?*

We reach a stoplight and the honking crescendos, even though there's literally no way anyone can go. Newspaper vendors trek from car to car, pressing the front page to the drivers' windows. Today's headlines, in big, bolded black and red letters, are about this weekend's protests and the murder of three protestors by the military police: **AL MENOS TRES MUERTOS EN TEGUCIGALPA TRAS EL DESPLIEGUE DEL EJÉRCITO POR LA OLEADA DE PROTESTAS.**

Peddlers come up to our windows, trying to sell us everything and anything: mosquito zapper rackets, bags of sliced mango verde watered in vinegar and lime juice, pirated movies. Two children that seem to have claimed this stoplight as their permanent location knock on Mami's window. They're not selling anything—they just want money. Some days, the older one of the two does a few balancing tricks with a stick and a ball while the younger one goes around collecting tips. Not today, though. Today they carry a piece of a cardboard box with the words *temenos hambre* written in black marker. Mami shakes her finger at them and mouths *hoy no tengo.* They move on to the next car.

A few men try to wipe the car's windshield, pero Mami honks and shakes her finger at them too. They're reluctant to step away—already drenched in sweat, foreheads glistening and shirt turning translucent around their armpits. For a second, they just stare in before moving on, willing her to change her mind.

Stoplights make Mom nervous ever since she was held at gunpoint for her purse and phone at one near here couple months ago. So now we keep the windows up, which sucks, because even in the morning, the coolest time of day, Tegus is warm and sweaty. The car's AC hasn't worked in years, and we won't be getting that fixed any time soon.

As the light turns to green, the voices of the hosts from *Despierta Tegus* fill the car. They hardly cover any news, just four dudes shooting the shit. But we listen to them every morning on our way to school.

I don't understand how they haven't run out of things to say. Today's topic is movie titles with terrible Spanish translations that are nothing like the original English. One of them says *Jaws,* called *Tiburón* in Spanish—*Shark.* The host with the low, raspy voice whose name I can never remember brings up *Pulp Fiction,* dubbed *Violent Times.* Javier, my favorite of the three, points out *Brokeback Mountain,* which in Spanish is *Secreto en la montaña.*

"They should've kept that movie a secret buried in some

mountain," Mami mutters, cutting someone off. They honk and yell something at her, but I can't make it out.

"What secret?" Alberto says.

Maynor locks eyes with me again. I close the sun visor a little too hard.

"Nada, Beto. Forget it," she says.

"Why?"

"Ay no, Mamá, don't say things like that. Aren't all your wedding designer friends—you know?" Maynor says.

"Bueno, sí, pero eso doesn't mean that I think it's—"

"It's just so ignorant," Maynor counters.

"Ignorant? Mira, Maynor, I don't know *everything* in the world, but I've been alive longer than—"

"Mami—" I cut in, coming off a little more desperate than I meant to. "I know you're super busy today, but is there any way you can pick up my phone from Texicell? I called yesterday and they said it's ready. Please?"

Mami sucks her teeth—a reflex she's tried to correct in the three of us for as long as we've existed. "Pucha. I don't know, Libertad. Can't you ask your abuela?"

"You know she can't, Mami. She came home at ten last night. She's too busy with the costumes for some school play, or the parade."

"I have things too, you know?" Her voice rises again. "I have two menu tastings for this weekend's wedding. But even mi Mamá thinks her work is more important than my job. I have to make time for everyone else's—"

"Ma. Porfa. It's been a month," I beg, turning to her, softening my voice. "I really, really need it. I had stuff for a school project on it."

Partially true. Not a school project, but a project nonetheless. At this point, I'd say anything to convince her.

Mami throws her hands up. "Fine. I'll try to pick it up during my lunch break."

"Gracias, Ma. Enserio." I breathe out a small sigh of relief, partly for my phone but also for the successful derail of the *Brokeback Mountain* conversation.

On the radio, the men have moved on to talking about the protests. This, too, they discuss in their signature comedic tone. I pray Maynor doesn't say anything else that puts Mami in a worse mood. When I turn to look over my shoulder, his eyes are closed, his head resting against the window.

Twenty minutes later, we drop him off at la UNAH, the National Autonomous University of Honduras. The campus is huge—hundreds of people walk in all directions, with purses and backpacks slung over their shoulders. Some are dressed in suits and formal skirts with dress shirts. Others wear T-shirts or fútbol jerseys with ripped jeans. The wall next to us is covered in graffiti: a bunch of blue spray-painted fuera joh and chepos asesinos—a call for the president to step down, and "killer cops," respectively.

Soon I'll be a student here too, just about ten more months of high school to go.

Maynor mumbles something that sounds like "see you later" and slams the door. I half expect Mami to get out right then and yell at him in front of everyone, but she really is late today. She spits out *mico malcriado* and speeds away.

Mami is the wedding planner at a local hotel, which sounds a lot fancier than it is—it's not her dream job or anything. Her official hours are from nine to five, but she usually makes it home at around nine at night, except on weekends, when she's there past midnight. Another underpaid job in this jobless city.

Her salary is crap. But she makes it work with Abuela, who's ran a small sewing workshop for the past thirty years. Mostly school play costumes, ballet show outfits, and quick patchwork jobs.

"Here," Mami says as we pull up to school, handing Alberto and me seventy Lempiras each. "I didn't have time to make you anything for lunch, Alberto. But I'll ask Miss Lezama if you spend it all on Chilly Willys and candy. Get a pizza or a baleada, at least."

"Ay, Mami." Alberto rolls his eyes.

"Libertad, make sure he makes it to the classroom. I love you both. I'll see you tonight."

"Te amo, Mami." Alberto's already out of the car.

"Bye mami, te amamos. Don't forget my phone," I remind her.

"See, at least two of my children love me. Tell your brother when you see him that I'm not waiting for him tomorrow—either he's on time or he can walk. I just don't understand this . . . this *person* he's turned into. Always late, malcriado, all sensitive, calling me ignorant over a movie."

I can't tell if she heard me about my phone. I close the door gently, careful not to make Maynor's mistake.

TWO

I walk Alberto to his fifth-grade classroom. The door is deco-rated with different national symbols for the upcoming festivities—poorly drawn pine trees and macaws with hand-written explanations of national symbolism. Alberto runs inside without saying good bye, his Real Madrid backpack bouncing with every step. There's nothing inside except his FIFA World Cup album and lunch money, all of which he'll spend on stickers of whatever fútbol players he's missing.

His teacher isn't here yet, but there are enough of his classmates nearby that I don't feel the need to wait around. Plus he's already talking about some fútbol player's injury with a few boys.

It's still twenty minutes before classes start. I walk down to the concrete soccer field where most of the senior boys play before school every morning. They stay sweaty for the rest of the day, but it's the best time to play, weather-wise.

A match is well underway—about ten boys with their pants rolled up halfway to their knees pass and fight for the ball. One of the goalkeepers yells something to a player, waving his arm to the right. His words get lost in the wind.

I spot my friends sitting at our chosen plastic picnic table to the side of the court. Usually, they're all gelled-back hair in place and sleepy eyes, but today they seem caught in a heated argument. I can't make out what they're saying yet, but Valeria punctuates every word she says by tapping the table with her index finger.

Ever since my phone died before the beginning of the school year, I get this small panic attack that something huge will happen between three p.m. and seven a.m. the next day. Something everyone will know and be talking about, but I'll have no idea what's going on because no phone means not knowing shit.

Chisme is life.

I walk to the side of the table Valeria and Carla are sitting on. Across from them are Miguel and Pablo. I stand to the side waiting for the girls to scoot over—Carla is copying someone's homework, so it takes her a second to look up and see me.

"That's what I heard from Vicky. But you know that girl will say anything." Miguel shrugs.

"I mean—" Pablo begins, then stops to take a drink from his Coca-Cola. "That doesn't make sense. Why would Vicky keep her nudes on her camera roll and not on some app with a password lock? And then just let him—or anyone, really—scroll through her pictures? It sounds like she wanted him to see them."

"Doesn't matter." Valeria's finger stays pressed to the table. "He shouldn't have sent them to himself. She didn't even know he did that, pobrecita."

"I'm just saying that maybe he doesn't deserve to be, you know, expelled."

Pablo follows the last word with a swig from his bottle of Coca-Cola. His fingers leave prints in the condensation covering the plastic bottle. He's always drinking Coke, even at seven a.m.

"Except he's not getting expelled for sending the pictures to himself. He sold and spread them throughout the whole freaking school." Carla glares at Pablo, pen hovering over her notebook, frozen midair. "Maybe the city."

Pablo rolls his eyes. "Don't be dramatic. I'm telling you, she *wanted* him to see those pictures. Just, think about it, okay? Why would you keep naked pictures of yourself and then let someone see all of your camera roll, *unless—*"

Carla leans forward, cutting him off. "What if she forgot she had taken those pictures? Huh? And you know what? That's not even the point. Selling someone's nudes is like, illegal. Not to mention child pornography. Vicky is seventeen."

Pablo slouches back with a loud exhale. "All right, okay."

"Also." Valeria continues where Carla left off. "It's not like he's getting expelled just because of *that*. My mom told me that Mrs. Gomez told her that it's officially going down as an accumulation of suspensions and detentions. This was just the last straw. La gota que rebalsó el vaso."

"I heard that too." Miguel nods.

This is some old chisme. The debate has been going on for the last week, ever since Vicky's nudes spread throughout the school, courtesy of Daniel Ramírez. Both Vicky and Daniel are in our class.

Pablo showed us all five of Vicky's pictures and a video. He sent them to our group chat, said they'd been sent to the boys' soccer team's group chat. He's the team captain.

Honestly, I looked. Pablo didn't give us any warning—he just sent it all out of the blue.

I mean, I tried to not *look* look, as in spend too many seconds actually staring at any of the pictures, but I did look for a second there. Felt sick during and after. But I figured if everyone else had already seen them, what did it matter if I did too? Besides, it was Pablo who showed them around. I wouldn't put it past him buying them directly from Daniel.

"Would you do the same to Camila?" Carla asks Pablo, snapping her notebook shut and sitting up straight.

I shift uncomfortably on the bench. There it is. The reason why we let Pablo hang with us: Cami.

Top reason I need my phone, too.

"That's different." Pablo's tone turns defensive. "Camila's my girlfriend. She would never do that. Vicky and Daniel were just . . . fuck buddies or something. Camila and Vicky don't have a thing in common." He caps his empty Coca-Cola bottle, squeezing the plastic hard enough that it crinkles.

"Speaking of, where is Cami?" I ask. Valeria darts a glance my way.

"Late. Her bus got stuck behind some car accident or something." Pablo glances down at his phone.

I dislike Pablo for many reasons. He goes hard with the nice-guy act, then gets away with saying some of the most sexist, ignorant shit. And his voice is too loud, especially at seven a.m. But the top reason? A guy like him with a girl like Cami is just . . . off.

Exactly one week after my phone died, they started dating officially. Though they had been talking for a while, I guess. I didn't even hear about it from Camila. It was just a random Monday morning at this very table—Pablo's self-satisfied smile was unbearable as he retold every detail of how his grand gesture (taking Camila out for dinner) had come to him weeks before, and he just *knew* that was the perfect way to ask her to be his girlfriend.

My stomach hurt the whole day.

Pablo's phone chimes. "Her bus is pulling up. I'm gonna go meet her." He smirks at us before jogging off toward the stairs that lead to the school entrance.

I miss when he would just play fútbol in the mornings, before he took an interest in Camila.

"Move to the other side." Valeria nudges me. "It's three of us on one side and only Miguel on the other."

I grab my bag and sit next to Miguel. He's on his phone playing Fortnite.

Without meaning to, I keep glancing up the stairs. Moments like this, I *really* wish I had my phone. Something to do with my hands.

"Do you think Vicky will come to school today?" Miguel says without looking up.

"I doubt it. I mean, would you? I'd change schools or something. Beg my parents to homeschool me." Carla shrugs, but she still seems flustered from the argument with Pablo.

"She's already missed, like, a week and a half, hasn't she?" I ask.

33

"Maybe she's keeping up with homework or something." Valeria drums her fingers on the table.

"She's been totally silent online since it happened. Except for the weird Snapchat story she posted last night," Carla adds.

"What Snapchat story?"

"You don't know?" Carla sounds surprised.

"Uhm, no phone, remember?"

She grimaces. "Right . . . So she posted this like, all-black screen snap and wrote over it with something about moving on or letting go and finding yourself."

"It was: 'When you let go you will lose many things from the past, but you will find yourself.' I saved it," Valeria adds, holding up her phone.

The sunlight hits us square in the eyes, so I can barely make out Valeria's phone screen without squinting. I swipe at the sweat beading on my forehead.

Miguel snickers. I feel bad for Vicky, but it's hard to get away with cheesy Tumblr-adjacent quotes on black-background Snap stories without someone making fun of you.

Cami and Pablo appear at the top of the stairs. They don't hold hands, but their arms brush against each other with every step, and he's telling her something that requires a lot of hand motions. I shield my eyes from the sun to be able to look at them. I follow their bodies' movements.

We still wear those buttoned-down, white- short-sleeved shirts with the school's logo monogrammed over the front left pocket, despite most schools having moved on to polos. Plus, our pants are an ugly pale green that fit baggy on everyone. But on Cami, it's like the uniform was made with her in mind.

"Good morning," I say when they reach us.

Valeria side-eyes me. Carla's gone back to transcribing whoever's homework, and Miguel doesn't even glance up from his phone.

"Hey," Cami says, sitting next to me. Pablo slides next to her.

"So what happened?" I ask, turning my head to look at her for a second.

"Some huge accident—at least three cars and a motorcycle. The police took forever to get there. Like, forty-five minutes. There was a body on the side of the road, that's when I stopped looking," she says, scrunching up her face and shaking her head.

"Probably the motorcycle person." Valeria purses her lips.

"Be right back." Pablo stands up and squeezes Cami's shoulder. He lopes toward the small food store on the side of the court, probably to get another Coke, then turns around. "Want anything?"

"I'm good," Cami responds with a quick smile. "Thank you."

"Cute," Carla adds.

I can't tell if she's being sarcastic. Camila doesn't meet her eyes. A second of tension moves through the table, as it does whenever Carla acknowledges Pablo and Cami's relationship.

"Hey, when are you getting your phone back? It's been, like, what, a whole month?" Cami asks. She doesn't look up from her phone.

"Today, I think," I say. I wish I had my own phone right now to scroll through instead of having to find anywhere to look at that is not her.

35

"Finally," she says, looking up. For the first time today, our eyes meet.

It hadn't occurred to me once that maybe she wants me to have my phone back.

Or maybe she just means it's been a minute.

I hold her eyes. In the sun, there's a mellow gold-green to them. "Yeah. Finally."

"We need to head in," Carla says, glancing at the time on her phone. She reaches for her backpack and slides the notebooks in. Pablo appears behind Camila with another soda, put his hand on her shoulder. We look away from each other.

The soccer match has ended. The boys on the court are changing shirts, pulling them over their sweaty heads and grabbing clean ones from their bags. It's already too warm to sit outside comfortably. I can feel the bench under my pants heating up.

"Fuck. I didn't even get time to finish calc," Cami groans.

I, too, feel robbed of time. I'm annoyed at the bus, the route, the police, and Maynor, even if he isn't the reason Cami is late.

Mostly, I'm annoyed at my mom. For the phone and the honking. For not seeing that her son isn't sensitive about a movie, not really.

THREE

"Make sure your parents read the permission form all the way through. This year isn't like any other, muchachos," Mrs. García says. "The school wants to make sure we're doing everything in our power to keep you safe." She splits us into groups according to our roles en el desfile, the upcoming parade. Las palillonas discuss the final details of their outfits, then head out to practice.

Palillonas are the girls that march and dance in beat with the marching band, all while twirling a baton. They dress up in what looks like a cross between a cheerleader's and a soldier's uniform. It's a big deal to be a palillona, both here and in Nicaragua. Some of them even get awards and scholarships, for their patriotic spirit and shit.

While the marching-band people head over to the auditorium, the rest of us pick up where we left off with our hand-painted banners and flags last week. Of course, the boys on banner duty will spend most of the class period playing Fortnite on their phones or showing each other videos: Sometimes it's fútbol, sometimes it's porn.

September 15 is one week away—and with it the big Independence Day parade, and my eighteenth birthday. Honduras was independentized from Spain on September 15, 1821. And I was independentized from my mother's uterus on September 15, 1999.

Independencia didn't ring right to my mother (thank god), so instead she called me Libertad. Not that Mami is particularly patriotic, but I like to picture her in the hospital bed watching the parades and feeling moved enough that it seemed right to name me after the occasion.

It also adds intrigue to my narrative, since my last name is Morazán, like Francisco Morazán, the guy over-credited for doing some of the work behind the battle for independence. No relationship though.

I'm in the flag and banner group. We're arguing over the last few hand-painted details: The bottom blue feathers of a guacamaya, our national bird, or the pale-green leaves of an orchid, our national flower? Civics with Mrs. García is the class period devoted to these life-or-death questions.

Schools from all over the capital participate in the parade. The rest of the school year we'll focus on Honduran law and history, but las Fiestas Patrias is what this class is really about.

I'm grateful for a hands-on project. It's way better than learning about the Honduran Family Code, which inevitably means an in-class debate about why same-sex marriage can never be recognized in the eyes of God and thus our law. A debate we've been having since eighth grade. A debate that is strictly one-sided. Although this year, us being seniors and all, we'll probably use the rest of the school year to do stuff like college applications or résumés.

Carla reaches for the red watercolor paint next to me. "So—Friday. Big one-eight. What are we doing?" she asks.

"Hmm. I don't know yet. I mean—who knows if anyone will be able to, you know, do anything. I'm not even sure the parade's gonna happen . . ."

"Yeahhh. If anything goes down with the protests, I don't think my parents will let me go anywhere after," Valeria adds.

Mrs. García is right: This year is not like other years. It's an election year, and for the first time in Honduran history, a president—the current president—is trying to reelect himself, against every constitutional law. If Juan Orlando wins, again, that'd be four more years under his presidency, eight overall. The right wing party has ruled the country since the 2009 coup.

It doesn't help that he's been tied to drug cartels. Or that his first candidacy was financed with social-security money, which resulted in over three thousand deaths because of missing funds for medicine and medical equipment. Some people were even given pills made out of flour—or worse, road-marking paint. On top of all that, Juan Orlando appointed his sister, Hilda Hernández, as director of strategy for his presidential campaign, and now she still holds a major position in the government.

Protests from the opposition have exploded all over Honduras ever since Hernández announced he was once again the candidate for the national right-wing party. No one expects a fair election—and the September 15 parade is the perfect opportunity for a big uprising. Maynor said that the National Police is planning to have thousands of agents on the streets of Tegus that day.

"Do we have any yellow paint?" Carla asks. She's working on the crown of our national shield, which currently looks oddly like one of those old-timey judge wigs.

I wish Cami was here. She can really paint. But Camila is a palillona, currently practicing synched-up marching and fancy baton twirling on the soccer field.

"We used all of it." The tip of Valeria's tongue pokes out the side of her mouth as she paints white spots of a sickly-looking deer.

Carla sighs. "I'll ask Mrs. García for more." Her chair scrapes the floor as she gets up.

I finish painting the last blue star on our flag, right in the middle. My fingers are stained blue, and I think about asking Mrs. García if I can go to the bathroom to wash them off. There's a big window on the way to the bathroom with a perfect view of the soccer field: I imagine las palillonas there—including Camila—the sun hitting them at full force. Even inside, cool drops of sweat keep sliding down my neck.

"Do you think Juan Orlando will actually win?" Valeria interrupts my thoughts.

My body stills reflexively. I look up at her. She's holding her long black hair with one hand and fanning air onto her neck with the other. I go to offer her the ponytail holder on my wrist before realizing I don't have one.

Truth is, I don't know what I think. Juan Orlando and the

nationalist party have gotten away with a lot. Like, *a lot* a lot. Why would this election be any different?

"If he does," I being to say, slowly, "it probably won't be fair. I think everyone hates him. He's, you know . . . cost us a lot of lives."

"The UNAH shooting was just a few months ago." Valeria cracks her knuckles. "People can't forget that fast."

My chest tightens. Months ago, Juan Orlando Hernández ordered the military police—the MP—to take to the streets in major cities like Tegus and San Pedro to "mantener el control." When I still had my phone, I saw videos all over Twitter and Instagram of the MP beating protestors, firing tear gas and rubber bullets.

And the worst—the one that still pops into my head when it gets too quiet—of four MP walking into the National Autonomous University, la UNAH, and shooting into a crowd of students. Real bullets. The video was recorded from a phone. It's all blurry and pixelated, but you can hear the high-pitched screams of two women in the background, and the *fuck, puta, Dios, nos están matando,* of the person recording it, followed by the drumbeats of the soles of his shoes hitting asphalt as he runs away.

Maynor wasn't there that day. The university had been on strike for months—no classes held, and whole buildings blocked off by student fronts.

I didn't really understand what the strike was about. I still don't, not really. Maynor said it had to do with students not being allowed to participate in the democratic structure of the university's academic guidelines, and then being denied the right to pacific protests.

I do remember hearing that a student leader's dad was killed outside his home the day after he'd done several interviews in support of his son and the cause.

The night of the shooting, I sat in front of Mami's TV, switching between news channels, waiting for someone—anyone—to say something about the shooting. Maynor kept walking from one end of the bedroom to the other, cupping his face with his hands. We waited for the names of the dead students. Why the MP shot them in the first place. Nothing came.

Instead, a thirty-minute special about the first Walmart to open in Tegucigalpa in a couple of months was aired. There was a small note about it buried in the newspaper the next day, with no names or specifics. Just "enfrentamiento en la UNAH." It was almost as if nothing had happened, except for the video and the three corpses. And the Instagram stories reposting the video. And my poems. Or rather, the poems of @InsurreccionPoeticaHN.

I started the account the very same night of the university shooting. After many *no puede ser* and *this country* and Maynor brushing his scruffy beard with his fingers over and over and biting his nails, we went to bed.

I tried to fall asleep. My chest felt heavy, like someone was sitting on it, or pushing me down into the bed. I kept turning and turning, but there was no relief from the images of my brother running through the halls of la UNAH, screaming with no sound coming out of his mouth or the cameraman's footsteps as he escaped, y mi mami with a gun to her face at that traffic light months ago.

I sat up and opened my phone's notes app, typing out eight uneven-rhyming lines about the president, and the students, y la corrupción and no change. I read them over a dozen times, enough to memorize them. And then I knew I had to say them to someone.

But Cami was asleep by then, and things between us were already weird. I'd heard the creak of Maynor's window as he snuck out. I would never post it to my personal account. I'm not stupid—I've seen and heard what happens to people who speak out against the government. And I guess a part of me felt embarrassed, or maybe nervous, about being perceived as too intense or virtue signaling or something.

A few years ago, Valeria made the mistake of pushing back on Mrs. García's views during our Family Code same-sex marriage debacle. It was a small thing—she said something like *why should we care about who other people are attracted to?* Mrs. García was appalled, of course. But the worst was the way our classmates reacted to it: The boys would not stop teasing her, calling her *la defensora de los pobres* and over-the-top and abogada. It was a quick lesson about how uncool it was to care too much about anything. And that was just the people in our class. I can't imagine what people on the Internet would have to say.

So I created another account. I didn't even have to think of the username—it seemed to have lived in my head for a while. Then I took a screenshot of the poem, posted it with a bunch of hashtags related to the shooting and the president, and went to bed.

The next day, the post had more likes than any of my personal account photos, and over a hundred shares. People from school—from my own senior class—reposted it with GIFs and stickers and their own words. It was exciting but weird. Somehow, I knew that if they knew the identity of the person writing the poems (regardless of who it was), they wouldn't have been as willing to share. Something about the anonymity made it okay to care. To be "intense."

I couldn't resist telling Maynor about it. He was almost giddy with excitement as he climbed into bed next to me, reading the poem out loud a couple of times. It felt good to see him happy and proud, instead of the storm of grief he had been the night before.

"I had to go all the way to the first floor for more paint." Carla sits down next to us with a huff, dissolving my tangle of thoughts. "So," she says, turning to me, "did you decide about your birthday?"

"Not really," I say, shrugging. It's not that I don't like birthdays—I actually love them. It just feels pointless to plan for a day that will probably almost certainly most likely be a mess.

"I say we just wait and see. Make a small plan, like, dinner somewhere and drinks at La Esquina?" Valeria comes to my rescue. "And if anything goes down, then we move it to the next week or something."

"Sure. That sounds great." I smile at her.

"Okay, who do you want to invite?" Valeria asks.

"Um, you two, obviously. Miguel and Cami . . ."

"If you invite Camila, you have to invite Pablo too, you know," Carla chips in.

" . . . and Pablo." It takes a lot of willpower not to roll my eyes.

"Ok, so the parade is at eleven and will probably go until three or something. If you give everyone time to shower and stuff, I'd say dinner at like, eight, and then La Esquina."

Again, planning my birthday the same day as an anticipated

uprising feels like planning an extremely fantastical thing. I hold out hope though. It'd be the first in a year full of firsts: My first time getting into La Esquina with my real ID. My first time voting in November. My first time drinking (legally).

"Chicas, ¿cómo vamos?" Mrs. García singsongs from behind me, looking over our flora and fauna banner—we finally compromised on feathers *and* leaves.

"I think we just need to draw a couple more orchids and animals and it should be good," Carla decides.

"Yes, and the flag?"

"All done," I say, pointing to the center star, which has already dried.

"Perfecto, chicas. Please make sure to go over the form with your parents. It's pretty straightforward: The school buses will take you downtown. The parade should be around two hours long. You need to bring your own water bottles, but you can buy food at the stadium. Then we'll bus you back to the school. The school reserves the right to make changes to this plan if needed, or to cancel our participation in the parade if we think it might endanger the lives of our students in any way. Okay?"

We nod. Her words sound rehearsed—she must have given this same explanation a dozen times today. She's the Civics and History of Honduras teacher for grades 9–12. As she stops to examine our drawings a little longer, I notice that her usual super-tight-and-slick bun has loosened, a few graying black hairs curling around her ears and neck. She looks flushed, her blinking just a little slower and longer than normal.

She must be exhausted. I can't imagine planning el desfile del 15 this year, never mind the last twenty-five.

I take a deep breath, and then turn to look at her. "Mrs. García . . . Do you think there will be a parade?"

She releases a shaky exhale, then pastes on a smile that looks like it hurts her face.

"I don't know, girls. I think we're in for a historic quince de septiembre."

FOUR

Camila leans against the side of my bus, scrolling through her phone. Her hair, which was down this morning, is now up in a bun. Sweat licks baby hairs to her forehead and temples. Her cheeks are sunburnt from being under the afternoon sun for the past hour. The light brown of her skin and its yellow undertones with the reddish glow of the sun makes me think of a sunset, sort of. I cringe at how cheesy that sounds, even in my head.

The end of the school day is usually the only time I get to see Cami alone—Pablo is off at fútbol practice. Everyone else either stays in some after-school club or their parents pick them up. But Cami lives too far from the city for any of that, and Mami y Abuela could never leave work to pick Alberto and me up.

Camila used to wait for me outside my bus every day, but she hasn't in a long time. Not since February. I've concluded that she must speed-walk from her last period to the bus and hustle inside before I can even spot her.

But not today. I tell Alberto to get on our bus without me, that I'll be there in a few. He ignores me, of course, and runs straight to Cami.

They hug, and she asks him about his day. He makes a big deal of explaining a goal he scored during recess, even re-creating the kick with an imaginary ball. He beams when she congratulates him and sends him off with a forehead kiss.

"Listen to your sister," she says, "go grab your seats."

Alberto blushes and hurries off.

At what age do you learn to have some chill about a crush?

"Hold on—" Cami touches my arm before I can follow Alberto, then pulls out her phone and finishes typing whatever message she'd started before. I wonder what it is that can't wait, but she has to make *me* wait for.

Yet another moment where I miss my phone, when it feels like my hands aren't meant to be empty. I stay and wait in silence, staring awkwardly at my shoes. It just feels good that she wants me to stick around: Like maybe things are slowly going back to normal. To before.

She finally puts her phone in her pocket and looks up at me. Her eyes are somewhere between green and brown, depending on the light. Our bus partially blocks the sunlight from hitting us directly, so her eyes are closer to brown right now. Her eyebrows rise with her mouth as she smirks. "So. . . . If you're getting your phone back today, can we expect a new poem soon?"

She's the only other person aside from Maynor who knows that *the* poem is *my* poem. Because, well . . . I've told Cami pretty much everything since forever. Even though shit was super awkward between us, texts far and apart, it felt so good to tell her about the poem—to have something else to focus on besides the sticky tension between us.

"Maybe," I say, "September fifteenth is probably a good occasion for it."

"Who knew your birthday was such a big deal?" Cami's smirk softens into a smile.

"You did." I smile back at her. "How are my gifts coming along?"

This is one of our things too—elaborate birthday presents, extra points if handmade. Camila is an amazing painter, so this year I gave her three handmade painting canvases made of linen. Abuela helped me find the perfect fabric for them, and the stretching bars too. We built them together at her sewing workshop, all three in different, special sizes that you wouldn't find in a store. Abuela even wrapped them up herself with the wide pink ribbons she usually uses for ballerinas' buns.

Luckily, Camila's birthday was in January. I don't know what I would've done if it had been *after* we kissed. Come to think of it, maybe she wasn't planning on getting me anything.

I open my mouth to say *just kidding* but she cuts me off.

"Vos tranquila y yo nerviosa. I'm doing something a little different this year. Eighteen is a big birthday."

She smiles. We smile at each other.

"Can't wait," I say, feeling warm, but then I add, "I mean—if there even is a birthday, you know."

"Yeah," she sighs, then leans her back against the bus. "We'll see. I heard my mom on the phone last night saying the MP's locking down, like, ten blocks, including the hospital."

Camila's mom is a nurse at the downtown hospital. When I used to spend the night or she drove us somewhere, she'd tell us the most messed-up stories. Not what you'd expect, not grotesque injury stories. More like whispered accounts of doctors and nurses getting forced into cars by mareros, taken somewhere to treat a wounded member of the gang.

The deal was simple: If the wounded guy survived, the doctor or nurse got to leave—and live.

"I don't even know why they're holding a parade this year, with everything that's been going on," I say, leaning my back against the bus next to her. Our shoulders and arms touch. Her skin is soft and sun-warm.

"Because of that," she says. "To make it seem like it's all normal, like this could be any other year, any other election."

I scratch my neck. "Yeah. You're right."

That's when I notice that my hands are still covered in blue paint. I tug at the dried blue tendrils, and they come off like thin pieces of skin. I stop, though, when Cami reaches for one of my hands and starts peeling away the paint herself.

Her hands are steadier, more careful, her fingers long and soft. The pieces she pulls come off easily, in whole sections. I feel dizzy again, and the hand she's holding begins to sweat.

"Better to have blue hands than a sunburn," she jokes, pointing to her face.

"All for independence." I roll my eyes.

"Mhmm."

After a couple minutes there's barely any paint left, but she still brings my hands up to her eyes, as if checking for any missed spots. The driver turns on the bus and our backs shudder with the motor. Cami gently drops my hands.

"Text me when you get your phone back," she says, turning to walk to her bus, which is just two spots away.

"I will," I say.

I watch her walk away. I stay watching her as she goes up the three steps, finds her seat all the way in the back, and pulls out her earbuds.

Before Cami and I kissed, we would text all day and call each other for hours, even after having been together for most of the school day. After the kiss, we started talking less: The more days that passed, the more and more awkward it felt to bring up what happened at La Esquina. Then it was summer break, and we only saw each other a handful of times at parties and group hangouts.

When school started again, I hoped enough time had passed for things to go back to the way they were before. But then my phone died. And she started dating Pablo. And now we're here.

It's like, I think I can still tell Camila anything, except this big important thing that she should already know. That of course she knows. Because it's happening to both of us.

Right?

FIVE

That afternoon, I'm doing homework with Alberto at the dinner table. Mine is on the key elements of the Baroque movement and his is to trace the political map of Central America, labeling every lake, volcano, and river. We have the radio on, set to the new hits station. Ozuna's voice peaks over a fast beat—I turn the volume down after reading the same sentence four times without taking in any meaning.

We hear the key turning in the front door lock and look up. We're not used to anyone being home before seven or eight.

"¿Cómo están mis hermanitos?" Maynor is home much earlier than usual, fake-hiding a plastic bag behind his body. It's green-and-blue-lined, clearly from Pulpería Las Flores, the corner store on our street.

"What's that?" Alberto's eyes widen as he stands up and reaches toward Maynor.

"A surprise." Maynor holds the bag just out of Alberto's reach. His mood has clearly improved since this morning.

"For me?"

"For us, Beto. I thought we could use some hermanitos time before Mami and Abuela come home." Maynor puts the bag down on the dinner table and takes out a packet of plantain chips and a two-liter cold Coca-Cola. Alberto claps and runs to the kitchen to get three cups, a knife, a bowl, limes, and hot sauce.

This is our favorite tradition. It was our dad who taught us—Maynor and me—many years ago. When he was still around.

Maynor cuts the lime in half and squeezes it over the plantain chips in the bowl. To get the most juice out, he does this weird thing where he presses the lime halves against each other, making them kiss, sort of. It works even on the driest of limes. I pour three cups of Coca-Cola and Alberto adds a bunch of hot sauce to the chips.

"Okay, what is this crap you're listening to?" Maynor jokes, grabbing the radio and turning the volume up.

"First of all, that's the new Ozuna song, and it's *good*," Alberto says.

Maynor's expression turns mischievous. Then he brings his fingers to his mouth, and I realize what he's about to do a second too late. Before I can cover my ears, the loudest, most horrible whistle bursts out of him.

"Maynor!" I flinch, yelling at him over the ringing in my ears. "Why?"

Alberto presses his hands to his ears and grimaces. We've both been victims of this trick our whole lives.

"Because." Maynor grins. "I had to clear your ears of this shit.

53

You only think Ozuna's new song is good because you don't know your old reggaeton, Beto."

"Okay, yes, old reggaeton is always gonna be the best. But Ozuna and Bad Bunny aren't bad," I say. "You sound like un viejito when you're all 'the good old days,' Maynor."

He laughs. "Okay, okay—top three Daddy Yankee songs, go!"

We do this for an hour. Maynor pulls out his phone and plays the songs we name. We make our way through all the major artists. Then the conversation shifts into who Alberto thinks will win next year's FIFA World Cup and Maynor disagrees—he's a hard-core Brazil fan, while Beto believes in Argentina whole-heartedly.

I listen to them argue, but don't know enough to weigh in. After we finish all the Coke and plantain chips, Maynor tries to show us how old reggaeton is danced and Beto almost falls out of his chair laughing. Our hands are sticky with hot sauce and lime juice.

As the sun starts to set outside the windows, Beto leaves to wash his hands. Maynor stops the music and sits on the chair next to mine, turning his body to face me.

"Hey—I'm sorry about this morning," he says.

"What are you sorry for?"

"I don't know. Trying to fight Mami over the movie comment thing," he says. "I never seem to know the right thing to do. But I also don't want to—you know, make you uncomfortable or think I don't have your back or something."

"It's okay." I shake my head. "I don't want you to feel like you need to fight everyone who says something dumb. Especially not Mom."

"But I will," he says, holding my eyes and leaning forward. I believe him.

"It's okay." I reach for his hand, giving it a good squeeze.

"Okay," he says, squeezing back. "So, how's little Cami?"

He raises his eyebrows and smirks like one of the señoras at the beauty salon asking if I have a boyfriend yet. I drop his hand and roll my eyes.

"Hay, Maynor. How's *your* girl? What's her name—Pamela? No, no, that's the one from last week, right? Or was it the week before that?"

He slaps my arm playfully. "Okay, fine, fine, forget I asked."

I slap him back and he flinches. I forgot about the bruise on his arm.

"Oh fuck, sorry," I say. "How did that happen? Soccer?"

"Yeah," he says, and I think he'll say more, but instead he picks up our bowls and cups. "I'll wash these."

Alberto comes out of the bathroom as the front door opens. We can barely see Abuela's head behind the crinkly bags of groceries spilling out of her arms.

"¿Qué quieren cenar?" she asks as the three of us rush to take bags out of her hands and start putting things away.

Maynor and Alberto fight over what we should eat for dinner, baleadas or tacos de pollo. We go with baleadas. Abuela assigns us each a part: Maynor slices plantains. Alberto sets the table. I heat some frijoles up, and she begins to make tortillas. She tells us about the orders she's making for the September 15 parade. All the palillonas outfits, and a guacamaya costume that took her three days having to glue-gun all the feathers.

Mi abuela is the smartest and most talented artist I know, but she would never call herself that. Una artista. She says that her work is the work of a woman who didn't have any other options. That she would have loved to be a doctor or teacher. That's what she wants for us, *better* and *real* jobs.

I don't know what a real job means. I *do* know that her feet swell like water balloons every day. That I've never seen them in any shade other than purple. That the blue veins that bulk and wrap her ankles are longer than the rivers Alberto traced today for his homework. Longer than the rivers that run across our small piece of dirt on this continent.

Mami comes home when we're already washing and drying dishes. Maynor gets up to fix her plate. I try to wait more than a few seconds, but as soon as she's sitting down, I ask about my phone.

"I tried," she sighs. "But I had no lunch break, and then I got there too late. They'd just closed. They're not open until Monday."

I take a deep breath. I can't lie, I'm upset: It's been weeks. And now I have to spend yet another weekend without a phone.

Not to mention that I won't be able to text Camila tonight. Our conversation next to the buses today felt—for the first time in a long time—like our friendship might finally be returning to normal.

Mami glances at me. "I'll go then, I promise."

She looks exhausted. After a beat, I nod. "Okay," I say. "Please."

I'll for sure be reminding her Monday morning.

Mami tells us about her day, the crazy wedding clients she had to deal with and more hotel drama. Abuela asks her if there are any foreigners staying at the hotel coming to see the parade, and if any of them are single and could get her a marriage green card.

We laugh.

This is how it's always been: Mami will never have time for anything other than planning someone else's wedding. Abuela will always ask her the same question and make us dinner and dress other people up in feathers and sparkles and expensive-looking fabrics—but not herself. And las baleadas will sit warm in our bellies, while Alberto shows us the kick motion of the goal he scored during recess, again. Maynor, playing goalie, will let the phantom ball slip through his fingers and let his brother score.

MAYNOR

MAY 7, 2009

"Mira hijo, all you need to remember is that fútbol is just like this city. Gana el más fuerte. And as captain, *you* are in charge of how strong of a game your team gives."

Maynor nodded. He'd heard this speech before—his father liked to repeat himself. Still, he had to admire the way Diego delivered the same advice every time—like gospel, like he alone held the secrets of the universe. Or soccer. Or women.

"Dios is with us," his dad continued, signaling with his hand for Maynor to turn left. "I put you in my prayers this morning. If it's his voluntad, you'll win today. And, of course, Olimpia will too—we'll crown ourselves three-time champions. You just leave everything in God's hands. Like I do."

"Sí, Papá," Maynor mumbled. He was still too new to driving to comfortably hold conversations and focus on the road. But something kept him from confessing this to his dad.

Mami would've understood. But then again, he didn't feel this nervous about messing up when it was her in the car.

The radio played a Luis Miguel song. Diego tapped his knee to the beat.

"Are you watching Olimpia's game later at home?"

"I don't know." Maynor scanned the parking lot for a spot. "We might all head over to Mauricio's house after our match. Watch it there. I'll call if I need you to get me."

"Dale, hijo. I think I'm gonna go watch it with Gerardo. Trying to convince your mom to come with me."

Maynor turned the car off. Outside, the sun reflected bright shards off the metal of the cars. He had forgotten to put sunscreen on, again. He could already feel the soft burn over his skin tomorrow.

"That sounds fun," Maynor said. "Salúdame a Gerardo."

He fetched his soccer bag from the back seat, unzipping it to make sure his lucky gloves were inside. The smell of sweaty laundry filled the car, for a second overpowering Diego's flowery cologne. Before he could reach for the door, his father put his hand on his back. Maynor flinched, instinctively.

"¿Qué te pasa?" his father asked.

"Nothing, sorry. Just pre-game jitters."

He'd flinched at his touch for years now. Usually, he could regulate himself enough that it wasn't noticeable.

"I told you to not be nervous already." There was a hint of annoyance in Diego's voice. "It's all in God's hands. And you know what I was gonna say? Y'all should invite some *cheeses* to watch the game with you at Mauricio's. Girls love soccer players. When I was your age and on the team—it was *bam bam bam*. Just girl after girl. It drove them crazy to see me on the field."

Maynor met his eyes and forced a smile. "Sure. That's a good idea, Papá."

"I'm telling you. If you just listen to my consejos, things will always work out for you. You're seventeen—your whole life por delante. You just listen to me."

Maynor nodded. "I know, I know."

Full head of black hair slicked back, thick eyebrows, and clean-shaven, his father was young. He was only sixteen years older than Maynor, but he was also just . . . *young*. At times, talking to him felt no different that talking to his buddies.

Once, Diego had seemed like the most impressive man in the world to Maynor. He knew everything there was to know about the things that mattered. Where there once had been awe, all he could find now was fear.

His father continued to rub his back in small circles. Maynor tried not to move this time.

"All right, good luck with the game. Call if you need to—we'll celebrate your and Olimpia's wins this weekend. And remember to pray before the game."

The game ended without any goals—still, it hadn't been an easy match. It was clear the boys were overexcited, pumped with anticipation of the Honduran Soccer League final later that day.

Olimpia was playing Motagua. Whenever these clubs—both teams from Tegus—faced each other, the city was a mess. Fights that often ended in death broke out over the city. Traffic was even worse than usual. And random bursts of fireworks could be heard throughout the day.

"You're gonna hate me," Mauricio said. He'd walked off to call his mom and let her know the game was over—that he and Maynor were ready to be picked up.

"What's up?" Maynor was untying his tennis shoes, looking for fresh socks and slippers in his bag. Both boys were shirtless, hoping to dry off some of the sweat.

"My dad got last minute tickets for me and him to go to the game," Mauricio said, with an apologetic smile.

"Oh man, that's sick. Fuck you, dude." Maynor reached for his wet T-shirt and tried to flick Mauricio with it, but he side-stepped the strike.

"Sorry, man," he said, reaching to pat Maynor on the back. "I wish we had one more ticket. Is it okay if we just drop you off at your house? We can still get food though."

After burgers at Bigos, Mauricio's mom drove both of them home so Mauricio could change. As Maynor waited for his friend to get ready, he considered his dad's advice: Should he text a girl and try to watch the game with her? He ran through the possibilities. And the realities. Like the fact that he was covered in dried-off sweat that had turned his skin sticky. He could smell himself. He'd need to go home and change. Maybe ask one of his parents for money. There were just too many steps and not enough motivation.

Mauricio showered in record time and put on the season's Olimpia jersey. It was white with a blue neck and *Coca-Cola* in red letters across the chest, the blue and red lion sigil on the left pectoral. As he slicked back his hair, he caught Maynor's face in the mirror. "Why don't you hit up Laura or Marcela to watch the game with you? You know they'd say yes in a heartbeat."

"I don't know, man." Maynor stretched his arms over his head. The adrenaline from their game was wearing off—he could feel his muscles growing sore. "I'd have to go home and shower first, get dressed and shit. I don't think there's time."

Mauricio looked at his watch. "Sure there is. Just shower here and borrow something. We'll drop you off wherever you want."

Maynor sighed, then reached for his phone to call Marcela. He knew his father would be pleased about this turn of events, and something about this knowledge furthered the exhaustion of his muscles.

He showered and borrowed jeans and a plain white polo from Mauricio's closet. The boys were almost the same size, save that Maynor was a few inches taller. He looked in the mirror: Clean shaven, short black hair. He thought of his dad and tried to find traces of him in his own face.

"So, we're dropping you off at TGI Friday's?" Mauricio said, reaching for his wallet on the dresser.

"I need to go home first. Get some money from my dad. I'll ask him to take me."

"Man, he's gonna *love* that you're going out with Marcela. One hundred Lempiras says he'll try to meet her."

"Probably." Maynor ran his fingers through his hair.

Traffic was as bad as it got. Everyone seemed pressed to their horn. Mauricio's dad, like most other capitalinos, was a fearless driver: He drove over median strips and even against traffic at times to move forward.

Dark blue Motagua flags and white Olimpia flags were attached to most cars. Where there wasn't any team-color publicity, the city was covered with banners that read NO A LA CUARTA URNA or SÍ A LA CUARTA URNA.

Maynor felt resentful of this election year. He would turn eighteen on January 1, just a month too late to vote. The president, Manuel Zelaya, was trying to install a new ballot, la cuarta urna, that would essentially give the people the option to re-elect him. Maynor knew this was a big deal—something his parents and his grandparents were often talking about. He didn't know if he should feel in favor or against it.

On second thought, maybe it was a relief that he couldn't vote.

By 7:30, thirty minutes before the game began, they pulled up to Maynor's house. "Let me know how it goes with Marcela," Mauricio said with a knowing smirk.

"Thank you for the ride, Don Fabio," Maynor said. Mauricio's father reached out to shake his hand.

"Anytime, buddy. Say hi to your parents for me."

Maynor took a deep breath before reaching for his keys. The billiard bar across the street was already pumping loud music. A couple regulars stood outside, smoking cigarettes. Up the road, the piñata stores were closing for the day.

Both of his parents' cars were in the garage. Usually, his mom was at the gym at this time. And she wouldn't skip it for the game, regardless of how much his dad insisted. She hated being around Diego during games.

Maybe it meant that she could drive Maynor to his date. The thought filled him with relief.

He turned the key, pushed open the iron gate, and walked to the front door. The house seemed quiet—by now, his father would usually have the TV at full volume, listening to los reporteros making their predictions about the game. Or he'd be in the shower, getting ready to head out, '90s music turned up high. Maynor's siblings, Alberto and Libertad, would also be home—watching TV, running around, maybe doing homework on the dining room table.

He pushed the door open. The loud creak of the hinges cut the air.

The first floor was empty. It smelled like nothing. No one was cooking. No one had recently eaten. The hairs on his arms and back stood up. Because he had lived in his body, which had lived in this house, he knew. He knew to know. Something was wrong.

It was the silence that filled him with dread. Because he knew it wasn't silence at all, but the appearance of it. He closed his eyes. And then he could hear it. The muted bam, bam, bam that seemed almost underwater. A soft crying underneath it.

Maynor stood at the foot of the stairs for a second, his soccer bag still hanging from his shoulder. His heartbeat was fast and hard against his chest. He thought he could feel it in his throat. He knew exactly what was happening upstairs. And for a split second that Maynor would spend the rest of his life thinking about, mostly with unbearable shame, he thought of how easy it'd be to just turn around. To walk out the door, which was still half-open behind him, and out the iron gate. He wasn't even supposed to be here.

But something was different about this time. There were no screams. No screams at all.

He took the stairs two at a time, his legs feeling more and more liquid with each step. At the end of the hall, his parents' door was closed. It couldn't lock—his parents had broken it years ago in a fight. The banging behind it was clear now: A fist hitting a body, a face. Because he lived in his body, which had lived in this house, he knew the sound a fist made against a face versus a torso.

Finally, he heard his mom's voice, carried on a sob: Please stop.

The door next to his parents' cracked open. Small fingers appear around its edge, and above them, a face: Libertad.

Her cheeks were wet. They locked eyes, and he put a finger over his mouth. He slipped inside the room, closing the door behind him as silently as possible. Four-year-old Alberto sat on the bed, his eyes were wide-open and eyelashes wet, like he too had been crying.

"What happened?" Maynor asked his sister.

Libertad looked up at him, her hands locked together in front of her. In the next room, a crash—Alberto jumped.

"Okay." Maynor took out his phone. "Lock the door, okay? And don't open it until I say it's okay. Do you understand? Only open for me. Not for Papi and not for Mami."

His sister nodded. Maynor dialed 911, then prepared to burst into his parents' room—for the first and last time ever.

SIX

"Switch the thread to royal blue. There should be four cones on the top shelf," Abuela says. I wrap the white thread on the sewing machine's spool pin around my finger and pull. It snaps just when I think I can't take my circulation being cut anymore.

The blood returns to my fingertip, returning color to my skin.

Occasionally on Sundays, Abuela drags me with her to the workshop. On weekdays, the rest of the women who work with her are here. Some of them have been here for years—even before Mami was pregnant with Maynor, back when the workshop was a few rooms of our current house.

But on Sundays, it's just Abuela cutting and sewing and threading and never giving it a rest. She likes me to come along, even if there's not much I know how to do. At least I can bring her a glass of water or change the thread color on the machine. Mostly, I think she wants my company.

The radio on Abuela's old phone plays over the hum of the

machine's motor. She's always listening to some Catholic sermon. She'll pray along for a bit, but most of the time I think she just likes the background noise. The same way she likes us to keep Mami's TV on all through the night.

Abuela is used to voices and the sounds of life happening around her. She grew up with six siblings, and had three children herself: mi tío José, Mami, and mi tía Martha. Tío Jose lives in San Pedro Sula—SPS—the big industrial city to the north. He does something related to installing security cameras for la Alcaldía or the government or something. We're not really close, but he comes back to Tegus on Christmas with his children—mis primos—and his wife. They usually stay over at our house for a couple days, then drive back before New Year's.

Maynor talks to Tío José the most. I suspect it's because Tío feels like he needs to be Maynor's dad-figure. Tía Martha died eight years ago.

"Amén, amén," Abuela repeats after the radio priest.

"Done," I say, tying the last blue thread to the white leftover.

"Gracias, hija." Abuela stands up and stretches. "What are you wearing on Friday, then? You need to tell me today, porque I don't have time this week to make something last-minute."

"I told you, I don't need anything. I'm just carrying the flag and banners. I'm gonna wear jeans and a blue shirt of Mami's or something."

Abuela presses her lips together. I can tell this disappoints her: Any other girl in my position would probably squeeze the juice out of having my abuela—she'd be the palillona with the best fit or get Abuela to make her a traditional Honduran dress with multiple layers and colors.

"What are your friends wearing?" Abuela sits at the machine and pushes down on the pedal to pull the rest of the white thread out.

I shrug. "I think the only one of my friends who is a palillona is Cami."

"And she has an outfit?"

"I think so."

"Well, I'm sure she'll look beautiful. That girl has a nice waist. All of you—so young." Abuela's eyes pull her concentration to the fabric in her hands: a piece of something, a shirt or a skirt or a dress.

She's right—Camila does have a nice waist. I feel my face get hot at the thought and rub my shoulder. "What are you making?"

"It's one of the skirt layers for a dress." Abuela doesn't look up—she squints through her huge drug-store glasses, the fabric pinched between her fingers. She dyed the roots of her hair black this morning, like she does every week, and some of her swollen fingers still bear the evidence. "This woman's daughter—she's been my client for years—is dressing in a vestido típico. She wants it with interspersed blue and white layers, a long skirt so she can lift it and dance with it. You know, so it looks pretty when she moves it around."

I have no idea how the piece of fabric she's holding will become a skirt layer. But Abuela's hands move instinctively. She's been doing this longer than I've been alive. There's something magic-like to the workshop, to the way pieces that appear shape-less come together to form a whole.

She must have made thousands of dresses by now. I wonder how many of those were for us—for any of her daughters.

"Did Tía Martha like to dress up for the fifteenth?"

"Uy no," Abuela says, a smile hinting on the corner of her mouth. "Marthita was so, *so* particular. Every fabric was too itchy, too thick, too thin. She wanted me to let her go dressed in the men's typical robes—said they were more comfortable."

She stops to adjusts a thread. I'm fascinated by the piece in front of her that's suddenly begun to take on a recognizable skirt shape.

"Imagine. Carmen, your mom, was always excited for the parade. All week before the fifteenth they'd both spend it sitting in front of me, watching each thing I made, trying it all on even if it didn't fit. Carmen wanted me to make her a copy of every dress and Martha wanted to just complain about it. My daughters are—were always opposites of each other."

The left end of her lip lifts slightly.

Abuela's memory is long like her workdays: She can remember anything, even if it happened twenty or thirty years ago. Sometimes she tells the same story more than once, but she never changes or adds any details—her recollection is unmoving. It's one of the things I love the most about her.

But I also think it's one of the reasons that sadness sits on her chest. Why she sometimes cries all through the night, then pretends we couldn't hear her the next morning.

"One time," she begins, and I move closer to hear her over the sewing machine's growl. "Tu papá . . . I mean, César, your grandfather . . . he was stationed in Argentina. I was alone with the three kids at home and needed to go do something—un mandado, ya no me acuerdo de qué." She stops to extend the fabric in front of her and pull at the just-sewn stitches, testing their stretchability. I am patient for her to return to the story, knowing its exact course.

"I asked our neighbor back then to look after them for an hour, told him I'd be back rapidito. I come back and Marthita, she was four or five at the time, was just waiting for me to leave to play with César's old guns. She had seen where we hid them. They weren't loaded, of course. Come back and the neighbor tells me he doesn't know where she got them, imagine." At this she looks up to see my face, to approve my reaction. I smile and shake my head.

"Ah, and he tells me Carmen, she was eight or nine, has been taking a bath since I left. I go and see because I know something's up: She's bathing in milk. Imagine, ¡con lo que nos costaba todo! No money, and this girl is bathing in milk while the other one plays with the guns."

I laugh. I've heard it before, though I always flinch a little when Abuela talks about Abuelo. He's not dead . . . but his absence still carries a sting.

Mi abuelo is a retired colonel from the coast. He lived with us for a long time, but a few years ago he just . . . went back home, to his small town next to the Caribbean Sea. He still calls once a week and asks how we're doing. But he and Abuela have a weird marriage.

No one has ever said anything directly to me about it, but I remember years ago overhearing Maynor and Mami whispering about Abuelo's other family. Abuela will often say she just doesn't care for him, but when anything important happens—a political scandal, a friend of the family's death, anything—he's the first person she calls. They can talk for hours like old friends.

When Abuelo lived in Tegus, he'd spend hours giving us the most random history lessons. He seems to know everything, from information about centuries-old empires to the Central American colonies and how we all got here. One time, he told me that—although un-google-able—most of the wealth in Honduras, Guatemala, and El Salvador can be traced back to twelve families, dating back to colonial times.

I don't know how he knows stuff like this. Maynor says Tía Martha would call him a walking library.

"Hija, go make us some coffee." Abuela stops working abruptly, glancing at my hands. I've been biting my nails without meaning to; she's good at noticing when people need something to do.

"Can I borrow your phone?"

She looks at me over her eyeglasses, then raises her eyebrows and nods.

I grab the phone and go to the workshop's small kitchen, where the women keep their lunches during the weekday, and Abuela her old French press. I set the water to boil and type in a number I know from memory.

I haven't called her in months, even before my phone broke. She hasn't called me either. But something about how excited Camila seemed for my birthday and me getting my phone back makes me feel brave today. I know she has this number, Abuela's, saved. She picks up on the third ring.

"How's your parade fit coming along?" Cami asks.

"You know it isn't."

"So, your mom didn't pick up your phone on Friday?"

"Nope. Tomorrow, though," I say, smiling to myself in the empty kitchen. It feels good how much she seems to want me to have my phone back. "What's up with you?"

"Not much. Finishing calc. Did you get it done?"

"This morning. We've been at the workshop since, like, seven. Abuela asked if you had your palillona outfit—said you'll look great."

"Yeah, that's a mess, but tell her I say thank you. I wish I could've just gone to her, but you know my mom. I'm low-key excited for Friday though."

It's crazy how normal this feels. Like the last six months didn't happen at all.

"You know the parade is the same every year, right?"

"I meant your birthday."

"Your parents said it's okay for you to stay over, then?"

"Yup. If everything's okay, yeah."

"Awesome. And my gift?" I'm biting my nails again but have self-awareness to stop.

"You know I'm not telling you anything about that."

Her voice is light. I can picture her in her room, in bed with her notebook and textbook open.

The water boils. I turn off the stove and pour it over the ground coffee, letting the mixture sit for a minute. The rich aroma fills the room.

"Okaaaay. But know that I'll definitely remember this when it's your turn," I say, faking annoyance. The phone about slips from my hand as I push down on the press's plunger. "Ay. I've got to go, Cami. See you tomorrow."

"Tell your abuela I said hi."

I hang up. I'm about to pour the coffee and bring it to Abuela, before deciding to make one more call. I go through her call history and find a number that's purposefully unsaved, but with multiple calls back and forth. He picks up immediately, like his phone was in his hand.

"¿Aló?"

"Abuelo. It's me, Libertad."

"Hola, colocha bella," he says, his voice rising, excited. I can tell he's just sat up. In the background, a loud TV plays what sounds like a soccer match. "¿Cómo estás?"

He always calls me that, colocha bella. Abuelo, more than anyone, loves my curly hair. When I was a child, he'd try brushing and styling it for me himself if Mami and Abuela weren't around. He'd get disappointed whenever he visited and my hair was straightened: *But what about los colochos?*

"Bien, Abuelo. At the workshop. How are you?"

"Bien, bien. Gracias a Dios. How's school?"

I tell him about the Baroque movement project I just finished. He asks me questions about Spanish Baroque architecture that I can tell he already knows the answer to. I wonder, not for the first time, if he would've been a schoolteacher in another life. He, too, comes from a big family—tons of siblings I can't ever remember all the names of. Growing up, joining the military was his best shot at an education.

I finish making Abuela's coffee and bring it to her, still on the phone. She doesn't ask me who I'm talking to, nor does she pipe up with anything like *say hi to him for me*. She has that face she gets when she starts thinking about *the before:* Before Mami got pregnant at sixteen. Before Marthita died. Before Abuelo left.

Her house remains full—it's still her, another parent and their three children. The very same, on paper. But it's another life, a new timeline. One in which her hair no longer stays black.

Before we hang up, Abuelo asks how Abuela is doing and reminds me to be good to her, like always. *She needs a lot of love*, he says.

What I don't say: *Then why aren't you here to give it?*

Instead, I end the call and hand the phone back to Abuela. She turns the volume up on her radio show.

"So," she says, threading a new needle. "How about I make you a nice shirt or skirt?"

"Abuela, I told you. I don't care about the parade like that."

"Not for the parade." She sucks her teeth. "For your birthday, hija."

"Oh. I'll . . . look at the fabrics and pick something," I say, realizing I hadn't given what I'd wear for my birthday a single thought.

SEVEN

"It's still not right. It's gonna pinch me—or worse, fall off,"
Camila complains. Her top is too loose. Carla keeps trying to tighten
it with pins unsuccessfully.

We're in the bathroom with a bunch of other girls, figuring out
the last few details of our outfits and makeup before hopping on
buses that will bring us downtown for the parade. The air smells
like hairspray, synthetic and clean. This is one of the few days of the
school year we're allowed to ditch the uniform and wear makeup
beyond mascara and foundation. Still, those of us who are not palillonas or in the marching band must abide by a dress code: only blue
and white clothes, like the Honduran flag. Some girls wear outfits
that are nearly wedding-appropriate, others visited the hair salon in
the early morning. The air is charged, electric.

Cami's palillona fit is a white cheerleader-like skirt with a blue
hem, and a blue strapless top with five silver stars across her chest.
The tan lines from our school uniform are visible on her arms and
neck. When I notice them, I feel a desperation to trace them with my

finger, to follow this record the sun left on her body. But, of course, I don't. Instead, I look away and force myself to notice the rest of room. Most of the other palillonas wear something similar. I'm pretty sure all are hand-me-downs from previous years.

"Ouch." Cami winces. "You stabbed me!"

"Here, I'll do it," I say, nudging Carla aside. "Let me try."

Carla rolls her eyes and hands me the pins. One sticks my palm a little. Carla grabs mascara out of Cami's red-and-white-striped makeup bag and goes to the mirror on the other end of the bathroom. Cami gives me a look like, *okaaaaay.*

"Turn around," I say, avoiding eye contact but reaching to guide her by the waist, positioning her to face away from me at the angle I need her at. I secure the fabric around her torso with my left hand and insert two pins above her bra band with my right—back, out, and lock. I'm careful to not come close to her skin with the pin.

Abuela asks us to do things like this whenever we hang around the workshop, Maynor and I, but mostly me. As soon as we were old enough to follow her instructions and developed any fine motor skills, she'd drag us to ballet schools' show fittings to help her write down measurements or glue-gun the last few missing fake diamonds on headbands. I found it near torturous, all those hours paying close attention to twenty or thirty girls and their tutus and leotards and demands. I didn't get why *we* had to do it, and not one of the costureras who work for her. But in this moment, I know it's paid off. And I'm grateful to know—to be the one in this bathroom who knows how to do this last-minute, temporary fix.

I repeat the process a few inches lower, closer to her waistband.

I'm about to lock the last pin in place when I feel her back arch slightly, the most unperceivable tension in her body. I stop, nervous I might've hurt her somehow, though I know it's impossible. I've been careful to a ridiculous degree.

"Are you okay?" I say.

She grabs my fingers, my right hand free of pins, and squeezes for a moment. Electricity zings up my arm. I look at our reflection in the mirror. We're nearly the same height, so I'm mostly disappeared behind her. We lock eyes and I feel weightless, like I'm suspended by the gravity of her sight alone.

Then Valeria walks out of the stall where she had been trying on a white shirt Carla brought her and Camila drops my hand.

"Yeah," she says. "Sorry. Just, uhm, escalofríos." Her goose bumps match my own.

I lock the last pin. "You should be good."

She turns around to look at the pins in the mirror. She's perfect.

"*Okay*, birthday girl. Abuela has shown you some tricks, clearly." She smiles. As much as I like the shape of her face when she smiles, I can tell the thickness of the moment we shared is over—vanished into the air like the hairspray.

"Some," I say, trying to keep any grief from seeping into my voice, and grateful, really, that she can't tell just how sweaty my hands are now. Two more seconds and I wouldn't have been able to hold that last pin in place.

"So, the plan is still to just head over to your house after the parade, then dinner and La Esquina?" Valeria cuts in from behind us.

"If everything goes okay, yeah."

"What did your fam get you?" Camila asks, still looking at herself.

"Abuela made me a blouse and skirt for tonight," I say. "Mami will probably take us all to get dinner somewhere this weekend. And she promised to get my phone today, for real."

It's been another week, and Mami couldn't grab my phone on Monday, Tuesday, or any day, really. Her hours have been crazy with all the fechas patrias events happening at the hotel. But she's off today for the fifteenth, and we called to make sure the store was open. Hell, she might even already have it by now.

I should be used to not having a phone by now. I mean, it's been *months*. But ever since Camila started being less weird, it's been triple hell. I'll be sitting in class or in the bus or lying down at home and swear I feel a vibration on my thigh. I'll reach for my phone and find my pocket flat empty—phantom notification.

"Finally," Cami says. "For real, that's like, the *best* gift. After mine, of course."

I catch her eye and arch an eyebrow. She smiles, and I feel it again, that thickness, and then she turns away.

It takes five buses, fifteen teachers, and forty-five minutes to get grades ninth through twelfth downtown for the parade del 15 de septiembre.

It's a hot day as ever in Tegucigalpa. The vinyl of the bus seats sticks to the back of my thighs, damp with sweat. The boys don't smell like their usual morning soccer match; it's all fathers' borrowed cologne. It may be the most exciting day of the school year: no class, out in the sun, and all the food we can buy and eat downtown. The parade is a big deal, even the president and first lady attend. It occurs to me this might be the last time I participate, at least in this way. One year from now I might watch it on TV with Maynor and Mami, sitting in bed eating plantain chips and commenting on the outfits and twirling.

The gel on most of the guys' hair has melted away—tendrils stick to their temples and foreheads. Some of the girls have given up and tied their hair up into tall ponytails, me included. But most fight through and keep it down, not ready to dismiss the hours spent styling.

Sitting next to me, Valeria sweats through her shirt. She fans at the small stains forming around her armpits.

"This is ridiculous," she says. "It's not like the school doesn't have the money to afford AC."

"Oh, they would never," I say, shaking my head.

Camila and Pablo sit across the aisle from us. I want to keep my eyes out the window but can't help looking over. They hold hands, but Pablo lets go every few minutes, wiping his hand on his pants. I try to overhear their conversation, which is sparse, mostly Camila pointing things out the window.

The streets are absorbed. Over thirty schools just from el Distrito Central participate in the parade. And then there's others, from the more rural parts of the country, that make the daytrip to la capital. Peddlers fill the sidewalks, selling flags, bags of mangoes and nuts, fans with hand-painted designs like five blue stars or a guacamaya. Food stands crowd most corners, indistinguishable from each other: women with scarves wrapped around their hair and strong, thick hands shaping and flipping tortillas that will become baleadas and burritas and pupusas.

There's the military police too, carrying guns longer than their legs. Must be hot as fuck confined in those uniforms. El centro de Tegucigalpa is a thrum to the senses any day—an over-pollution of smells and sounds—but everything is heightened today.

Feliz 15 de septiembre . . . and happy birthday to me.

The buses get us as close to the National Soccer Stadium as they can—which is where the actual marching takes place, around the field. The stands are at capacity. Camera flashes go off at the presidential box. There's over a dozen local TV channels here, men with long, heavy cameras over their shoulders, and women with microphones with big spongy heads pressed to their chests as they talk. "Sopa de Caracol" plays on a loop, loudly. The excitement is inescapable, contagious. I almost don't mind the sun toasting through my hair.

Our school takes its place in the parade—we're near the middle, number 13. Leading our group is the marching band, followed by las palillonas, and then banner people—the order repeats for every grade. Three teachers are assigned to each grade, ready to supervise and make sure everyone is doing what they're supposed to. They take headcounts over and over, as if they didn't right before we left the school.

Military police swarm every entrance. If anyone tried to leave it would be hard, if not impossible, without an adult chaperone.

Before the parade begins, the host—Salvador Nasralla, a TV personality—stands on a wooden stage in the middle of the soccer field and asks us to join him singing the national anthem. He's famous for narrating fútbol matches. He's also rumored to be gay. Boys often mock the way he moves his body or tease one another by calling each other a "friend of Nasralla."

His voice comes out staticky through the enormous speakers at his sides.

A Honduran flag stands next to the stage. I stare at its still folds of blue and white as the familiar instrumental music begins. We put our right hands over our hearts and open our mouths to sing the song about a loud ocean striking a naked volcano, and the honor it'd be to die for a land with a name: *Serán muchos, Honduras, tus muertos, pero todos caerán con honor.*

When it's over, everyone returns to making visors out of their hands to shield their eyes from the sun. The sweat on my face makes my eyes sting. We melt as the schools in front of us kick off the parade and begin to make their way around the track. Trumpets and drums hurt my ears. Despite it being an open field, every inch of air feels precious and finite.

Several schools are dressed in trajes típicos—the Honduran traditional robes, now mostly used in patriotic formal events like this. I'm unsure of their origin—I remember Abuelo saying it's a mix of colonial influences but most likely modeled after the clothing of different Indigenous groups, like los Lencas.

Boys wear hard cotton fabric pants, mostly white or the color of clay, and a long-sleeved baggy shirt that matches the pants in the same fabric. Three embroidered ribbons in different bright colors run around the neck and wrists, making it look like they're wearing three long necklaces and three bracelets on each hand. A red handkerchief tied around the neck and a farmer's sombrero complete the look.

But the boys look simple next to the girls, with their long dresses with skirts of multiple layers and colors. A single skirt can have a blue layer, a red layer, a yellow layer, and more. It's beautiful—no dress is exactly like another. With every other step the girls take, they hold open the edges of their skirts, like birds' wings in flight. The movement produces the illusion of color waves in the wind.

The school in front of us begins to move and, finally, we get in formation. The marching band goes first, then the palillonas, and behind them my group, carrying Honduran flags and the banners we've been hand painting from the beginning of the school year. Every step is slow, giving the palillonas time to twirl their batons and dance around, coordinated in their movements.

At first I can't really see Camila—she's too far ahead. I try to stand on my toes, but that doesn't help. I keep bumping into the people in front of and behind me. Finally, after peeking around bodies and angled arms, between heads and flags, I catch a glimpse of the back of her head, one bent elbow resting on her hip.

She's a natural performer—her hips and the beat locked as one.

Sweat slides down my back and all the way to my waistband, making my shirt stick to my skin. Camera flashes blink at us from every angle, making it even harder to see anything. We make it halfway around the track. Someone screams ¡Viva Honduras! And the rest of the crowd yells back ¡Viva! The drums and trumpets are deafening, louder by the second, and the cheers still manage to ascend over them.

So loud, no one hears the first explosion.

EIGHT

And we don't hear the second, either, but the fire is impossible to ignore.

It spreads throughout the left-side stands, black smoke flapping behind it. The music dies down in parts. A trumpet is insistent somewhere until someone nudges the player, pulls their arm, says *look*.

Cheers transform to screams. One minute, we stand in neat lines. The next, bodies begin to crash. People fall on the track, hands-first, stand up and run. They run to the exits, to the tunnels that lead back downtown.

But the tunnels are already flooded with protestors trying to get *in*. Men and women with covered faces, only the slit of their eyes visible. Red flags tied to their necks and fingers wrapped around rocks, glass bottles, and signs.

"¡Niños, mantengan la calma!" Mrs. García yells. "Grado doce follow me; each grade, follow your advisors. We'll move to the side. Listen! ¡Por favor, chicos, escuchen! ¡Calma!"

The other teachers repeat her commands down the line of

students. It's useless. We can barely hear them. Everyone shoves toward the nearest exit, a west-side tunnel labeled #6. After a few minutes that feel both like hours and seconds, it becomes clear that the protestors aren't even coming onto the track field.

They move around us, headed for the presidential box. Some of them pass close enough to touch, but they don't engage. There's no way to count, but it can't be less than a hundred people—they chant something, but it gets buried in the din. Military police run behind them. They're a wave of bodies across my field of vision, ants fleeing a colony that's just been stepped on.

One of the younger male teachers takes charge. Mr. Rodríguez steps into the middle of our student body, puts his fingers inside his mouth, and blows a loud, high-pitched whistle that pierces the ears of everyone closest to him. For a second, I think it must be Maynor—I've only ever heard him make that ear-splitting noise. He raises one hand in the air, then brings it down and cups both hands around his mouth. "Okay, everyone!" he yells. "We're exiting the stadium using tunnel five, which is mostly clear. Grade nine will walk in front, and then ten, eleven, twelve. I'm leading the group. Follow me. Hands on your head, both hands. Like this. No hands in pockets, please. Everyone! Everyone! Follow me. Please! Just follow me."

Tunnel 5 isn't far away. The protestors and MP move one way, and we jog toward the other, like cars on a two-way, narrow street. The smell of smoke is thick, but there's none around us—it's all on the stands above.

My elbows bump into other people's elbows, our hands wrapped around our heads. My hair is slick with sweat, and I get a whiff of the curl product I put on this morning, something coconut-y. But it's gone just as fast, the acrid smell of the burning overpowering everything.

Someone steps on the back of my ankle, pushing me to do the same to the person in front of me. The bumping and screams blur. We're last in this formation—the seniors. It made sense to turn around and walk back the way we came in, order reversed, the youngest in front.

I spot the tunnel up ahead. Around me I hear a million *Dios mío* and *Por favor, Dios.* Terse prayers. Protestors keep running in, next to us and around us. They yell with their hands raised. I make out a sign that reads NO HAY INDEPENDENCIA.

The explosions must've been Molotov cocktails. I feel someone touch my lower back and turn around to see Carla and Valeria.

It's not until I see that terror in their eyes that I feel my own chest tighten—I've been holding my breath. Suddenly, I spot Camila directly ahead of us.

"Let's go," she cries over her shoulder to me, as if we're not already running. "We're almost th—"

One shot. Two shots. Three.

Any calm, any order, *anything* that had been there before—goes.

Everyone's sprinting now. People behind us push forward. Someone bumps my arm. Someone else steps on my feet and ankles. I hold Camila's and Valeria's hands—the three of us can't stop coughing. We pick up the pace, then we drop our hand-holding because it makes it harder to move around people.

Valeria somehow gets ahead of us. We're still heading for tunnel

5. I keep looking at the ground, at my feet, trying not to fall. But it's not me who goes down.

Cami crashes against a man, a protestor. I hear the thump of their bodies as they slam. They both drop to the ground, shielding their faces with their hands.

I turn to pick Cami up, but another protestor, one that was running next to the man she crashed against, is already helping her. His face is covered with a red scarf. I can only see his back. Like almost every other man, he wears jeans and a soccer team jersey. Cami's lip is bleeding.

"I'm sorry," he says. "Are you okay?"

If his voice wasn't as recognizable, the half-moon shaped mole on his elbow around his fading bruises is.

"Maynor?!"

"Fuck."

"¿Qué putas—? What are you—"

Four shots. Five.

"Go!" he says. "Both of you, run. Tunnel five is empty. We left all west-side tunnels open."

We?

"Maynor! What the fuck? Where are you going? Come on!"

He turns to look at the presidential box. There's a lot more smoke than there was a minute ago. Then he unwraps his face, murmuring *puta puta puta* under his breath. He looks at us, then back at the box, then once again at us.

"Come on!" he screams. "¡Vamos!"

He grabs both our hands, and we run to tunnel 5.

"Let *go!*" I yell, shaking my arm up and down. Maynor's fingers are clenched around my wrist. A layer of sweat sticks his skin to mine. "Maynor, for real, *let go*! You're hurting me!"

"Just a little further—" he grunts. My resistance barely affects his grip, but the sweat makes his hand slide. He holds Camila with the other hand. She hasn't said a word—but she keeps running with us, away from the stadium. Maynor holds us, leading, taking what feel like random turns. It feels like we've been running for at least ten minutes, but I'm not sure I can trust the thing in my body that understands the passage of time right now.

Sirens ring out nearby. My arm feels like it's burning, my legs like they could give out at any second. And I know my wrist will bruise.

Finally, Maynor stops in front of a pulpería covered in Coca-Cola and Pepsi and Lays stickers. Inside the store, a radio belts out news reports about the stadium and the parade. I'm too tired to make sense of the words.

Maynor lets go of our wrists. His face glistens with sweat. I want to scream at him, but I'm out of breath. My face burns. I rest my hands on my knees, bent over, and take deep breaths. My throat. I look at the stormwater drain under my feet, blockaded by glass bottles and wrappers, and think *this is my throat.* Obstructed with glass shards.

My lungs ache. All three of us cough. Maynor sits on the curbside, takes out his phone, and begins to type out a message. Cami takes out her own phone and scrolls through it. I can't fucking believe I don't have a phone right now.

"Fuck," she says. "They're looking for us."

"Who? What do you mean?" Maynor stands up, wipes sweat from his eyes with the back of his hand.

"Mrs. García," she says. "Everyone but us is back on the buses. They saw us leave with a man—with you—and they think something happened to us."

"Fuck. Call them. Call someone on the bus to tell her. I can talk to her," Maynor says.

He had Mrs. García for civics class all through high school too.

Cami calls someone—maybe Pablo or Carla or Valeria—and tells them to pass the phone to Mrs. García. Then she hands the phone to Maynor.

"Sí, Mrs. García, hola. ¿Cómo está?"

With his free hand, he pulls at the end of his shirt and uses it to wipe his forehead, exposing his abdomen for a second.

"Sí, I have them both with me. I was at the parade with friends . . . Yes, when I saw the whole thing go down, I went to get my sister—"

He nods. I can't make out what she's saying, but I can tell she is raising her voice.

"Yes, of course. I understand. I'm really sorry for scaring everyone—I wasn't thinking of how it'd look for the girls to just run out with me. I'll bring Camila back to school—"

There's more from her side. Maynor nods.

"Mhm. Yes. No . . . yes. I already spoke to my mother. Sí, Mrs. García. She knows Libertad is with her brother. Yes—of course. Yes. I'll see you soon. Again, I'm very sorry."

He hangs up and hands the phone back to Camila. She wipes the screen on her pants, the glass wet with his sweat.

"You're such a fucking liar," I snap, pushing him. He barely moves. "Sos un mentiroso. Does Mami know you're here? Does she know *we're* here with you? Or is she just worried sick watching the news, wondering if we're okay?"

Despite the rugged texture of my throat, words come out clear and loud. "What the fuck were you even doing there, your face covered—you weren't 'at the parade with friends' or whatever." I make air quotes with my fingers around his words.

"I saw you. I *know* you were there to—I don't even know. You're so dumb. Sos un estúpi—"

Maynor holds his palms up. "Okay, okay, listen. I *will* explain, but not right now. Not here. We need to get Camila back to school. I already texted Mami to tell her I'm with you, that we're okay and will be home soon. She's stuck in traffic anyway because of all this," he says, waving his hands in the air.

"I'm still not going anywhere until you explain what is going on," I say, crossing my arms.

"All right," Camila cuts in. "I'm gonna go buy us some water. You two need to . . . yeah—"

She turns on her heel and walks up to la pulpería's front. The store owner takes her order through the holes of the iron gate. Behind him, strings of chip bags hang from the ceiling, and ads for the lottery and phone companies cover every wall. I overhear the radio: Someone confirms that the stadium protest is almost totally dispersed now, the president and his wife safe at home.

"Libi, we really can't do this here." Maynor's voice is lowered now. "First of all, Camila needs to get to school. Her parents are gonna be there to pick her up. I could get in trouble if we're not there before them. Second, it's not safe."

"Oh, I *know* you're not worried about trouble *now*, Maynor—"

"Please Libi. I promise, okay? When we get home, I really will explain everything. If we hurry, we can get there before Mami does—it'll be easier that way."

Camila comes back with three plastic bags of water. She hands Maynor and I one each and cuts a corner of hers with her teeth, then sucks the water out of it. I start to say something but stop myself. I'm too exhausted to fight. I want to go home. I want to be somewhere familiar, somewhere that makes sense.

"Fine. But how are we gonna get to school? Or home? It's too far to walk."

"Same way I got here." Maynor bites his water bag. He takes a few desperate gulps, then squeezes the rest of the cold water out over his head and down his back. "We're riding a motorcycle."

"What? What motorcycle?"

"I borrowed one for today. From a friend."

I didn't even know he knew how to drive a motorcycle.

"Okaaay . . . So where is it?"

"A few blocks away. I parked it far from the stadium and walked the rest of the way. Let's go." He turns, and I catch Cami's eye. She shrugs.

I shake my head, and the two of us follow Maynor down the street. In the distance, gray and black smoke columns rise. The sirens don't stop.

NINE

Forty minutes later, Maynor and I are home. There's no one else
here. Abuela is at work, of course, and Alberto was at school all
morning for the younger grades' own Independence Day activities.
Mami was planning to pick him up early and run errands—they
must still be stuck in traffic now.

Maynor walks to the kitchen and pours two cups of Coke. He sits
at the dining table and turns the radio on. I turn it off.

"Okay," I say. "Go on. Explain. We're home now."

Maynor sighs, scratches the sides of his patchy beard. "I need you
to promise not to say anything to Mami."

I stare at him for a second, then pull back a chair and sit. "Okay,"
I say, "fine."

He stares down at his hands. I think maybe he won't say anything, but then he beings to speak.

"It all started before the shooting. The UNAH shooting, a couple
of months ago. You remember."

I nod. It takes him a beat to begin talking again, like he's figuring out where to start. His eyes seem far away, and mine keep gravitating to the small pool of perspiration over his upper lip. I want to reach out to wipe it for him, but I'm too angry still.

"The university had been on strike for months, right. No classes—buildings blocked off by student protestors and so on. They were demanding stuff that made sense. Like a voice in the creation of the university's academic policies. For students to not be academically penalized for participating in peaceful protests." He grimaces. "And to actually investigate a fuck-load of student murders. Those of students who were known to be involved with the resistance."

I stare at him. "I . . . didn't know that. I mean, not that part."

Maynor wraps his fingers around his cup, holding my gaze. "Do you know what the *Autonomous* in 'National Autonomous University of Honduras' means, Libi?"

I shake my head. My eyes still sting from the smoke, and every so often I have to hold my eyelids shut.

"It means it's free from el estado, from the government of Honduras. It gets to make its own decisions about what's taught, where the money goes, and who can teach or study there. It doesn't abide by the state or the church. The only . . . entity, I suppose, the university needs to respond to is its own student body. And the faculty."

He coughs and takes a sip of his drink. I want to offer him water, but something keeps me in my chair. I can hear the effort in his voice to tell this story, and I know I can't disrupt the flow of it without risking losing it.

"It's like embassies. You know how the American embassy is its own thing here? Even though it's in Honduran territory, the

Honduran military can't go in there, right? It's considered like an extension of gringo-land. If the Honduran government sent military in there, it would be seen as an attack, right?"

I nod. It would. I can't even picture it.

"The university is like that, except instead of being another country, it's like a student country. This is why the police or MP can't go in there, unless la rectora—the dean—invites them in or there's some sort of crime they're investigating. When those MP came in and opened fire, that was an attack on the autonomy of the university."

Maynor pauses, giving me a second to process. I'm not surprised by any of this. I hadn't heard it before, but it's not a far reach from everything else. My wrist hurts from his grip earlier, and I rub it, gently. He reaches over the table and grasps my hand, starts massaging it himself.

"But they knew that was going to happen. Everyone in the student fronts, which is basically almost everyone in the journalism track—plus the general comm department and social sciences wing—knew. Because they had a . . . man on the inside. Someone who'd been told by a family member with ties to that kind of thing how it would go down. He'd been told it would be the Monday before Semana Santa. The MP expected there'd be less protestors than usual, with people from rural areas leaving to go home. And at that point the strike had been going on for so long that the numbers were already depleted. So it was gonna be a warning, more than anything, with rubber bullets not aimed at anyone in particular. A way to hit the already low morale."

He rubs his eyes using his free hand. There's a tightness to his body that is both familiar and new. It's been there for a while, months, but it isn't native to the brother I have known my whole life. When he's done rubbing, we lock eyes again, and I nod for him to continue.

"We thought we'd be ready. We'd built our base in one of the buildings that had been taken during the strike, using tables and chairs for makeshift defenses. Collected our own stuff to throw at them, plus set up cameras to live-stream it all. We thought we'd flip the situation on them. But it didn't happen like that. They came on the Friday before. They had real bullets. And no one was expecting them."

"Wait, wait, wait. Hold on. 'We'? What do you have to do with the student fronts and journalism or whatever?"

Maynor freezes. His gaze on mine wavers, and I can tell he's doing some mental calculations. Finally, he shakes his head and sighs.

"Yeah, okay . . . That's one of the things, Libi. I'm not a medical student: I haven't been a medical student for a long time. I tried it—I really did, for a term. It just wasn't for me."

I close my eyes for a second and lean back. Mami and Abuela will kill him. I can't believe he's kept a secret like this.

Maynor reaches for my hand again, lowering his voice. "You know where most medical students here end up, Libi? Call centers. They end up becoming medical interpreters for American call centers all over the city. Paid less than seventy Lempiras an hour. That shit would never be legal in their own country. Imagine: Two dollars an hour?"

Maynor lets go of me now, scrubbing his hands down his face.

"Everyone I know working in those places is miserable. And then—yeah. I met people from the student fronts, and with everything going on, I just knew that . . . there was more. There *has* to be more."

My mind is still spinning. "More . . . what?"

"More we—more *I* can do to actually have an impact. To make a fucking difference. Another Honduran with a medical degree who can't help other Hondurans won't change anything."

His eyes are pleading. I know he wants me to understand. To say it's okay. I think of that day after La Esquina in February, when I must've looked at him this same exact way.

"Okay," I say, taking a deep breath. "So you're not a medical student, whatever. That's fine. I mean, Mami and Abuela might kill you. But that still doesn't explain . . . this."

I wave both arms above my head. Even as I say it, though, I know it's not just *whatever*. The decision of what we study here is never whatever.

Journalism is not a popular career. Journalism is a bullet in your head.

Maynor stays quiet for a minute. I can't tell if he's trying to come up with something else to say, if there are actual words stuck in his throat. He looks down at his hands, like that morning last week, when I found him sitting on the edge of his bed, shirtless. He looks just as small. Displaced, I think. Here, but stuck somewhere else.

"The contact that was wrong, Libi, the man on the inside . . . that was me. We had heard an attack would happen in March, but we didn't know any of the details. So I started calling Tío José more and more. You know how he works installing security cameras in SPS and is part of the public safety projects and stuff? I knew he must know something, or someone he knew had to."

His eyes are glossy. I know it's not the smoke anymore.

"Everyone talks. Especially in the government, everyone talks.

So, I started talking to him a lot, feigning interest in his work. Telling him I might want to go into his line of business instead of medicine. Complaining about the strike and the fronts."

I hold my head with both hands, massaging my cranium in circles, soft and movable under my fingertips. The adrenaline must've kept me from noticing the splitting headache now pulsing against the backs of my eyes.

I can't believe Maynor could keep something like this from us—from *me*—for so long.

"We'd spend hours on the phone, me asking about our cousins and stuff. Then, one day, I said to him that a friend had heard about the possible attack and how it'd be great to finally end the strike and he just . . . told me about it. Said the boss of his project had told him it would be on the Monday before Semana Santa. That they would end that strike once and for all. And to of course keep quiet about it."

A tear surfaces at the corner of his left eye, escapes down his cheek. "But he was wrong. Or his boss was wrong. I don't know."

I don't know what to say. He rests his head in his hands, and I think that he's going to fully cry now because his breathing is so loud. I feel angry, still; but seeing him in pain, I can also sense his guilt. And I hate that he's hurting. I hate that he's been hurting for this long.

"Maynor, it's not your fault." This time, I reach for his hand.

But he waves me off, the urgency in his voice raw. "So they came, and we weren't ready. And those students—I mean, I didn't personally know them or anything . . . but they killed them."

His words come fast now, collapsing out of a place I can tell he'd kept closed and buried for as long as he could. "And I know . . .

I know I didn't pull the trigger, but . . . it still *felt* like it."

Finally, my brother sobs. Desperate, breathless sobs.

"I'm so sorry, May," I whisper, scooting in my chair to wrap my arms around him. He buries his face in my neck and cries.

A minute goes by, two. The emptiness of the house seems to come down on us, with just his moaning and the fizzling of the Coke in our cups to disprove it.

When he finally pulls back, I hand him a napkin.

"I never planned on joining the actual protests." Maynor wipes his eyes and nose with the back of his hands. "I know I'm the man of the house. I know I need to take care of Mami and Abuela and all of you. If not with money, at least by being here, alive. I just went to the student front meetings, listening, and thought that if I couldn't be there, at least I could help somehow."

The man of the house. I think of all the times I've heard my mother and grandmother call him this, how it never occurred to me it was a burden he was receiving rather than a title. A fact based, primarily, on the absence of the men before him. The men who left us, and him too.

"But after the shooting, it all changed for me," he continues. "I felt guilty and—no one said anything was my fault, but maybe some thought it. I started going to the protests and to every student front meeting, even if it was at midnight."

"Yeah. I can hear you sneaking out," I say, rubbing my hand up and down his back. He's all bone. A scrawny, scared kid.

Maynor winces. "I know you can. It's so bad, Libi. You'd think we have it rough with Mami and Abuela working all day, but the testimonies at the front are just . . ."

He leans back in his chair, a little more clear-eyed now. "Most of the students, they ride the bus or taxis to la UNAH, right? Every first of the month, without fail, mareros come by to ask for their war-tax from the drivers. These people who barely make enough to live have to pay them thousands of Lempiras to . . . *delay* being killed. And of course, the police and MP know—they're in on it. They get their own percentage. The student fronts have been protesting against it all, demanding that investigations be done, that this and a lot of other messed-up stuff stops, but . . . nothing. It's useless."

I'm still looking for the right words to say. It's shit, all of it. The MP and the government . . . it's like every day they push a little further with what they can get away with. And it's all an open "secret"—I remember scrolling through some of these stories when I had my phone, posted by independent journalists or student front pages.

"I'm sorry about today," Maynor says, his voice a smidge more collected now. "I'm sorry I hurt your wrist and pulled you and Cami like that. I freaked out—I didn't know what would happen. I just wanted to get you all as far from the stadium as possible."

I nod. "It was scary."

"I know." Maynor takes a deep breath and holds both my hands.

I can't imagine how terrified Camila felt. Even the memory of the terror that devoured my body feels far away now. But I do know one thing—Maynor's greatest fear is hurting others. Especially women, especially with his hands.

Our history haunts him, stays in his nostrils like tear gas.

"I don't think you should be doing this, May," I say, pulling away to look at his face. "I hear what you're saying about guilt and powerlessness. But think about it: Think about how long this has been going on, all of it, and nothing ever gives—"

The quiet *snick* of a key turning in the lock: Both of us sit up straight in our chairs, our heads turning toward the sound. Maynor wipes his face again.

Mami and Alberto burst through the door. Mami's carrying a white box with what I'm sure is birthday cake inside. Alberto looks like he just woke up from a nap, his hair flat on one side of his head.

"¡Gracias a *Dios*!" he exclaims. "Finally, home! We were in the car *so* long and there were *so* many people out there and we saw them walk by with rocks, right Mom? And then the police kept stopping every car and they stopped us and asked us where we'd been and Mami had to show them her ID and then they wanted to look in the trunk and I was so scared, but they just let us go."

Mami doesn't say anything. She has her headache face, which I would too if I'd just spent hours trapped in the car without AC on a day like today, with Alberto talking nonstop for most of it. She walks over to the table and sets the box down, then pulls my phone out of her pocket, setting it down too. Its metal back clinks against the wood.

The screen lights up immediately. I see a bunch of notifications from WhatsApp and Instagram. Despite everything going on with Maynor and this day, I feel my face light up. Fucking *finally*.

"I need to talk to you," she says.

Maynor flinches. He's so screwed.

"Okay, Mami." He goes to scoot back his chair.

"Not you. You," she says, looking at me.

TEN

"Come," Mami says. "Sit."

She points to her bed and closes the door behind me.

Her door is rarely closed. Maybe only on Saturday nights, while she gets ready for weddings, trying on dress after dress—all made by Abuela. The ones she doesn't wear end up piled on the bed with white deodorant marks and small sweat stains drawn around the armpits. Sometimes she calls me in and asks for my help zippering or pulling it over her head.

But there are no dresses laid out today. We sit at the edge of the bed. The mattress bows under us. I wish she'd turn on the TV, if only to have some noise to distract from the beating in my chest. She holds my phone firmer than she needs to, fingers wrapped around the screen. Trying to breathe through my nerves and unable to look her in the eyes, I lock in on her hands. I've always admired her beautiful, naturally square long nails—nothing like my bitten-down, boy-like hands.

I know whatever this is, it has to do with my phone. For the past five minutes, I've tried to think of everything I had on it and figure out if there's anything bad. The obvious thing is the poetry account. But I have a hard time believing Mami would be this upset about a poem. And my phone was password-protected before it died, so I don't understand how she'd be able to go through it anyway.

She's also just not the type to do that. Mami got pregnant with Maynor at sixteen, after sneaking around for a year to see our dad. Abuela was so strict. Mami says that strict parents make good liars out of their children and she's not about to do that with us. Or she doesn't think she is. Not the way Abuela was with her, at least; she claims to trust that we're smart enough to learn from her mistakes.

"I picked up your phone this morning," she says, staring down at her feet.

She looks a lot like Maynor just an hour ago; the way it seemed like our confrontation pained him more than it could me. Something shame-like sizzling off his skin. With Mami, it unnerves me even more.

"¿Mamá, qué pasa?"

After a long, unbearable second, she continues.

"The technician said he had to do a bunch of stuff to it, and he ended up taking off the passcode. He said some data or media might've been deleted, chats for sure. Some contacts may be missing too."

"Okaaay," I say slowly, still unsure of where any of this is going.

"He gave it to me, and I turned it on to make sure it worked. I didn't want to have to go back. You had a lot of messages and stuff come in. I was just going to try . . . try to call myself or send myself a WhatsApp, to make sure it was really fixed. And then you got a message from an unsaved number, probably one of the lost contacts."

She takes a deep breath. "All your chats from before with this person are gone, so all there is left are the new texts between you and this gir—person."

She hasn't looked at me once. My mouth feels dry.

"What new texts?"

She taps my phone screen a few times and hands me the phone. Just holding it again feels weird—it's heavy and cold in my hand. A WhatsApp chat is open, with a one-sided stream of messages that span several weeks, ending one week ago—last Friday.

Libi

Ok you're not getting any of my messages so you probably haven't gotten your phone back

You won't read any of this until you do but I don't know how else to say this .. so you'll read it when you get your phone back and maybe I'll regret saying anything then

Ok. Here it goes

I've been thinking about our kiss en febrero en La Esquina.

I think I was a little drunk and I don't know if you were. I don't remember. You didn't say anything about it the next day so I thought maybe you were too and that it was less awkward to just let time pass and say nothing about it.

You know how things have been going with me talking to P and he asked me to be his girlfriend yesterday and I said yes.

Maybe you don't know. But I guess you'll know tomorrow at school.

What I wanted to say is that I'm sorry that happened and that I don't want anyone to know. I know you tell Valeria a lot of stuff so I just really would appreciate if you didn't tell her this.

You know how people react to gay stuff here and I don't want to deal with all that dumb drama for a drunk stupid thing.

So, yeah. Just let me know when you read this.

I'm sorry

Libi?

I guess you haven't gotten your phone back. Let me know when you read everything I said before.

Libertad

Hello? You said you'd get your phone back today?

Text me when you can.

It takes me seconds to read through it all, but I have to go back and reread certain sections because my eyes keep trying to get ahead, to scan it all while not reading any of it at the same time. Long after I'm done, I keep staring at the screen—maybe to make sure I'm not missing any words. Mostly to avoid looking at my mother.

I swallow. I think my heart began to beat so fast, it eventually must've just stopped, because I can't feel it anymore. My chest is tight, and my vision goes blurry around the corners.

Eventually, Mami estimates that I've had more than enough time to read.

"So," she says. "I didn't really know what any of it—I don't know. And I don't know if I'm reading the situation or the messages right, especially after I . . . I went through your camera roll."

I look up at her, confused. I *know* there's nothing in my gallery that could possibly relate to this. She takes the phone from me and goes to my pictures, scrolling up, trying to find the next piece of evidence in this trial-by-ambush, building her case against me.

She clicks on an image I don't recognize at all.

"This." She turns the screen toward me, this time not handing me the phone, pulling it a bit away even—like there's something toxic about the object.

Fuck. Fucking Pablo. Fucking Pablo resending Vicky's nudes to our group chat. Fuck my phone saving everything to the gallery automatically. I didn't even know those were there.

"Mom . . ." I start. "Those photos aren't mine. That's not me. I promise you."

"I know it's not you. I didn't think you were . . . the girl in the picture. I thought someone, the person from the messages, sent—"

"No. No, they're not mine. It's not me, and no one sent them to me specifically."

"Libertad—"

"No, Mom, listen: That girl in the picture? It's a girl from my class. You know her. She—she didn't send those pictures to anyone and I *promise* you, not to me. This guy from our class, he—he stole them from her, sort of, and sent them around. It's on my phone because someone resent them to a group chat and my phone saves everything to my camera roll automatically. I think I can—maybe I can show you the group chat if it hasn't been deleted or something."

She doesn't say anything. I can tell she doesn't believe me, or that maybe I haven't explained myself well enough and none of it makes sense to her. She looks at me, but it feels more like she's seeing *through* me.

"Mom. If you give me the phone, I can show you."

"What about the chat?"

At this, I have nothing to say. I feel nauseous. A part of me is hoping I pass out so I don't have to have this conversation anymore.

"Who is the gir—the person from the chat?"

She stares me down and I lower my gaze to my feet, our roles reversed now.

"You're not going to tell me?"

"I—You—You saw, you read the message. It was a dumb drunk thing. And it's no one you know. It's not from school—"

"The message says 'tomorrow at school,' Libertad."

"What I meant is, like, it's someone from another class. I don't really see them, her, and—"

"Okay," she says, clasping her hands, the phone between them. She knows I'm not being honest. "Okay, fine."

We sit in silence, my eyes promised to the floor. I count the drawn-on pebbles on each individual tile in my head, fixating on finding a pattern. Then she turns the TV on, which makes me think the conversation is over, but I sense that doesn't mean I'm dismissed.

"Ma?"

Without turning to look at me, she raises her hand to gesture *one moment*.

I glance at the news flashing across the TV screen. More of what we already know: Parts of the city on fire, roads blocked, MP everywhere. They show footage of an MP pickup truck, the bed crammed with shirtless men, their hands cuffed behind them.

We both watch—pretend to watch—in silence. The TV is muted. For a second, I consider what a different day we might be having if Maynor was one of those men in the pickup truck. How maybe this—me—would seem small in comparison. I hate myself for the thought.

Mami lays back in bed, her upper body propped up by the headboard, legs dangling over the edge. Her worn emerald heels are still on, and my phone is still in her hand, and I hold my own hands to make sure I'm still here. I don't know how long it's been when she speaks again, but outside, the sky has turned the depleted color of dusk.

"When everything happened with Diego, I was so scared of what my mom would think of me as a mother."

It's been so long, but I still feel struck when she calls him by his name, and not Amor or "tu papá."

Despite everything, my ears are not yet untrained to the ways in which she once loved him. To the ways their union was the primary fact of my life.

"I thought your abuela would see me as a failure. She was so young when I got pregnant too, just forty years old. I can't imagine becoming a grandmother at that age, my age. I would die if you or Maynor . . . and I was a child, just sixteen. Una cipota. Everyone from your dad's family agreed we should get married. Even my own father. But not her."

Her eyes stay on the TV, allowing me to look at her without the dread of being looked back at. The screen colors wash her in blue and purple hues. The tension of her forehead and jaw pull her face inward, drawing a face I don't recognize in my mother.

"My mom said there was no need, that she could help me raise Maynor, that I could still have a normal life. Everyone was so shocked—my Catholic mother saying I could have a child out of wedlock. Abuelo had to convince her to sign the papers that allowed me to get married underage."

I don't know where she's going with this—I suspect something about how mothers know best. I want her to get to the punchline. I want this to be over.

"Of course, I don't regret anything. If I hadn't married your dad, I wouldn't have you or Alberto. And the three of you are my life. I couldn't imagine not having any of you. But my mom was right, at the time. She just wanted her child to have a normal life."

Deep in my gut, something turns. I can't remember the last time I ate, and I imagine the room of my stomach empty except for a puddle of fizzling Coca-Cola and black smoke.

"It's what every mother wants, I think. For life to be a little less hard for our children than it was for us."

Drops of anger starts bubbling up in my chest, seeping into my shoulders. Within seconds, I can feel the heat down in my toes, a burning along the edges of my skin.

Is she seriously saying I'm doing this to myself?

"Yeah, I know," I snap. "I'm obviously not *trying* to make my life harder—"

"Déjame terminar," she says, silencing me with a raised hand, again.

I exhale, maybe a little too loud. Finally, she looks over at me.

"Whenever it would go down with Diego over the years, you know . . . the hitting and stuff . . . he always made sure I didn't tell your abuelos. He knew that the day they found out—the day I got to them—would be the last day he'd be able to reach any of us. He'd always asked for that specifically, my silence, when he got on his knees to beg."

We look at each other. There's something blank to her expression that makes me feel invisible.

"A part of me always thought one of you—Alberto or you—would let something slip with Abuela. I was always hoping it would be one of you, as children do, that would say something about hearing or seeing something. I was so stupid," she says with a hollow laugh, "so stupid, waiting for my infant children and parents to save me. I tried to tell my mother so many times, and I just couldn't. Until . . . that day."

That day, when Maynor called the police. That day, for ten-year-old-me, is a blur. I don't remember much, and what I do remember I suspect comes from others' retelling. Pieces I've stolen from their memory to make mine. All I know is, finally, after many screams and impact noises on walls, the four of us—my mom, Maynor, baby Alberto, and I—were in Abuelo's car with the few changes of clothes Mami and Maynor had quickly packed for us.

That's the day we moved to Abuela's house. Forever.

"Maybe you remember, I don't know. You were so young. All of you. I'd cry every night when we first moved here. Every single night. Suddenly I was back in my parents' house, needing them to provide everything for me and my three children."

Tears slide down her cheeks and hang from her chin. I want to listen—to feel what she's saying. My heart breaks for that Mami, the one on her own with three children and nowhere else to go. But the thought of her implying I'm "choosing" a hard life like she did is an ocean in my ears. It's deafening, this fury. I keep swallowing, hoping it'll relieve the pressure.

"My mom, she's a great woman, you know that better than anyone. No one would've saved us the way she did, the way she has. But she can be so cruel. In those first few months we lived here, she'd say the most horrible things about how I allowed you kids to live through that, to see Diego as a monster, to be part of an unstable home. She made it sound like I *chose* that for us, like it was a thing I wanted and not something that happened to me too."

Bile claws my throat. I know Abuela isn't perfect, of course, but . . . I don't know. She's Abuela. She's our wonder woman. She's the one who does it all, somehow. And I still can't figure out what my mother is trying to say.

"Every day of my life I'm so scared for you—all three of you. I was so dumb at your age. I always think life or God is going to get me back for what I put my parents—my mother—through. And all three of you are so good—mi mamá always tells me that she wishes my children had been hers." She smiles at this, not a gentle smile, but a disfigured hurt that overcomes her face.

"Now I can't stop thinking about how you really are her children too. How she has to do this mother thing all over again. How any of you could break my heart, yes, but her heart too, like I did all those years ago."

"No te entiendo," I cut in. "I don't understand what you're trying to say. If you mean that—me and this message thing—Abuela will never find out about that. I told you it was a dumb drunk thing—"

"She'll blame me, Libertad." Mami's voice is pleading now. "She'll say it's because of how you saw me and your dad fight. That I didn't provide the example of a good man for you. That I did this to you . . . and maybe she would be right."

I feel like I've been punched in the throat. Now I wish she *had* been heading toward *moms know best* and not *you hate men and now you'll make Abuela hate both of us.*

She stares at the TV again, like I'm not even here. And maybe I'm not. But whatever assemblage of body parts are weighing me down right now, I know I need to get them out of this room.

I stand up, a pinch of tears behind my eyes. I want her to say "¿Dónde vas?" I want her to say "We haven't finished talking." But she doesn't. Her eyes stay trained to the TV.

She lets me go.

I leave and lock the door of my room behind me. I don't mean to slam it, but it hits the doorframe so hard, the walls shake. I throw myself onto my bed and wait a second, to hear her footsteps or screams. I press my face against a pillow, waiting.

But then I can't hear anything beyond my own crying, violent and messy. My eyes burn from the salt of my own tears. My chest rises with each gasp. I'm drowning.

I tell myself to breathe. To calm down. With each second, I convince myself that she's just about to knock on my door, so gently I might miss it. That the next thing I'll hear is her voice, soft and kind, saying *Libertad, I'm sorry. I'm new at this. I don't know the right thing to say. I love you so much.*

But that doesn't happen. Eventually, I do get my breathing to settle. I fall asleep, my face wet with snot and my stomach churning. My muscles are sore from running.

Mami never comes.

ELEVEN

Sunlight seeps through my eyelids, tugs my mind awake. I attempt resistance, but I'm pushed into consciousness, remembering I'm eighteen now, officially an adult—the minute that parade preparations began, and everything else unraveled.

It seems almost like an echo from a past life, like my mind can't fathom a day that both flooded my heart and emptied it within the span of twelve hours. Of course, all birthdays happen on the same day as horrible things, whether we're aware of them or not: A mother lays her eyes for the first time on the face of her child. Somewhere else—or maybe right outside the door—a finger pulls a trigger that erases a face, one that another mother will spend decades reconstructing in the corners of her memory.

I squeeze my eyes shut, trying to mine my mind for the details of everything good that happened before the parade, trying to hold it all close to my chest.

I had woken up before my brothers, but knew better than to get out of bed, so I wouldn't spoil our birthday traditions. I could hear the host of the morning talk show *Frente a Frente* on Mami's TV repeating, *It's 196 years, people. Yes, 196 years since Honduras and the rest of Central America became independent nations.*

Mami's hairdryer hummed its familiar white noise over the chatter, and I pictured her standing in front of the bathroom mirror, the air around her heavy with makeup powder. Her big, dark eyes would already be highlighted by eye shadow and eyeliner, years-old smudges on the mirror distorting her reflection.

I could also hear Abuela up. She mopped outside my room, some of the Fabuloso lemon fragrance filtering through the crack under my door. Abuela is always up before four for her prayers, followed by cleaning. She takes out the trash from the two bathrooms—daily— then mops. I shifted in bed then, making the old spring mattress groan so Abuela would know I was awake.

She got the hint. I heard her walk to my mom's room, where Alberto was sleeping like he does most nights. I could imagine Abuela nudging his small limbs, bent with sleep after gravitating to the spot where my mom's night heat had settled. Then I heard her knock on Maynor's door. All their footsteps and whispers as they prepared to barge in. I closed my eyes, trying to control my facial movements, my mouth itching to smile.

In they burst, all four of them: Mami dressed up and perfumed, my brothers with sleepy eyes and tousled hair in their long boxers and T-shirts, my grandmother on the verge of heading out the door for yet another day at the workshop. I felt their weight on the mattress, my mom's hand on my face.

I finally let my eyes flutter open then, a grin pouring out of me.

Everyone I loved with everything in me sang "Feliz cumpleaños," then "Las mañanitas"; Maynor played Vicente Fernández's version on his phone. Alberto clapped, and none of them could hold a tune. It was messy, some singing ahead of others: *El día que tú naciste, nacieron todas las flores.*

Even though I've just woken up, I'm exhausted again, and the golden memory of yesterday disintegrates as the gray edges of reality seep in.

Today, my body feels like a shirt left out in the sun for too long. Toasted hard and rigid, it hurts to move, to bend. I have a headache. Possibly from crying, or not having eaten anything since before the parade, or running under the sun, or smoke inhalation, or a broken heart.

I have no idea what time it is because I still don't have a phone, but the sky and the heat hint at late morning. Outside, one of our neighbors is playing Anuel AA's new song, and I can hear fruit vendors' voices through megaphones yelling out papaya prices.

It's Saturday. Abuela and Mami must be at work. Still, I feel scared to leave the room. If I could bear the headache and hunger enough to fall back asleep, I wouldn't even go out there. But I can't bear it. When I crack open my door I notice two things—someone's cooking with a lot of garlic and Mami left my phone on the table between my room and hers, in front of our family pictures.

The photo right behind my phone is of me at five years old in Mom's lap and Maynor at fourteen standing behind her. Mami wasn't even pregnant with Alberto yet. Next to it is a photo of Tía Martha. She looks the age I remember her, twenty or twenty-one. I shift my right hand—already reaching toward my phone—and pick up Tía Martha's photo instead. A thin layer of dust coats the glass, and I wipe it away with a corner of my T-shirt.

Even though I pass these pictures every day, it feels like I haven't looked at Tía Martha's face in a long time. Right away, I notice a resemblance to Maynor around her mouth. And maybe to me around her eyes.

I set the photo back down and grab my phone. My first instinct is to go through it again—all of it—starting with Camila's messages first.

But it wouldn't take much to get me crying again and this headache is killing me. I need to get some food first.

I find Maynor alone in the kitchen, wearing his long red basketball shorts and an old white shirt with the sleeves cut out that reads *Solo el pueblo salva al pueblo.* "Only the people will save the people." He looks tired, maybe even worse than me. He has his big cheap headphones on, and I recognize the fast political trap from this Venezuelan artist that was murdered last year spilling out from the speakers.

I want to touch him, to let him know I'm here, but I don't. I don't know why—even a simple touch feels scary now. I sit and wait for him to notice me instead.

"Libi!" Maynor turns and jumps when he sees me, almost losing the wooden spoon in his hand.

"May."

He slides his headphones over and off his head, then wraps me up in a tight embrace. He knows. Mami must've gotten to him first.

"Did she tell you?" I ask, my voice muffled in his shoulder.

"Yeah. She asked me if I knew and who the girl is."

"What did you say?"

Maynor lets go of me, holding me out at arm's length for a second.

"I told her I didn't know anything, but that it didn't matter to me either way. Not that it doesn't matter—it does. But it doesn't change anything for me . . . And that I thought she could've handled things better."

"She told you what she said?"

"Yes—she thought Abuela would blame her and take it as a sign of her failing. She talked about dad too. I'm guessing that's what she told you?"

I nod. He sighs.

"Lo siento mucho, enana." He rubs the back of his neck. "I don't know what to say. I always thought Mami would be, I don't know . . . better about this. She's young and—yeah. I don't know. I'm really sorry, Libi."

"I know."

We stay quiet for a minute, just sitting next to each other as oil and garlic sizzle on the stove. I can tell he's trying to figure out the right thing to say but is coming up blank.

I don't blame him—I also don't know the right thing to say, the right thing to feel.

"What are you thinking?" he finally asks.

I take a deep breath, closing my eyes for a second. "I don't know. I feel . . . guilty, I guess. Like I did something wrong? No—more like I *am* something wrong. I mean, I know that's not true but . . . I can't help it."

"That's not guilt." Maynor narrows his eyes. "That's shame."

Air escapes me in a wheeze, and Maynor pulls me closer. "Listen to me," he says, holding my gaze with his. "There's nothing you should feel ashamed about. You haven't done anything wrong, and you are *not* anything but good. You are good, Libi."

I nod, feeling less and less capable of holding back the wall of tears building at the corners of my eyes. The logic center of my brain knows that if our roles were reversed, I would be thinking the same things. Saying the same things. Which must mean that there's truth in what he's telling me . . . but it doesn't release the weight on my chest.

"Is Mami gonna tell Abuela?"

The words leave me before I can think of saying them. It's now that I realize that this is my biggest fear, bigger even than my fear of Mami's disappointment: Abuela's.

"No." Maynor's answer is quick, firm. "She specifically asked me not to tell her, or Alberto. I think—I think maybe she thinks that she can handle this without Abuela ever finding out. Like, maybe you'll change your mind or something. Or maybe she just wants to keep it peaceful as long as possible. I don't know."

"Well, I'd actually prefer not to let Abuela find out. Not . . . not right now, anyway."

"I know." Maynor gives me a small, albeit defeated-looking smile.

Just a few months ago, a little boy—one of her client's sons— asked Abuela if she could make him a dress like Elsa from *Frozen*.

He must've been two or three years old. The client, who was there to pick up a school play costume, had laughed it off with a "maybe next time," grabbed the little boy's hand, and left the workshop.

Abuela left too, practically busting down the front door just as we were starting dinner. She paced around the kitchen, screaming about the importance of gender roles. About how parents who let their children "cross-dress" were abusers.

Abuela wouldn't just not be okay with me and . . . this. She would hate it, hate *me*. It would break her heart, and seeing it shatter would break mine too.

Maynor gets up to stir the beans. "Are you hungry?"

The quick change of subject makes my head spin. But it also stymies the pain in my throat. At least, for a moment. "Starving," I say.

"Beans and eggs and tortillas and plantains?"

"So, a deconstructed baleada?"

"Yup. We can go watch TV with Alberto in Mami's room while we eat. Also—there's birthday cake."

I flinch at the thought of being in her room but force myself to nod. It's the only TV in the house, and she won't be home for hours. Eating in bed with my brothers—which we could never, ever do in front of Mami—feels like the thing I need to stay away from my phone just a little longer.

TWELVE

We're nearly done eating when Maynor's phone rings. We've been watching an old Disney Channel movie that happened to be on a local channel. Alberto's head is on my chest, and he jumps a little when Maynor's phone vibrates on the bed.

Maynor checks the screen, frowns, and turns the phone around to show me the name of the caller: Camila. I reach for it. "Um, hello?"

"Hello—hi. Are you home?"

I look around at the three of us in pj's and nestled in Mami's bed, dirty dishes and silverware lying in the crooks of our arms and legs. "Yes . . ."

"Can I stop by for a while? I couldn't give you your gift yesterday with everything, obviously, and my parents are running errands in the city, so they said they could drop me off and pick me up in a couple hours."

It's the first time I don't immediately respond to Cami's self-invitation with a *yes, of course.* I consider everything that could go wrong: She might see my phone, and then I'd have to tell her I've read her texts from a week ago, her weird breakup/not-breakup texts. That Mami knows about me. About us, but not about her . . .

But how can I talk about an *us* when we haven't ever said anything to each other about it? And what if Mami comes home early and puts two and two together? Fuck.

"Libertad?"

"Yes! Of course. Stop by." I slap a palm over my face.

"Okay, be there in five."

I toss Maynor's phone into his lap, then get out of bed and brush my teeth, twice—I can't tell if the smell of garlic is in my head. Minutes later, a silver Toyota Corolla pulls up in front of my house and Cami gets out of the back seat.

As I open the front door, Cami's mom waves and yells an excited *happy birthday* out the window, then speeds away. It's the second day in a row I'm seeing Cami out of our school uniform and it all hurts in my stomach: Her jeans and cropped orange sweatshirt. The gift bag hanging from her wrist. The outline of her phone in her front pocket.

"Hey!" she says, hugging me. Like nothing has happened.

"Hey you," I reply, following her in.

Cami greets Maynor, and Alberto leaps into her arms. She hugs him tight and spins him around, then plants a kiss on his cheek. He blushes.

I get it. I get what my ten-year-old little brother is going through.

"Cami." Maynor steps forward, a worried expression creasing his face. "I am so sorry about yesterday."

Cami shrugs a shoulder. "I know. It's okay. We were okay, and no one even knows about you being—yeah. I mean, I didn't say anything . . ."

"Thank you." Maynor looks down.

"Of course." After a beat, Cami adds, "I hope you're being careful."

Maynor nods. Alberto begins to ask "Careful about what?" and "Who doesn't know what?" But Maynor ruffles his hair and tells him to stop being tan metiche, then ushers him back to Mami's room to watch the end of the movie. Cami follows me into my room, the gift bag still swinging from her wrist.

It strikes me then that my bed is unmade and maybe my pillowcase is still damp with tears, but Camila doesn't say anything. She sits on my bed and looks up at me. I hesitate. She notices, patting the space next to her, and I sit.

"Okay, you ready?" she asks.

"Lista."

She hands me the bag, and from its depths I pull out a rectangle-shaped present. The wrapping is stunning; handmade, clearly by her—I'd recognize her line work anywhere. It's off-white paper covered with all sorts of black-inked doodles. "Doodles" doesn't feel like the right word, though: They're clean and intricate and detailed. There's an old camera, a paper plane, an umbrella, mangoes, a boombox, and a Honduran flag. Down the middle in a vertical line is my name in beautiful, big letters, each one bedecked with flowers. This wrapping paper is a gift in itself.

"Overkill?" Cami asks.

I look up at her. Her eyes are wide, her gaze searching my expression.

"It's beautiful," I say. "God, you're so good at this. How long did it take you to draw all this?"

Cami smiles. I can tell my face is giving her the reaction she wanted. "I've been at it for a while." She nudges my hands. "Okay, now open the actual gift!"

"If I tear this paper, I'm gonna freak. Like I might actually cry."

"Okay, start here," Cami laughs, pointing to one of the taped edges. "Just be careful."

I am. It takes me longer than it ever has to unwrap a gift, but I don't tear it even a little. When it's done, I place the wrapping paper on the bed and hold Camila's gift in my hands.

Her gift is two things, actually. First, an expensive-looking tan leather-bound journal with my initials monogrammed on the bottom right corner: *LMM*. Libertad María Morazán. The second is a book of poems by Juana Pavón, or as she calls herself, Juana "la Loca." Cami knows she's my favorite poet ever since we (accidentally) saw her perform about a year ago.

We had been heading to the movie theater inside Mall Multiplaza, and there was Juana on the steps between the entrance and the street. A group of people surrounded her as she recited a poem about Tegucigalpa from memory, words about privilege and heartbreak and bridges. She moved her hands and her body as she spoke—it was clearly an improvised kind of situation. When she was done, people clapped and yelled *Juana la Loca* over and over, her words hanging, ghostly, in the air around us.

Though brief, that moment—that poem—stayed with me. And I guess with Cami too.

"Jesus, Cami," I breathe.

"Yeah? Do you like it?"

"I love it. This is the best gift ever, seriously."

"Yeah?"

I nod, holding both books in front of me. Cami looks maybe even more excited than me, like she's the one getting the gifts. I free up one of my hands and hug her to me so tightly. I can smell her shampoo. With my face in her shoulder, I blink back the tears that just won't stop today.

"Looks like your only gift," Cami says, breaking our embrace. "No phone?"

There's a major dissonance between the girl who sent me those *I don't want anyone to know about this drunk stupid thing* and barely talked to me for the past six months, and the girl sitting next to me, who hand-drew gift wrapping for one of the most thoughtful presents I've ever received. It feels like a wound inside my throat and cold sweat on my forehead.

"Um, I did, actually. Get my phone back."

"Oh," she says, her voice dropping. "When?"

The early afternoon sun bleeds through the window and bathes her skin in golden light. It's enough to knock the wind out of me, but I force myself to speak, to sound casual: "Yeah. My mom gave it to me this morning."

"And you didn't text me?"

Cami's face changes. She frowns, waiting for me to say something about her texts. To confirm I know. To tell her that, yes, anything more than a friendship between us is dead now . . .

But I can't. Maybe it's my own wishful thinking, but I see a hint of regret in her face. Fear and grief for what could end if I saw those texts. I don't want that grief for her. And I definitely don't want it for me.

"I couldn't—my phone's been wiped. I have no numbers and no texts and no media. They basically returned it to factory settings."

Her eyes widen, and the smile that was there just a second ago returns.

Relief. It's relief that I see blooming across in her face. I was right.

"Oh damn, that sucks," Cami says, smiling.

"It does. But I guess it's a new beginning of sorts too, you know?"

"Totally." She nods, then raises her eyebrows. "So . . . you want my number?"

I grin. "I'd love that."

Cami and I spend the afternoon watching movies on Mami's TV with Maynor and Alberto. We caught Maynor's favorite—*Spider-Man* from 2002—halfway through, and *Transformers* from a few years back all the way through. We manage to fit into the bed: Camila on one end, me on the other, Alberto between us, and Maynor at our feet.

During the commercial breaks, Maynor switches the channel to local news to see if they're saying anything new about yesterday, but it's all the same as before. The attack by protestors keeps being called an attempted murder of the president. The MP keep getting praised for keeping him safe. About a dozen arrests. No information about possible dead or hurt.

Cami's parents are running late, stuck in some line somewhere— a bank or grocery store or pharmacy. It doesn't matter—their annoyance is my bliss. At some point, Maynor walks to la pulpería for plantain chips and Coke, and we eat in bed, all hands digging into the same big bowl, followed by more birthday cake. Mami got an all chocolate one. I'm not big on sweet food, so I usually just leave it up to her or Alberto. It's good—but eating it makes me sad, so I let Alberto finish my slice.

For the first time since my phone broke, I don't feel like I'm missing anything at all. Everything I want to be a part of is happening in this room. My headache lifts and I feel something peace adjacent.

That is, until Mami comes home at eight, honking her familiar beat in the driveway. All of us scurry up from the bed, straighten the sheets and shake out the crumbs before moving to the living room. My hands feel numb—I don't know if I'm in trouble after last night, or what that even looks like. I've never been grounded before.

My stomach drops: What if Mami takes one look at Camila and know she's the girl from the texts? What if she catches me looking at Camila, or even Camila looking at me?

When Mami comes through the door, I have to take a moment to gather my resolve, to force myself to look at her. I get the sense that she's also avoiding eye contact, but maybe that's just in my head. When I finally do wrestle my gaze off the floor, I see that she looks exactly how I feel: Her eyes are red and her face is swollen, as if she also cried all night.

But she hugs the boys and Camila, and I breathe out a sigh of relief. There's no hint that she thinks anything about Cami being here is wrong.

"Hola Doña Carmen. ¿Cómo está?" Cami asks.

"Bien, nena. How are you? We've missed you—I haven't seen you in a minute. How's your mom?"

If Cami has any reaction to Mami pointing out that she's been gone for a while, she doesn't show it. They slip into conversation like they always have. Mami doesn't really talk to me, but it's not obvious. Not to Camila or Alberto, anyway. The only ones who must be able to feel it are Maynor and her and I.

Halfway through dinner, which we all make and eat together, Mami addresses me for the first time—to pass her a plate—and Camila's parents call to say they're outside. She apologizes for leaving in the middle of a meal, but Mami assures her it's okay and kisses her cheek.

"What about me?" Alberto's cheeks are swollen with catrachas, crumbs spilling from his mouth back to his plate. I shoot him a look, but he doesn't notice. He giggles as Cami plants a noisy smooch on his cheek.

"Libertad?" Cami turns to me, and I almost throw up at the thought of her kissing me too. She pauses, then reaches for her phone, face-down next to me. "Don't forget to text me."

She winks, and I breathe. Nod. Then she's gone.

Mami, Alberto, Maynor and I stay in the kitchen. I want to book it to my room but not without clearing my plate. No need to give Mami another reason to be upset at me.

"Is Camila's mom still working at el Hospital Escuela?" Mami asks as I reach for the dish soap, my back to her.

I nod. Just because she's ready to speak to me, doesn't mean that I am. Then I realize she can't see me nod and that I definitely don't want to leave her hanging and get accused of being disrespectful, on top of everything.

"Yeah," I say in a quiet voice.

"I heard they were making massive cuts," she says. "I didn't want to ask her in case it made her uncomfortable."

When I don't say anything, Maynor rushes to my rescue, says he heard that too, something about identifying the doctors that have been taking part in the anti-government protests.

"Do you know if Cami's mom knows anything?" Mami presses on, getting up to put her plate next to the sink for me to wash.

I can't make myself speak. I shrug and reach for her plate.

"Ay, ojalá que no," she says. "They're good people. How's her dad doing?"

"Same as always," I mumble, already rinsing the plate and getting ready to leave.

Cami's dad has been sick for some time. It all started with a stroke two years ago, and ever since he's had a couple of other medical situations come up. For the most part, he's stable, just home a lot.

"May God give him health and keep that whole family safe," Mami says.

I dry my hands and leave.

Later that night, I relish lying in bed with my phone for the first time in weeks. My eyes burn from crying last night, and from watching TV pretty much all day today. Still, I start going through all my unread texts and notifications, the ones that were not lost, anyway. I can't resist reading Camila's texts one more time, but her words bring up a fresh wave of hurt. My finger hovers over the thread for a second, and then I delete them.

If she didn't bring them up—didn't say anything about them to me—then she must regret them. I'm more than happy to give her a clean slate with this, even if she didn't ask for it. I text her, *hey there*.

The rest of the messages are random, less important. Some Snapchats from people trying to keep streaks, a few spam texts from unknown numbers with government propaganda. I text Carla and Valeria to let them know I got my phone back. I delete so many pictures, starting with Vicky's nudes. I save people's contact information, guessing from their profile pictures. It strikes me then that Camila doesn't have a profile picture—otherwise Mami would've seen her. Something about that feels fateful.

I scroll through my friends' group chat information to find Pablo, who does have a profile picture: Camila and him. They sit next to each other in a restaurant I recognize but have never been to, their bodies pressed together. The picture was taken by someone standing up, making them both look small. I sigh.

Finally, I check Instagram: I have a few notifications on my personal account, old likes and a few DMs of random memes from Valeria and Cami and Carla. I like them all. But it's my poetry account that's buzzing.

I have over a hundred new likes on just my one post—my one poem—and twenty-two personal messages. Some ask when I'll post the next poem. Others are encouraging and sweet, telling me they resonate with my words.

A few messages, though, are not good—and those are the longest. Blocks of text defending the government. Calling me ignorant and stupid. Even a Bible quote, something about divided nations signaling the end of our times. I'm unsure of how this relates to the poem but decide to just delete all the bad messages and keep the good ones. Most of them are from weeks ago anyway.

Except for one: a DM is from this morning. It's long, and from a girl with a private account—Daniela Castillo.

> Hola! I just wanted to say that I really love your poem. I'm from Copán but I moved to Tegus this year and I feel like it said everything I've been thinking for so long. The helplessness and hopelessness of everything, in every corner of the country, no poder hacer nada. Feeling like the only thing left to do is leaving. I'm doing my first year en la UNAH in literature and would love to talk to you more about poetry and just . . . life, I guess? Is that weird? Me llamo Daniela, by the way, I go by Dani.

I click into her profile, where I can only see her bio and profile picture. In her bio there's a Honduran flag and it says she's a litera-ture student in la UNAH. She's cute—long, straight black hair, big smile, a hint of dimples, maybe? The profile picture is too small to tell. But what gets me is the flag next to the Honduran one in her bio: a gay pride flag. I like her message, send a brief but polite response, and request to follow her back.

My eyes are killing me. I put down my phone for a second and open Camila's gift, the leather-bound journal. Inside the front cover she's written a message I didn't see this afternoon: *Fill these pages with everything there's left to say—Cami.*

I brush my thumb over her handwriting, then grab a pen off my desk and turn to the first page. There are some words that have been bouncing around my head since yesterday. They burst to the forefront of my mind now, whether in response to Daniela's message or Cami's gift or both. I can see them hovering on the page even before I write them down: *The only thing left to do is leave.*

My phone buzzes at my hip, and I pick it back up. There are two notifications on the screen: Cami texted me back, and Daniela Castillo accepted my follow request.

THIRTEEN

"In the next two months, we'll have more than a dozen interna- tional admissions counselors from all over the United States and Canada visiting us. For those of you interested in applying to colleges outside the country, this will be a great opportunity to make connections, ask some questions. Applications to most places are due December first, and you should hear back from their admissions departments in the spring. Then you'll have the summer to get your student visa arrangements sorted."

Miss Katherine, our college counselor, hands out a thick package of brochures to the students in the front so they can pass them down. The whole senior class is crammed into our tiny auditorium. I grab one of the brochures and keep the pile moving. The glossy, thick paper in my hand is filled with pictures of white people sitting on grassy fields and smiling at each other, too many notebooks and laptops spread out around them.

I glance through the brochure half-heartedly. I've never thought about studying abroad much—Mami and Abuela barely make enough to pay for my and Alberto's school, not to mention food and gas and medicine when we get sick. I always figured I'd just go to la UNAH, like Maynor.

Of course, some schools offer partial financial aid and scholarships. I think of everyone else in the whole world, in other countries like this, looking at the same brochures, fighting for the same limited scholarships. Long shot.

"Are we gonna have any sports recruiters come?" Pablo asks.

"No, but you can always try to schedule a Skype interview."

She goes on to explain the logistics of recruiting internationally, and my mind wanders to the awkward car ride with Mami this morning, the still air between us punctuated only with Alberto's musings about his World Cup album stickers. For one brief, fleeting second, I wonder what it would be like to live somewhere else—somewhere I was surrounded by less people like Mami. With more people like me.

Sure, I know *of* people like that here. But even those people—decorators and florists that work with Mami, maybe someone's aunt we heard of once—seem to exist in rumors. They're never seen living publicly like that, and it's easy to blink the truth of who they love away.

My phone vibrates against my thigh. It feels good to have real, non-ghost notifications back. Before pulling it out from my pocket I already know who it is: Dani.

Usually, I wouldn't use my phone at school and risk having it confiscated all week, but I don't want to wait to message Dani back. We've been texting constantly over the past few days. It only took a couple messages back and forth for me to feel safe telling her who I was, the person behind the poem she liked. Since then, it feels like

I've told her more than I've ever told anyone. Except for Maynor. Or Camila, maybe. I even told her about what happened with Mami. She didn't try to give me one of those empty *things will get better* speeches. She just listened and said how sorry she was.

I've learned a lot about her too. She's been living in the city since February. Before, she lived with her aunt in Copán. Both her parents are dead—or rather, assumed dead. They left many years ago, when she was a child, hoping to cross the Mexican-American border and come back to get her after they were settled in the US. The last time she heard from them was right before they got to Juárez. A brief check-in phone call, then never again.

Things are crazy at UNAH today. The fronts might be organizing for some pre-elections marches. Also, I think I saw your brother?

"I want each and every one of you to make a list for tomorrow, of five potential places you'd like to apply to," Miss Katherine says, breaking into my thoughts.

"What if we don't want to study abroad?" David, one of the always-has-known-he-would-be-a-doctor-here asks.

"Then write a one-page explanation of your plans. I'd still like you to make a list. You should have more than one option. There are multiple places where you could study medicine in Honduras, David. There are also several good programs in México or Costa Rica or Chile. Just give it some thought. That's all I want from you."

David rolls his eyes, but Miss Kat doesn't catch it. I hear someone murmur "This is a waste of time." I silently agree with them—this *is* a waste of time for most of us. Everyone knows there's only a handful of people who'll be able to leave the country—those with relatives already living in the US or rich parents. Maybe a couple lucky ones who do manage to get a significant scholarship.

I flip through the thickest of all the brochures and stop at a page listing every club at this college in the Midwest. Right between Latin Club and Mountain Biking Club is the LGBTQ+ Club, plus a brief description. I read it one, two, maybe seven times. Then I notice the photo of six people beneath the description. Most of them have dyed hair, tattoos, and piercings. They have their arms looped around each other's' shoulders.

Behind the brochure, I type and send three back-to-back messages to Dani:

> Are there any social student groups at UNAH?

> Yeah, I heard Maynor talking about the fronts this week.

> You should say hi to him sometime. You two would like each other.

"Miss Kat, I gotta say what everybody's thinking. Most of us can't afford any of these colleges. It's a waste of time just to think about it," this kid named Cristian says. His face is flushed red from playing fútbol earlier.

Miss Katherine looks pissed now. "Listen, muchachos. I get it. I know that's how most of you feel. But this year the school has been contacted directly by these colleges. They *really* want you to apply and are offering generous financial aid packages."

A few audible sighs ring out through the auditorium.

"Fine. Okay. I'm not really supposed to say this . . ." Miss

Katherine crosses her arms, lowering her voice. "But I want you to trust me about trying. This isn't business as usual for these colleges. They *need* to recruit some of you. They receive funding and donations and other sorts of . . . help . . . if they take on a certain number of students from our . . . background."

Valeria leans over to whisper in my ear, "She means poor and from a third-world country."

I snort, then quickly stare at the floor in case Miss Kat looks my way. "Yup."

"Promising though," Valeria adds, opening another brochure.

Dani messages me back:

> Social groups? No, I don't think so. That sounds too much like organizing. And you know how they feel about students organizing.

"I think you should do it," Valeria says, gesturing for me to move so she can sit next to me.

We're at the tables outside the cafeteria, facing the soccer court—there's a match on its way between the senior and the junior boys. The plastic bench is sun-warmed, and I can feel the heat through my pants. On the side of the court, Camila and Carla sit on the ground, sharing a gray jacket to cover both of their heads from the sun. Pablo is playing, but every so often he jogs to them and takes a sip from his Coke, which Cami holds out for him.

"Do what?" I ask, even though I already know what she means. I have at least nine different brochures in my hands.

"Your grades are good. Your extracurriculars are fine."

"Have you seen these application fees?" I tear my eyes away from the field to look at her. "Where am I going to get eighty dollars per school from? That's—what—almost two thousand Lempiras for just one application. Applying to five schools would be more than half my mom's salary."

"Look, don't worry about that part yet." Valeria squints against the harsh noon sunlight. "There are fee waivers we can apply for. It doesn't hurt to just . . . gather everything they're asking for. Just in case."

"Why do you think I should do it, though? Are you doing it?"

She nods. "I talked to my parents about it, and they think it's a good idea. My dad's half sister lives in Virginia—she'll help me out."

"That's pretty lucky."

"Yes," she says, peeling a mandarin she's just pulled out of her backpack. "It *is* lucky. But it doesn't mean you need to have someone already there for it to be possible. Plus, well . . ."

She pauses for a second. I watch her fingernails digging into the skin of the mandarin, the soft lines of dimpled orange folding inward. It feel like I'm avoiding her gaze, but maybe she's the one avoiding mine.

"If you stay here, it'll probably never feel like you just get to . . . be. And I mean that in so many ways. Like, look at your brother. He never wanted to be a doctor, right? But he still *has* to do something that's acceptable and safe and profitable, eventually. If we stay here, we have to be doctors or lawyers or engineers or . . . well, I guess that's it. Maybe dentists. But we'll always be struggling."

Valeria rips off a big chunk of the mandarin peel and sets it aside. I keep my eyes on her hands. I can feel the sun burning my hair and scalp.

"If we stay here, we'll be going to college with the same people we've known all of our lives. Maybe we'll marry one of them. And that's it, Libertad. That's all."

Valeria's eyes narrow. She stares past me, toward the horizon. "I want to *try*. I want to study something I care about and go a week without having to worry about all of this . . . mess. All the protests and stuff. I don't think . . ." Her voice goes soft. "I don't think you lose anything just by trying."

I sigh. Both of us look down, staring at the naked orange in Valeria's hands, its fractured peel strewn across the table. Valeria shakes her head, as if coming out of a trance, then hands me a slice of mandarin.

"I know," I say, taking it from her with one hand and wiping the sweat beading along my hairline with the other.

"There's no harm in trying."

"Yeah, but . . . I'm scared. I'm scared I'll get my hopes up and then . . . you know." I pop the slice into my mouth and bite down, gathering my thoughts as the sharp, sweet taste of citrus coats my tongue. "Also, I guess I've never considered not living with my family."

"We can't live with them forever."

I think about it for a minute: It sounds logically right, of course. But also not true. Not about us, here.

"The thing is, I think we can? Look at my mom—she's forty. She lives with her mom. And Maynor is twenty-five and he lives with his mom. And, I don't know, if Maynor suddenly got some girl knocked up or something, they'd live with us too, you know? Most households are just like, multiple families from the same main branch. Different generations under the same roof."

Valeria bites into another piece of the mandarin and offers me a second slice. I take it: It's soft between my fingers, and I'm tempted to squeeze it, let the juice run down my fingers and wrist and arm in itchy streaks.

She swallows. "Okay, yeah. I hear you. But doesn't that just make applying somewhere else sound better?"

"Mmm. I guess so." I think about our home. It's always felt safe—every room familiar, welcoming. Living with my father wasn't like that.

The past few days, though, I've started thinking twice about leaving my room. I've started texting Maynor to confirm that he's the one in the kitchen, that no one else is there. Mami and I will occasionally say something to each other at dinner or in passing. But more than once I've caught her in a quiet corner, by herself, wiping tears from her eyes. It's made me feel nothing but angry.

Maybe living at home forever isn't a real option. Not for me, anyway.

"So. You're gonna do it?" Valeria asks, her voice hopeful. She's finished the mandarin and is sweeping the fragments of peel toward her, building a little mountain on the table between us.

I hear cheering and turn back to the field. It looks like the junior class boys have scored a goal, but the sun is too bright to make out any faces. When I try, blue spots appear at the corners of my vision. The players all become faceless bodies moving around, dirt clouds rising from their feet.

"Yeah. Maybe it's time to get out of here," I say, letting the blue spots blind me, just for a second.

MAYNOR

Before he could open his eyes, Maynor knew the power was out.
He couldn't say *how* he knew. He just did. Power outages were common, one or two a week, and perhaps the recognition had become coded in his body.

Maybe it was the absence of electric humming. There was a crispness to the air. Sunlight flamed on his face. The birds' chirping was clearer than ever. Cleaner than ever? Yeah, that was it. He knew the power was out from the cleanness of his senses—like a curtain of fog had been lifted from the air.

It was Sunday. Sundays in the new house were different; in the old house, his father would sleep in until noon. They all knew to be as quiet as possible until he woke, careful not to enrage him. Once up, he'd drive all of them to DK'D for vanilla lattes and sugar donuts. The rest of the day was spent in bed—all in the same room, watching fútbol games and movies on cable. Except for his mother, who'd clean and make sure his and his siblings' school uniforms were ready for the week. As well as his father's clothes.

In the new house—which wasn't really new, but rather his grandmother's house that he'd known from birth—Sundays were for cooking and cleaning. And everyone had to pitch in. He could smell coffee and hear the clanking of dishes being dried off and put away. Maybe the power had just gone out. He recognized the voices of his mother, grandmother, and Tía Martha but couldn't make out any words—they were talking too fast. Outside, he thought he could hear the chopping of a distant helicopter. It was a hot day.

He turned to the other side of the bed, expecting to see his sister still asleep: They'd been sharing a room since May. But she was gone. He sat up and closed his eyes, counting down sixty seconds in his head. A habit he couldn't pinpoint the beginning of: At the old house, he'd count down five minutes, even ten. Today, he only needed one. When he reached zero, he threw his legs over the edge and sprang up in a quick motion. Bathroom, then kitchen.

"¿Qué tanto alegán tan temprano?" he teased, scanning for the French press.

"Good morning, Sleeping Beauty," his aunt sing-songed.

She pulled out a kitchen chair and sat next to his mother. It still surprised him, sometimes, how different they looked despite being sisters. There was a general resemblance, of course, but it was almost muted by the ways in which they held themselves so differently. Martha was tiny, not taller than five feet, with short, straight black hair and big square glasses. Her features were pointy and small. His mother, on the other hand, commanded the room. She was tall with an athletic build. Her black hair was long and thick. Her eyes, which she had passed down to Alberto, were big and round. The black bruise on the right was almost all gone—barely a hint now. The cut on her lip had healed.

"It's not even . . ." He checked the clock, forgetting the power was out.

"Son las ocho," Mami said. "Do you want some pan and coffee, bebé?"

Abuela stood by the sink peeling a mango. She wore her navy-and-white house dress, her hair covered by a shower cap. Maynor could smell the hair dye across the room.

"How did you heat up the water?"

She had driven up the street to one of the many atol stands, Mami said, where the ladies used an open flame to cook various corn drinks and foods. They'd done it happily as a favor—she often bought fritas and elote asado from them. Mami patted the empty seat next to her, gesturing for Maynor to sit down, then turned back to the conversation with Martha and Abuela. They were gossiping about one of Abuela's clients, who seemed to have a new boyfriend every time she came by the workshop. Maynor sat.

The next hour was peaceful—a reminder of everything they'd gained in the past month and a half. The women gossiped and teased him. The coffee got cold, but still they dipped their bread into their mugs and sipped. His aunt prepared a bowl of mango verde for them to share, squeezing lime juice over the thin slices in that funny way of hers—making the halves kiss: maximum juice rendering. There was no use in asking why the power was out or when it'd come back. No one knew the answers to those questions.

He was about to suggest driving up to buy some charcoal for a carne asada, when Libertad, fresh from the shower, rushed into the room with Abuela's phone.

"It's Abuelo," she said, handing the phone to their grandmother.

Abuela made a face. Maynor couldn't tell if she had meant to. He knew little of their current situation, except that Abuelo had been gone for a year now, and was staying in his hometown in the north, Puerto Cortés.

"¿Aló?" his grandmother said. There was a long pause. Her face changed—first to confusion, then dread. "No," she uttered. "No puede ser."

"¿Mamá?" his aunt stood up. "¿Qué pasó?"

For a moment, Maynor thought maybe something had happened to his uncle, José. Or one of his children—they also lived in the north. It'd make sense for Abuelo to know first.

But that wasn't it. Abuela put the call on speaker. Maynor didn't quite understand, but it seemed like no one else did either. At some point, in the middle of the night, military men had entered the president's house. They'd escorted Manuel Zelaya out of his home, still in his pajamas, and boarded him on a plane en route to Costa Rica. International news outlets all over the world were already covering it: an American-sponsored coup. Honduras was officially under military rule. It wasn't a power outage in their area. It was all of Tegucigalpa that was power-less.

The rest of the day was a blur. Power returned after noon. Abuelo called again, as did Tío José, as did everyone they knew, trying to piece together any information they had. The family sat in front of the TV, flipping between local and international reporting.

Protests began as soon as word spread: American chain restaurants burnt to their bones, major roads barricaded with rocks and tires ablaze. Footage of soldiers and protestors en enfrentamiento. A baton snapping down on a spine. A forehead slit raw, blood cascading in sheets down a face. And so many war tanks making their way down every street he'd ever known. His siblings lost interest in the commotion before long, but the women remained glued to the screen.

At nightfall, an announcement went out over the airwaves: a six p.m. to six a.m curfew that would be in place for the next two weeks. To be extended as necessary. Abuela cursed and cried—"How are we going to get any work?" she begged. "Everything is going to get cancelled."

He understood this part—no ballet shows, no quinceañeras, no weddings meant no money would come into the workshop. People would cancel these events until any sense of normalcy returned, and there was no way to predict when that would be.

"It'll be okay, Mamá," his mother said. "We'll leave at six and come back at five thirty. We'll bring whatever we can to finish at home."

After the night his father didn't kill his mother—the night he fractured her jaw and punched her right eye shut—his mother lost her job selling publicity for a small magazine. The owner was a close friend of his father. There were six of them in a single house now. Six mouths to feed, and only one source of income: the workshop.

"All because of that stupid ass of a man," Abuela said. "Ese pendejo."

She meant the now exiled president. If his understanding was accurate, the reasoning behind Zelaya's outing was that he had been trying to remain in power after his term ended next January. He was associated with other leftist governments: Hugo Zelaya and Fidel Castro. The Americans had intervened before he could establish what they believed would be a leftist dictatorship.

"That man," Martha began, "is, like it or not, Mamá, the democratically elected president. He had half a year left in his term. This is happening because the Americans intervened as if our government, our country, is some monopoly game they can just manipulate however they want."

"No, Martha," his grandmother replied, in a slow tone. "Te voy a decir una cosa. You haven't lived long enough to know. Look at Nicaragua. Look at Cuba. Los gringos know what happens when one of these locos decide they want to stay in power. They will live in their palaces, and you won't have enough to eat."

She didn't yell. She didn't even raise her voice. And somehow, this was even more terrifying. His aunt, however, did scream. They went in circles, repeating the same arguments over and around each other. They had been at this dance for the past few months, but it never got this loud. For a second, Maynor blinked and thought he was back in time. Eventually, his mom intervened.

"Bueno, ya," she yelled over Martha. "Neither of you has any control over any of it. We will do whatever we need to get by."

"You know why you think like that?" Martha said, turning to his mother. Maynor felt a tug in his stomach. "Porque you got knocked up at sixteen and then again at twenty-three and then *again* six years later. 'Cause you've spent your whole life raising kids and playing wife to a piece of shit. You've never thought you had control over anything. But this"—she gestured to the TV screen—"is real life."

Martha stormed out of the room and seconds later they heard the scratching of her bedroom door against the floor, followed by a slam.

"Ella no entiende," his grandmother said.

His mother stayed quiet. Maynor's chest felt like it might explode.

He didn't cry on the night his father had almost killed his mother. He didn't cry the weeks after, when all the way from his new room he could hear his mother crying herself to sleep. He didn't cry when his grandmother noted that it would take Alberto some time to begin talking again. He didn't cry when his father left voicemail after voicemail, or even after he stopped.

But looking at his mother now, at the smallness of her shape, he felt the tears well behind his eyes. He didn't know what to say. So he walked to her and put his hand on her shoulder and he hoped. He hoped that over the voices of the men on the screen, over the sirens in the distance, and her sister's words, she could hear his silent promise: He was here. He would never leave her. This was real life.

FOURTEEN

Tell us about a time you had an idea or belief challenged.

What makes you unique?

Who is your biggest inspiration?

How do you contribute in your community?

Why do you want to pursue a career at our institution, and
what are your long-term goals?

I read the list of possible scholarship essay prompts over and over again, hoping one will suddenly jump out and hit me in the face with an obvious, *Yes, of course!* answer. I have to choose one and write a 700- to 1,000-word response that will convince a group of strangers I'm deserving of some scholarship money.

Nothing happens. Nothing's happened for days. It's not that I'm at a loss for words. The words come. I *know* the answers they want for all these questions. I know how I need to appeal to the hypothetical readers of this essay. But when I approach a page with the pen, I freeze. I'm a clogged sink.

I give up. I sigh, then make a paper plane of the list and fly it across my room. It crashes into the door and lands in front of it, soundless. I pull an old pair of earbuds from my desk drawer—the plastic coating the wires is darkened with dust and peeling in places. I plug it into my phone and play a random Bad Bunny playlist from YouTube. The music comes through choppy, textured by the low-quality earbuds like an old carpet. I push through a few songs before the ding of a notification bounces off my ear drums.

> You need to come to this. Make Maynor take you. He's probably gonna be there anyway.

There's a post attached to Dani's message: It's publicity for an event at a place called Cien Años. A poetry reading four weeks from now, near the end of October. Cover is a hundred Lempiras.

I scroll through the bar's Instagram account: They seem to host events like this often—local bands and poetry readings—the proceeds almost always in benefit of different people's medical procedures. I'm halfway down their feed when I see a picture of Berta Cáceres, the Lenca environmental activist. I click on it to read the caption. The post is from last March, for the one-year anniversary of her murder.

Te recordamos hoy y siempre querida Berta. Exigimos justicia. Acompáñanos hoy para conmemorar la vida de Berta Cáceres.

It feels surreal that so much time has passed since Berta's killing. It feels like yesterday we woke up to the news. Per usual, things were phrased so differently between local and international mediums.

CNN and *The Guardian* and *The New York Times* and so on talked about her activism for the Lenca people. They broke down who would benefit the most from her death: the government and the international companies trying to build a dam that would destroy the water source that Río Gualcarque is to her community. Berta opposed the construction of the dam fiercely and organized her people to protect the river.

Local news channels focused on her friend from México, another activist, who was there during the attack on her life but survived. It was clear they were trying to frame it all as inside job, to absolve any outside parties—the government, the military—from even being mentioned. So much has surfaced since: Texts and calls that point to local powerful families with monetary interests set in the dam, and with deep connections to government officials. Time has uncovered so much, but there's yet to be a single arrest. I get a bit nauseous thinking about it even now.

I like Dani's message about the poetry reading and text back:

> this sounds so good.

At the realization that I'll be meeting Daniela in person for the first time, something crackles electric in my chest, the way my arm hairs do near a television screen.

I'm about to send the post to Maynor and ask if he has plans to go, when the guy in question bursts into my room. He dives onto my bed without a word and wraps his arms around my face, suffocating me. He plants a comically delicate kiss on the top of my head as I struggle against him.

"What. Are. You. Doing. Here?" I gasp for air.

"I came home early." He loosens his arms from around my face and goes still, deadweight now. "What are you doing?"

"Maynor, get off! You weigh more than a house."

He laughs. This is what Alberto used to say, when he was four or five and Maynor would lay on top of him like this. Maynor rolls over to lay next to me, and I scoot over to make space.

"I came home early," Maynor says again. "A friend gave me a ride—I have so much homework to do tonight. Have you eaten yet?"

I shake my head. "I'm not hungry. I have a question for you, though: Have you ever been to Cien Años?"

"Yeah—a few times. They have a cool space. Sometimes, after student front meetings, we'll go for a drink and stay for whatever's going on. It's a good crowd."

Over the past few days, Maynor has begun talking with me more about the student front meetings and protests. At first it felt like he was testing me, waiting to see if I'd shut him down or demand he quit. I didn't. In part because the more I talk to Dani about all the shit going on—the things that led her parents to leave, the shit that happens outside Tegucigalpa, which is somehow even worse—the more I understand the work Maynor's doing.

At home, we talk about the issues. But it rarely feels like there's space to dwell on them. Whenever Mami or Abuela complains about living conditions or crime or murder, the next thing they say is a version of "pero ni modo, we gotta keep moving. Hay que sobrevivir." And that's that.

Maynor is *doing* something about it. As scared as I am for him, it feels good to be included in this part of his life. It feels good to know he can trust me with this important piece of himself.

"Look at this," I say, showing him the post about the upcoming event. He takes my phone from my hands, which he always does and is *extremely* annoying. I wish he'd just read the screen and let me hold my phone.

"Sounds interesting," he says after a beat, before handing my phone back to me. "You want to go?"

"Yes." I lean my head on his shoulder. "But Mom—"

"Would you read your poetry?"

"Oh. Um, I don't know—I hadn't gotten that far."

"It's an open mic." He points to the post on my screen.

Is that why Dani wants me to come? I think about it for a minute, rereading the post as I consider. "Maybe?"

"I think you should." Maynor ruffles my hair.

"Okay . . . but what about Mom?"

"What about her?"

"I don't know if I'm grounded." I really don't know—it's been over a week since everything happened. Mami and I haven't talked about any of it again, but we also haven't talked about anything else.

"Hmm." Maynor scratches his chin. "I don't think you are. I mean, I don't know . . . But I don't think Mami would say anything if you're coming with me."

I nod. "That's what I think too."

"Do you know anyone who's going?" He smirks, and I know he knows exactly why I want to go.

"Dani." I smile, heat blooming across my cheeks. "She sent me the post."

Maynor wiggles his eyebrows. "How old is this girl again?"

"Nineteen? Maybe twenty? She's a first year."

"All right. Now you know I gotta ask around about this Dani, just to make sure. But I *think* I can take you."

I roll my eyes but can't help grinning. "You do that."

My phone vibrates. Instinctively, I go to the notification, even though I can feel Maynor reading over my shoulder:

> Talk to your brother and tell me what he says.

"Tell her I said we're going." Maynor's voice crackles loudly in my ear, making me jump. "I'll take you."

I turn quickly and drop the phone, grabbing Maynor's ears with my hands before he can move. I rub my nose against his. Dad used to do this with us, years and years ago. He called it "naricita." Little nose.

"Thank you, thank you, thank you."

"Yeah yeah," Maynor laughs, pulling away from my grip. "Four weeks is a long time from now, though. Why don't you come to la UNAH with me next week, just one day? You could meet your friend."

"You're forgetting about this little thing I have called school . . ."

Maynor shrugs. "Nothing will happen if you miss one day." Then his eyes light up. "I have a plan. I'll tell Mami a friend is going to give me a ride in the morning and we can take you to school while we're at it."

"What about Alberto, though? Wouldn't she just ask us to bring him with us?"

"I mean, we can actually drop him off at school, that's fine."

"Oh. Okay . . . yeah."

"Okay enana." The bed creaks as Maynor gets up. "Are you sure you're not hungry?"

"What are you making?"

"Whatever there is to make." Maynor stops by the door, spotting my forlorn-looking paper plane. He stoops down to pick it up and unfolds it. "No luck yet?"

Maynor is the only person—besides Valeria—that I've talked to about applying abroad. I'm about to make something up when sunlight moves from behind a cloud and bursts through my window, bisecting the room—and Maynor—in half. He blinks away the light; his skin looks golden, and the soft brown of his eyes is startling in the moment.

"No," I sigh. "Not really."

"Come on." Maynor smooths out the crumpled paper and rests it on top of my desk, then stretches his arms over his head. "Come help me in the kitchen."

FIFTEEN

Saturday morning, Maynor and I are in the middle of washing
dishes and putting things away after breakfast when we hear the
front door open.

Mami and Abuela are both at work. Alberto's still asleep—he
usually doesn't wake up until noon on the weekends. We stop what
we're doing and look at each other, both of us frozen in place. I can't
imagine who else could possibly have keys to the house.

Maynor presses a finger to his lips, then slowly makes his way
to the living room. A booming voice interrupts his sneaky steps:
"¡Buenaaaas!"

I drop the plate I was halfway through scrubbing with a loud
clank and run toward the front door. Maynor straightens up and
smiles.

"¡Abuelo! What are you doing here?" I leap toward him, arms
extended. Abuelo sets his bags down and squeezes me to him tightly.

"I had a meeting in Tegucigalpa, so I thought I'd come over
and stay a few days. ¿Cómo estás, colocha bella? How are you, my

boy?" He releases one arm from around me and pulls Maynor into a half-hug.

"I'm good, Abuelo," Maynor replies. "How are you? How are things in the coast?"

"Hot—I haven't been able to sleep all week. I thought I'd take a meeting in Tegus to get out of it for a while."

"Have you seen Abuela?" Maynor asks.

"Yes. I went to the workshop first, got the keys from her. She didn't know if you'd be home."

"Libi and I were just cleaning up. Are you hungry?"

"I'm okay, son. I'm all right—I ate in Siguatepeque on the way here."

After we help Abuelo with his bags and finish cleaning up the kitchen, Abuelo lies down in Mami's bed and turns on the TV. Maynor and I sit at his feet while upcoming election coverage scrolls across the screen.

"It's gonna be a whole mess." Abuelo shakes his head. "What's the talk like at the university, Maynor?"

"Not good, Papá." Maynor runs his fingers through his hair. "Everyone thinks the National party is gonna cheat. The usual, you know: Votes thrown out, dead people voting and so on."

"Habrá que ver." Abuelo lifts the remote, changing the channel to yet another news station. "It's all the same in the end: Right, left—they go home and have dinner with each other, keep the money within the same five families. They laugh and drink together while people kill each other over them. Look at los locos from the student fronts, how they made you miss, what—three months of classes?"

I glance at Maynor. He looks like he's about to say something, then thinks better of it and nods. I turn back to the TV, and the two of us stay at Abuelo's feet until his snores are louder than the newscasters' voices.

At some point, Maynor tells me he's gonna take a nap in his room. I stay a little longer with Abuelo—just watching him sleep, his face illuminated by the TV light. I wonder if he misses it here. Tegus and this house. Abuela. Us.

I know so little about his life in the coast. He lives with one of his sisters there; or at least, he used to. We haven't visited in over five years, maybe more. I can't even remember when it became clear he was done pretending he just worked there, and we were done pretending he would ever come back.

Through the years, I've heard rumors of him having girlfriends. It only makes me sad because I know it once made Abuela very sad. It doesn't anymore, though. She moved on. She barely acknowledges his presence when he's here. He's like an old roommate, a long-lost friend—not a partner nor a lover.

My gaze moves up to Abuelo's nose—hooked and big, white hairs poking out of each nostril. He's gotten so much older, and I don't think I've taken the time to notice. He's been bald for many years now, but I remember the dark hair that once was there.

I wonder what our lives—and his—could have been like if he had stuck around. If he had been Abuela's husband, for real.

I wrestle all afternoon to begin the scholarship essay, but my heart just isn't in it. There are other thoughts bouncing around my head, itching to get out. I reach for the journal Cami gifted me. I leave the first page blank, and in the second page, I write a question on the top margin: *¿Te sentís independiente?*

My handwriting comes out small and all cramped together, no space between words and letters. I stare at it for a minute, considering both the craft of my handwriting and the question I'm asking. Honduras doesn't *feel* like an independent nation. I mean, sure—we're our own country, but even from a young age I understood we were always at the mercy of bigger, more powerful nations. What does that even mean, really, to be independent? And from whom? We're a small country. Small, like my handwriting, too insignificant to take up any space.

I think of the coup nearly a decade ago now. The way I understand it, one morning the US government decided our democratically elected president wasn't fit to rule anymore. They drove him out, imposing a military state and right-wing government instead. How can we be independent if another country—bigger, richer, more powerful—can swoop in at any time and upend everything?

¿Te sentís independiente?
Pues, a vos la historia te miente.[1]

I get going, returning to the same question over and over, answering it for myself differently each time. My thoughts begin to shape into a poem, and I feel a familiar tingling zinging down my body.

I lose sense of time. The page is full of scribbles and crossed-out lines by the time I stop to text Dani about going to la UNAH this week. Short, one-line messages pour in: She can't wait. She's going to treat me to mondongo from Corina's. And show me her favorite garden on campus.

I start typing a response, asking her why she loves the places she's chosen. But I get too excited and, in a moment of bravery, decide to call instead. I've never talked to her on the phone—I'm not even sure she'll pick up. The call rings. By the fourth beep, I'm ready to hang up and pretend it was a butt-dial, but she picks up.

"Hey! Hold on," her voice comes through, followed by some shuffling.

I get nervous. Maybe this was a bad time? What if she's busy? People don't just call without texting first about calling. I should've asked. I'm about to apologize for calling, when she comes back again, her voice much clearer this time.

"Okay, hi. I had to find my earphones," she says.

I like her voice. There's something surprising about it—it's lower than I expected it to be. Low and warm.

"Hi!" I reply, suddenly hyper-aware that this is also *her* first time hearing *my* voice. "Um, can you talk? Is this okay? I should've asked—"

"Yes!" she says. "This is great!"

"I was texting you back to ask about all those places you like but then I just kind of . . . wanted to hear you tell me about them."

I talk too fast, but if Dani notices, she doesn't say anything. I get up and pace around my room to calm myself down and not give away how nervous I am. Because that wouldn't be very cool of me.

"Okay, so," Dani begins, "the first woman to graduate from la UNAH did so in 1936. Her name was Corina. This soup place I'm taking you for lunch is named after her. I should've asked you though—how do you feel about mondongo? I know it can be a divisive—"

"I love it," I say, before she can even finish talking. I haven't had mondongo in a minute but the memory of the hearty flavors makes my mouth water. "Okay, what else?"

She tells me about the garden. Listening to her talk reminds me a bit of how Abuelo tells history facts. She knows so much, and she loves to know.

I ask question after question, and she has an answer for almost everything.

The light outside my window fades to a soft blue. My phone gets hot against my cheek, so I grab my own pair of earbuds. The cicadas get loud enough Dani can hear them through the call. She asks how writing my essay is going.

"It isn't," I admit. "I gave up and ended up writing a poem instead."

"Read it to me," she says.

"What?"

"Read it to me, Libertad."

Hearing her say my name feels so good, I almost forget her request.

"Come on, I'd love to hear it," she insists.

"Right now?"

"Why not?"

"Um . . ." I reach for the journal. Suddenly every word I've written seems wrong, like there might be better words for all words I chose. "It's a rough, rough draft," I say.

"That's okay," she says. "I can keep that in mind. Just read it."

"Okay," I say. "All right, fine. You ready?"

"Ready."

I take a deep breath and begin to read. My voice is quiet at first, shaky, but as the poem goes on, I try to get it together and sound more confident. After all, I do mean these words.

I finish on a rush of air, then wait for Dani's response. The line on the other end is silent for a second, two.

"Hello?" I ask, at the same time Dani says, "Damn. I love it."

"Really?"

"Really. It has such good rhythm and a well-rounded take on both our history and current events. It's . . . full of urgency."

It strikes me just how good Dani is at articulating what she loves about something. How she's able to express her joy, her enthusiasm, in such a way that I can't help but feel the same.

We keep talking until Dani's phone is about to die and it's late enough Mami and Abuela will be home any minute.

"I'm glad I called you," I say.

"I'm glad you called me," she replies. "And I'm so excited to see you."

After we hang up, I lay in bed, feeling all warm and shit. I google Corina's Mondongo, and other things Dani mentioned. My room is dark and I haven't bothered to turn on the light, but the phone's brightness is enough to notice my hands are full of blue ink marks. This always happens when I write. It must be something about how I hold the pen.

I'm about to get up to wash my hands when I hear the front door open—

Mami and Abuela are home. I hesitate at my bedroom door but force myself out because I want to have family dinner with Abuelo, even if Mami is there. Of course, the first person I run into is her.

"We got groceries," she says—not unkindly, not like anything. "Go help."

I see Maynor and Alberto carrying bags in and join them in putting things away.

"What do you want to have for dinner?" Abuelo asks. He's the best cook in the world. Famous for his carne asada, and his mole.

"¡Tacos de mole!" Alberto and I shout in unison.

"I knew it." Abuelo turns to Abuela, eyes sparkling. "I told you, didn't I?"

"Yes, yes. I brought the mole," Abuela says. "And this." She pulls a three-liter bottle of Coke from a grocery bag, like a magician pulling a rabbit from a hat. Alberto cheers.

Abuelo assigns each of us a task. Mami says she's too tired to help, so she sits at the table and eats plantain chips with queso.

"How's work?" Abuelo asks her.

"Insane."

Mami crunches down on a chip, then covers her mouth as she speaks. "I just sold the most expensive wedding of the year. Guess the date for it."

"Christmas," Maynor says.

"No."

"New Year's?" Abuela asks.

"Nope—the Saturday before election day."

"Bold," I say. It feels weird to address her after days of not speaking, but the word escapes me without thinking.

"That's what I said. I told the couple—this woman, she's from here, the fiancé is some gringo—we can't refund them if they end up having to cancel because of any protests. They went right ahead with it."

"Well, it's getting cancelled," Abuela says. "Tenelo seguro."

"Their problem now." Mami shrugs.

The conversation, per usual, morphs into a heated discussion about the upcoming election. Abuela has strong opinions, perhaps the strongest of us all. Usually, these talks end up with her half yelling at us, even if no one is disagreeing openly. We all know it's best to just nod and stay quiet once she gets going. Maynor, Mami, and I have made the mistake of sharing our thoughts before to grave consequences. The woman can go on for hours.

"What the young people of this country don't understand," Abuela says, finger raised in the air, "is that it can always, *always*, be worse. Just look at Nicaragua! They kept saying, 'Mejor que Somoza cualquier cosa' but the cualquier cosa—the anything else—was so much worse. Now they're living under the communist system they wanted, with no toilet paper in stores, como Venezuela . . ." Abuela flings her arms out, and Abuelo quickly turns the handle of a sizzling pan on the stove away from her.

"Look at me," she continues, as Maynor and I shoot Abuelo small, grateful smiles. "I work more than fourteen hours a day. Yes, the Nationalist party is a bunch of rats, ladrones, drug dealers. But at least they don't threaten the small businesses . . ."

When I'm done chopping the chiles Abuelo asked me to, I sneak out of the kitchen and back to my room. I know I'll have to return soon, but a twenty-minute breather goes a long way with Abuela's rants. I lie in bed and grab my phone: I have messages from Dani and Valeria, plus a missed call from Camila. I call her back, and she picks up on the first ring.

"¿Aló?"

"Hey—what's up? You called?"

"Yes, just wanted to say hi. What are you up to?"

Something about her voice throws me off. It feels like there's something she wants to say that she isn't, but I shrug it off. I tell her about dinner, and Abuelo being home. I begin to tell her about the new poem I wrote, then realize I mostly want to tell her about sharing my poem with Dani.

I stop myself, though. I don't know why. It feels weird to talk to Cami *about* Dani . . . but there's no reason it should be. I've known Dani for less than a month—we're friends. And I don't owe Camila anything, not like that. I confuse myself enough that I don't notice I've stopped talking midsentence until Cami's said my name twice.

"Libertad?"

"Yes, sorry. What was I saying?"

"Your new poem. You had just finished writing it, and then . . ."

"Right. So . . . I ended up reading it over the phone to Dani, a new friend. I met her on Instagram . . . which sounds weirder than it is. She actually messaged my poetry account, and we got talking and I told her who I was and so on. She's a student at UNAH—"

"Wait," Cami interjects. "You told some strange girl from the internet who you were and the poems you're writing? Don't you think that's a little . . . dangerous?"

Her tone is more annoyed than concerned. I will myself to keep the annoyance out of my own voice when I respond, "No, it's fine, really. Dani is very much anti-government. She's reliable. Trustworthy."

"You can't know that about someone you haven't even met," Cami snaps.

"Well, I'm meeting her this week." My voice rises, comes out more defensive than I meant it.

"How?"

"Maynor is gonna take me with him to the university. I'll skip school."

"That's pretty dumb."

"What do you mean?" I try to fake a laugh, but it sounds too canned and sharp.

"You shouldn't skip school just to go hang out. It's our last year— what if you miss something important?"

"It's one day, Cami. If I miss something important, someone will tell me."

"Okaaay," she says. But it doesn't sound okay. I know the smart thing is to let it go, to not read into whatever this is. But right now, anger has a direct current to my chest.

"Maje. People miss a day all the time. Isn't Pablo always skipping to stay home and watch fútbol matches or whatever?"

"Yeah, exactly, whatever. I said okay."

"Okay then."

Cami stays quiet for a minute that feels more like ten. Her breathing from the other end is loud but slow. I'm tempted to break the silence but can't make myself open my mouth.

"All right, I have to go," she finally says. "I have homework. Good luck with the poem."

"Thanks," I mutter. I don't wait for her to say anything else. I hang up and throw my phone down beside me.

The screen lights up as it lands. I have more messages from Dani, and I was only on the phone for fifteen minutes. I'm shocked no one's come get me to help in the kitchen, but when I turn my head to the closed door I realize why.

There's yelling outside. Real yelling. I hadn't noticed it before, and I have no idea how long it's been going on for. I freeze, trying to make out a word or two, to distinguish the voices, when there's a knock on my door.

"Libi."

It's Alberto. I open the door. His face is pink and wet with tears.

"What happened? What's going on?"

"I don't know." Beto's lower lip trembles. "Abuela and Maynor started fighting about something—the president. I don't know. Then Abuelo yelled at Maynor, said he was being dis-dis-disrespectful to Abuela, that he should go get his own house if he thinks he can say whatever he wants—"

164

Alberto sobs and stutters too much for me to understand the rest of what he's saying. I lay a hand on his shoulder.

"Okay, breathe. Take a deep breath with me." I raise my shoulders with my next inhale, and Alberto mimics the motion.

I can hear Mami's voice now. She's telling someone—probably Abuelo—that they can't talk to her son like that. There are heavy footsteps, then Maynor's bedroom door slams. I close my own door, pulling Alberto inside.

"It's okay, Beto. It's gonna be fine."

"Is Maynor going to leave?"

I swallow. Where would he even go?

"No. Not at all. They're just saying things 'cause they're upset right now."

I text Maynor to ask if he's okay. I motion for Alberto to climb into my bed, then lie down beside him, covering both of us with my comforter. He fits his head in the crevice between my arm and torso. The faint smell of mole and onions wafting from his shirt makes my stomach hurt.

"Did you get to eat?" I ask him.

"No. They started fighting," he whispers.

A loud growl—I can't tell if it's his or my belly rumbling.

"Here." I reach under my pillow, grabbing my earbuds, and hand one to him. "Let's listen to some music. What are you feeling?"

He sniffles. "¿El conejo malo?" His breath is warm on my neck.

"I was thinking the same." I smile at him, type "Bad Bunny" into YouTube, and hit play on the first song that pops up.

Despite how loudly I blast the music, we each have one ear

exposed to the screaming outside. It goes on and on, though I can't make out any of the words. I try my best to concentrate on the beat of the song, moving Alberto's head to lay over my chest. The pressure and weight of it helps settle my breath.

Alberto's sniffles and hiccups slowly subside, until he finally falls asleep halfway through the fifth song. I pause the music. Outside, I hear footsteps to Mami's room, and a door being shut.

Maynor finally texts me back:

It's the same shit as always.
I'll tell you later. I'm going out.

Ok. Be safe.

I'm sorry, Maynor.

I lay my phone down on my stomach. Minutes later, I hear the window in the room next to mine open, then a thump as Maynor hits the ground.

I lie in bed for another hour, just listening to Alberto's breathing and responding to the messages Dani sent since we talked on the phone. I think of texting Camila, even going so far as to type the beginning of an apology I don't mean. Ultimately, I decide against it.

When I finally sneak to the kitchen for food, I don't run into anyone. Everyone's locked themselves away. The tortillas are cold. I eat, but with nowhere near the same hunger as when I'm competing with my brothers for the last scoop of mole.

SIXTEEN

I barely see Maynor over the next couple of days. He comes home late and leaves early or waits to leave until we're all out of the house. Abuela makes snarky comments about him here and there, mostly calling him stupid and disrespectful. I bite the inside of my cheek every time.

Abuelo tries to ease the tension—he's not the type to dwell on anything for too long. Of course, he's never here long enough to deal with the fallout. "Ya pasó, ya no piense en eso," he tells Abuela over breakfast Wednesday morning. But if anyone can hold on to things, it's Abuela.

Finally, after breakfast, I decide I can't take it anymore. It's me, Alberto, and Abuelo in the car with Mami driving—Mami's taking Abuelo to a meeting after she drops Beto and me off at school. I decide it's now or never to ask Mami what happened.

"It's complicated . . ." she begins, stopping at a streetlight. Honking pierces the air. "Mi mamá has very strong feelings about these things. And we all have to understand her. You and

Maynor—you're jóvenes. Idealistic, as all young people are. You think change is always better, that the right-wing is the worst possible power. But she's seen the other side of it. The other extreme."

Mami's voice is distant this morning, tired. I stare outside from my seat behind her, nervous to accidentally make eye contact through the rearview mirror. The car to our left gestures for a cacahuate-peddler to approach. A young girl rushes to slip the driver a small bag of peanuts, and he hands her ten Lempiras.

"The sewing workshop is her livelihood. And ours—you know I don't make enough to support us. Without Abuela working, I don't know what we would do. She's terrified to have a government that doesn't value small business owners. The candidates from the opposition, they have ties to Venezuela and Cuba. Their ideas could ruin los micro-empresarios."

The light changes, and we move forward. I look at the girl selling cacahuates on the side of the road as we pass her and think back to what I've heard from Maynor and Daniela. To all the stuff I've read online.

"I don't get what she means by ruined," I counter Mami, willing my voice to stay neutral. "How is she not ruined right now? She gets up at four in the morning and doesn't come home until after ten. She pays taxes and still can't go to a public hospital and expect to be treated in time. Or even know if the medicine she's given isn't expired. Or worse."

A couple of years ago, news broke that the president's election campaign had been financed through social security funds. Thousands died due to a lack of resources. But even worse, some were given expired medicines or pills made of flour.

"Ya, enough—" Abuelo starts.

Mami breaks hard after a motorcycle cuts her off. The cars behind her honk.

I sigh. I know what he's going to say—what he always says. Something about how Abuela is a stubborn woman. How we just need keep our mouths shut. How we'll never change her mind even if there's stuff she is wrong about, and it doesn't really matter at the end of the day.

But to my surprise, those aren't the words that Abuelo says.

"She wasn't always like this," he murmurs once the car starts moving again. "It's more complicated than left or right for her. When Martha died . . . was killed . . . it changed things—"

"Papá," Mami interrupts him gently. "No tenemos que hablar de eso."

I don't know if she doesn't want Abuelo to have to talk about it, or doesn't want me and Alberto to hear of it. Or, maybe *she* doesn't want to hear it. Either way, Abuelo clicks his tongue and flicks his hand, gesturing that he doesn't wish to be stopped.

"Abuela will always blame the left—the protestors and the resistance and so on," he says.

"But Tía Martha was protesting *with* them, right?" I ask.

"It's more complicated than that, colocha bella. A ver, listen. Martha was at a protest three days after the coup, July first of 2009. How old were you? Seven? No, you would've been—"

"I was nine," I supply for him. "Almost ten."

"You remember, then." Abuelo slowly shakes his head. "The city was a disaster. Restaurants and hotels burnt down. Rocks being thrown everywhere. We didn't know how long it would all go on for." Abuelo closes his eyes for a second, like a very long blink. When he opens them again, he seems focused on some faraway point out the windshield.

"Martha was young, twenty-three or twenty-four—just a little younger than Maynor right now. And she was a hothead, always ready to fight about this or that. She was against the coup, yes, but she also let herself be influenced by the company she kept. People who hated los gringos for their intervention or whatnot." Abuelo tsks. "Not good company."

His expression turns somber, and I'm filled with questions. *What kind of company? Why does he think she was influenced, and not the other way around?* But I see Abuelo swallow, then open his mouth to speak again, and I hold my tongue.

"The military police were there because . . . well, of course. The protestors wanted to burn the whole country down—locos. There were shots fired from both sides. I—it doesn't matter whose bullet it was that . . . If that insane man hadn't tried to stay in power, to create ties with Venezuela, los gringos wouldn't have intervened. There would've been no coup, no protest. *That's* how Abuela sees it. Without him . . . Marthita would still be here." Abuelo stops and rubs his forehead with his thumb.

Silence descends over the car.

I knew a less-detailed version of this, of course. I knew Tía Martha got in a lot of fights with Abuela about the coup in the days leading up to her death. I knew that Abuela hated Martha's friends. I also have a feeling, in this moment, that Abuelo knows *exactly* whose bullet it was that killed her.

I want to say that there are so many faults to this logic. If Abuela blames the then-president for trying to stay in power, how can she not hate this guy who is *also* trying to stay in power? At least the president then, Zelaya, tried to let the people vote on the option of reelection. Juan Orlando just decided to run again, no questions asked.

But I don't say anything else for the rest of the car ride—something about Abuelo's face warns me not to.

Finally, we get to school. We kiss Abuelo goodbye, and he tells us he'll try to make a special dinner tonight. His heart isn't in it though—I can tell he's still thinking back to his younger daughter, and what happened to her eight years ago.

Alberto heads over to his group of friends on the playground, like usual. But I feel too shaken up by what Abuelo told us to watch the junior and senior boys' before-class fútbol match. Or to sit next to my friends while they finish up homework and gossip. Or even to see Camila, who's been weird to me ever since our phone call.

Instead of heading to the picnic tables, I go straight to my first-period classroom. It's empty, and all the lights are off, the smell of Fabuloso hanging heavy in the air. I find the desk I always sit at, take out my phone, and google Tía Martha's full name plus "murder" and "coup" and "protest."

The first few results are from big local newspapers. I don't even click them—I know who pays them off, what they'll say. I scroll down until I find a source that seems attached to the resistance, no corporations or government agencies.

Her name is one in a list of a dozen people, all of them killed on July 1, 2009. I skim through until I find what I'm looking for, the detail that Abuelo says doesn't matter. All deaths are attributed to bullets only the military police have access to. No mystery there, then: killed by the state.

I find another source with a more detailed reporting of the events and start skimming through it. One paragraph jumps out at me then, sending icy tendrils of recognition down my back.

The protests of July 1 targeted three different locations: the Presidential Palace, the Supreme Court, and the Public Ministry. Organized by local groups, such as Colectivo Unidad Color Rosa, the demonstrations came after a series of murders targeting LGBTQ+ people following the Coup D'état on June 28, including the violent assassination of Vicky Hernández, a transwoman, sex worker, and activist. In the scene of most of these murders, military bullets were recovered.

I read this paragraph over and over. Was my aunt protesting for queer people's rights? For their lives? Is this what Abuelo meant by "not good company"?

Tía Martha was killed by a military bullet in the protests following the coup. She was there, presumably, to advocate for the lives of gay people. She was there to oppose the coup, American intervention, and by extension . . . well, the current government.

The current government that is now doing exactly what they condemned and used to justify the coup—trying to stay in power. They're trying to reelect a president when reelection isn't legal.

Except eight years ago, the leftist government didn't just up and change the constitution while we slept. They tried to hold a vote first, ask the people if it was something they wanted. Then American soldiers kidnapped the president in the middle of the night, and the protests began . . . as did the burning, the fighting.

How can Abuela support a government that killed her daughter? I don't get it. I don't get how she can be a person who has suffered the unthinkable because of these people, *and* a person who would rather have them in power.

Neither side feels totally right or totally wrong. What I do know is that we live on the unsealed scars of what happened in 2009, and things are about to get really bad with the election just a month away. I look down at my phone again, at my aunt's name on the list of the dead and blink fast, trying to make it go away and trying to make it stay. Trying to make it be someone else and not be not by anyone at all.

SEVENTEEN

The list, my aunt, my brother, my grandmother: It all stays jumbled in my head throughout the day. My brain feels like a big pan of refried beans forgotten on the stove, burnt and stuck down. Unwashable.

At the end of the school day, I stand outside the bus home, leaning against its cold metallic side. Alberto's on already but waiting inside is unbearable—the heat gets trapped in there like a greenhouse. I watch people walk by, climbing aboard my bus or others, when I feel my phone buzzing against my thigh.

> So are you coming tomorrow or Friday?
> Or are you gonna stand me up?

It's Dani. Maynor hasn't said anything about going to UNAH since the fight with Abuela happened. It's been hard not to pester him about it, but I figured he had enough going on. Time's running out for this week, though, so I text him to see if we're still doing it, then tell Dani I've asked—she knows everything about the fight.

> Let me know what he says. I get it
> if he's not up for it this week. It'd be
> great though, I'm really excited!

"That's *very* understanding," a voice in front of me says. Recognizing her shoes, I keep my gaze glued to my phone.

"You must have 20/20 vision to read my texts from over there." Though really, she's not too far away. I can smell the tanginess of her perfume and sweat mixed together. After a second, I glance up: Camila's hair is in a bun, as it usually is by this time. The sun bisects her face horizontally, right above her nose.

"So, you're still missing school for your little field trip?"

"I don't know. It's up to Maynor. He's . . . having a rough time at home."

Cami's face changes, and she takes a step toward me. "Did your mom and grandma find out about the protest? The student front?"

My eyes widen. "No! God no. That'd be the end for him. He just got into a bad argument with Abuela." I sigh, then click my phone screen off. "It's dumb, but it was kind of scary—lots of shouting. Alberto cried."

The lines on Cami's forehead deepen with concern. "Why didn't you tell me?"

Her question takes me aback. Cami is the person I *would* usually tell all of this to. But the rules changed after February. They seemed like they were changing back after my birthday, but now I'm not so sure.

"I . . . I don't know. It happened when we got off the phone on Saturday."

She nods, pressing her lips together. I can't read her expression—whether that pains her or not.

"It's gonna be okay," she says, her voice softer than before. "So many families are fighting over the same thing right now. My dad and his brother even stopped talking to each other for a few weeks . . . But at the end of the day, your grandma loves Maynor, and Maynor loves her. They don't have to agree for it to be okay."

A cloud moves, and the sun shines in my eyes. I squint, and Cami moves to stand next to me, our shoulders touching. The bus shakes behind us every time a kid gets on.

Things still feel off with Camila, but I'm exhausted from this morning . . . And from every other time I've been scared for what happens next. For the elections. For Maynor and Abuela. For Mami and this huge hole between us I can't tell anyone about. For the first time in months, I let my head fall onto Cami's shoulder. She rests her head over mine—her hair is warm, sun toasted.

"I'm just . . . I'm scared something will happen to Maynor," I say quietly. "And that when it does, he'll be in the middle of a fight with Abuela. I'm scared it could all happen again."

"What do you mean *again*? You're scared they'll fight again?"

"No . . . I don't know. I'm just worried. Tired."

"Yeah," she half whispers. "That makes sense."

I take a deep, audible breath, then exhale.

"Why don't you try writing about it?"

"Like journaling?"

"No. I mean, sure, you could do that too. But I meant like a poem. Did you finish the one you were telling me about?"

"No, not yet."

"Maybe try finishing it."

"Maybe," I say. I haven't had the energy to return to the poem at all.

Behind us, the bus motor roars to life. I feel the shaking in my skull and pull away from Cami reluctantly.

"Let me know how it goes?" she says.

I'm about to respond when my phone vibrates in my hand. It's Dani—I see Cami notice.

"If you get a chance or whatever," she adds, pushing herself off the bus.

I nod, but I don't know if she notices; she's already walking away. I pull my earbuds from my front pocket and plug them into my phone.

The bus ride home is long, but a good break; liminal time to sit and listen, to watch and decompress. I take a window seat and Alberto moves in next to me, flipping through the soccer player stickers he acquired today. He must spend all his lunch money on them.

Since the buses don't have any AC, we keep all our windows down. The honking and yelling around us comes through crystal-clear. So does the smell of exhaust fumes and food. At a stoplight, I scan the newspapers' front pages displayed on the stands on the median: CIENTOS DE MIGRANTES SALEN DEL PAÍS EN CARAVANA HACIA EE.UU.

This year, whenever news outlets aren't covering the elections, they're talking about the caravans leaving the country every other week for America. It's crazy how a few months ago, I never considered it as a possibility for me. I understand why people leave, of course—I just never thought *I* would try to.

The lights change, and we speed forward. There's a faint pounding in my head—I lay it against the warm window and close my eyes.

> **Let's do it on Friday**

Maynor replies about an hour later.

Alberto and I are home alone. The house feels peaceful and quiet. I text Dani the good news as I wander into the kitchen. She replies:

> **So we'll meet the day after tomorrow!!!**

My knees go soft at the thought. I stare at my phone, smiling like a person with a secret. Alberto gives me a weird look, then goes back to microwaving the grilled chicken that either Abuelo or Abuela or Mami left for us. I rub at the sore spot on my hip while grabbing hot sauce and the last quarter of Coca-Cola in the fridge. I set both down on the table.

As we sit, I want to ask Alberto if everything's okay. He's barely said a word. But he starts talking before I can open my mouth.

"Is Maynor moving out?" Grease and hot sauce from the chicken are already smudged around his lips. His eyes are always big, but they seem even bigger now.

"No." I shake my head. "Where would he go?"

"To our dad's," Alberto says, and I frown without meaning to. The idea is so ludicrous, I can't begin to imagine where he got it from.

"Maynor doesn't talk to him, Beto. And he would never live with him again—you know that."

Alberto shrugs. I stare at a crumb of dried food stuck to the table, scrambling to think of something else to say, of some other question to ask. But by the time I lift my eyes, he's already finished his food and dropped his plate in the sink. He walks away through the kitchen door.

After washing his plate and mine, I go to my room and pull out the journal. I re-read the poem draft. It feels close to done, but I want to revisit it once more. Not today, though.

I've been thinking about the first message Dani ever sent me:

> Sometimes, it feels like the
> only thing left to do is leave.
> Salir de Honduras.

At the time, it reminded me of the story we've all heard from an early age about how Honduras got its name. Supposedly, in his fourth and last trip to the Americas, Cristobal Colón reached the northeast coast of the country, disembarking in what today we call Gracias a Dios. The sea was furious, full of sharp waves. Perhaps the ocean could sense the horrible acts that would be unleashed from Columbus's ship—and the violent legacy to follow. So, the tale goes, when the colonizer set foot in Gracias a Dios, he exclaimed, "¡Gracias a Dios hemos salido de esas honduras!": *Thank the lord we've made it out of those deep waves.* The coast got the name from the first part of the sentence—Gracias a Dios—and the country got Honduras, "deep waves."

The story has been disproven, so I don't know where Honduras's or Gracias a Dios's names came from. Though I do know that many others—Tegucigalpa, for instance—come from Indigenous languages. Still, the story of the colonizer—the murderer—exclaiming in relief to have survived deep waters, then naming a country after them . . . it swirls around my head. That, plus the news we hear at least every other week about massive caravans leaving Honduras, praying for safe passage out. Words for a new poem come to the front of my mind, and I write down the first few lines:

> *Cuenta la leyenda que al pisar tierra Hondureña por vez primera,*
> *Colón exclamó a quien oyera,*
> *"¡Gracias a Dios hemos salido de esas honduras!"*[2]

I write all afternoon, teasing out more and more of the nuances of this parallel: The impossibility and danger of both staying and leaving. After a few hours, it's still unfinished. But I can't figure out what about it feels undone. I read the poem out loud to myself a few times.

As excited as I am, there's a distance between me and the poem. A lack of self-implication. Am *I* leaving? Will I feel like thanking God if I do? It's too removed from myself, like I'm people-watching and not participating.

I cross out a few lines and go at it again. This time, I think about my brother and my aunt. I think about Vicky Hernández and the murders after the coup. This time, I let the words come from the bottom of my stomach, and I think about me.

EIGHTEEN

Most days, I need my alarm or Mami's knocks on the door to wake up. Not today, though. The eagerness to go to la UNAH and meet Dani kept me up almost all night. When I finally manage to drift off, my sleep is light enough that Abuela's mopping wakes me up at four a.m. The citrusy smell of the disinfectant climbs up my nose. I lie in bed: eyes open, texting Maynor, scrolling through Twitter.

Last night, Maynor told Mami he'd give Alberto and me a ride to school with a friend. She was suspicious at first. He's barely been around all week and suddenly he wants to give us rides? But Maynor told her he wanted to buy us breakfast, do something nice to make up for all the fighting. She let it go after he promised to text her as soon as he had dropped us off.

The early morning feels eternal. I've scrolled to tweets from three days ago by the time Abuela, Mami, and Abuelo leave. As soon as I hear the car engines, I jump in and out of the shower, but it takes me longer than ever to dress. Both Maynor and I ignore

Alberto's questions of "Where are we having breakfast?" and "Why isn't Libertad wearing her uniform?"

Finally, Maynor's friend calls to let him know they're outside. For a split second, I'm scared they might be riding a motorcycle, that my brother is insane enough to believe all four of us will fit. But then I see the small, old white car. Something about it is vaguely familiar. As if I should already know the girl with shoulder-length hair in the driver's seat, even though I've never met her before.

"Buenas," she says as Alberto and I get in. "Feel free to move stuff, I know it's a mess back there."

It really isn't—there's a stack of books and a pair of sunglasses, all neatly stacked in the middle. Alberto and I climb in the back and Maynor gets in the passenger's seat. He kisses her cheek and says good morning in the softest voice I've ever heard come out of his mouth. Alberto immediately meets my eyes and raises an eyebrow.

"Alicia, mucho gusto." She meets Alberto's and my gazes in the rearview mirror. "It's a pleasure meeting Maynor's little siblings."

Alberto and I introduce ourselves, and then the car goes quiet as Alicia pulls away from the curb. Her voice is sweet, and something about her demeanor feels safe and comfortable. I don't worry about having to make small talk.

After driving through Espresso Americano for breakfast, it only takes half an hour to get Alberto to school. But in that time, he's managed to ask Alicia every little detail about her life that could possibly be relevant to him: Which fútbol team does she root for? Is she excited for the World Cup? Who are her favorite reggaeton artists?

He asks me again why I'm not in uniform. I tell him the seniors are having a color day, which he will obviously find out is not true later in the day. And then, at last, we drop him off. Maynor walks him to his class, and when he comes back, he switches seats with Alicia and drives us to la UNAH.

"So, you're a senior, right?" Alicia asks me, finally free from Alberto's interrogation. "Do you know what you want to study?"

"Not really." I shake my head. "I've always figured I'd go into medicine. I'm applying to some schools in the US as a bio major."

"That's great!" She turns to look at me from the passenger's seat. Her light brown hair frames her small, heart-shaped face in straight, even curtains.

"Yeah, I guess so," I reply. But even I can hear the apathy in my tone. Truth is, I haven't thought about it much—I just figured the thing to do was become a doctor. I'm not great with math, so engineering isn't an option. Lawyers here get killed, so that's a no-go either.

"I'm in my fourth year of medicine," Alicia says now, turning back around. I catch Maynor's eye in the rearview mirror, and he grins.

The line of cars outside the entrances to the university is insane. Desperate honking and the muted beats of different music playing loudly inside cars fill the air. I drank my coffee too fast. My stomach hurts, and I'm hyperaware of my coffee-breath. Dani texts every few minutes to ask how far, how much longer, where are we meeting.

"Where are we parking? Daniela is asking," I ask Maynor once we've gone through the gates.

"Okay, hold on." Maynor's brow furrows. "You can go meet

your friend in a minute. I also have things I want to show you, you know." There's a hint of annoyance—maybe even hurt—in his voice.

"Yes, of course," I say quickly. This day is supposed to be about me and Maynor spending time together too, I remind myself.

"Tell her you'll meet her in an hour or two at the taco stand by the sciences building." Maynor nods at my phone as the three of us climb out of the car. Alicia moves to Maynor's side and kisses his cheek, then turns to me.

"I have class in a few minutes. It was so nice to meet you, Libertad."

"Thank you for the ride," I reply.

Alicia waves an *it was nothing* gesture. She squeezes Maynor's hand, and then the two of us watch her walk away until she disappears behind a white building.

When she's gone, Maynor grins at me. His face is a little red, I notice, his expression reminding me of a younger version of him—a giddy child caught mid-mischief. I will definitely be questioning him more about Alicia, I decide, though not right now.

"You ready?" he asks. I nod.

I have to nearly jog to keep up as the two of us make our way across the campus. Maynor's legs are long and he moves like a cat—careful, but agile. He points out almost every building as we go, telling me what careers are studied where. Every inch of sidewalk is packed, and I swerve and side-step to avoid colliding head-on with students or peddlers trying to sell food and goods. The sun is in my eyes no matter where we turn, and the humidity sticks to my skin. I'm just about to complain when Maynor finally leads us into a building he calls the social sciences' main hub.

It's . . . depressing. The overhead lighting is the greenish off-white color I associate with horror movies. It's even hotter in here, somehow—the body heat of students and teachers trapped without AC. To my surprise, though, Maynor walks straight through the central hallway, exiting out the double doors on the opposite end.

I jog again to catch up and find myself in an open-air atrium—like what you'd find in the middle of an apartment complex. Building walls surround the square; there's no trees or vegetation here, unlike the rest of the university. I have a feeling that if we were alone, just me and Maynor, we could hear our words echo, bouncing off the walls around us.

But we're far from alone. Music plays from different speakers around the square. People congregate in small groups, laughing and whispering and gesturing, all deep in conversation. What ultimately catches my eye, though, are the walls around us.

Nearly every inch of building space, even incredibly high up, is covered in graffiti. A lot of it is the same as what I've seen in the city: *FUERA JOH. CHEPOS ASESINOS. BERTA VIVE. GRINGOS FUERA.* But there are also dozens—no, hundreds—of faces.

Some of the faces seem familiar, like maybe I've seen them before. Many of them I don't recognize. There are names scattered all around too, some of which identify the faces. Most of the portraits are stenciled in different styles, clearly done by different artists. Some are spray painted in red, others blue or black. A few have more details, like eye color and wrinkles.

I can't stop looking—and looking and looking—at all the eyes staring down at me. I spin slowly in place, my breath caught in my lungs. There's something that feels holy about this space, like a church of sorts. A place of worship.

"Who are they?" I ask Maynor. He smiles, but it doesn't spread to his eyes.

"Los desaparecidos."

"Students that have gone missing?"

"Yes." Maynor sits on the one empty concrete bench near us. I lower myself next to him. "Some of them were students, but not all.

"Some are from over thirty years ago," Maynor begins. "When the military death squads would just pick up people—suspected of anti-government involvement—off the street. Most of them were students." Maynor lifts his feet from the ground and sits cross-legged, like a child, turning to face me. Without thinking about it, I mirror him.

"The death squads would torture and then kill them. For some, their remains have never been found." Maynor grimaces.

"Some of them have died more recently though, right?" I probe.

Maynor nods. "Some of them were in the coup a few years back. Others from the protests just months ago. People the military police have . . . vanished. Their faces and names are here—so we don't forget them," he says.

Maynor catches my eyes, and I nod for him to continue.

"This quad is where most people in the fronts hang out. It's a sacred place. A place to remember and grieve and see how long this battle has been going on. . . . How much it's taken from us."

Maynor spreads his arms out, gesturing to the walls around us.

The two of us fall silent for a minute and just look at everything. Me, taking in all these faces for the first time. Maynor, for probably the hundredth or so.

"I'm scared for you, Maynor," I say, finally. "And worried. The fight with Abuela . . ."

"Abuela will always be Abuela." Maynor sighs, rubbing his palms together. "That's not a battle I'll ever win."

"I think it's different this time, Maynor," I say, covering my eyes from the sun to be able to look straight at him. "Abuelo talked to me and Alberto about Martha. . . . How she died."

He frowns—it's clear this has caught him off guard. After a moment, he nods. "You were little when it happened, both of you. But I wasn't—I was your age now, eighteen. Martha was only twenty-four. I was there when she had her last fight with Abuela the night before she was killed. I was there when . . . when Abuela got the call from one of her friends." His voice trails off. I take his hand and squeeze it.

"I'm so sorry, Maynor," I whisper.

He stares at the sliver of bench between us. I want to ask him more about our aunt, specifically what I read about a few days ago. But it doesn't feel right in this moment.

"I'm not stupid," he breathes.

"I know you're—"

"I'm not stupid, Libertad," he repeats louder this time, cutting me off. "I know that thing's aren't left or right. I know that stopping that asshole from reelecting himself won't fix everything. The things Abuela fears—they're real and valid and true." He slides his hand out of mine, meeting my gaze now.

"I'm not some dumb idealistic kid—I know Abuela has lived through so much. But things are bad right now, Libi. And they're only getting worse. There are whispers everywhere: JOH's party is using social security funds again, this time to finance their reelection campaign. Meaning a few weeks from now, there won't be any medicine in public hospitals. Doctors won't get paid. People will die. And this is just the beginning." Maynor blows out a long, slow breath. "If the nationalist party can get away with staying in power four more years . . . I don't know how we'll ever get them out. They'll be invincible."

I nod, trying to wrap my mind around the enormity of Maynor's words. "So how do we—how is it stopped?" The question comes out of me clunky, awkward. I feel young and stupid, though nothing in Maynor's face hints that he thinks this.

He shrugs and scans the wall behind me. "We do as much as we can, Libertad. On election night, people from the fronts will stay at the voting centers all day. Watching them count each vote. Making sure they don't cheat us out of it. If they do, we'll take to the streets. We'll make it impossible for them—for anyone—to have peace. Solo el pueblo salva al pueblo."

Only the people can save the people. His words turn over and over again in my mind as, a few feet from us, a man in black skinny jeans and a gray tank top bounces a soccer ball on his knee. It distracts me for a second, but Maynor doesn't mind—he looks with me.

Eventually, the man drops the ball. As it rolls away from him, I turn back to Maynor. "Are you still talking to Tío José? Are you still trying to get information out of him?"

"Yes," Maynor says simply, scratching the back of his neck. "Everyone who has some sort of connection is."

"But what if you get information that's wrong again?"

"I don't know." Maynor sighs. "We try to double-check everything."

"Maynor . . ." I start. There's a question on my tongue that he must've considered already, I know. But I still have to ask—no matter how much it makes me sick to my stomach.

"Yeah?" His eyes get a little wide at the anguish in my voice.

"Have you ever thought that, maybe . . . maybe José knew what you were up to? That maybe his ties to the government go deeper than he'll admit." I gulp, forcing myself to stumble through the question. "I mean, what if he told you the wrong date on purpose? Like, counting on you to spread the wrong information."

"It's possible." Maynor responds quickly—I'm relieved that he's thought of this, at least. "But I don't know how to find out the truth."

I scratch at the grainy concrete next to my shoes. My phone vibrates in my pocket, but I ignore it.

"Okay," I say finally, taking a deep breath. "Okay. Tell me more."

Maynor raises his eyebrows. "About?"

"I don't know. . . . Everything. What happens next. Martha. You. A-*li*-cia." I sing her name, batting my eyelashes. The tension around us eases, if only for a second.

Maynor laughs and stretches his arms over his head. Around his armpits, his blue shirt has turned translucent with sweat. Then, he points to a face spray-painted in green on the building to our left. It takes me a few seconds to find it.

"That's Roger González," Maynor begins. "He was taken by the military after the protestors burned down the American embassy in '88 . . ."

Over the course of the next hour, Maynor tells me everything he can think of. Events from before either of us were born. Stories about our aunt. Stuff he's learned from people that have been doing the work of preserving our history for years—a lifetime even. Shit we're never taught in school.

"The war between Honduras and El Salvador was called the fútbol war, though obviously it wasn't about soccer. The games were just the last straw."

My phone vibrates again, but I can't seem to pull away from my brother. At some point he gets up to grab us some water and snacks from the nearest vending machine. It's only then that I notice I've been itching at my arms uncontrollably; they sting so bad, they feel cold despite the sun.

"I should've told you to put some bug spray on," Maynor mutters, handing me a bottle of water. "Los zancudos son unos hungry motherfuckers here."

"I better not get dengue," I tease him, pouring some of the cold water on my arm. It's a joke, but barely—back in May, at the start of rain season, Mami got a bad case of dengue. She was on bed rest for a week.

"You won't," Maynor says. "*If* you stop scratching." He bats my hand away, softly.

I click my tongue at him. Maynor's always been good about not scratching bug bites, not picking at his face whenever he gets pimples. I, frankly, don't understand how he does it.

We finish our bag of tajadas con encurtido, and Maynor takes our trash to the nearest garbage can. The sun has shifted since we first sat down—the slanted shadows of the buildings around us slashing the space in two. I grab my phone to check the time: a little after twelve p.m. We've been talking for nearly four hours. I have two missed calls from Dani and a bunch of texts.

"You should probably go find your friend," Maynor says when he returns, hands in his pockets.

I nod, but as excited as I am to meet Dani, I remember one more thing I wanted to do with him today. "Wait," I say, stuffing my phone back in my pocket. "I actually have something to show *you*."

He sits back down. "Oh yeah?"

"Yeah! You're not the only one who has cool stuff to share."

Maynor smiles. "Okay then. Show me."

"Actually, I'll tell you. It's this poem I wrote the other day." I open the small backpack I brought with me, pulling out Cami's journal. "I don't know if it's dumb or repetitive or if it only makes sense in my head. . . . I guess—I mean, what I wanted to say is . . . that when you really think about it, Honduras—"

"Libertad," Maynor interrupts, laughing. "Enana, just read it. It's all good."

"Okay," I say, nodding and breathing out slowly. I'm too aware of all the people around us now, but I try to focus on my brother. I open the journal, then clear my throat. "This is called 'Por fin hemos salido de Honduras.' Here it goes:

"Cuenta la leyenda
que al pisar tierra Hondureña
por vez primera
Cristóbal Colón le dijo al que le oyera:
'Por fin hemos salido de esas honduras.'

"Colón, por supuesto, se refería
a las olas del mar del que venía.
Colón, por supuesto, lo decía,
por las ondas que abatieron al Santa María.

"Lo que Colón no sabía—
lo que Colón, por supuesto, no se olía
es que 500 años más tarde,
sus palabras se repetirían:

"'Por fin hemos salido de Honduras.
Por fin hemos salido de Honduras,'
es lo que yo imagino dice
mi gente al coger la mano de sus hijos
y despedirse de sus raíces.

"'Por fin hemos salido de Honduras,'
es lo que yo imagino dicen
cuando se bendicen
para comenzar un viaje de 5000 kilómetros
y diez mil cicatrices."[3]

I can tell I've read it a little too fast: I'm out of breath by the time I finish. I stare at the words on the page for a few more seconds, then glance up at Maynor.

A beat of silence goes by. "Fuck," Maynor breathes, staring in shock at the words in my notebook. He has the same faraway, out-of-it look he usually does in the mornings, when he sits in bed half-dressed, peering at nothing in particular.

"It's not finished," I rush to say. "I know it needs something more, I just got stuck—"

"Libi, it's *so* good," Maynor cuts in.

"Really?"

"Yes—it's simple, but powerful. Potent." The corners of Maynor's eyes crinkle as he smiles, and I know he's being sincere.

"Thank you," I say, reaching out to squeeze his hand. Both our fingers are sticky with the vinegar from el encurtido. "I feel like it needs something else, though. Just one more thing to wrap it up . . ."

"Can I see it?" Maynor asks, pointing to the journal.

I hand it to him. His eyes scan the lines, left to right. With his free hand, he drums against the bench.

"Okay," he says, after a few minutes. "What about:

"'Por fin hemos salido de Honduras,'
es lo que mi gente canta
desde la garganta,
aunque el alma se les quebranta
y la piel de los pies se les levanta."[4]

I can't believe how fast he did that. "Yeah," I breathe. "Totally—that's so good. Damn."

"It's your poem, enana," he says, handing the journal back to me. "You don't have to take my advice, okay?"

"I know, Maynor. It's just that good."

"Wanna keep going?"

"Like writing? Right now?"

"Yeah. Right now," he says, smiling.

I beam at him. "I do, actually."

"Okay." Maynor scoots closer to me. "So, I was thinking we could shift some of the rhyme here and here . . ."

The two of us crouch over my journal, writing and rewriting the stanzas together.

NINETEEN

By the time Maynor and I are done writing the poem, I have too
many messages from Dani. I decide to just call her. She picks up on
the second ring.

"I'm so sorry," I say immediately. "Maynor and I got talking and
lost track of time. Where are you? I can go wherever—"

"Turn around," Dani says. "And look to your left, by the trash
cans."

I do as she tells me and scan the crowd, worried I won't recognize
her; there's a lot of people out here having lunch. I hear some of the
sounds coming through the call in my free ear as well, doubled in a
disorienting way. I'm starting to panic when, finally, I spot her. She's
a few feet away, phone to her ear, long hair blowing gently behind
her. I wave, and she hangs up the call as we walk toward each other.

"Oh my god, hi!" I say, when we're face-to-face. "I'm so sorry.
I know you were trying to get ahold of me. Maynor and I got to
talking . . ."

"It's okay, really," Dani says, smiling. She's beautiful—her eyes are big and dark. I can't stop staring at them. There's a small mole above her left eyebrow, a dimple on her right cheek when she grins.

"I figured Maynor would want to show you los desaparecidos," she continues. "When I got there, you both looked so excited and into the conversation, I decided to wait."

"That was kind of you," I say, laughing a little. "We can really get going when it's just the two of us." My stomach swoops—I feel a little nervous at the thought of her watching us. Watching *me*.

"Are you hungry?" Dani asks.

"I could eat," I reply. As skittish as I feel right now, the encurtido wasn't substantial.

A flash of Dani's dimple, then: "That's what I was hoping you'd say. Come on." She beckons me toward a stretch of road lined with food trucks on either side, and I follow her.

All the trucks have long lines of people in front of them. The smells of onions and garlic and beans and meat sizzle in the air. Dani and I line up in front of a truck near the end, and I recognize it as the mondongo stand Dani had texted me about.

"You still want to do soup? It's, like, five million degrees," I say, tugging at the neckline of my shirt.

Dani laughs: "Trust me."

Before I can say anything else, it's our turn. Dani orders two sopas de mondongo. The woman who runs the place clearly knows her—she smiles, takes Dani's money, and almost immediately hands us each a closed foam container and plastic spoons. I start to open mine as we move away from the truck, but Dani stops me.

"Not here," she says, and gestures for me to follow her.

Dani isn't a fast walker like Maynor. I don't struggle to keep up. We fall into an easy, synchronized rhythm strolling across campus. Our arms brush occasionally, make my skin feel charged. We go into a tall, cream-colored building and I follow her up the stairs.

By the time we reach the third floor I'm out of breath. The soup container burns my hand through the foam. Dani swerves into a small, empty room. The walls are covered with a greenish foam-like material, and there are two microphones set up on a desk in the middle. The table where the microphones are propped up is covered with words and drawings: Anti-government slogans, random love declarations, dicks, sex jokes. There's something halting about it, seeing all of these real, messy human experiences tangled together, inscribed in one place. Dani glances back at me, and I raise an eyebrow.

"This is one of the radio cabins," she says. "For student-run programs."

"Can we eat here?"

"If we're careful." She closes the door, and I understand why she picked this room now. It's air-conditioned—almost too cold—and I can't hear anything going on outside anymore. Completely soundproofed.

We sit next to each other at the table and un-lid our containers. The steam off them mixes between us. The room is small enough that sitting next to each other, our arms, and legs touch. I can smell Dani's perfume over the soup, something soft and earthy—like amber.

"So," Dani starts, blowing delicately over her soup. "What do you think so far? Did Maynor show you around?"

"A little. He took me to the walls and told me about their history and stories—los desaparecidos. It was heavy, but important to see. I'm having a really good time," I say.

Daniela nods. If she feels my leg jiggling beneath the table, she doesn't say anything. "I felt the same way my first few days here. Really wide-eyed, like there was something new to take in at every corner." She grabs her plastic spoon off the table.

"You don't anymore?"

She stops, spoon hovering over her soup, and considers this without breaking eye contact. I don't think anyone's ever looked me in the eyes for this long.

"Sometimes, yeah. I guess the longer you are in a place, the more you start to notice all the cracks too."

"Yeah," I say, my gaze falling to the table. "I get that. Earlier today, Maynor walked with me all the way to the bathroom. I thought he was worried I wouldn't find it, but then he waited outside, said to yell if anyone gave me trouble. He told me about all the . . . the sexual assault and stuff."

I scratch lightly at a heart with an arrow through it on the table in front of me.

"Mmm." Daniela nods. "Some of the bathrooms are safe, well kept. . . . But most aren't. Everyone knows to carry their own toilet paper and not use the bathrooms at the edges of campus."

Unable to think of anything comforting to say, I shake my head and purse my lips. She receives my answer-less gesture.

"Yep. We do what we can to take care of each other, at least."

I wonder who she means by *we*, but don't ask. Now that I'm not being blitzed by the sun and the cacophony of sound, my body begins to process how nervous I am. We're alone, Dani and I, and close. I can hardly believe she's sitting next to me right now, not just a text in my DMs or a voice over the phone—a real person.

A beat of cool silence passes between us before Dani takes a sip from her soup. "Go on," she says. "It's cooled down some—try it."

I do as she says. It's still hot, but I can handle it. It's also delicious: Lime-y and garlicky, filled with tender meat.

"Okay, yeah," I say. "I get it now. Está buenísima."

"I told you!" Dani beams, then squeezes my shoulder. Her palm is warm, and I still feel the heat through my shirt even after she's pulled her hand away.

It goes quiet again as we both devour our mondongo—I hadn't realized how hungry I was. As I take in spoonful after spoonful, Dani tells me about the different radio programs that friends of hers record here. I listen intently. There's something hypnotizing about her voice—it's even in tone, neither deep nor high-pitched. It's mellow, soothing.

"How much of the population do you think has access to Wi-Fi, Libertad?" she asks me now, snapping me out of my thoughts. Something about her tone—authoritative, teacherly—tells me she already knows the answer.

"Less than half?" I guess.

"Less than *thirty percent*. Not even TVs are as common as we think, much less computers or cellphones. The thing most people have access to? The radio."

She spreads her arms out, gesturing at the room like it contains the radio itself.

"It's the single most important tool we have right now in terms of widespread education. Just think about it: A lot of people can't afford to go to school or come into the city or go to a doctor to ask even the simplest questions. That's where the radio comes in. We do tons of different programs—educational, medical, political. There are almost no constraints."

"That's so cool," I say, setting my empty cup aside. "I hadn't realized how important the radio is for, like, getting the word out."

Her excitement is contagious. The corners of her mouth lift as she grabs our empty containers, stacks them together, and deposits our napkins and spoons in them. I watch her hands move back and forth in the space between us—there's a precision to them that entrances me.

"It sounds crazy, but . . . the future might be radio, Libertad."

I can hear the pride in her voice, the and-I'm-a-part-of-the-future.

"That is something," I say. "I'd never thought about it."

"What's this?" Dani touches my arm, red from the mosquito bites and my incessant scratching.

"Oh." I groan a little. "I got eaten alive out there."

"Hold on." She reaches down, pulling something out of her purse. It's a travel-size Vicks VapoRub. I'm about to protest that I don't like the smell, but she's already opened it and plunged her finger in.

"It will help with the itching." Dani nods. "Trust me."

I sigh, a bit dramatically, but proffer my arm to her. She smiles and rubs the ointment onto my bug bites in small circles. I do immediately feel relief, but I can't tell if it's the camphor or just . . .

Dani. Her fingers are warm, the Vicks cold. The contrast is pleasant. There's a soft pressure to Dani's touch, and I feel it in my chest.

She looks up at me and we lock eyes. Five seconds go by, and she still has her fingers on my arm. A soft tingling sensation moves across my face, and I have to look away.

"What about you, though?" I ask finally. "Do you have a secret radio show I don't know about?"

Dani clears her throat. "No," she says, closing the tub and putting it back in her purse. "I do have an idea, though. It's just, maybe . . . a little dangerous to execute."

"Tell me," I say, leaning forward.

"I mean, it's also probably impossible." Dani hedges, lifting her gaze to meet mine again. Our faces our closer to each other's now— just inches apart.

"Okay then, whisper it." I murmur.

Dani laughs, then bites her lip. "Okay, so . . . Maynor told you about the disappeared, right?"

I nod. *Serious conversation, this is a serious conversation,* I remind myself. But as hard as I try to concentrate on whatever she's about to say, it feels like a Herculean task with her face so close to mine.

"Well, los desaparecidos are not a thing just here, in Honduras. Argentina had over thirty thousand desaparecidos during the cold war. El Salvador has had so, *so* many over the years. And have you heard of what's been going on in Colombia?"

I shake my head slowly. "Kind of, but . . . not really."

"There are a lot of similarities between what's happening in Honduras and what's happening in Colombia. They're facing some of the same disputes over territory, places where the rule of law is whatever the cartels say. In Colombia, there is a criminal group that kidnaps people—journalists, activists, protesters—and take them into the jungle until their loved ones pay a ransom or do whatever they ask."

I nod, keeping my eyes locked on hers.

"There's this radio show in Colombia," Dani continues. "It started decades ago. Family and loved ones of the people who are gone come in and just . . . talk to them. Let them know that they love them. That they're still looking; that they won't stop. The show is always on at the same time, on the same days. Family after family talks to their missing loved ones. Just in case they can hear. In case that—wherever they're being held—a radio is on."

Though Dani's expression is steady, something shifts in her eyes—something deeply, endlessly sad. I wonder, in this moment, if she's thinking of her own parents."Damn," I whisper.

"Yeah," she exhales. I'm nervous the vibe will turn too sad, that she'll move her face away from me. But she doesn't—she stays close, and neither of us says anything for a few seconds. My gaze drops to a few tiny freckles splashed across her nose. My chest pounds—once, twice. I feel it in my ears.

"Why do you think it's impossible?" I ask, if for no other reason but to drown out the sound of my heartbeat. "To do something like that here, I mean."

"I don't know . . ." Dani sighs. "COFADEH has already been working for decades on getting answers to these people's whereabouts. At best they get ignored. Usually, they face a lot of harassment and intimidation. From the cartels or government officials that are part of the disappearing—or of covering it up."

"COFADEH?" I ask.

"Committee of Relatives of the Disappeared in Honduras. For years, the mothers of those who have been taken get together the first Friday of every month in Plaza la Merced to commemorate, demand justice. Some of them have been doing this since the group started in the early '80s."

"Jesus." I feel a tug in my chest. "After all these years?"

Dani shrugs. "Sometimes, giving up hope is not an option, you know?"

I nod. I do know—or, at least, I think I do. "Well, for what it's worth . . . you have the perfect radio voice." I smile at Dani, and the corners of her lips tick up. She leans into the already small space between us, and I can feel her warm breath against my nose.

My breath stutters. I think she's about to say something else, to tell me more about her impossible radio show. Instead, she closes the space between us, pressing her lips gently against mine. For half a second, I freeze. Then my eyelids flutter shut, and I lean into her, deepening the kiss between us, pressing my whole body into hers.

Heat races along my skin, down my head and chest and arms. The kiss lasts for a couple minutes, but when Dani pulls away it feels like seconds and hours. Like time isn't a real thing.

"Wow," I breathe. Dani grins, and it might just be the most beautiful sight I've ever seen. Then she stands up and offers me her hand.

"Come on," she says, nodding toward the door. "I still have to show you my favorite garden."

Halfway across campus at the Sendero de las Orquídeas garden, I'm still dizzy from our kiss. Dani points to flowers and plants, tells me their names.

I squint at a bright red heliconia, its petals splayed under the bright afternoon sun. "It must've taken you forever to learn all the names."

"Yeah." Dani laughs, and I notice the softest flush of pink bloom across her cheeks. "It did. It wasn't really about the names, though. I . . . I'm trying to be a better listener when it comes to nature. And learning the names of the plants I walk by every day feels like a step in that direction, you know?"

I nod, expecting Dani to say more. But she doesn't. "Wait—what do you mean?"

Dani runs her hand through her hair and blinks. "It's like . . . you need to really notice to remember which is which, right? The number of leaves, the edges, the shapes. You really need to stop, to take your time, to shut up and look and listen to what the plants are telling you."

She bends down, then holds a leaf up to the light as she talks, twirling the stem between her fingers.

It takes everything in me not to pull my phone out and snap a photo of her. But I don't want to ruin the moment. Instead, I do everything I can to commit every single detail of this time between us—of Dani and the leaf and sunshine—to memory.

"I really like that," I say, brushing her hand with mine. Dani grins at me again, and my heart speeds up in my chest.

After spending nearly four hours with Dani, I get a text from Maynor telling me it's time to head home. Dani walks me to the parking lot. When we're about fifty feet away, I spot Maynor and Alicia leaning against the hood of her car. They're holding each other, kissing. Maynor looks young, happy and giggly in a way I haven't seen him look in years.

Dani, noticing them too, catches my eye and laughs.

"I guess I'll go interrupt that." I roll my eyes.

"You do that," she says, dimple all out. She pulls me in for a hug, then whispers in my ear, "Text me later?"

Something like a tickle, but better, makes its way up my spine. I want to fold into myself.

"Yes, totally," I mumble into her shoulder.

She gives me one last squeeze and walks away.

"Wait—Dani!" I call after her. She turns around.

"Um . . ." I clench the fingers of one hand in the palm of the other. "About the—you know, the kiss." The words rush out of me. "I don't want to pretend it didn't happen."

Dani smiles quizzically. "Yeah—why would we do that?"

"We wouldn't," I agree, shaking my head.

I don't stop smiling the whole ride home.

TWENTY

We pull it off. No one finds out I missed school, especially not Mami. Over the course of the next two weeks I try to talk Maynor into doing it again, but he refuses.

"That was a one-time thing," he says every time I bring it up. "You're not gonna keep blowing off school."

He's right, Dani texts. *As much as I wish you could. But the reading isn't too far away.*

It doesn't stop me from feeling frustrated. I mean, easy for Maynor to say—he sees Alicia all the time. Which, now that I've met her—that I know Maynor has a girlfriend—it's so glaringly obvious he's in love. The way he smiles at his phone. His quick laughter at even the cheesiest jokes Alberto and I tell him. How he still sneaks in late. I had assumed he was going to student front meetings, but it occurs to me now that he's probably with her a lot of the time.

Not that I don't get it—Dani and I talk on the phone every day.

The Saturday after our meeting at la UNAH, I lay in bed as she tries to talk me into reading at the Cien Años open mic.

"But you know for a fact people love it," she says. "This would just be a new channel to get it out there."

The day after la UNAH, I went over the edits and additions Maynor and I did to the "Por fin hemos salido de Honduras" poem and, at last, decided to post it to my poetry account. Within hours, it had accumulated over a thousand likes and dozens of reshares. It brought in a bunch of new followers to the account too. The craziest part was seeing several of my own classmates reposting the poem to their own story.

Still, the thought of standing on a stage and reciting it out loud in front of a crowd of strangers fills me with nerves—like a swarm of bees buzzing around in my stomach.

"Come on," Dani wheedles now, breaking into my thoughts. "What's the worst that can happen?"

"Do you really want to know? 'Cause me and my anxiety are more than up to that challenge."

"Okay, okay," Dani laughs. "Just promise me you'll think about it, yeah?"

I smile, glancing out my window at the setting sun. "Yeah, okay—I'll think about it."

The sky transitions from cotton candy colors to night as we talk. Dani is so open and honest with me—no hesitation in her voice whatsoever as she lays everything out there—that it scares me a little. She says she loved a girl from Copán, but things didn't really work out once she moved to Tegucigalpa. I admit to only having kissed Camila that one time.

"What happened after you kissed?" Dani asks.

"Well . . . nothing." I lie down in bed, my eyelids growing heavy. "That's kind of the point."

I yawn. My phone feels hot against my cheek. I pull it away from my face and see that's it's nearly two in the morning.

"You should go to bed," Dani says gently as I press the phone against my other ear. But it takes the two of us at least thirty more minutes to say goodbye.

Mornings turn cooler as October flies by. Rain season is nearly over, and we've been spared any major hurricanes this year. Jacaranda trees blossom bright purple, flame trees a deep vermillion red. I love the city this time of the year. I can't wait for the election to be over so we can move on to all the Christmas festivities.

On the downside, we leave for school earlier. Mami's had us leaving at six every day for the past week or so. She's working on the big wedding scheduled the night before the elections, ten days away now. She comes home late too, and almost immediately passes out in her room. In some ways, it saves me from having to see her—the awkwardness between us is still there, still palpable.

In other ways, I miss her . . . a lot. I miss her hotel gossip, and hearing about her day. Without her, our dinners are mostly Maynor and Alberto talking fútbol, Abuela and I barely following.

At least there's Dani. She texts me good morning, and I text back a smiley face as I walk to the usual table between the cafeteria and soccer field. None of my friends are here yet, so I sit and lay my head down, pulling my jacket over my face. All I want to do is nap, even if just for ten minutes. Staying up late to talk Dani is worth it, but most days I feel like I'm not gonna make it to lunch.

I'm near drifting off when I hear steps and feel a presence beside me. I'm hoping it's Valeria or Carla—or even Cami, though we haven't talked much lately. But when I emerge from under my jacket, Pablo is standing next to me.

"Hey," he says, raising an eyebrow. "No one's ever here this early."

His hair is still wet, slicked to the side. He smells like fresh laundry and deodorant. My eyes gravitate to the tip of his nose, pink from the cool breeze.

"Oh. Yeah, my mom . . . she's been dropping us off earlier and earlier. Busy at work."

He nods and sits across from me. I don't think we have ever been alone together before. Have ever talked, just the two of us.

"If you want to *really* nap, you should go to the library," Pablo says, and I can't tell if he's being kind or hinting that I should leave.

"Thanks . . . but I'm okay." I cross my arms and set them on the table, resting my chin on top of them. The wind picks up a strand of my hair, tossing curls into my eyes, as a heavy silence descends between us.

"I'll get you a coffee!" Pablo says. He stands up so fast it startles me. Before I can tell him I don't want anything, he's jogging toward the cafeteria. Five minutes later, he walks back with a small black coffee and a Coke.

"Thanks," I say, taking the hot foam cup.

"No problem." A ding, and Pablo pulls his phone out from his back pocket. He sighs. "Cami's bus is stuck in traffic again. Another accident or something," he says, eyes glued to the screen.

"Sucks," I hear myself mumble. I reach for my phone in my own pocket, mostly to avoid having to say anything else. It's 6:30. Soon, students will arrive in hordes. I go to Dani's chat and start typing a new message.

"Hey, can I ask you something?" Pablo says.

I stop typing and look up at him. I can't imagine what he could possibly have to ask me.

"Did you and Camila get into a fight or something?"

"No. Why?" I snap. I can't believe she said something to him.

"Whoa, nothing. She just . . . I don't know." His gaze drops to the table. "She seems upset. I keep asking her what's up and she said she was worried about you . . . but she won't say anything else."

Pablo looks worried now, his expression genuinely concerned. Something in me softens.

"We aren't fighting," I say, gentler this time. "Stuff's just been . . . weird."

"Okaaay." Pablo nods. "In that case, maybe you could, I don't know . . . talk to her? You're still her best friend, you know."

For all my hang-ups with him, maybe Pablo isn't the worst person in the world.

"Bet." I nod at him, though I'm not sure that I will.

"Did you do the worksheet for bio?" he asks, taking a sip of his Coke.

We talk about the one class we have in common for a few minutes.

He drinks his Coca-Cola, and I finish my coffee. Then Valeria gets here, Carla, everyone else. Even Camila makes it ten minutes before the bell.

"So. Any plans this weekend?" Valeria asks,

"We should do something! The election is in two weeks. After that, who knows if we'll ever get to go out *again*." Pablo's voice drops to a dramatic whisper with this last part.

"Let's go to La Esquina," Carla suggests, sitting up. "Saturday?" She claps her hands in excitement as everyone around me nods.

"Um, I . . . can't, actually," I say.

"What? Why?" Camila asks. It's the first thing she's said to me since she got here.

"I have a thing." I play with the zipper on my bag, avoiding both her and Valeria's eyes on me.

"So get out of it! Come on, Libertad, this is important," Carla whines.

"Okay, well, my thing is important too," I say evenly. I'm not sure how a spontaneous plan to go out got "important."

"What is it?" Valeria asks.

I exhale. I don't know why it feels so weird to tell them, but I'm suddenly nervous.

"All right . . . Have you heard of Cien Años?"

Carla shakes her head, but everyone else nods.

"It's this bar near la UNAH. Chiller than Esqui—they hold lots of poetry readings there and stuff. Anyway, they're doing another open mic this Saturday, so I said I'd go with my brother and a . . . a new friend." I cross my legs, once again avoiding Cami's eyes on me. "I really can't get out of it." Not that I'd want to, though I don't add that last part.

No one says anything for a second, before Pablo breaks the silence: "Why don't we all just all go there, then?"

Fuck.

"Yeah! It'll be nice to try a new place," Carla cheers.

I nod, though everything inside me is screaming no. I don't really want them there, but I also feel bad saying that. I finally lock eyes with Cami from the other end of the table. Her hair rests in one thick braid over her left shoulder. She hasn't plucked her eyebrows in a minute, which is rare; little hairs out stick near the ends, out of shape.

"Should be fun," she says—but the smile on her face doesn't quite reach her eyes.

TWENTY ONE

"I liked your new poem," Camila says from behind me. I jump in my seat.

I'm reading through some additional application questions that one of the colleges I'm applying to asks, stuff about volunteering and hobbies. It's five minutes before lunch is over, but I decided to head to our español classroom early.

"Thanks," I reply, looking up at her. She lowers herself into the desk next to mine.

"What are you doing?" She gestures to the papers in front of me.

"College application stuff. They ask *so* many questions."

Cami nods. We haven't really discussed anything related to me applying—and eventually studying—abroad.

"So, I guess you're really trying to leave, huh?" Her tone isn't unkind, but there's something cold about it.

"I guess so." I shrug.

We sit in silence for a couple minutes. I'm about to tell her I need to go to the bathroom just to avoid the awkwardness when she speaks again.

"Look, Libertad . . . I'm sorry about going off on you on the phone the other day. And being weird about it afterward. I don't want things to be weird."

I'm caught off guard by Cami's directness—apologizing isn't usually her thing. "Okay." I nod. "You're right. I'm sorry too." Though I'm not really sure what I'm apologizing for, Camila nods.

"All right," she says. "Well . . . I'm excited for Cien Años. And to meet your new friend."

"Awesome." I smile. "Maynor will be there too, and his new girl-friend. Wait, did I tell you he has a girlfriend?"

"Really?" Cami raises her eyebrows.

"Yeah! Her name is Alicia—I like her a lot." The lunch bell rings then, and other students start arriving as Cami and I talk. While it doesn't feel like all the tension has dissipated between us, it's definitely a step in the right direction. Valeria sits down on my other side. A few minutes later, Miss Torres walks in and asks everyone to take out notebooks and pens.

"Muy bien, chicos," she starts, once the rustling around me has settled. "As all of you know, the presidential election is right around the corner. Many of you are of voting age now, and it's important that you have developed ideas of what's at stake here. So today, we're going to do an exercise on articulating our stances, providing evidence, and listening to others. For the first ten minutes of class, you're going to write down three reasons why you support one of the candidates, and then we'll share.

"*Ojo*—muy respetuosos," she adds, moving to walk down the aisles of desks as we hunch over our papers and start writing. "No insulting anyone or any of that."

Ten minutes later, I have three vague reasons as to why I think Pedro Romano, the opposition's candidate, should be the next president. Though really, my reasons are more about why Juan Orlando *shouldn't* be. Miss Torres makes her way back to the front of the class.

"All right, who wants to go first?" she asks, hands on her hips. "Don't make me call on you."

Davián Arita's hand shoots up immediately. I brace myself for it. I know he has some messed-up opinions. His dad works for the government, though I'm unsure doing what. To my right, I clock Valeria rolling her eyes.

"Go ahead, Davián. Tell us the candidate and your three reasons for supporting him.'

"Okay, miss." Davián clears his throat. "My candidate is Juan Orlando Hernández, obviously. In my opinion, there simply isn't any other choice. First, in his time as our president, JOH has militarized our streets more than ever—making our country a safer place. Second, he's improved our relationship with the US government by supporting them in United Nations votes. For a country as poor as Honduras, it's important to have a good exchange with one of the most powerful nations on the planet." Several other boys nod as he speaks, and Davián smirks a little to himself, as if he knows he has this in the bag.

"Finally, Hernández knows we need to focus on developing

small businesses, so he's created many loan options for micro-empresarios. Keeping him as our president for four more years will improve the country's economy as a whole."

My hand is itching, I want to raise it so badly. But anonymous online poetry is one thing. Saying something directly to my classmates, people I have to deal with on a daily basis? No way.

"Muy bien, Davián," Miss Torres replies. "Okay, now let's hear from someone who supports Pedro Romano."

Valeria—face flushed now—raises her hand. I know she can handle herself, but that doesn't stop the nerves fluttering in my stomach. Miss Torres gestures for her to speak.

"Well, to start, I think the most important reason Pedro Romano should be our next president is because it's not *illegal* for him to be a candidate. Our constitution states that no person should be allowed to rule for more than a single term. *His* candidacy isn't unconstitutional." Though Valeria's voice is calm, I can see the passion—maybe fury—blazing in her eyes.

"Second, Pedro is in conversation with leaders from different organizations that defend Indigenous groups who are protecting the country's biodiversity and vital water sources. Which literally means preserving life, both for current and future Hondurans. And finally, Pedro's candidacy is supported by equal rights organizations for women and queer people."

My body goes still, cold. Valeria's barely uttered her last word when Davián starts talking again.

"So we should support someone who wants our family values destroyed?"

"You need to raise your hand—" Mis Torres begins, her brow furrowing, but Valeria cuts her off.

"How are *your* family values affected by what someone else does?"

"Not *me*," Davián says, clearly just stopping himself short of saying *duh*. "But what about children who would be exposed to seeing *maricas* en las calles? Are they supposed to think that's okay?"

"That's enough." Miss Torres raises her voice. "Do *not* use that language in my classroom."

"Miss, Davián is right," this kid named Julio jumps in. "Honduras is a Catholic country—"

Valeria leans forward in her desk. "You mentioned having a good relationship with the US," she says to Davián, ignoring Julio. "Why not copy them? They legalized gay marriage in 2015—"

Miss Torres slaps the whiteboard behind her. "The next person to speak *better* raise their hand," she booms.

The classroom quiets. We sit in silence for a few minutes. By the time the next person raises their hand to give their answer, I've closed my notebook. There's no way in hell I'm saying anything.

That night, I look through my poetry account's DMs. Most of them are positive, like the comments, but I open the few that I can tell from the preview are not.

> I hope every marica leaves the country like you say, porque if I see them in the streets I'll fuck them dead.

> Honduras is a country of God. It is
> because of so many homosexuals
> "living their truth" now that we're
> being punished with so much violence.

> You don't know what you're talking about.
> You're probably just another culero angry
> with their sickness. It would be a mercy
> to kill you all.

I think, for a second, about replying. Then I swipe left and delete the messages instead.

TWENTY TWO

At Cien Años the lighting is dim but pleasant, a soft yellow glow across the small cozy space. It couldn't be more different from La Esquina. La Esqui is always full of people around our age, between sixteen and twenty-one or so. Cien Años feels older; the people around us are older. It only carries local beers. The music is from another time, much of it live. There's a stage at the end of the wall opposite the entrance. On it are a drum set, a couple of guitars, an electric piano, and a bass.

Everyone figured out rides with Carla and Pablo. I got here before them, with Maynor and Alicia. When we walk in, I spot Dani by the bar. She wears white jeans and a short-sleeved black button-down that looks soft, like silk. I can't tell if she's wearing makeup, but her hair looks recently straightened. I feel immediately mesmerized and unbearably nervous at the sight of her. I'm tempted to get a drink just to calm my nerves but figure it's best to take things slow.

After I introduce her to Maynor and Alicia, the four of us grab a table, and Dani and Alicia talk about a professor they have in common for a while. Daniela sneaks discreet looks my way as she tells a story about a horrible group-work experience, and my face warms.

I don't know what happens when my friends get here. How do I introduce Dani? As my friend? She *is* my friend. But what if someone can tell that Dani and I aren't *just* friends? Someone who would make a big deal about it—like Carla or Pablo.

"You okay?" Dani asks me, low enough Maynor and Alicia can't hear. The music playing isn't so loud it's unbearable, but our table still shakes with the beat. Alicia shows Maynor something on her phone.

"Anxious," I say.

"Do you want a drink?"

I nod. She takes my hand and leads me to the bar. We get two Salva Vidas. When we get back, Maynor and Alicia are kissing. We sit and they pull away from each other, giggling.

I'm still struck by how light Maynor looks around Alicia. His lips are parted as if caught mid-laugh, instead of the usual solid purse. It reminds me of the version of him that would get picked up onto other boys' shoulders after stopping a goal from the other team, his arms raised above his head in celebration, always.

I'm studying my brother's face when Valeria texts me to say they're all on their way over. I guzzle down the rest of my beer a little too quickly. Dani squeezes my hand and opens her mouth to say something, when a man with waist-length, chestnut-colored hair hops onstage. Someone cuts the music.

"Thank you so much for joining us tonight!" The guy's voice comes through the giant speakers in front of the stage. "My name is Santi. Tonight is just one of many in our poetry open mic series. For those of you who are new, Cien Años is a place of community, and these poetry readings are a time to celebrate poetry, local artists, and each other, no matter what's going on in the world. This night will be full of celebration and remembering and demanding . . . all that fun stuff."

A few people from the crowd cheer and whistle. Santi pauses for effect and runs his free hand through his hair, pushing it away from his forehead.

"Before we get to the poems, we're gonna start the night off with a beloved local indie-pop band. Their new EP has been playing all over the capital; they'll launch us off with a few songs before we get to the readings. You know them. You love them. This is Pez Luna!"

A group of boys jumps onstage. They take their positions with each instrument. They thank everyone for coming and remind us to sign up to read at the table next to the entrance. When they start playing, I almost immediately feel more relaxed.

After a couple of songs, Dani and Alicia and Maynor and I are all vibing with the band, moving our heads with the beat. I take a sip from Dani's Salva Vida, and she offers to get me another one. I'm about to stand up to come with when I feel a hand on my back. My friends are here.

"Hi!" Carla yells excitedly over the music.

"Oh my god, I love it here!" Valeria adds, squeezing my shoulder before moving to help Carla pull up some extra chairs to our table. Camila and Pablo walk up behind them, holding hands. And behind them is Miguel and a guy I've never seen before. Pablo introduces him as Héctor.

Cami's wearing a dress, plus more makeup than I've ever seen her put on before. Pablo looks like he always does, hair slicked to the side and a polo shirt over jeans. Héctor and Miguel are dressed nearly identical to Pablo, just different color variations of their polo shirts. They all move their eyes around the place, lingering on the band, taking everything in.

I introduce Dani when she gets back with my beer, yelling over the music. Everyone's nice, but I can tell Camila is not herself tonight. Her responses to Dani's questions are short, and she keeps avoiding my eyes while constantly looking Dani up and down.

So much for being excited to meet my new friend.

"This is our last one!" the lead singer from Pez Luna shouts, and he grins at the ensuing groans around us. "Thank you so much, mi gente, for coming out tonight and joining us at Cien Años. Se les quiere."

The crowd cheers the band off the stage when they're done. The host takes over again, asking us to give it up one more time for Pez Luna.

"And now," he continues when the applause has died down, "let's get this reading started."

Santi pulls a piece of paper from his pocket and leans closer to the mic. "First off is Lucía López. Where are you, Lucía? Come onstage!"

A girl with short hair and an eyebrow piercing moves around a table to the left of us, hopping onstage with an easy familiarity. She hugs the host before taking the mic from him. I wonder how many times she's done this.

"¡Buenas noches, Cien Años!" she calls out. "I'm so happy to be back here. This poem, on brand with the rest of my work, is about the violence women in this country face every day—violence that the state continues to ignore."

The audience claps and whistles. Our table is the quietest, probably because we're still figuring out how this all works. Lucía pulls a notebook from her pocket and clears her throat. And then she reads.

Her poem begins with an anecdote about her walking home late at night, fearing for her life as two guys follow her. The bar goes pin-drop silent. Dani reaches over and digs her fingers into my thigh, her eyes glued to the stage. When she lets her hand rest there, my head spins, heat flaring in my stomach.

Valeria locks eyes with me, her gaze dropping from my face to Dani's arm disappearing beneath the table. I shift in my chair. Dani's hand falls away.

"¡Gracias a todos!" Lucía shouts from stage, wrapping up her poem to enthusiastic whistles and applause. "I would let Santi introduce the next reader, but I'm too excited. Santi, is it okay if I . . . ?"

From his table to the right of the stage, the host with long hair laughs and nods. Lucía introduces the guy who reads next, a man named Adrián. Adrián has a buzzcut and wears a black T-shirt bearing a sketch of the president's face drawn in red, devil's horns on his head. The drawing is cartoonish but appealing, direct, the words *FUERA JOH* scribbled under it.

"This one goes out to my girlfriend, Lucía," he says, pointing to Lucía, who blows him a kiss from offstage. The crowd sighs a collective "aww" as he breaks into an ode to first love. As cheesy as it is, I can't stop grinning as he reads, my own cheeks warm.

A few more poets go after him. Most are so good, it's hard for me to look away, to be distracted by anything. At some point, Dani gets me another beer, and when she returns, I realize Camila is no longer sitting with us.

"Where is she?" I ask Pablo over applause, the host lending a hand to the person who just read down from the stage.

Pablo shrugs, tilting his head as if he has to think about it. "Bathroom, I guess?"

Before I can respond, the host takes the mic again. "That's it for the list! We're going to take a short break. If you didn't sign up but want to read, come find me!"

There's more clapping and whistling before the overhead music resumes.

"You should do it," Dani half whispers in my ear.

"No way." I turn to her. "You do it."

"*I* don't have anything to read. You do."

She pulls gently on my earlobe. I feel hairs on my nape stand tall. From the corner of my eye, I notice that Camila is back, standing next to Pablo, sneaking wary glances in our direction. I pull away from Dani quicker than I'd like.

"What do you mean?" I ask, willing my eyes back to her face.

"The one you just posted—'Por fin hemos salido de Honduras.' It's so good, Libertad, please." She pouts, and I laugh.

"Nah—public speaking makes me nervous. You can read it, though, if you'd like."

"For real?" Her eyes light up. "You know, I would . . ."

I try to still my mind, to force my heartbeat back down. Her immediate "yes" tripped me—I didn't think she'd actually take me up on the offer. But the more I consider it, the more I really, truly love the idea of her reading my words aloud.

"Yes. For real."

Dani beams, and everything around us disintegrates in the glow of her smile. I forget where we are for a second, pulling her closer to me by one of the belt loops of her jeans. Our faces are mere inches apart as I breathe in the faint scent of beer off her mouth, feel the warmth of her lips so close to mine.

Then our backdrop comes into sharp focus again. Everyone—Carla, Valeria, Miguel, Héctor, Camila, Pablo . . . hell, even Maynor and Alicia—is staring at us.

Carla arches an eyebrow. Pablo's eyes go wide. Dani clears her throat and stands quickly, which startles me.

"I'm gonna go tell what's-his-face that I want to read next," she announces, walking toward the stage.

I nod, though everyone around me looks confused. It hits me then that, in addition to not knowing what they've just witnessed, they also don't know what's about to happen. I lock eyes with Camila, used to finding some sort of comfort there, but she looks away. My brother smiles at me, though, and so does Alicia. I take a deep breath and release it slowly.

Onstage, Dani and Santi stand next to each other. His hair is longer than hers. His hair might be the longest in the bar. Daniela looks taller up there, radiant in the bright overhead lights. Even though I'm not the one onstage, my heartbeat pounds in my throat. I take another sip of my beer.

"Okaaaay, damas y caballeros, we're back!" Santi announces. "Up next, we have . . ."

"Daniela," she says, leaning into the mic that Santi hands to her. "Daniela Castillo." She smiles at him as he gives her a thumbs-up and jumps offstage.

"¡Buenas noches, everyone!"

Her voice does not betray any uneasiness. It comes out smooth and stable through the speakers. A few people from the crowd yell back some form of hello. Maynor moves to take Dani's spot next to me, resting his arm behind my back. "What's she doing?" he whispers.

"I do have a poem to read," Dani says. "But it isn't mine. Some of you might have already read it online, but I wanted those of you who haven't, to get to hear it tonight—it's just that powerful. The author gave me their permission to share."

She clears her throat, pulling her phone from her pocket—going to my poetry account, I assume.

Maynor raises his eyebrow and laughs, finally getting what's going on. He squeezes my shoulder and Dani reads.

TWENTY THREE

"That was amazing," Valeria says, wide-eyed. Daniela sits back down next to me, applause still going. "*So* good," Carla and Alicia echo.

"Thank you." Dani smiles, shrugging. "Like I said, though—not my words."

My skin feels like it's on fire. Hearing her read my poem aloud, getting to see everyone's reactions around me in real time . . . I don't think I've ever felt prouder of anything I've done before.

"Doesn't even matter," I tell her as Maynor returns to his place next to Alicia. "You were so good. I—" I lean in close to her, murmuring, "I don't think I've liked anything I've ever written more than right now. Seriously. I never could've done that the way you did."

"Yes, you could." Dani grins. "But thank you. I'm glad you thought it went well."

"It was incredible, Dani."

"It was beautiful," Camila echoes from Dani's other side, and I jump—I hadn't realized she could hear us. She's been so quiet all night, for a second, I almost forgot she was there.

Cami's voice is soft, and something else—I wonder if she's being sincere. Then Dani turns back to me, squeezing my knee, and I feel a little dizzy from it all. The poems, *my* poem, the crowd's cheering, the beers, my seesawing emotions . . . her.

"All right, folks," Santi says from the stage. "Looks like we don't have any other readers for tonight, so we're going to close here. Thanks as always for joining us! Remember, Cien Años is open until two a.m. every Thursday, Friday, and Saturday. Feel free to stick around until closing time to grab a beer or two. The kitchen's also open for another half hour if you're craving our famous chicken wings. ¡Buenas noches!"

He raises his hands as we clap, cheer, and whistle. Then he turns the mic off. Our table becomes an island against the tide of people suddenly flowing around us, getting up to mingle or use the restroom or grab a beer or leave.

"Does anyone want food?" Carla asks the group.

"I could eat!" Valeria yells over the hubbub.

"Same," Pablo, Miguel, and Héctor all say at the same time.

"Actually—" Maynor starts, his arm draped around Alicia's shoulders. "Alicia and I were just thinking—her place isn't too far from here, and her roommate hasn't moved in yet. Instead of buying an overpriced plate of wings, we can stop for a cheap pizza and head there, if y'all want."

Ten minutes later, we've figured out rides and calls to mothers and are on our way to Alicia's. I mean to ride with her and Maynor,

Dani, and Valeria, but we all get mixed up with whose car is too small or too big and who should take more people and who is going to get the pizza or more drinks. I end up in the back seat of Pablo's dad's car, which he's borrowing, with Miguel and Carla, while Pablo and his friend Héctor sit up front. Camila sits on my lap, just like she did that night months ago at La Esquina.

This time, though, it feels awkward and sweaty. Her sit bones dig uncomfortably into my thighs. I keep readjusting, which makes her keep shifting, and we're stuck in an endless cycle of mumbled "sorry's."

Pablo blasts reggaeton so loud I can feel the beating of his car speakers against my thigh. Only after we start driving, careening through side streets away from the bar, do I wonder if he's too drunk to be doing this.

Within seconds we're at el Boulevard Morazán, American fast food chain signs a blur around us. Pablo pulls into the gas station before Popeyes and runs inside with Héctor to buy more alcohol, leaving the car on.

"I need to stretch my legs," Cami says over the music. I nod, though she can't see me, and the two of us practically roll out of the car as she opens the door. The night air is cool against my skin, the white lights emanating from the gas station sobering. It smells like diesel fuel and frying oil. Cami crosses her arms. She looks cold or pissed or both.

"It's hot inside the car," I say, trying to break the silence.

She doesn't respond. Instead, she looks toward the gas station, at the boys waiting in line to check out.

"Okay. What's your problem?" I blurt.

She turns her head back to me, but there's something unrecognizable about her eyes, distanced and closed off.

"What's my problem with what?"

"You've been weird all night, and now you're ignoring me."

"I wasn't ignoring you." Cami shrugs. I wait, thinking she might say more. But she doesn't.

"That's it?" I raise an eyebrow. "You don't know? What happened to not wanting things to be weird? Being excited to meet Dani?"

"I don't know."

"Cool then. So, it's all in my head."

Cami rolls her eyes. "I didn't say that either."

"Then what is it?"

She sighs, dropping her arms to her sides. "I don't know, Libertad. I don't know why it feels weird."

"Make a guess for me," I spit.

"I *said* I don't know."

"Okay, then stop! Stop acting weird!" I yell, throwing my hands up.

Cami scoffs, and I narrow my eyes. "What?" I ask.

"Maybe *you're* the one being weird. Taking us to new places with random people. Acting like an entirely different person."

"So this *is* about Dani!" I laugh, but it's dry, humorless. "She isn't some *random* person, Camila. She's my—. . . she's important to me, okay?"

Cami doesn't say anything for a second, which is enough to make me regret everything that just fell out of my mouth. We stare at each other. I can't read her face.

"She's your what?" Cami finally asks, her voice deadpan.

"Nothing," I say weakly. "She's just . . . important to me. And you've been so weird to both of us tonight."

"*I've* been weird?" Cami's the only to laugh now, sharply. "I feel like I don't even know you anymore."

"That's a little dramatic—"

"Okay, well, I'm just telling you how I fucking feel because you asked."

Cami so rarely swears that it takes me aback. Before I can respond, Pablo and his friend burst out of the gas station.

"Let's goooooo," Pablo yells, slapping the front of the car with his palm twice. I look toward Cami, but she's already turning away, following them into the car.

This time, she sits on Carla's lap instead.

Alicia lives on the top floor of a two-story apartment in the southern part of the city. Upstairs, in the mostly empty living room, our voices echo off the empty walls. The floor is an all-white, cheap ceramic. In the middle of the room is a plastic table full of drinks and ashtrays, with a single pot of flowers in the middle. I don't know what they are, but their color is shocking: Hot pink with a single yellow stem in the center. There are a few plastic chairs too, but not enough for everyone. It's clear Alicia's just moved in.

Maynor sets a gigantic pizza box on the table, and Alicia turns on a Bluetooth speaker while the rest of us stand around awkwardly. Finally, she gets some reggaeton going, the echo in the room making everything twice as loud. Maynor turns off the overhead light and plugs in a string of Christmas lights hung around the ceiling. I can't help but stare at how easily the two of them move around the room, as if this is a routine for them—as if this place is just as much his as hers.

Pablo is the first to try to break the awkwardness, grabbing Cami's hand and pulling her to the empty space just beyond the table, swaying to the beat. Cami dances with him reluctantly, mostly trying to hide her face in his neck. From the brief glimpses I catch of her expression, she looks just as upset as I still feel. Then Carla drags Pablo's friend to the makeshift dance floor, where they dance closely, sloppily, with too many turns that make them bump into each other. I watch Pablo and his friend passing a bottle of whatever they bought at the gas station back and forth, taking shots over the girls' heads.

Maynor and Alicia sit on the floor by an outlet they use to charge their phones, their faces visible only from the screens lighting up with notifications on their laps. Every once in a while, I hear them giggle, see them sharing a soft kiss. Dani and Valeria nab the chairs around the table, opening the pizza box and grabbing slices. Miguel stands next to them, devouring a pizza slice he's folded in half with one hand and scrolling through his phone with the other. I reluctantly take the last chair next to Dani, though I feel too anxious to eat.

Valeria and Dani talk about Valeria's college plans. I nod along, adding one-word agreements every now and then. I keep checking my phone for the time and placing it back under my thigh. I'm all shaken up from Camila, practically nauseous. Though that could also be from the beer, or the too-fast drive here.

The third time I go to grab my phone, Dani intercepts my hand mid-motion and interlaces her fingers with mine. She doesn't break eye contact with Valeria—who I notice noticing. I take a deep breath, letting the heat and weight of Dani's hand settle me. I try my best to really listen to her and Valeria's conversation, to pay attention. Though it takes a few songs, I do finally start feeling a bit better. Dani and Valeria clearly like each other, and that makes me happy.

An hour goes by like this. At some point Miguel tries to make Valeria dance, but she tells him she's too full from the pizza. He accepts defeat and joins in on their conversation, telling us about his own plans to become an agricultural engineer. Then Maynor announces that it's time for anyone who isn't planning on sleeping over to leave.

"There's one extra room," Alicia adds. "Lucky for you all, the previous tenants left behind some beds."

"Wait—what about Mom? Are you taking me home?" I ask Maynor, standing up. He stops the music. I feel unsettled by the sudden silence, exposed.

"No, relax. She's sleeping at the hotel tonight. I told her you're with me, that everything's okay."

"So, we're staying here?"

"Yes. Anyone else?" Maynor asks, turning toward the others.

"I'd love to." Dani raises her hand. "As long as I can get a ride back to campus in the morning? I don't want to wake up my roommates."

"No worries," Alicia replies. "You and Libertad can sleep in the other room."

My face gets hot and I have to avoid eye contact with absolutely everyone.

"All right—I'll drive the rest of you home." Pablo yawns and stretches, dangling his dad's car keys over his head.

"Hell no." Maynor snatches the keys from his hand. "You've been drinking all night. Alicia and I will drive everyone back. I'll ride with her after we drop you off."

For a second, Pablo looks like he's about to protest, but then he shuts his mouth. His eyes are half-lidded now, his body still swaying to nonexistent music.

"Okay, we'll be right back," Alicia tells Dani and me as the others file out into the hallway. "Make yourselves at home. The sheets are clean. You can go into my closet for sleepwear—second drawer to the left."

"Amazing." Dani grins. "Thank you."

"See you on Monday!" Valeria calls over her shoulder. Everyone else echoes, except Camila, who's the first out the door.

"That was a *great* poem," Pablo slurs in Dani's direction.

"Thanks, but it wasn't—"

He pulls the door shut behind him, and the slam echoes across the apartment.

There's a beat of silence, and then Dani turns to me.

"Are you sleepy?"

TWENTY FOUR

Wordlessly, we navigate the boxes in Alicia's room as we move toward the closet. I grab a shirt I recognize as Maynor's from the drawer before noticing the heap of his clothes on top of the dresser. His stuff is littered throughout the room, mixed with hers—even his rosary drapes over the edge of her bedside table.

I go into the bathroom, closing the door behind me, and change into Maynor's shirt and some loose, pink shorts of Alicia's. I brush my teeth with my index finger and some toothpaste I find in the cabinet. Then I take about ten deep breaths, watching my chest rise and fall in the mirror.

I look better than I thought I would: Normal. Fine. I feel a little anxious again, but the source is something different this time. Nerves? Excitement?

I'm about to share a bed with Daniela.

Dani knocks on the bathroom door and I jump, hitting a drawer handle under the bathroom counter with my knee. "Mierda," I mumble, rubbing what I know is going to be a bruise tomorrow.

"Everything okay?"

"Yes—yes, coming."

When I open the door Dani's right there, also changed into borrowed clothes. The T-shirt she wears is so long, I can't see her shorts.

"Sorry—I really need to pee."

"All yours," I say, sliding between her and the door frame.

The second room is smaller than Alicia's but looks larger without all the boxes. There are the two twin beds pushed together, forced to share what I assume are queen-sized bedsheets. Headlights from passing cars appear in the street-facing window every few seconds, throwing light and shadow along the opposite wall.

I don't know what to do with myself. I get in bed and burrow under the covers, pull out my phone. The toilet flushes, and the faucet turns on. I have messages from Valeria saying that Pablo made Maynor pull over to vomit on the side of the road.

I scroll down my messages until I find my chat with Camila—it's been a while since we've texted.

I replay our conversation outside the gas station in my head but it's already getting blurry around the edges. I can't remember how much Camila had had to drink, if at all. I just know I had had a bit much. Nearly sober now, I feel less angry and more sorry. Maybe she hadn't been that weird? Maybe I was weird and that made her weird?

I don't know. I don't know anything. I just don't want to be in a fight with my best friend.

I'm really sorry about tonight, I type, and send before I can change my mind. The *online* under her name pops up immediately, the blue checkmarks next to my text letting me know she's read it.

She starts typing, and I'm staring so hard at my phone, I don't notice Dani's in the room until she closes the door behind her. I set my phone face down on my chest.

"Hey," I say, in a weird, high-pitched voice. "How was it?"

Dani raises an eyebrow. "Peeing?"

"Yes . . . peeing," I say, smiling, doubling down.

"Peeing was great, very pleasant," she plays along. "Are you cold? Do you want me to find another blanket?"

"I'm okay," I say. "A little hot, actually." But I don't move from my burrow under the covers.

"Ooookay," Dani says. "I'll just—" She turns off the overhead light, standing in the dark for a second before making her way slowly, hesitantly, toward the bed. Finally, she gets in under the covers, moves around a bit.

"So . . . what was up with you tonight?"

"What do you mean?" I ask, even though I already know.

"Something seemed up when you got here. Also, Carla said y'all stopped at a gas station and she thought she heard you and Camila fighting."

Dani shifts so she's lying on her side.

I sigh, slip my phone under my pillow, then turn so the two of us are facing. "Yeah."

"Do you not want to tell me?"

"No." I backtrack. "I mean, not that I don't want to tell you. It's just . . . I don't know what there is to tell."

It's quiet for the moment as the two of us look at each other, warm breaths tangling together in the small space between us.

"I asked her why she was being so weird all night," I try again. "I was kind of mean about it, honestly. And I . . . I asked her if it was about you."

My voice dissolves into a whisper, and I'm not sure if Dani can still hear me. But the faint orange light coming through the window is enough to see her eyes widen.

"Did you want it to be about me?" she asks after a beat. Her eyes are boring into mine, and I have to force myself not to look away.

"I don't know. Maybe," I admit. "Not that—I mean, I don't want you to think—"

"I don't think anything," Dani says softly. Her tone, though kind, is tired. "I think it's all complicated. But I don't think anything negative. Not about you, Libertad."

"Okay." I exhale, giving her a small smile. "Okay—good."

"We should try to go to sleep," Dani murmurs, closing her eyes. "Tonight was fun. Thanks again for letting me read your poem."

"Thank you for reading it." My smile stretches into a grin now. "It meant a lot to me. You did a great job."

"It was all you," Dani whispers.

Her breathing slows, deepens. For the life of me, though, I can't close my eyes. Every few seconds a car drives by, throwing moving light on the back wall and Dani's face. The ends of her long, dark eyelashes spark gold in the flashes.

"Dani?" I whisper.

"Yes?"

"I'm not sleepy."

"I thought you said you were," she says, without opening her eyes.

"I was lying."

Dani smiles. "Why?"

"Because . . . I was nervous about sleeping next to you tonight. Or, like, whatever happens before the sleeping part."

Dani's eyes flutter open.

"What did you think would happen?"

"I don't know," I say. "That's why it was scary."

"Okay," Dani says slowly. "Well, what did you want to happen?"

Another car drives by, loud and squeaky, like it could use a trip to the mechanic.

The car's headlights move from Dani's face to her feet, to the wall across from us, until they disappear and leave us in darkness again.

I roll over so all my body weight is on my side and lean forward, toward Daniela. I place my lips lightly on hers—a question. She answers me, kissing me back. Then her lips open, and she wraps her hand around the back of my head, through my hair, pulling me closer.

Our kiss is urgent, demanding, as if everything is ending and beginning at the same time. Dani kisses my neck, down to my shoulder and back to my mouth, and I shiver. I kiss her with everything in me, again and again and again, until Dani finally pulls away.

"How are you?" Dani pants, her hand resting on my waist.

"So good." I grin.

Dani laughs then, and I swear I can make out the pinkness of her cheeks even in the dark. "No," she says. "I mean, like, are you . . . okay? Like you're not drunk or anything, right?"

"No." I shake my head firmly. "I'm okay."

"You sure?" Her eyes search my face.

"Yes, I'm sure. Are you okay?"

"Yes." Dani smiles, leaning in to kiss me again. "Can I—" she starts, whispering against my lips. "Is it okay if I . . . if I take your shirt off?"

I nod. Little by little—question by question—in between kiss after kiss, all our clothes come off. With Dani, my body feels like someone else reading a poem I wrote, instinctively knowing where all the pauses and emphases belong.

I wake up to a door slam, followed by giggles and shushes. At first I think it must be morning, but outside, it's still dark. I check my phone: four a.m. I have a bunch of texts but can't make my eyes focus on the screen long enough to read them.

Dani is asleep beside me, her breaths deep and long. My throat and mouth are dry—it hits me then how unbearably thirsty I am. I stare up at the ceiling, trying to muster the willpower to go get water, taking in the feel of both my body and Dani's together on the bed.

A part of me still can't believe what happened just a few hours ago: Dani and I had sex. I had sex with Dani. It was good and surprising, and it made me feel so close to her. I think, for a second, that no two people ever been as close as we have—as we just were.

I always thought that if I ever got to have sex with a girl, it would happen later in life, and definitely not in Honduras—maybe because the thought of doing anything explicitly gay seemed impossible here. So I told myself this wasn't important. That it was okay if it took a long time to happen, or even if it never did.

But here I am. It happened, here, with an amazing person I really like and who really likes me back. To my horror, I have to take deep breaths against the tears welling up in my eyes. What an impossibility this was, and it just . . . happened. Holy shit.

Careful not to move too fast or make too much noise, I get up. The bed springs squeak some, but Dani doesn't move. The floor is cold under my bare feet. I dress fast and slip out the door, closing it as gently as I can behind me.

"What are you doing up?"

"Jesus!" I jump.

The yellow glow of streetlights streams through the living room window just enough to make out Maynor standing next to the plastic table. He's in his long basketball shorts and a threadbare T-shirt. Next to the empty pizza box is now a five-gallon blue water bottle. Maynor tilts it over the edge of the table and fills a plastic cup up. He gestures for me to sit with him, offering the cup.

"Did you just come in?" I ask.

"No—we got back an hour or two ago. Your friend made me pull over so he could throw up, by the way."

"I know." I take a sip of the cool water. "Valeria told me."

He pours himself a cup of water. "I don't miss being eighteen . . ."

I roll my eyes. "Okay, old man."

"Aging is a privilege denied to many, Libi," he says, wagging a finger in my direction. "So I take a lot of pride in every single year."

I can smell him—a mixture of tang and musk.

"Maynor," I sigh. "Who talks like that at four in the morning?"

"I do," he replies, nudging my arm with his.

It's then that I notice something on the table I hadn't caught earlier. I move aside the pizza box, seeing Sharpie scribbles, signatures, and drawings that start at the center of the plastic table and radiate outward—it reminds me of the table in the radio cabin that Dani showed me. Some of the drawings are expected, like penises. Others say FUERA JOH and slogans you'd find spray painted across the city. There's also a bunch of names in different inks and handwritings. Maynor's hand rests next to a red heart drawing with an arrow across it. The inscription inside the heart reads *Maynor + Alicia*.

"Where did Alicia get this table?" I ask him.

"I got it for her. Well, technically I stole it for her." Maynor rubs his neck. "From this tacos place at the university, where we had our first date. And she scribbled this heart with our names in it. I got it for her on our six-month anniversary."

I laugh. Because of course Maynor didn't get her some ordinary gift. "That's really sweet, Maynor. . . . And annoying for the tacos place? Another guy would've gotten her flowers."

"I did." Maynor points to the pink flowers with the yellow tongues. "Anthuriums. My favorite."

"They're beautiful," I say, raising my eyebrows. I had been meaning to ask Dani the flower's name, but kept forgetting. I didn't know Maynor had a favorite flower. Though I guess there's a lot I might not know about him.

"You're so weird sometimes." I shake my head.

"Weird how?"

A car drives by outside, its headlights moving through the room, bisecting my brother's face for a second.

"I don't know. . . . Just the things you love, I guess. They're all so random. No clear pattern."

"That's how all people are." Maynor shrugs, staring into his cup of water. "But I mostly love simple things, you know? Fútbol. Alicia. My family. Your poems." Maynor glances up at me. "And anything that makes it easier to believe things will get better for us—including your poems."

My breath hitches in my throat. "You're a good brother, Maynor."

Just then, Maynor grabs something from behind the vase of flowers. He offers me a black Sharpie. "Here—write something."

"I don't know, May," I say, uncapping the marker slowly. Now that I'm not dying of thirst, I mostly just want to go back to bed.

"Write your name, then, something like that—anything you want."

I sit there for a second, staring at the table and thinking. About Dani, whose amber perfume I can smell on me. About Cami, my friends, our family, my poems. Nothing feels quite right—a stolen plastic table shouldn't be this demanding.

I look at Maynor, who stares back at me assuredly—as if he has no doubts in me whatsoever. Something in his gaze reminds me of when we all lived in the other house, before Abuela's. When Maynor and I were children seeing our dad hurt our mom and not knowing what to do. When we'd hold each other through the screaming and fists on the walls. I remember a thing we used to say to each other.

I touch the tip of the marker to the table now, writing it in a small space between a heart and a curse: *Maynor y Libertad juntos contra el mundo.* Maynor and Libertad against the world. I look up at him when I'm done.

"Perfect." Maynor squeezes my arm, so much love in his eyes, I can barely take it. "That's perfect, Libertad."

TWENTY FIVE

I wake up to my brother's knocks. I know I've been dreaming but can't remember what about. Next to me, Dani's eyes open too. We spent most of the early hours wrapped in a mess of sweaty limbs but moved apart at some point in the morning and ended facing each other, nose to nose. When she meets my eyes, her face opens into a smile. I kiss her lips, a smile itching across my face.

Maynor knocks again. "Libi, let's go! We have to make it home before Mami."

That gets me up. Dani and I bound out of bed and put on our clothes from last night, sneaking glances and smiles and kisses all the while. It feels like my whole body is glowing. I grab my phone from under the pillow. I want to know the time, but it's dead.

"What time is it?" I ask Dani.

She taps her phone. "Almost seven."

When she opens the door, the smells of fried eggs and refried beans with chorizo drift in. Maynor and Alicia made us breakfast.

We sit across from them at the table. The empty pizza box has been stuffed into a trash bag and moved to a corner by the front door.

"Thank you so, so much," Dani says. "For everything—letting me stay, food, seriously."

Alicia waves her off. "Not a problem. This one did all the cooking." She points at Maynor with her lips. "Did the cars keep you up? It's a busy street."

"I was out like a light," Dani says.

"Same here," I echo.

"This smells incredible," Dani says to Maynor.

"I *am* the best cook in the family. Ask Libi." He winks.

"He's okay," I tease, rolling my eyes.

"Just wait till you try the beans," he says, reaching over to scoop some on her plate.

"Gracias, Maynor," she says, then turns to Alicia. "I love anthuriums." She taps the yellow center of a flower lightly.

"I know, right? They're so beautiful" Alicia replies, giving Maynor eyes.

"It's the best flower," he says, a pride in his voice like he invented them himself.

After that the four of us eat in silence, too hungry to make small talk. The sounds of our eating are punctuated by the bustling of people and traffic outside. When we're done, there's no mess to clean—every plate and cup disposable. We throw it all in the trash bag and Maynor carries it outside.

On the ride home, Dani rubs my palm with her thumb as we hold hands in the back seat. With each small circle, my back tingles. I never want this morning to end.

As Alicia drops us off, I stand on the curb and give Daniela a long, slow kiss. I'm so lost in her, I barely care who sees us. When we pull away, I catch Maynor kissing Alicia too, overhear them making plans for tomorrow.

"So—" Maynor says once we're inside. "You and Dani?"

"Yeah, yeah, yeah," I say, shoving him lightly.

"Oh, you gotta tell me more."

I yawn, which makes him yawn. "Maybe after I get a good nap in."

"All right, all right," he says, ruffling my hair. "But I won't forget."

The house is quiet. Alberto is still asleep, and Abuela's left for work. She probably didn't realize we were gone at all.

In my room, I plug my phone in. The battery symbol comes on, and only then do I remember the text I sent to Cami. As I wait for my phone to turn back on, though, my eyelids get too heavy, and I fall asleep.

A small buzzing in my ear is what wakes me up hours later. I slap at my ear, still half-asleep, before noticing that my legs, arms, and neck also itch to the point of burning. I scratch at the spots but find little relief—my nails are too short to make a difference.

I sit up. The room feels like it's a hundred degrees. From the soft blue light cutting through the window, I can tell it's early evening. My window screen is open, which explains all the zancudos buzzing around me. I get up to close it and climb back into bed, instinctively reaching for my now fully charged phone.

It's a little past five. Notifications litter my home screen, messages from Valeria, Mami, Carla, Dani. But there's only one that makes my stomach drop. I scroll down until I see it: Cami's chat.

Despite the quickly growing pit in my stomach, I take a deep breath and open our conversation.

> I'm sorry too

> You weren't wrong when you said I was acting weird

> Or that it was about Daniela

> I don't know what to do. I'm sleeping over at Pablo's. My mom thinks I'm at Carla's. He's passed out now. But he was supposed to drive me all the way home

> Anyway, that's not really important right now. I'll figure it out in the morning

> It is about Daniela because it doesn't feel good that things that were ours you now suddenly have with her

> And I don't know . . . how close you two are?

> Does that make sense

> Do you know what I mean

> Are you two just friends

> Are we just friends?

Then, a couple hours after the other messages:

> Because I don't think I can be just your friend.

TWENTY SIX

I don't know how something we think about every day and haven't stopped talking about all year creeps up on us, but a week's gone by since my friends and I all went out, and it's suddenly Saturday again, the morning before election Sunday.

Things at the house are better, though not lighter—it's more a sense of fake-peace that surrounds us. At some point in the last week or so, Abuela began addressing Maynor again, asking him to move this or that, inquiring about a friend of his she hadn't seen in a while. Maynor played along, and eventually things seemed back to normal between the two of them.

The same sort of thing happened between Mami and me. We act like our usual selves in shared spaces. We laugh lightly together in the kitchen or talk about the news, but rarely are we ever alone together. When it does happen—like when we find ourselves waiting in the car for my brothers—we say next to nothing. We scroll through our phones, pausing only to ask each other "What's taking them so damn long?"

Before our fight, before she saw the texts on my phone, I used to get into Mami's bed and listen to her talk about her day and then tell her about mine. Sometimes my brothers would join us, Abuela stopping by occasionally to check in on us and add her two cents. Sometimes I would even fall asleep with Alberto and her, waking the next morning to the sounds of Mami getting ready in her bathroom. None of that has happened in weeks now, and I can feel the ache of it in my chest.

At least I have Dani to distract me. The past week we've kept up our streak of calling each other every night before bed, talking about the elections and her classes and my college applications. Mostly, we talk about us, and the night at Cien Años.

> Maybe after this weekend, if everything goes okay, we can try to go out again somewhere

Her text lights up my screen. I glance up from my essay and grab my phone to respond.

> I'd really like that. Fingers crossed

It takes me all morning before I finally decide that my scholarship essay is done. There's nothing else I can do for it: It's time to send it off into cyberspace with two of my applications.

With Valeria's help, I managed to get fee waivers. While I still technically have three more days before both schools' deadline, I promised myself I'd be finished before the elections. Best to play it safe, I figure—in case all hell breaks loose and we have power cuts. I'm about to go ask Mami if I can borrow the hotel's laptop she carries around when Maynor knocks on my door.

"You're awake," he says, raising his eyebrows.

"Yeah." I stretch my arms over my head, leaning back in my chair. "Some of us have been up for hours, you know."

"Hey—I'll have you know that Abuela made me sweep the whole house *and* the sidewalk in front at five this morning."

"Jesus." I make a face, and Maynor laughs. I notice now the gray dirt spots on his face, long sweat prints around the armpits and neck of his shirt. "If it was up to her, you'd be cleaning the street too."

"What are you doing?" he asks, tapping the pad of paper in front of me before moving to sit on my bed.

"Finishing my college essay. Well, I *am* finished—I was about to ask Mami for the laptop to type and send it. And then you walked in."

"Do you want me to read it?"

"No! I mean . . ." I start over. "You can, I guess. But I don't want any more pointers. I'm ready to be done," I say firmly, brushing stray curls out of my face.

Maynor raises his palms. "Okay, okay, no pointers. Just reading. What prompt did you end up choosing?"

I hand the pad of paper to him. "The person who's my biggest inspiration."

"Oh, so it's about me?" Maynor winks, and I roll my eyes.

As Maynor leans back and begins to read, I grab my phone. Dani hasn't texted me back yet. I scroll down to Cami's chat—which I do at least a few times a day now—scanning again through her messages from the night of Cien Años. At this point, I could recite them from memory.

I never texted her back—a dick move, I know. I didn't know how to respond; I still don't. We haven't talked at all at school either, though; to be fair, she's been avoiding me as much as I've been avoiding her.

Also, if I'm honest with myself . . . I'm still a little pissed at her. I've spent years watching Camila be courted by dozens of boys. Shit, I've spent the past three months putting up with Pablo. And she couldn't do the same for me? For one night? And *now* she wants something more? And if Dani had never come into my life—would she have even said anything?

"This is really great," Maynor says, snapping me out of it. "Good job, enana."

"You mean it?" I ask, putting down my phone.

"Yes, I promise. I'm so proud of you," he says, squeezing my knee. His voice is so tender, I know he must mean it.

"Okay, okay, you big softie," I tease him. "Now give it back—I need to submit this and not think about it anymore."

Maynor starts to hand the pad back to me but pulls it away again just as I'm reaching for it.

"Maynor," I groan. "Come on."

Maynor pulls me in for a sudden, sweaty hug.

"Ew—you stink," I say, pretending to gag.

"I love you too."

"Yeah, yeah." I shove at him gently, and he ruffles my hair before finally—for real this time—handing the paper back to me.

Once I hit submit on my applications, I feel like I can breathe again. I know the hardest part—waiting—is ahead, but at least the ball's not in my court anymore. It's time to let go and let God. After returning Mami's laptop to her, I flop onto my bed and text Valeria to let her know I'm done.

Woooo! I'm about to hit send too, she texts me back. Then:

> Now we just wait like three months :/

Three months from now—February. I wish the month meant anything to me other than that it'll be a whole year since Camila and I kissed in that dirty bathroom en La Esquina. But that's where my mind goes, immediately.

I go to Cami's chat again, this time clicking on her WhatsApp profile. She changed the picture a few days ago: It's a photo of her at the beach from a family trip she took this summer. She's wearing a bright yellow two-piece bathing suit and sunglasses. The ocean glitters behind her, and she's standing sort of sideways, the curve of her perfectly round ass unmissable. Not for the first time, I use my fingers to zoom in, staring for so long my mouth gets dry and I feel a pressure between my legs.

I've felt this way about my best friend for as long as I can remember. It's so glaringly obvious to me now. And now—finally, maybe—she's willing to admit that she feels the same way about me.

I have to respond to her. I have to say something, anything. But I don't know what. I breathe in, hold my breath for five seconds, and breathe out. Applications is a big one off my checklist . . . but now I don't have an excuse to keep stalling on Camila's texts.

I go to her chat and type the first thing can think of. The first thing that needs to be addressed:

> I'm sorry I haven't responded to this.
> I didn't know what to make of it.
> I still don't, if I'm honest

> Do you still feel this way?

> Like you don't think you can just be my friend.

I hit send on each message before I can change my mind. My heart beats so fast, it's making me nauseous, and I have to sit up. I switch the ringer on and turn my phone face down. Waiting is a little less painful this way.

I'm not sure how long has gone by—maybe a couple minutes—when my phone dings. And it's her.

> Yes. I still feel this way.

I can hear my pulse in my ears. I type and delete, type and delete. Under Cami's name, I can see she's online. I picture her staring at our chat, waiting.

I make myself stop typing, to take a moment and gather my thoughts, when she texts me again:

> How do you feel?

Air wheezes out of me like a popped balloon. That's the question, isn't it? And fuck, I wish she was asking me two months ago, because this would be so much simpler.

> I haven't wanted to be just
> your friend for a long time

I text.

> But things are so complicated now.
> I need a little more time to think.

> Can we talk after the elections?
> Maybe at school on Monday?

It takes her a few minutes to reply. I see her type and stop and type again. Finally, she says,

> Yes. Let's talk on Monday

I lie down, setting my phone on my chest. My feelings for Cami and Dani are a tangled mess, twisting tighter and tighter in on themselves, suffocating all rational thought. What does it mean to not be just friends with Cami, when we're barely friends now? What about Pablo? And where does that leave me and Dani? Should I be telling Dani about any of this?

A few days after Cien Años, Daniela asked me about my fight with Cami again. I brushed it off, said it was just a weird drunk argument that didn't matter anymore. But of course it does.

When I close my eyes, my mind scrambles to put everything back to the way it was before. It'd be so easy for Cami to come over again all the time, like she used to. We could sleep over at each other's houses. We could kiss again. We could go back to before things got weird, but this time, we'd both know what it means.

TWENTY SEVEN

The next morning—election day—Mami wakes us all up early.
She, Maynor, and I all vote at the same center a few blocks from our
house. Abuela votes elsewhere, deeper into the city. I don't really
understand all the specifics and logistics, but she's taking Alberto
and the car to wherever she votes, and we're walking to our center.

When we arrive, I get why we're so early. The line is unending,
circling around the block. Street dogs lie in the sun all around us,
flies buzzing in our ears. People in line fan themselves with papers
or books or their hands.

"Put your phones away," Mami tells us, her eyes warily roving
around our surroundings. I don't think we're gonna get mugged
right in front of the voting center but do as she says anyway. Maynor
kicks a small rock forward with every step. Mami hugs herself and
looks around every few seconds. The sun gets more and more
unbearable as it arcs up into the sky.

My fingers itch to take my phone out again as it buzzes in my
pocket, over my thigh. It won't stop—it hasn't stopped since last

night. After submitting my college application essay and texting Camila, I finally felt free again to return to the first poem I had drafted in the journal she gave me: The poem about whether Honduras is—or will ever feel—fully independent. I read the poem over and over again, switching a few words around before finally typing it up on my notes app and posting screenshots of each stanza to my Instagram poetry account before bed. I figured that if there was ever a time to share, it was right before election day.

Immediately, my phone was swarmed with notifications. I got thousands of likes in a few hours. Half a day later, there's no sign of it slowing down.

After a few minutes of the line coming to a complete standstill, Maynor pats his jean pockets and pulls out a twenty-Lempiras bill. "I'm gonna run across the street and get a Coke," he says, nodding in the direction of the pulpería.

"Hold on." Mami pulls twenty more Lempiras out of her purse, glancing over her shoulder. "Get me a Coke Zero too. Do you want anything, Libertad?"

I shake my head.

Maynor comes back a few minutes later with their drinks, condensation dripping down the sides of the plastic bottles. He takes a long sip of his Coke before recapping it, holding it loosely in his hand. The line moves forward a few inches, and I reach for his bottle, pressing the cold, wet plastic against the nape of my neck.

By the time it's our turn to go inside the voting center, we're sweaty and grumpy. It must be closer to noon—the air is thick and moist. I go to the table I'm directed to, realizing that the building we're in is a public school. The conjoined desk and chair I squeeze myself into to vote was built for a small child.

I stare for a second at the long paper on the desk in front of me, full of the congressional and presidential candidates' faces. I'm thankful for the tri-fold cardboard, the kind we used for science projects in elementary school, that conceals me from the person at the desk next to mine. It takes me a moment to process that this is really happening—we're making history, one way or the other, and I'm finally old enough to get a say in what happens.

Despite the hours-long wait in line, it all seems over too quickly. I pencil in my votes and cast my ballot. Not even five minutes later, someone's pressing my finger into an ink stamp, tinting it to prevent double voting. And then I'm walking back home with Maynor and Mami.

The rest of the day goes by unbearably slow, all of us taking turns watching TV or cleaning around the house to keep ourselves occupied. Finally, a little after eight, we make our way wordlessly to Mami's room and position ourselves around the TV, waiting for the current trend results. Everyone keeps checking their phones as if it's going to be texted to us; when I go to Instagram, I see that my new poem has over six thousand likes and more than a hundred reposts.

Mami steadily flips through the channels. For a few minutes, the stations keep flashing the same footage of different voting centers that they've been showing us all day. It's not until 8:14 p.m. when we spot something new: a bar graph, showing that the left's candidate is up by 5 percent with more than 60 percnt of all votes counted.

Maynor and I exchange wide-eyed glances, hugging so hard and fast, we bump heads.

"No puede ser," he whispers into my ear. "Gracias a Dios."

As we pull away, I think I catch Mami smiling as she texts someone. Alberto asks if we can go make dinner now. Abuela, who was leaning against the door frame, turns and leaves the room without another word.

Abuela doesn't eat with us that night. I think I hear her on the phone with Abuelo, or maybe one of the workshop ladies, though I can't be sure. Maynor, Alberto, Mami, and I eat fast and hungry, reheating leftovers from the fridge as we go. Food sticks to Maynor's beard, and Alberto's hands are visibly sticky from across the table. As we start clearing dishes, Mami reminds us to keep things down, to be considerate of Abuela's feelings.

"Remember," she says, repacking leftover rice into an old Tupperware container. "At the end of the day, this is her house. What Abuela has done for us, no one ever will. Not any of the presidential candidates. No one."

Maynor nods, but nothing can wipe the smile off his face. He practically bounces as he wipes down the table. From the corner of my eye, I see him sneak out his phone, texting Alicia, *we did it, amor.*

I, too, have texts from Valeria and Dani, echoing the celebratory feelings. I feel like we're in a movie, like nothing this big and good has happened before.

Suddenly, I feel more exhausted than I've been all day. As if my whole body had been holding its breath, just waiting for the elections to be over before I could get back to my normal life. Now I feel something in my chest untangle, the tension from grinding my teeth all day pinching the ends of my jaw.

Tomorrow, at school, I'll talk to Camila about . . . well, about us. Then I'll talk to Dani. And then I know something will change, though I'm not entirely sure what yet. Dread swells in my chest, and I know better than to try to fall asleep before it eats me alive.

"Does anyone need the bathroom before I take a shower? I'm going to bed soon." I yawn, grabbing a dirty plate from the stack on the counter and rinsing it in the sink.

"I'll wash the dishes, Libertad. Just leave them," Mami says, before laying a gentle, tentative hand on my cheek. At first, her touch shocks me, since it's the most physical contact we've had in weeks. After a second, though, I find myself leaning my head into her palm.

"Thank you," I say with a small smile.

Just outside the kitchen, Maynor stops me. "We did it," he says, grasping both my shoulders and shaking me a little. His eyes are shinier than usual—I can't tell if he's just tired or teary-eyed.

"We did it," he says again, then whispers, "All of it was worth it. Everything each of us did. The fronts. The protests. Your poems, enana. All of it."

Maynor's grin is huge, all teeth—radiant with joy. He looks so young like this. Like in the photo I've seen of ten-year-old Maynor leaving the movie theater after watching *Spider-Man* for the first time, in an actual Spider-Man suit made by Abuela—all the black spiderweb details Sharpie'd-in by her hand. Or from all my memories of teenaged Maynor dancing a goofy, celebratory dance after blocking a particularly good shot during a fútbol match, his fists raised high in the air.

And I wish I could take a picture of him, just like this.

I should have.

The next morning, I wake up to my mother's screams.

MAYNOR

"My parents met at a barbershop," Maynor said, passing the joint in his hand to Alicia. They sat on her car's hood, the metal warm underneath their bodies. "My dad had known about my mom for months. A mutual friend showed him pictures of her. And he wanted an introduction *so* badly, but everyone told him my mom had strict parents. There was no way."

Alicia blew smoke out of her mouth. It swirled between them for a second, before dissipating into the dusky sky. "So how did they end up at the same barbershop?"

"Fate, I guess," he said, tugging at the cross dangling from the chain around his neck. "My mom was there with my grandpa. He was getting a haircut, this is back when he still had some hair left. My dad just happened to be there at the same time. And get this—" Maynor raised his eyebrows. "My mom was the one who approached my dad. She just came up to him and was like, 'You're Diego, right? I've heard you've been asking around about me. Here's my house number—if anyone but me picks up, hang up.' And that was that."

Maynor shook his head as Alicia handed back the joint. "Had me two years later."

Alicia smiled and ducked her head, tucking a strand of hair behind her ear. It struck Maynor that this was the first time he didn't feel like shit talking about his dad with someone outside the family.

"I can't imagine your mom having to introduce herself to anyone." Alicia nudged him. "She's so pretty."

Now it was Maynor's turn to smile. He put the joint out carefully, slipping it over his ear.

"Yeah—I'm really glad you got to meet her."

For a moment, there was so much more he wanted to say, words tripping over themselves in his throat to get out. He wanted to make sure Alicia knew how much he cared about her, like *really* cared about her. How much joy flooded his body with every single second they spent together. He wanted to ask her more about the future, and the two of them, and did she want to come over to meet his siblings soon? Because he couldn't wait to introduce her to them—he knew they would adore her just as much as he did.

But then the moment passed. The words fell back, whisked away from him like smoke disappearing into the evening air. *Another time*, he told himself.

"You wanna go?" Alicia finally asked.

"One more minute," Maynor said, wrapping his arm around her. She leaned into him, and the two of them stared up into night sky. The lights of Tegucigalpa blinked back at them.

Alicia's phone dinged then, and she pulled it from her jacket pocket.

"What is it?" Maynor asked.

"Un compañero," she mumbled, and Maynor watched her eyes race through the block of text. "He's warning anyone who's out tonight to be careful. La policía's raiding bars across the city."

"What? Why?"

"They're looking for some students," she said, her eyes still on the screen. More messages began to appear under the first text block. "Student front leaders, I think. Trying to bust them for something like drunk driving so they can detain and interrogate them. Or just find them out in public, so they don't have to take them from their houses."

"Fuck, seriously?"

"Mhmm." Alicia shivered, slipping her phone back into her pocket. "Maybe we should go back to my place. It's getting cold anyways."

Maynor nodded, sliding easily off the hood and stretching. Then he froze, icy terror running through him. "Hold on. My sister's out at La Esquina right now."

Alicia wrapped her jacket tighter around herself, pushing hair out of her eyes. "Do you want to call her?"

"I don't think she'd pick up—she hasn't been responding to any of my texts." Maynor ran his hand through his hair, pulling his own phone out to double-check. "She's underage, Alicia. Fuck. I need to go get her."

Alicia tossed him her car keys and moved to the passenger's side. "Better hurry, then."

264

By the time Maynor had dropped off Libertad and a few of her friends at their respective homes and made it back to Alicia's, it was past one a.m. He'd dropped off Alicia at her home earlier too, first thing out of La Esquina, since her place was close, and the car was cramped. Now he was especially grateful for the last-minute decision; he couldn't have confronted his drunk little sister about the lipstick on her neck with Alicia in the car.

Outside Alicia's apartment building, Maynor killed the engine and took a breath. All of the hope, the expansiveness that had filled him just hours earlier had deserted him. He was tired, though it was hard to say from what, exactly. He hadn't had classes in a while—the latest student strike had been going on for two weeks, and it didn't seem like the university and the student fronts would reach an agreement any time soon. His half-hearted job hunt had fizzled out a few days ago, when he learned that all the call centers he'd applied to required weeks of unpaid training. By then, the university might be back to business as usual. Nothing seemed worth investing his energy into if he didn't know when things might change again.

So the days went by. He played soccer with friends, occasionally, and smoked and hung out with Alicia most nights. The only marker of time became this feeling in his chest, gradually expanding to every corner of his body. First he called it boredom. Then it graduated to restlessness. But tonight, sitting alone in Alicia's car, new language came to him: He felt totally, utterly powerless.

Up in Alicia's apartment, Maynor closed the front door behind him with an absurd amount of care. The gesture was pointless though.

Alicia was sitting at the little table in the kitchen, waiting for him.

"Thank God," she sighed, setting her phone down. "My calls weren't going through."

"My phone died on the way here." Maynor kicked his shoes off. "Where's Julia?" Though Alicia's roommate was rarely home, he always asked.

"She went out." Alicia rolled her eyes. "She'll stumble in in a few hours and bring the party with her, I'm sure. My friend and I are talking about looking for a new place together this fall.

"Come," she added, before Maynor could respond, filling two cups of water and motioning her head toward her room. Maynor followed her in, closing the door behind them.

"I was worried you'd ran out of gas. Or worse," Alicia murmured, once the two of them were changed and settled under her thin comforter. Headlights from her bedroom window, which faced the main boulevard, flowed through the otherwise dark room.

"I'm okay," Maynor sighed. "Just exhausted. Definitely not how I thought tonight was gonna go."

"That's not how I thought meeting your sister for the first time would go, either." Alicia rolled over to rest in the crook of Maynor's arm. Maynor laughed softly, twirling a strand of her hair around his finger.

"Oh, I don't think it counts as meeting if she can't remember."

"That bad, huh?"

"She passed out as soon as we dropped you off."

"Are you gonna have a stern big-brother, man-of-the-house conversation with her about drinking?" Alicia teased.

Maynor kissed the top of Alicia head gently, inhaling the sweet, flowery smell of her shampoo. "Maybe just about being careful."

"*Especially* if she's hanging out around boys," Alicia said sagely. "And she probably is, at her age."

Maynor's smile slipped from his face. "I don't think so," he whispered, after a beat. "Not like that."

"What do you mean?" Alicia lifted her head from his shoulder. Her gaze was probing, luminous in the glow of headlights sweeping the room.

"Nothing," Maynor replied quickly. It wasn't his place to say anything before Libertad was ready, he knew. But that didn't stop the worry, the dread, that crept up on him again. He cracked his neck and rubbed at his eyes.

"What's up with you?" Alicia asked, laying her head back on his chest. "You've been off for days."

It took him a second to consider her question. What *was* up with him, really? Finally, after a minute, he said, "I feel so stuck, Alicia."

"What do you mean?"

"I just—I feel like I'm not moving. Like the days are passing by, and shit's all the same here, or worse. I'm so scared that one day I'll wake up—" Maynor paused, swallowing. "That I'll wake up, and realize I'm just like my dad. Full of big ideas and no follow-through. Harmful to the people I love." Maynor ran a hand over his face. "I'm twenty-five years old with no degree and no job. I live with my mom and grandma. They work insane hours to put food on the table *for* me, you know? And what do I do every day? Smoke weed and play fútbol?"

"That's not true." Alicia shook her head, moving her hand in small circles on his chest. "You're getting your degree. Then you'll get a job. Things take time."

"Where, though?" Maynor grunted. "I'm studying *journalism*. A joke of a career. If you want to get hired, you have to decide you're fine being paid off. Not even you—getting a degree in medicine, for God's sake—know you'll have a job at the end of it." Alicia stiffened, and Maynor forced himself to pause, to lower his voice.

"And then what's the point?" Maynor squeezed his eyes shut as Alicia resumed stroking his chest. "Look at all this fucked-up stuff going on with the student fronts, and no one's willing to report about it honestly. At least the protestors are standing up for something real. For a better place, somewhere we can all just *live*."

"I know," Alicia whispered. "I know, Maynor. I get it."

Maynor kept his eyes closed, feeling Alicia's head and her hand rising and falling gently with his breath. A few minutes or maybe an hour went by, and Maynor wondered if she had fallen asleep.

"La ley del más fuerte," Maynor whispered. "There has to be something more than that, right?"

Alicia didn't reply, and Maynor was certain now that'd she'd fallen asleep. Outside, the first streaks of dawn washed over the buildings in the distance. His city began to rise.

TWENTY EIGHT

No one will ever be able to tell us how, exactly, it happened.

On election night, Sunday, November 25 of 2017, I went to bed early, earlier than usual. Maynor helped our mother clean the kitchen—he was too excited to go to bed. Then Mami said good night to him; she was tired from the day before, when the gigantic wedding had taken place without any major issues after all. Maynor hugged her, reassuring her that everything would be okay. Nothing was ever as extreme as Abuela made it sound.

If Mami or Abuela or I had had Maynor's rush of energy, we might've been awake at one a.m., when the power went off for about thirty minutes. After texting a few friends and scrolling through social media, we would've learned that it was a country-wide power outage. When the power finally returned, around two a.m., the election results had been updated: Juan Orlando had gone from being 5 percent behind to 10 percent ahead. It was clear, then, that he was going to win. But he had already won, hadn't he? He had won before we even walked to the voting center that morning.

If Mami or Abuela or I had been up then, we might have heard the squeaking of the front door's hinges. This was the last time Maynor ever left our house, and he didn't use his window, as he had so many other nights. It was closed and locked from the inside the next morning.

What happened next? Here's where the details begin to collapse. Here's where my imagination must reconstruct what it doesn't want to see but *has* to know.

Maynor probably walked to the building where the voting count was taking place—the Supreme Electoral Tribunal. It's not a particularly short walk, but my brother was fast. I imagine the air was pleasant, full of whisper and soft heat, like the best of Tegucigalpa's November nights, the wind a relief from the sweat accumulating on his forehead and neck.

Because Maynor, I know, was furious. Furious of how the rest of his life and those of the people he loved would play out if we—if he—didn't do something about it.

Maynor got to the Supreme Electoral Tribunal and found that a massive crowd of protestors had already begun to gather, their chants uncoordinated but deafening. *¡FUERA JOH! ¡LADRONES! ¡CORRUPTOS! ¡EL PUEBLO MANDA!* In my mind's eye, I can see my brother yelling with them, shouting, *¡FUERA!* I can see his elbows bumping into bodies, someone pressing their hand to his back as they tried to move around him.

I can see Maynor making his way to the front of the crowd then, closest to the main gates of the tribunal, painted dark blue. I see him banging on the metal, his knuckles bruising. The sweat stains on his shirt like lakes, misshapen around his torso. I imagine my brother turning around, surveying the ocean of people behind him, their faces and fists raised to the sky, and thinking to himself, *They won't get away with it. They can't just steal our voices like that.*

At some point, between three and four in the morning, the military police showed up, as expected. They wanted, like Maynor, to get to the front of the line, to the gate. So they pushed and fisted their way through. *¡Váyanse a sus casas!* I imagine them shouting. *¡O los vamos a matar!*

It wasn't long before a fire broke out. It wasn't long before the bullet that inaugurated the post-electoral crisis of 2017 was fired. Then tear gas tore through nostrils. People ran and crashed into each other, covering their mouths.

I see Maynor pushed away from the gates by one of the MP. Maynor pushes back, maybe flicks away the hand or gun pressed to his chest. But el militar is stronger.

Maynor loses his balance, falling back, scraping his elbows on the sharp pavement. He stands back up though, fast. He screams, *How can you do this to us?! Don't you see what's happened?!* I see Maynor's fists swing, his black hair plastered to his temples with sweat, his eyes fighting to stay open, burning with gas.

I see the bullet that finds its way to his ribs, lodging into the left side of his body.

That's where my imagination stops.

Pictures and footage revealed in the next few days will show the protestors carrying red flags and torches, but not any noticeable weapons. Maynor isn't in any of it. I know, because I've examined every second that exists trying to spot his face, the back of his head, his half-moon elbow mole. Nothing.

But he was there. He was there because this is where his body would be found the next morning, next to three other men. All of them, including Maynor, without any ID or wallets on them.

What were my brother's last thoughts? What was the last thing he saw, when he closed his eyes?

Maybe he pictured his girlfriend, intertwining their initials in a red-inked heart on a plastic table.

Maybe he saw his family gathered together in the kitchen of our house, eating and laughing and telling stories over each other, loudly, the only way we knew how.

Maybe he saw himself, stopping the last ball of the game, securing the win for his team, lifted onto his friends' shoulders. Arms raised high, a champion. My champion, my brother.

MAYRA

At forty years old, she wasn't the youngest soon-to-be-grandmother in the waiting room. Under the white, fluorescent lights of the La Policlínica waiting room, this was obvious to her. The faces of the two younger women in nearby chairs bore the same lines of fear that hers did—except this wasn't their first time. Grandchildren waited at home for them already, they told her.

"Todo va salir bien," la señora with the sharp red acrylics repeated over and over, holding her hands. They were cold and damp, but Mayra held on to them tightly. "Your girl will be just fine. And so will her baby. Do you want us to pray again?"

She looked down at her own hands and for a moment was unable to recognize them. She fixated on the raised gray mole in the valley between her index finger and thumb. All her children had picked at it as babies. Even now, she could picture their small fingers trying to pull it. And the new set of fingers to come.

Mayra had never been one to let her walls down around strangers. But here she was, allowing this woman she'd met an hour ago see her en llanto. She nodded, unable to control herself enough to open her mouth and utter a simple *sí*. She closed her eyes and willed herself to focus on the woman's voice: *Padre nuestro en las alturas de los cielos . . .*

Carmen's screams pierced the air, from the hospital room where she lay straight into Mayra's chest. How could she pray while her fifteen-year-old daughter could be dying just feet away? How had this happened?

She opened her eyes and, without meaning to, met his—the boy's. He took this as a cue to break the course of his desperate pacing. Over the past few hours, he'd walked from one end of the waiting room all the way to Carmen's hospital room and back so many times, Mayra noticed, that he was now doing it with his eyes closed, whispering prayers under his breath as he went.

The boy approached her. Despite their differences—and how much she wished their lives had never crossed paths—he was the only one who seemed to share her panic in this moment.

"Doña Mayra," seventeen-year-old Diego Morazán begged, his eyes tinted red, the sides of his face streaked with tears. "She won't stop screaming. What do we do? What can I do?"

Her eyes fell to the scratches on his forearms. The blood there hadn't begun to congeal yet—it was fresh and bright. The pain her daughter was in had caused it. Next to her, the woman stopped her prayer.

"Is it her first?" she asked Diego, perhaps sensing that Mayra was unable to speak.

"Yes. But he wasn't due until the fifteenth," Diego answered, running a frantic hand through his hair.

"It's the full moon." The other woman, the one with the left eye that turned in, nodded. "Makes babies come early."

Diego didn't respond, his gaze turning back to Mayra. "Doña Mayra," he asked her again. "What do we do?"

"There's nothing you can do," the woman with red nails replied on her behalf. "This is normal—el primero cuesta. All you can do is wait. Why don't you sit down, muchacho? This could take hours."

Diego took the chair to the other side of Mayra. Instinctively, she shifted away. If he noticed, he didn't show it. And she didn't care. This was the relationship they've had ever since she learned of his name seven months ago.

Seven months ago, her daughter had brought Diego Morazán home, explaining that she was pregnant. They had been dating, in secret, for two years, despite Mayra's rules—simply put, her girls were not allowed to even *think* about boys until they had, at the very least, graduated.

And yet: "This," Carmen told her, cupping the sides of her not-yet-swollen belly, was something they wanted.

Her husband, César, had sat next to her, listening, asking the questions she couldn't bring herself to consider: Where were they going to live? When would they get married? Did his—the boy's—family know? How would he support her and the baby?

Diego and Carmen answered patiently, like they had rehearsed everything beforehand. All they needed now was their signatures. The signatures allowing their underage child to marry.

Mayra spoke only four words to them that day: I'm not signing *anything*.

The next morning, César told Mayra he was going to do it. And that she needed to as well. *She's a child!* Mayra plead. *She doesn't have to throw her whole life away—we can raise la criatura. She can still go to school, live a normal life.*

But César had made his mind up. *What's the point of having her resent us forever?* he spat. *This is the choice she's made. They say they want to handle it themselves. Let them.*

Three months later, she watched her fifteen-year-old daughter marry at a Seventh Day Adventist church, to which Diego's family had belonged for generations. Carmen was five months along then, but still so thin and small, her belly was barely visible under the white dress. Mayra hadn't even insisted on a Catholic ceremony. It wasn't possible for a pregnant woman.

With time, she had been forced to know the boy and his family. She couldn't stand any of them. Most of all, she despised Diego's mother, who seemed too enthusiastic about her teenage son's new life. And so it all happened, right under her nose. One day she'd had a teenage daughter she'd had dreams for, and now she was gone. Gone to live with a family of strangers.

Her daughter's screams shook the walls again, and Mayra dug her nails into the brown vinyl of the waiting room chair. Just then, César returned from trying to get a new update from the doctor. Both her and Diego stood up.

"They can't move her to the delivery room yet." He shook his head. "She has a few more centimeters to go."

"She can't take it anymore!" Mayra yelled at him. "Can't they hear her?"

Outside, fireworks exploded, making her jump. For a second, they were louder than the screams. César took a step toward her.

"Mire, Mayra." He took her hands. "We must calm down. This is going to take a few more hours. Remember how it was with José? She's okay—the doctor says she's fine. We just have to be patient."

Something about her husband's voice did offer her a sliver of peace. She forced herself to inhale deeply, willing her daughter's sobs to stop. "They can't give her anything for the pain?" she asked weakly.

"They already did," César replied. "It's going to take a minute."

She nodded, sitting back down. This time, César took the chair next to her, and Diego sat on his other side.

There was no TV, no radio. Nothing to help them pass time. The women who had led her in prayer were now strung along in a conversation of their own. The screams continued, though a little quieter now, more spaced out. After half an hour or so, one of the women's daughters gave birth, and she was allowed to go see her. Shortly after that, so did the other's. By two in the morning, they were the only ones in the room left waiting on a baby.

"I'll go get us some coffee," César said, standing up. "Do you want one?" he asked Diego.

"Sí, por favor."

César had managed a better relationship with the boy and their new in-laws. He was a practical man—he didn't dwell on the emotional. Diego Morazán had shown up at their house to change their lives forever, and not two days later her husband was discussing soccer with him.

As the metal double doors slammed behind him, Mayra rested her face in her palms. A moment of respite from the overhead fluorescent lights was a blessing to her senses. But she had only shielded her head for a minute before the screams started again. Despite the pain meds, they sounded sharper, more desperate than before.

Diego stood. "Doña Mayra," he begged her again, as if she had any power over their situation. "It's time. It has to be."

In her brain, it was only a flicker of a second. But that was enough for her to see him, really see him, the boy in front of her.

Despite the visible amount of gel he'd applied, his hair was a tangled mess of black curls. He'd put his hands through them so many times, they now stood at random peaks and angles. His eyes were red and swollen from crying. The blood on his forearms was finally dried, his fingernails bitten off around the edges.

Mayra saw the scared seventeen-year-old boy in front of her, and the only thing she could wonder was *Where were his parents?*

Maybe it was the way he was looking at her, a look she recognized instantly, because she was a mother. It was the look of a child asking her to fix something she had no control over. And it required both all her strength and no thought whatsoever to do the thing he needed. She stood, reaching for his hand.

Diego's eyes widened. He glanced down at their hands, then back to her face.

"I will go find the doctor," Mayra told him. "You stay here, wait for our coffees, and tell César that I'm with Carmen." She let go of Diego's hand then, stepping back. "She's going to be okay. This is normal. You will leave this place with your wife and son."

By the time Mayra found Carmen, nurses were rolling her into the delivery room. It was time.

"¡Mamá!" Carmen cried, reaching out a limp hand to her, and Mayra rushed to her side. "I can't do it anymore. Ya no puedo. Ya no puedo," Carmen panted, her hair pasted down to her temples and forehead with sweat. "This was a mistake, Mamá."

Despite her daughter's appearance, her cries, Mayra wasn't scared anymore. Or rather, her understanding of what she needed to do was bigger than her fear. She grasped her daughter's fingers with one hand, using the other to cup Carmen's face.

"Claro que sí podés, mi amor," she said, willing her voice to be calm, firm. "There is no mistake. You just hold on a little longer, and then it will be over. And it will be worth it," she promised. "A few minutes of pain for a lifetime of happiness."

Tears streamed down Carmen's face, but she nodded. Mayra followed her daughter and the nurses to la sala de partos, her fingers trembling as she tied a blue gown one of the nurses handed to her around her body. No matter that the fear had returned again—she was there. She held Carmen's hand as her daughter squeezed, and pushed, and cried. She held it as the doctor yelled *one more!* She held it until her daughter let go, and her grandbaby's cries rang through the air.

At forty years old, Mayra had lived through one natural birth, two Césarians, and one miscarriage. None of it had prepared her for the immensity of meeting her first grandson. Her new center of gravity could now be found in a little mass of black hair, whirlpooled atop the head of the baby her daughter held close to her chest.

"Maynor," Carmen said, beaming up at Mayra. "After you. Happy new year, Mamá."

TWENTY NINE

Mami honks again, this time letting the horn blare for at least five seconds. I pull the covers over my head and grunt into my pillow. I had been positive she would give up after the third honk, but no. *Just fucking go already.*

On the bedside table, my phone vibrates. I know it's her calling. I close my eyes as the buzzing dies down, hoping to hear the car pull away. Instead, a minute later, angry footsteps beat their way through the house, los insultos ringing under Mami's breath.

"We need to go. Right now," Mami says, slamming my door open.

"I told you I wasn't coming," I mumble without surfacing.

"We're all going. It's not optional. Your abuelos and Alberto are in the car waiting."

"I don't *want* to go. Can't you just do it without me? Please."

"No," Mami bites out. "You're coming. I can either drag you or you can do it por las buenas." I hear her sigh as she steps closer to my bed. "Por favor, Libertad. We'd already be halfway done if you had just gotten ready in time."

I take a deep breath. I do believe she'd find a way to carry me to the car herself, and I don't want to experience that. But I can't make myself move. I can't.

Mami rips the covers off my body.

"*Fuck*, fine then! Fine." I stand, and Mami moves back to the doorway. She stands there, arms crossed, surveying me as I begin to get dressed. It's clear she doesn't trust me not go straight back to bed if she left.

And she's right. I would. In a heartbeat.

"Apúrate," Mami says, motioning for me to hurry up. "I don't know if the flower people will even be there today."

"They're there every day," I snap. "People die every day."

"People also have families, Libertad. They might've left at noon."

"Okay, whatever. Someone will be there."

It's New Year's Eve—tomorrow is Maynor's birthday. He had the suckiest birth date anyone could have: January 1. No one ever had money by the time it came around, and everyone who drank was always too hungover to do anything.

He did enjoy the fireworks the night before. In a way, his birthday never felt like just another day, even if he'd wanted it to. And he liked all the reheated party food.

When I finally climb into the car, no one says anything to me about having had to wait or being late. Everyone is quiet, and I can't tell if they've just been sitting in silence the whole time or if I'm the cause. But I also don't care.

Mami turns the radio on as she pulls away from the curb. I think she's also bothered by the quiet. Of course, the first thing we hear is a discussion of the now counted and recounted votes. She turns it back off.

"Did you bring the wet cloth I asked you to get?" Abuela asks Alberto from her place in the front seat, and he holds it out for her to see.

I lean my head against the window and close my eyes, but the road is so bumpy, it makes me nauseous. I open them again and see that the traffic around us is insane. Everyone is rushing somewhere to get a last-minute ingredient or drinks or cuetes.

We're headed to the cemetery—Abuela wants to clean Maynor's grave, and Mami wants to place fresh flowers there. I personally don't care about either, and neither would have Maynor, I think. Though we never really talked about after-death wishes. Why would we?

After about twenty minutes, we finally make it to the flower stand before the main gate. Like I told Mami, there's plenty of people selling flowers. *Holidays are fake,* I remind myself. *Holidays are only holidays for some people.* At the stand, Mami and Abuela ask for a bunch of white flowers I don't recognize the name of, and really don't care to learn.

We drive as close as we can to the lot where he's buried. The place is packed, the whole garden and church full of people. I drag my feet as we walk to his little plot—I can't help it. The wind feels especially cold today as it whips across my face, though it hasn't been unbearably hot in a while. By the time I catch up to my family, Abuela is already on her knees, wiping down the plaque.

To my surprise, bright pink flowers already rest in the middle of his grave. Anthuriums. Fresh—maybe even from today.

"¿Y esas?" Abuela asks Mami, gesturing to the flowers. "Did you bring them?"

Mami shakes her head.

"Alicia did," I say softly. "It was his favorite flower. He got her some, one time."

My throat's dry, and I'm having trouble remembering the last time I drank water. Everyone nods, but no one says anything. Mami had known of Alicia for a while, it turns out, even before I did. She'd met her a few times too, though it sounds like she didn't really know how serious he felt about her until after his death. I learned all this at the dozens of church services they held for him, and completely against my will. I keep getting dragged places I don't need to be at, and it's pissing me off to no end.

What's the point?! I want to scream at them. None of the conversations or las misas or the days stick around in my head for long anymore. I woke up one morning, and my brother was dead. As will happen tomorrow. And the day after that. And on and on and on.

"Alberto, come help me," Mami says, picking away dried, dead leaves that had collected over Maynor's grave in the past week. She doesn't ask me to come help; she already has, every single weekend, and I've pretended to try for exactly thirty seconds before sitting down. Today, I go straight to the sitting down part, the grass wet under my butt.

Abuelo stands next to me, brushing my hair with his hand, before going over to help Abuela. Or hover around her—I'm not sure if he's being helpful or not. I watch my grandmother clean my brother's grave for a minute before my eyes inevitable pull to survey the families around us, all dressed in black. Familias de luto.

Before Maynor was killed, back when the world was a place with rules and patterns that I might've not always agreed with but ultimately understood, I found the phrasing of "de luto" strange. The word *luto* itself—mourning. Families in mourning, families of mourning. Luto: a short word, bisyllabic. A baby could say it. It's not one of those words that sounds like what it is. Too small to contain its meaning. Days after the funeral, I googled it, trying to pinpoint the Latin root. But it's not Latin at all; perhaps this is why it doesn't do what I need it to in a way my brain recognizes. It's Proto-Indo-European, from the root *lewg*, which means to break off, to shatter. Familias de luto, family in shatters. That's more like it. To break off. Before Maynor was killed, back when the world was—

I finally pull out my phone.

I forget about my phone all the time now. It went from being the center of my world to an object that's cold and foreign in my hand, removed. I even deleted most apps, deactivating some accounts. On the screen, there's an immense number of accumulating texts from Dani and Cami and my friends and unsaved numbers whose messages begin with, "I'm Maynor's friend, I hope you don't mind . . ."

I put my phone away again.

"Okay," Mami says after a minute, and I stand reluctantly to join my family. "Does anyone want to say anything before we pray?"

I shake my head. Alberto is crying again but being secretive about it. I think he's learning how to do this from Abuela.

"Do you remember, Carmen, how long it took, his birth?" The corner of Abuelo's mouth ticks up as the memory settles over him. "He didn't want to come out."

"Forever," Abuela says. "It felt like forever."

"Was he supposed to be born on January first?" I ask, genuinely curious about something for the first time in months.

"No," Mami replies. "He was due on the fifteenth."

"What happened?" Alberto asks, though this gaze stays lowered to his shoes.

"We were at a New Year's party, your dad and me—it was at his grandparents' house." Mami smiles to herself. "Around nine or ten I knew I had to go, that it was happening. I called my parents, and then Diego drove us to the hospital like a maniac. Somehow, your abuelo and abuela were already there." Abuelo moves to stand beside her, to squeeze her shoulder, and Mami rests a hand on his.

"That New Year's Eve," she continues, "there was a full moon. Everyone kept telling me not to look at it, as pregnant as I was. That it would make the baby come early. Of course, I didn't believe them—I kept looking at the moon all night. And then I felt it." Mami swallows hard, clearing her throat. "Maynor getting more and more jittery inside me, beginning to push around."

"Wait . . . so—Maynor had that horrible birth date because you wouldn't stop looking at the moon?" I ask.

Mami doesn't laugh, exactly, but breathes air in a soft chuckle. "Yes."

"Well, that sucks," Alberto mumbles, and that gets a chuckle out of the rest of us. "Did you ever tell him that?"

"Hmm—I don't remember," Mami says. "Probably."

I finally will myself to look at Abuela, whose tears have been streaming down this whole time. Abuelo rests a hand on her back.

We stay there like that for a while, my family and I, as if we're waiting for someone else to tell us it's time to go. At some point, my grandparents and mother walk over to Martha's grave a few plots away. Alberto tells me he has the car keys, and I follow him back to where we've parked.

My family's New Year's traditions are unusual. We don't make pork or tamales or any of that stuff. Instead, my grandparents cook a gigantic paella they learned about years ago, from some neighbor who had lived in Spain. Abuelo spends all day collecting the seafood and Abuela usually works at the workshop until five or six, then comes home and puts it all together with him.

While they're working or cooking, my brothers and I know every room needs to be swept, mopped, aired. By the time we sit down for dinner, it's around eleven or so. We talk and eat until we can say happy birthday to Maynor, then stand outside the house and watch the fireworks. We toast with grape juice. We hug and tell each other *¡Feliz año y bendiciones!* And then we go to bed.

But not tonight. After the cemetery, we stopped by El Patio to get un pollo asado. None of us are hungry, though. The chicken sits on the kitchen table, untouched.

Mami and Alberto lie down in her room as soon as we're home.

When Mami's not working, they've taken to watching any movie that's on TV without any discernment. I lie in my own bed, scrolling through my phone without stopping long enough to really take anything in.

What I want, more than anything, is to put in earbuds and lose myself in music. But every time I've tried, I've had to stop less than a minute in; nothing is enough to hold my attention for long. And so the hours go by, until I finally drift off sometime before eight. I jolt awake again around midnight, sweaty and scared, when all the fireworks go off.

It's my brother's birthday. He would have been twenty-six.

THIRTY

The only thing I find comforting these days is that, on the rare occasions I've stepped out of the house since November 25, Tegucigalpa looks exactly how I feel.

The protests after the elections were massive. I know because it was impossible to get places—like the church and the cemetery— until whoever was driving rolled down their window and told the protestors what we were up to. Who we are, where we were going. Then they'd try to build us a way out of it all, whistling and signaling to the ocean of bodies before us until they parted. Even then, so many roads were blocked off with rocks and burning tires. The military police had also secured the streets around most government buildings, turning the city unnavigable.

The news of those killed in front of the Supreme Electoral Tribunal fueled the chaos. Maynor's and the other men's names and faces were everywhere—on social media and TV, yes, but also stenciled on walls and written on sidewalks. Meanwhile, none of us cared about the electoral results anymore. Or at least, I didn't, and I don't remember anyone else around me talking about it.

The world was burning, and it had nothing to do with us anymore. Who gives a fuck about who gets to be president? It's all the same.

I let my phone die, not charging it again for days. I remember, vaguely, so many friends and people from school at the different church services. I remember Dani and Camila and Valeria and Carla and Pablo and Miguel. I remember their voices surrounding me, like walls, but little else. The memory of it all seems inaccessible, underwater, unfocused. Like it didn't happen to me at all. Like I wasn't there for any of it.

We leave the house again today—January 4—to get my mother a birthday cake. Usually, we'd get two at once on New Year's Day. There's a single panadería y repostería open on January 1, a fact we learned many years ago when we forgot to get any cake the day before. Maynor always wanted a lemon pie. Mami never wanted cake at all, but still we insisted on getting her something, mostly for ourselves.

Today, Abuelo drives and Alberto scrolls through radio stations. I lie down in the back for a few minutes with my feet pressed against a window, then get restless and sit up again. When we stop at a traffic light with a little newspaper stand on the corner, one of the front-page headlines catches my eye—**TOMA DE POSESIÓN TOMARÁ LUGAR A PUERTAS CERRADAS**. The presidential inauguration will take place behind closed doors, not open to the public as it usually is.

I pull out my phone—which I keep permanently silenced

now—and scroll through Dani's messages from the past two days. The last text I sent her was a simple *happy new year*. Before that, it's a string of messages from her asking if she can come over, if she can bring something, if she can talk to me. As well-intentioned as I know it is, I wish she'd stop.

It's not that I don't *want* her to come over as much as I don't know where to pull the energy to text back *yes, come at 4*. And then walk to my mother's room and say *a friend is coming at 4*. And then walk back to my room and try not to fall asleep or forget. And then open the door when she's outside. And then talk. And then say, *I'm ready for you to go now.*

I close Dani's chat and go to Camila's. It's pretty much the same story over there.

At the bakery, Abuelo keeps asking us to tell him what smells good, what looks good. Alberto says everything does. I say nothing does. Neither of us is really participating in the way he wants us to, so he finally grabs a tiramisu just so we can go. I'm grateful for it.

On the way home, Abuelo stops to get gas. A man in an Olimpia jersey tries to sell us pirated movies and windshield wipers while we wait for the tank to fill. He keeps flipping through the CDs quickly, bombarding us with titles and small details. I lie back down in my seat.

"¿Y música no tenes?" Abuelo asks him.

Great. Now we're going to be here forever.

"¿Qué música buscaba?" the man replies.

"Good music. None of that reggaeton stuff."

From the front seat, I catch Alberto rolling his eyes.

I can hear the man flipping through more CDs, stopping to show Abuelo some. They go back and forth for a while until Abuelo recognizes something that excites him. He pays the man fifty Lempiras for it, and we're finally free.

"Listen to this song," he tells Alberto and me, popping the CD into the player. I don't sit up. I pretend I don't hear him.

The song he wants us to listen to is immediately familiar, though I don't know why or how. I thought Abuelo was going to play something old and corny, but this seems modern, sad. It's not until halfway through that I realize it's not a song about a breakup, but about death: The God mention is what does it. The whole "God has decided it's time" sentiment.

For a moment, I feel angry. Betrayed, tricked. But still, the melody is soothing. And the lyrics circle back to the beginning, to the parts I liked.

When it's over, Alberto asks Abuelo to play it again, and he obliges. This time, I'm less upset about the God parts because I see them coming. Abuelo plays the song over and over all the way home, which takes longer than usual. Since I'm lying down, I can't be sure, but I think Abuelo drives us around a little bit slower than usual, just to be able to play the song again.

At Mami's request, we don't sing happy birthday to her. She cuts the cake for us, then does a silent prayer in her head that ends with tears traveling down her face. She wipes them away quickly, quietly.

After maybe an hour of sitting in silence, pretending to eat, there's a knock on the front door. Mami and Alberto and I look around at each other in confusion. Abuela and Abuelo headed out a few minutes ago to the workshop, so it can't be for them. For a split second, I'm terrified it's Camila or Daniela or someone else I might've said yes to coming over and then forgotten about. I go to check my phone, then realize I don't have it with me.

This keeps happening—I keep misplacing things, forgetting.

Mami opens the door, and all of us freeze—it's Alicia. I see Mami hesitate for a second before inviting her in, and I get it. Company—any company—is incredibly draining. But it doesn't take long for us to realize that Alicia won't be overstaying.

She looks like shit. I don't remember what she looked like at church the last time we saw her, but she's lost at least ten pounds, if not more. The bags under her eyes are pronounced, almost blue. In black leggings and an oversized T-shirt, she looks fragile and frail, like a sick child. In her hands is a bouquet of white roses.

"Hi," she says tentatively, stepping inside. "I tried calling but couldn't reach anyone."

"That's okay." Mami squeezes her arm. "We're at the table—come sit."

"Hey Libertad, hi Alberto," Alicia says, and we both wave at her. "Is this chair okay?"

I nod. We've never had assigned chairs, though it's sweet of her to ask. My mom sits again and offers her cake, but Alicia shakes her head.

"These are for you," she says, extending the roses out to Mami. "Happy birthday. I'm not staying long, but I did want to get these to you. I know that—well, I can't imagine . . . I'm really sorry." Alicia's eyes grow shiny. "I know this week is—was—your and his week. He talked about it a lot. The double cake and stuff."

Mami nods and takes the roses, lays them down on the table, and grasps one of Alicia's hand in hers. "Thank you, Alicia."

Tears roll down Alicia's face. "I'm so sorry," she whimpers. "I know you don't need another person to take care of right now—"

"Shh, it's okay," Mami says. "It's okay, nena. He'd be so happy you're here with us. I bet he is."

Mami squeezes Alicia's hand. Alberto reaches over to hold Alicia's other hand, and Alicia smiles, laughing just a little through her sobs. It takes me a minute, but I reach out too, and the four of us hold hands and cry.

Alicia stays for another hour, politely moving around a piece of tiramisu on her plate with a spoon but never bringing it close to her mouth. Mami asks her which classes she's taking now, how long until she graduates. She tells us everything, including just how much of her study plan Maynor and she had built together, thinking about what would work with both their schedules.

"I couldn't get him to give me a straight answer about when he would graduate," Mami says, shaking her head. "I thought he must have been flunking out of everything."

"He thought that maybe—" Alicia begins, then stops. For a moment, I think that maybe she's forgotten what she was trying to tell us; this has been happening to me too. Then she starts again. "He thought he'd graduate this coming June. He didn't want to say anything, in case it didn't work out. He was very, very close though."

I stiffen, feeling like I've been punched in the throat.

293

He was so close. So close to something he'd wanted for such a long time, and yet he was still being careful about saying anything. Just in case it didn't work out.

Maynor was never good at celebrating himself. He was good at making others feel good. He was good at being true to himself. I remember, now, thinking of him as Alicia's husband someday. As a dad. . . . He would've been such a fucking good dad.

I excuse myself from the table, the traces of tiramisu that actually made it to my stomach already on their way out. In a span of seconds, I ask Alicia to forgive me, hug her, then run to Mami's bathroom—the one farthest away from everyone—to throw up.

Later, in my room, long after my stomach has settled and Alicia has left, I text Camila and Daniela. I tell them they can visit tomorrow, for an hour. I tell them I can only do it all at the same time and at once.

They both say they'll be here.

THIRTY ONE

Mami's back at work now. Her mourning days—the accumulation of vacation days she didn't take over the years at the hotel—are over. She leaves the same as ever, at six a.m. and not a minute later. Though I'm awake when she's getting ready, it doesn't feel the same. I don't smell her perfume. I don't hear the hair dryer. I just know she's up because the light from the bathroom is on.

Eventually, I fall back asleep. It's just me and Alberto in the house; school doesn't start again for another few days. At some point midmorning, he knocks on my door, then climbs into bed with me. He's sweaty, and his shirt smells a little like spoiled milk, but I still hug him close, kissing the top of his head as my eyelids drift back down.

Hours later, we're both woken up by knocking on the front door. I check my phone. It's two p.m., and both Daniela and Cami have been calling and texting me to let me know they're outside.

"Who is it?" Alberto asks, still half-asleep.

"Camila. And Dani, a friend you don't know."

"Did they bring food?"

I shrug. In the past month, my lack of hunger has been compensated by Alberto's ever-present appetite.

I tie my hair up and put on socks. I'm wearing a soccer jersey that once smelled like Maynor over a pair of shorts. I think, for a second, about changing clothes, but toss the idea in the same breath. Whatever I do, their reaction to seeing me can't be too far from how it felt seeing Alicia yesterday: shocking.

"Hi," I yawn, opening the door. The white light of the outside world blinds me. For a second, Camila and Dani are just two glowing outlines. "I'm so sorry. How long have you been waiting?"

"It's okay," Dani says.

"Not too long," Cami adds.

"Good . . . good." I stand there for a second, scratching my neck, before remembering that this is the part where I invite them inside. "Come in," I say, backing up. "It's just Alberto and me."

I close the door behind them and rub my eyes violently against the brief flash of outdoor light. When I'm done, everything burns, and I can't make myself look at either of them directly. I focus on their nose or forehead for just a second before moving to a point behind or around them. Something about resting my gaze for too long on their faces makes the back of my throat close up.

They both smell amazing—like showers and sunlight. They're wearing similar outfits, jeans and thin, long-sleeve shirts in different shades of gray, which makes me wonder for a moment if they coordinated that. But why would they?

Dani is carrying two soup containers—I'm guessing mondongo from Corina's—and a three-liter bottle of Coke. Cami holds a notebook in one hand and nestles a pizza box into her hip with the other. I feel jealous of Alberto, who's gonna have a feast.

"Where do you want us to put all this?" Cami asks. "Are you hungry? Kitchen?"

I nod and follow her. It strikes me then that Dani has never been in this house, and I'm just letting Camila guide us both.

They both begin to unpack stuff, Dani asking where she can find cups and plates and spoons and napkins and Cami showing her. I nod along and shrug when they ask preference-based questions like "Do you want soup or pizza first?"

Watching them move around each other is, surprisingly, not as weird as I thought it'd be. They both seem calm and happy to be here. I don't know if it's wishful thinking, but they even seem comfortable with each other—maybe they've spoken with each other more than I realize.

Once everything is set and the girls are seated, I yell Alberto's name a couple times. But I don't hear him move or even yell back that he's coming. Before I even realize I'm doing it, I bring my fingers to my mouth and release the loudest, most horrible high-pitched whistle I can—just like Maynor taught me, years ago. Next to me, Dani flinches.

"Jesus," Cami says, rubbing her ear.

I laugh. As much as I hated it when Maynor whistled like that, it gives me immense pleasure when I do it. The air feels good sliding fast through my lips, my lungs fuller, powerful.

"What was that?" Alberto asks as he walks into the kitchen, looking stupefied.

"You weren't responding." I gesture to the table. "And the girls brought you all this food."

"I was coming!" He throws his hands up. "That was too loud."

"Fine, fine. I'm sorry," I relent.

"Hi, handsome. I agree with you, that was too loud," Camila says, reaching out to lay her hand on Alberto's head. He looks up as if just noticing her.

"Hello," he says, the least excited I've ever seen him be around Cami. "You brought food?"

"Yes. I brought pizza, and Dani brought soup."

Alberto turns to look at Daniela. "Hi."

"Beto, this is Dani," I say, pouring myself a glass of Coke from the bottle on the table and taking a sip. "She goes to la UNAH like Maynor."

"Hi." Dani smiles at him. "It's nice to finally meet you."

Alberto smiles back. "Are you also a doctor?"

I don't know why, but that almost makes me spit out my Coke.

"No," Dani responds. "I'm in communications."

"Beto . . . you know Maynor wasn't going to be a doctor, right?" I ask gently. "He was lying to Mami and Abuela about that. Maynor was studying to be a journalist."

Alberto's eyes go wide. For a second, I think he's about to ask me more. But then he just shakes his head, reaching for a slice of pizza. "How many can I eat?"

"As many as you want," I say, before adding, "Just leave some for Dani and Cami too."

Alberto grabs three slices and sits between the two of them. Everything goes quiet as he starts eating.

This is the part I most dreaded. When the shuffling and hello-ing ends, and you have to actually make conversation. Turns out my dread of silence isn't bigger than my exhaustion, though. I stare at the food at the center of the table, knowing that I'll just keep doing this until it's time to go back to sleep, if no one else attempts to carry the burden of talking.

"What do you want to do when you're older?" Dani finally asks Alberto.

He shrugs, taking a bite.

"You used to want to be a fútbol player," I offer.

"Soccer players here don't make any money," he says around the pizza in his mouth. "That's what Abuela told me. And I don't think I want to do it anymore, anyways."

We all nod. "Well, *you* could be a doctor," I say. "That would make Abuela and Mami happy." *Not that doctors make a lot of money here either . . .*

Alberto shrugs again. "Maybe."

"When do you go back to school?" Dani asks all of us.

"Thursday," Cami replies.

"So four—well, three—more days to rest," Dani says.

I'm glad no one's asking any stupid questions, like how we're doing or if we're excited to go back. Alberto and I haven't been to school since before the elections. Both our grades were okay enough that our teachers just decided they wouldn't factor in any remaining assignments. Which I would feel more grateful for, if I cared about things like grades and school projects anymore.

Also, I'm pretty sure everyone missed a few days of school in the week after the elections, between the protests and the MP shutting down most of the city.

"Y'all already back in school?" I ask Dani.

"We started today."

I nod. It doesn't pass me by that Alberto would normally be talking out of his elbows in the presence of two pretty girls Now, his focus lies solely on the pizza in his hand.

I stare at his plate, at the thin lake of orange oil accumulating there, and along his mouth and fingertips. I stare and stare, for I don't even know how long. But it must've been a minute, because I miss both Dani and Cami calling my name.

"Hey," Dani says, touching my elbow. I snap myself out of it.

"Hey," I say, looking from Dani to Cami and back. They wear the same expressions, eyes questioning, worried.

"I was just asking if you wanted me to give you my notes from the last few weeks of class in December," Camila says.

"Right," I say automatically, nodding. "Yes, that'd be great."

I know, even as I say it, that I will never look at them. But if I've learned anything over the past couple of months, it's just how badly people want to feel like they're helping. And how much easier it is to let them.

"Okay." Cami's lips tip up into a smile. "I copied them over for you in this," she says, handing me the notebook she'd been carrying. "They're divided by class."

"Thank you," I say, taking the blue notebook. "This is really helpful."

She nods, and it genuinely does make me a little happy to make her happy, in this moment.

"I need to wash my hands," Alberto declares, throwing down a crumpled napkin onto his plate. The three of us watch him walk out of the kitchen, and silence descends as the door closes behind him.

"So." Dani rubs her hands together. "Is there anything . . . what do you want to do? Should we watch a movie?"

I almost say yes before she's done talking but decide to think about it for another second. Do I want to watch a movie right now. Do I care about the fictitious life of fictitious people. Does it matter to me what happens to them.

"Uh—no. I won't be able to concentrate."

"Okay, okay." Cami nods. "Do you want to—um—"

"I—" I take a deep breath. "I'd like if . . . if the two of you could tell me what's going on, with everything. The elections and the inauguration and stuff." I catch Dani and Cami exchanging looks but decide to push forward anyway. "I don't know anything. I haven't tried to—well, I just haven't kept up. And I know I won't be able to avoid it forever, so I'd rather if the two of you could just . . . catch me up," I finish weakly.

As much as I really don't want to hear about any of this, I know, deep down, it's better this way. If I have to learn anything upsetting, I'd rather it be now through the two people I trust the most. That has to be better than overhearing it at school or the radio. It just has to.

"Okay," Dani agrees.

"I think that makes total sense," Cami adds softly.

It feels like they're both waiting for each other's permission to start talking, which irks me. Now that I've asked, I just want them to get it over with. "Okay," I say, glancing between the two of them. "Who's gonna start?"

"Right," Dani says, clearing her throat. "Where do you want to begin?"

"The power loss," I tell her. This is the last thing I understand—the last thing that happened before everything around me shattered.

"Okay. The power loss," Dani says. "So, when the power came back on, JOH was ahead in the polls. That's when the—the protests started." Dani clasps her hands on the table, leaning forward a little as she meets my gaze. I nod at her to keep going.

"They tried to say those things weren't related," she continues. "The electricity going out and the vote count. But obviously, no one believed that. Over the next few weeks, analyses done by international political rights groups showed indications that the voting system was messed with during the forty minutes it was offline."

"There were other signs too," Camila jumps in. "Like thousands of votes found trashed outside some places. Or whole centers where everyone somehow only voted for the Nationalist party. Or . . ." Cami's words stutter out, and I see her visibly recoil at whatever she's about to say next. " . . . Or votes by dead people. Ballots supposedly filled out by people who have been dead for years."

Dani takes over again, shaking her head. "The government agreed to do a recount. A week later, though, they officially declared JOH the president-elect again. The way they tried to make it explainable was by saying that those early projections didn't reflect rural votes. Only city votes—like Tegucigalpa and San Pedro."

"But no one believed that."

"No, of course not," Cami scoffs.

"So then what happened?"

"More protests." Dani's eyes are steady on me as she talks. "The airport was shut down for a while. But eventually, you know . . ."

"People need to go back to work," I say grimly, and they both nod.

I sit back, thoughts racing as I process everything. All of it makes sense. None of it is surprising. I only have one more question for them, I realize, and it's the one all the others have been building up to.

"Um, can you . . ." I take a deep breath against the nausea turning my stomach. I start again, trying to get the words out as fast as possible before I lose my nerve: "I want to know what's been said about Maynor."

Cami stiffens. Daniela shifts in her chair.

"You mean, like, on social media and stuff?" Dani asks.

"Yeah." I nod, then repeat, more firmly: "Yes. I want to know what people are saying online."

Cami sighs. "The usual, you know? A lot of people are angry, saying the MP need to be held responsible for murder. That Maynor wasn't doing anything wrong, which of course he wasn't. And even if he had been, they still can't just kill people off like that."

"Okay." I take a breath. "Yes, okay. What else?"

Dani crosses her arms, gaze falling to the table for the first time since we've sat down. "There are others—just like always—who are defending the MP. Who argue that they're there to enforce order . . .

even if that means murdering protestors." Dani's cheeks flush, and her eyes narrow as she meets my eyes again. "Those people are wrong, Libertad."

I nod. Things go quiet as the three of us sit there, Dani and Cami watching me as I take this all in.

"Thank you," I finally say, once I find my voice again. "Both of you."

They both give me little half-smiles. For the first time in I don't even know how long, a wave of gratitude, of peace, washes over me. I'm glad they're here.

"Oh! There's one more thing," Camila adds.

"Yeah?"

"Have you checked your Instagram account lately?"

"I deactivated it," I respond, brow furrowing.

"No, no, not your personal account. Your poems account."

"No," I say slowly, not sure where she's going with this. "I haven't opened it in a while."

"Okay, well . . ." Cami sits up in excitement. "All your poems have, like, over twenty thousand likes, Libi. The day after the elections, they went very viral."

"What?" I sit there for a second, stunned, sure I've misheard her. "Twenty thousand?"

"Yes! Maybe even more now." Cami grins at me, and I raise my eyebrows.

"Wow—that is . . . I'm not even sure how to feel."

"It's a lot," Dani agrees. "But your poems have really resonated with people. They're just so *good*."

I can't help it. For just a fraction of a second—maybe even less—I think, *Maynor is gonna flip when I tell him.*

I shudder, wrapping my arms around myself. It's true—Maynor would've been so proud, excited. It makes me incredibly, unbearably sad, to think of all these things that he just . . . doesn't get to know.

"Thanks for telling me," I whisper, swallowing down the lump in my throat.

They both nod, their smiles falling away at the sight of tears catching my lower eyelashes.

"Is there anything that would help you right now, Libertad?" Dani asks quietly.

I shake my head. I can't think of a single thing that would make any of this hurt less. But I don't feel ready for them to go, either.

"How about," Cami starts, tapping her chin. "Do you want to go outside—like just sit on the sidewalk in front of your house—and do that horrible whistle again?"

"That—" I laugh, her suggestion catching me completely off guard. "That's exactly what I want to do right now, actually." I nod, wiping my eyes.

It's the best time I've had in forever, whistling with Cami and Dani in front of my house. Even if I have to listen to them complain about their ears ringing for hours after.

THIRTY TWO

The rumbling of the sewing machines makes everything vibrate; even the inside of my mouth, my teeth clacking against each other.

We're lying on the floor, our heads propped up by thick rolls of fabric. We're not even that close to the machines. In fact, we've purposefully put as much distance as we could between us and their hot motors.

We're in the storage room, where all the fabric and elastic are kept. The concrete floor is cool, a sweet relief from the heat. More effective, even, than the old, loud fans Abuela has in every corner. There's sweat running down the sides of my face—I feel like I'm going to suffocate.

"It'll rain soon. Then this will be over," he says, rolling onto his side to face me. "I bet it'll rain on May first—it always rains May first."

"Says who?" I ask, turning to face him. He's always saying stuff like this, stuff that seems either too vague or too specific to be true.

"I don't know, people. Everyone always says it rains in Tegucigalpa on May first. It makes all the heat and black smoke go away."

"You're making that up."

"No, I'm not," Maynor says, rolling his eyes.

I see it then. He hasn't rolled his eyes in a long time. A habit of his teenage years, outgrown.

I touch his cheek. It's clean-shaven, smooth. No hint of a beard.

"I thought it was January," I say. "It's not hot. It won't get hot for a while."

"It's not January." He shakes his head. "Too hot."

"It is," I insist. "Your birthday was just a few days ago."

"Really?" He smiles. "How old am I?"

"Twenty-six. You're twenty-six."

"Wow—that's old." Maynor raises his eyebrows. "I'm so old."

"Aging is a privilege denied to many," I say.

"That's dumb," he counters.

"Yeah," I agree. "It's very dumb."

"When our parents were twenty-six, they already had, like, both of us."

"Yeah. I don't know how they did it," I reply.

Over the rumbling of the women working in the next room, Abuela calls out to us.

"Libertad!" she yells. "Maynor, come here for a moment. I need your help with something."

Maynor rolls his eyes again. "Come on," he says, dusting off his pants as he stands, grinning. "Let's go see what she wants." He offers his hand to me, and I stretch my fingers up toward his.

I wake up to the rumble of distant thunder, heart pounding against the hollow of my chest.

It's the first time I dreamt of Maynor since he died. I've had nightmares about his death, of course, but I haven't seen him in those—I just know something is wrong, that he's in danger. But I never even hear his voice.

My face is cold. When I touch it, it's also wet. I've been crying in my sleep. I take a few deep breaths, trying to bring myself back to reality, to feel the bed under my body.

My phone tells me it's 2:47 a.m. I lie in bed a few minutes longer, staring at the ceiling, before accepting there's no way I'm falling back asleep anytime soon. I throw the blanket off me. Maybe water or some tea will help. I stop just outside the kitchen door, though, as Mami's hushed voice drifts into the hallway.

"I don't know what to think anymore," she says. "There's a part of me that wonders if he *is* to blame in some way. I didn't know Maynor was calling him, asking for information about government attacks or whatnot." She pauses, and I realize she must be on the phone with someone. After a minute, she continues.

"But why would he even entertain that kind of conversation with him? I just—I don't know. I don't want to think the worst."

I walk into the kitchen. I know exactly who and what she's talking about, so there's really no reason for me to eavesdrop. Mami looks startled, her eyes going wide at the sight of me.

"Ay, Papá, I have to go. We'll talk later, okay?"

"¿Abuelo?" I ask. Mami hangs up the phone and nods.

"Yes. Tío Jose called him today. He asked if it was a good idea to come see us, after what happened at the funeral. He wants to talk."

I take a deep breath as I grab a glass from the cupboard, then move to grab the pitcher of cold water from the fridge.

"I don't want him to come here," I tell her, filling my cup. "I don't want to see him."

"I know," Mami replies. Then, more tentatively: "And I agree . . ."

"So what? Is it Abuela? Is she playing the 'this is my house' card?"

"No." She sighs and signals for me to sit down. I put the pitcher back in the fridge and take my water over to the table. "Not at all. She knows it's not a good idea for him to come here right now. This is hard for all of us, Libertad."

"Okay," I answer shortly.

Mami rests her hand on my back, rubbing it gently up and down. It feels good, soothing. I try my best to push down the sharp, hot pulse of anger in my throat.

"I just want the two of you—" Mami finally starts, after a minute. "Alberto and you—to be okay. I know this is the worst thing that's happened to us, and some days I don't know how we're going to survive it. But no matter what . . . I just want both of you to be okay."

"I know," I say, more subdued this time. And I do know—I see her eyes searching my face, tired and red. We're shells of ourselves, but she's still trying to keep us from tearing apart completely.

"Why are you up so late?" she asks.

"I had a dream about Maynor."

"A bad one?"

"No." I shift in my chair. "I mean, I don't know. I still knew he was

309

dead, in the dream, but he looked so alive—happy, young. No beard."

Mami nods like she understands, like she was there. And I guess she does, better than anyone else.

"Do you ever see him?"

"All the time." She smiles. "I see him grown and little and growing—all of it. I have a lot of dreams of him before he was a teenager, from around seven to twelve." She laughs. "He was horrible then, unmanageable. You have no idea."

I don't, but I remember the stories other have told me, anyway. From the sounds of it, Maynor was unstoppable at that age—thin like a feather, always running, knocking things over, teasing other kids. It took a long time for him to chill out, to find the right outlets for all that energy.

Mami and I sit together for a little longer, her rubbing my back while I take sips of water. When I finish the glass, I reach for her, stretching my fingers in her direction. Just like in the dream with Maynor.

Mami takes my hand and pulls me to her. Though her body feels soft, fragile, her grip is solid and warm. I hug her back as hard as I can.

"I love you so much," she whispers into my hair.

I clutch her tighter to me. "I know, Ma. I love you too."

Half an hour later, rain taps lightly against my bedroom window. My thoughts rush back to the stormy day of Maynor's funeral.

I hadn't considered all the people we didn't see in our day-to-day lives who would be there. I could barely think of myself being there.

But then I spotted him—Tío José in his black pressed suit, shaking water off his umbrella, that stupid Honduras flag pin government employees sport on their breast pocket.

Something snapped inside me. Maynor had felt so much guilt after the UNAH shooting, the faulty information Tío José had given him that he'd provided to the student front. And wasn't it the government, ultimately, that had killed Maynor? Who was to say that that hadn't been on purpose, that the two weren't connected?

In my head, I made the jumps and lines necessary to connect the dots. It was the pin, I told myself, that damn pin. I didn't want to see it anywhere, much less so close to my brother's corpse.

Before I could even process my body's movements, I was in front of Tío José, who had moved to stand next to Abuela. I shoved him. But he barely moved, his body firm like a rock.

"Did you know?" I yelled, turning to Abuela. "Did you know your son had phone calls with Maynor about the MP's attacks on the fronts?"

"What are you talking about?" José said, grabbing my wrists.

Abuela closed her eyes. When she opened them, tears were welling in the corners. I jerked out of her son's grasp.

"You gave Maynor fake information!" I screamed at him. "Did you *want* him to carry that guilt? That's what killed him. That fucking guilt and the fucking MP and this. Fucking. Pin." I grunted, pulling on it.

It didn't come off. The goddamned thing stayed secured to his chest.

The tears Abuela had been holding in cascaded down her face, and José wrapped his arms around her. Mami appeared next to me then, tugging me away to a private room. I tried to explain myself but kept talking too fast for her to understand.

"We all did this," I said, waving my arms around. Mami sat in a chair in the corner of what appeared to be a storage room, holding her head in her hand. "It's *his* fault that Maynor felt so guilty. And it's Abuela's fault that he couldn't share all the political work he was doing with us. And now what? We just go on pretending that she and José don't support the people who killed him?"

I pressed a finger into my chest. "And it's *my* fault for not telling you about his secret life. It's all of our faults that Maynor is dead," I sobbed.

The phone in Mami's pocket kept going off with message notifications. She took it out, silenced it, and put it back, then raised her gaze to meet mine. As hard as I tried, I couldn't read the expression in her eyes.

"Are you ready to go back now?" she asked me quietly.

I nodded. I realized then that there was nothing else I could do, nothing else I could say. I nodded, and Mami stood up and took my hand, walking me back to the room where my brother's body was waiting.

CARMEN

He might as well have been a stranger. Familiar dress style
aside—blue jeans, button-up shirt, sleeves folded elbow-high—the
man looked nothing like her ex-husband of seventeen years.

The last time she saw Diego, six years ago in a lawyer's office, he
didn't meet her eyes once. The room was small and cold; an aggres-
sive AC unit kept running the whole time. Both their lawyers were
present.

The agreements of the divorce were read out loud. They'd never
owned a house together or shared a bank account. The dissolution
of their marriage was simple: There was nothing to split. Not even
the care of the children.

After a two-year-long legal battle, in which Carmen demanded
Diego took responsibility for at least *some* of their children's educational or living costs, and Diego claimed over and over again
that he didn't have the means, they reached a settlement. Diego
would contribute, in no way, to his children's care. Custody would
be solely hers.

Now he stood in front of her, outside the church where their eldest child's body estaba siendo velado. His head was clean-shaven, and he'd gained some weight. Mostly, he just looked older, the wrinkles around his eyes and mouth more pronounced. She wondered if he, too, was taking in the differences in her body, her face.

"Diego," she said, gesturing with her chin. "Let's go to the side of the building."

He followed her. He knew she didn't want him to be seen here—not by her family. She'd said as much through text.

A part of her had expected him to complain. To say he had as much right as anyone in her family to be here. But he hadn't. He'd simply said he'd be here. He'd meet her outside.

"Has it—did it start?" he asked once they reached the side of the building, staring at his feet. The shadow of the church covered them from the sun.

"No, not yet. In a few minutes."

"Okay," he said, still not meeting her eyes.

Carmen grimaced. Her heart and body were in so much pain, it was hard to decipher if any of it could be attributed to the man standing in front of her. But she didn't think so—if anything, the only feeling he elicited in her was pity.

Diego Morazán was the father of her children. And he'd abandoned those children without looking back. Now they shared a dead child, one he hadn't even been in contact with in the past few years. At least, not that she knew about.

"When was the last time you spoke to him?" she asked.

"A year ago," Diego replied, finally glancing up at her. She couldn't read his eyes. She'd once been very good at it—at detecting any sort of brewing storm in them.

"He didn't tell me about it."

"We didn't see each other." Diego shrugged. "I texted him a bunch, asked if we could get together for coffee. He only responded once."

"What did he say?"

"That he was busy with school, but he'd let me know. He said Alberto had been asking about me. Thought maybe he could bring him too."

Carmen nodded—she remembered that faintly now. Alberto had had more questions about Diego, now that he was older. Now that, after nearly a decade, the painful memories of what he'd witnessed as a toddler had dulled. He'd even mentioned Maynor asking him how he'd feel about meeting up with their father sometime.

But then life had gotten busy, and neither Beto nor Maynor said anything else about it to her. Now she wondered, staring down her ex-husband, if he was thinking the same thing she was: the irony of Maynor's lack of response. Just how far the tables had turned.

A few months after they separated, Maynor had asked her if she'd be okay with him reaching out to his father. To see if he wanted to get coffee, watch a game. Anything.

He hadn't wanted a father-son relationship, exactly. Or at least, he didn't tell her that. But he did want to talk. To hear what Diego had to say about everything he'd done. To know what his plans for life looked like now.

Of course, she'd said yes. It wasn't easy, after all the ways he'd hurt her—hurt them. But Maynor was seventeen, nearly an adult, and she'd never dream of keeping her children away from their father. Not if that's what they wanted.

It hadn't even mattered, Carmen thought bitterly. After standing Maynor up a few times, Diego had completely disappeared from their lives. She only saw him again to sign the divorce, years later, and that was it. Until Maynor's death, after which she had texted him to let him know the details of the funeral. She had half expected his number to have changed. But the message went through.

"Okay," she said, after another long beat of silence. "I should head back."

"Was he happy?" Diego asked.

"Maynor?"

"Yes."

Carmen sighed. She hadn't slept for two days. Every muscle in her body hurt so much, at some point she'd gone numb. Inside the church her two youngest—her living children—were waiting to view their brother's body. They needed her to come back. There was no way they could do it without her.

Another memory came to her then—Maynor's first word. It had been *papá*. She remembered Diego's excitement when he'd first uttered it, and every other time after.

"I think so," she said at last, shifting her weight from one foot to the other. "He had a girlfriend he really liked. He was passionate, loving. A good brother . . . and a very, *very* good son."

Through the tears clouding her vision, Carmen caught Diego bowing his head.

Once, a few years ago, she heard from a mutual acquaintance that he'd remarried. She immediately asked to not be told any more. It wasn't that it hurt her; she hardly thought about him. She just didn't care. Why waste a second thinking about the man who had, in one way or another, rejected the three people she loved more than anyone else in the world?

"I have to go," she choked out, starting to turn away.

"Carmen," Diego called to her, softly.

She turned back around.

"I'm . . . I'm gonna go," he said, running a hand over his head, through his nonexistent hair. For a second, the gesture was striking. For a second, he looked just like Maynor.

"Go where?"

"I have a . . . a thing I have to do. That I couldn't move. I just . . . I thought I'd come to tell you, in person."

She didn't know what to say. She didn't feel hurt. She didn't feel upset. She didn't even feel disappointed. Her body had no room to hold even another ounce of pain.

"If I could move it, I would. I tried really hard. I didn't know this—"

"You didn't know your son was going to die?"

Diego didn't say anything. He looked again at his feet, and she looked at him. After a few seconds, she walked back into the church.

THIRTY THREE

"Just try to focus on what your teachers are saying. The day will go by fast," Mami tells Alberto and me before pulling into the school's parking lot. It rained all night. A thin, damp layer of gray coats the city.

"Tonight, I'll ask you to tell me one thing you learned, so you need to remember it," she adds, putting the car in park.

Alberto clicks his tongue, a new habit that's only strengthened over the last few weeks. I don't know how long he'll get away with it.

After we get out of the car and Mami drives away, Alberto stays by my side, holding on to the straps of his backpack with both hands. Usually, he sprints past me as soon as he can—eager for those few minutes before class when he can either play or talk soccer, exchanging player stickers for his World Cup album. Today, he drags his feet around the brown water puddles littering the ground.

"I don't want to go," Alberto mumbles.

"Me neither," I admit. "But I think we have to."

"Why?"

It's a good question. I tilt my head, considering for a minute. Even then, I don't have a good answer.

"Honestly . . . I don't know," I say slowly. "Because school is important?" That sounds right, logical. I nod, pressing on as we walk.

"Because if we miss any more days, they won't let me graduate, and they won't let you move on to the next grade. And we can't stay home all day forever. We need to get back to some semblance of normal."

"What does *semblance* mean?"

"Like, *looks*. A life that looks like normal. Resembles."

"But it isn't. It looks like before but it isn't."

I sigh. I mean, yeah. I can't argue with that.

"I know," I respond. "I miss him too."

Our paths split as the two of us move around a car, rejoining a few feet away from the school. Alberto clicks his tongue again. "Playoffs begin this week," he says.

"What?"

"Playoffs, para el mundial."

"Oh." My mind reels at the swift change in topic, but I try my best to catch up. "That's . . . cool. Are you excited?"

"No." Alberto sounds exasperated with me now. "Maynor and I were supposed to watch them all. Even the ones at three a.m. our time. Then we both needed to predict winners from the quarter finals on."

I stop walking, so he stops walking. I turn to him and kneel a bit so we can be eye to eye.

"Are you asking me if we can watch them together?"

Alberto nods. "But you need to learn all the names of the players and stuff."

I clutch my heart and release a dramatic, long-suffering sigh. That pulls a smile out of him. "Fine," I tell him. "I will learn all the players' names 'and stuff.'"

"Good." He points at me. "First one is Thursday at eleven p.m., Brazil versus Canada. Don't be late."

I roll my eyes for him, like Maynor would have in a moment like this. "I'll be ready."

Beto hugs me, then sprints away.

The rain starts back up, which means no morning fútbol match. I'm grateful for it—I was dreading, more than anything, that time when we all sit outside and everyone tries to make small talk around me. Or worse, with me.

Instead, I head straight to my first-period classroom, chem, which is empty, and put my head down on a table and my jacket over my head. I manage to sneak in maybe ten minutes of silence before people begin to trickle in. Then I take out the notebook Camila filled out for me and flip through the pages, pretending I'm reading and catching up.

But it isn't long before Valeria and Carla come in, telling me hi and sitting around me. Soon, even the notebook shield becomes pointless.

"This rain sucks," Carla whines. "I straightened my hair for literally nothing."

"Do you want a ponytail?" Valeria offers.

"No, I have one."

"I think your hair looks good, though," I say, testing my voice, forcing myself to try out a normal interaction with my friends. It's okay, I decide.

"Are you sure?" Carla asks, pulling up the camera on her phone to check for herself.

"Yeah," I reply.

"So—first day back in a long time. Is it weird?" Valeria says, turning toward me.

"More like pointless." I shrug, thinking about what Alberto said this morning. "Or like, weird in the way that it feels and looks the same as always. But it isn't."

They nod.

"That makes sense," Carla says, putting her phone away.

"We're here if you need help with anything, like catching up," Valeria adds.

The start of class is clunky. Heavy rain makes traffic worse than usual, so a bunch of buses are late. Every time Mr. Bodden begins to say something, someone opens the door and interrupts. The third or fourth person to do so is Camila. She sits on my other side, smiles as we lock eyes.

I'm glad to see her. After her visit, we started texting a bit more. Not as much as before, but still. Sunday night, she sent me a link to a pirated version of the 2002 *Spider-Man* movie. We pressed play at the same time on our phones, watched all of it together.

We're a quarter of the way through first period when the power cuts off, the overhead lights going out. A few minutes later, the door opens again and seven people come in, presumably from the same bus. They scatter around the class trying to find an open chair, rainwater dripping from their hair and backpacks.

One of them is Pablo. His hair is short, shorter than I've ever seen it. He moves around the room, trying to find a chair, but can't. I'm confused because there's clearly an empty one right next to Camila. I almost make the effort to call him over, when he spots it himself and, hesitantly, approaches our table.

"Is it okay if I sit here?" he asks Cami.

She nods. He sits. Everyone else around us shifts uncomfortably in their chairs, and no one needs to tell me they've broken up.

For the rest of class, I try my best to concentrate on the formulas outlined in green and red Expo marker on the board when someone else opens the door. This time, it's not a student, but the principal's assistant—Mrs. Gutiérrez. She tells us that since there's no power, the bell won't ring, but it's time to move on to second period.

"You heard her, guys," Mr. Bodden sighs. "Pack it up. Make sure you take a picture of the board if you didn't have enough time to get it all down. Oh, and one more thing—" he calls out over the growing clamor of people packing up, students from classrooms around ours flooding the hallway. "Miss Katherine wanted me to remind you that if you applied to any colleges abroad, you should check in with her regularly at her office for any mail."

By the time third period rolls around, I'm nearly caught up on most major points of gossip; Valeria and Carla seem to enjoy filling me in. Despite everything, listening to the highs and lows of their voices as they tell me about Pablo and Camila's breakup, and Vicky's return to school, and who got with who since I've been gone is exactly what I want to be doing right now. I'm relieved to be part of a conversation that has nothing to do with me, that requires so little thought on my part.

"Well, he says she didn't really give him much of an explanation," Carla says, opening her locker. "She just stopped answering his texts or calls. Eventually, she told him she wasn't feeling it anymore."

"When did this happen?" I ask.

"Before winter break," Valeria says, hugging books to her chest. "Maybe the week after the elections? But Pablo says she started ghosting him even before that."

I don't know why Cami didn't say something to me. Then again, I also don't know when she would have. I guess that'd be a weird thing to bring up to your friend whose brother just died.

"I thought they were doing good," I comment, holding Carla's locker door open for her as she searches its depths for a notebook. "They seemed just fine at Cien Años."

"I don't think they did though," Carla's voice echoes out, into the space between me and Valeria. "That was actually the first night I thought something was off."

I rack my brain for any signs of the two of them acting weird around each other that night. But I can't. I was so focused on Dani and the reading and my poem—at least, until Cami's and my fight at the gas station. Mostly though, I can't think about it anymore because Maynor pops up everywhere in those memories: Laughing with my friends. Kissing Alicia. Handing me a marker over the stolen plastic table.

I shrug. "Yeah, maybe."

It's not until the end of our last class before lunch, psychology, when the power comes back on. Over the ensuing cheers, Mr. Cruz warns us not to celebrate too early. The rain is expected to continue for at least forty-eight more hours.

Sure enough, the sky darkens to a shade of lead. The raindrops are heavy and cold against the backs of my neck and arms as Carla, Valeria, and I run between buildings to the cafeteria. There aren't enough tables for all the students eating inside today, so the three of us grab food and sit on the floor, our backs pressed to one of the walls.

The single TV suspended high on the wall opposite to us runs news footage. Reporters are covering the disarray that storms like this always bring to the city—flooded streets, trees falling into the road, neighborhoods being evacuated. The chatter of students around us makes is impossible to hear anything, and I lose myself, for a moment, in the captions scrolling along the bottom of the screen.

"So she didn't say anything to you?" Carla asks, bringing me back.

"Who?" I ask, disoriented.

"Camila," Carla says.

"No. But we haven't really talked," I reply, waving to Cami as I spot her in line to buy food. My phone digs painfully into my thigh from the way I'm sitting, one leg over the other. I take it out to put it in my backpack, but I see I have a message from Dani from less than a minute ago.

Have you seen the news?

My heart drops for a second, before I realize she must be talking about the rain.

Yes this sucks, I type. I'm about to hit send when Valeria touches my arm.

"Dude, look," she gasps, pointing to the TV.

It feels like I blinked and missed something, something big. Most students who were sitting on the floor are now standing, huddled closer to the TV. The chatter is gone—no one's talking. The footage on the screen has changed from flooded streets to a shot of black smoke bisecting a dark gray sky. A red box at the bottom of the screen reads **PRESIDENT'S SISTER PRESUMED TO BE IN HELICOPTER ACCIDENT—HAPPENING NOW.**

THIRTY FOUR

For the first time ever, the lady working the cash register pulls a TV remote out of one of the front pockets of her apron.

I've heard my classmates begging her for it since the first day that TV went up. She always had an excuse—we don't have it, we're not allowed to give it to students, the batteries are dead. Whenever the boys wanted to put on a game happening during our lunch break, they had to stand on a chair and manually change the channels.

But today, Doña Almita produces the remote, turning the volume all the way up. There's a bunch of teachers here now too; a crowd gathers by the front doors, their hair and clothes wet from the rain. I imagine that pretty much everyone who doesn't have a class to attend or teach has found their way here.

"According to a statement from the air force, the aircraft took off at 9:34 a.m. and made contact with the ground for the last time at 9:47 a.m., indicating that it had less than ten minutes left to reach its destination, the city of Comayagua," a reporter says. He's standing in a field of unkept grass, his rain jacket hood over his head. Water drips from his arms as he gestures to the city behind him, shrouded in smoke from the crash.

The scene cuts back to one of the news anchors in the studio. "La Casa Presidencial has not yet confirmed that Hilda Hernández was in the helicopter that crashed down a few kilometers outside of the city of Comayagua," the reporter says. "Por el momento, there are no confirmed deaths. Hilda Hernández is, of course, President Hernández's older sister, as well as the appointed minister of Communications and Strategy."

The air stills in my lungs. I feel out of my body—like I'm watching a movie. Like I can see myself, the back of my head, and the heads of everyone around me, our eyes all glued to the TV. It all seems staged, somehow.

"There's no fuckin' way," someone near me mutters. "This is fake, right?"

"Maybe it's real, but it wasn't an accident," someone replies. "Los Hernándezes run the biggest cartel in the country! This could've been one of their enemies, some other cartel."

Whispers amplify around me. It feels like my ear is pressed to the inside of a shell, the incessant *whoosh* of an ocean of theories reverberating through my skull.

The president's sister is dead, maybe killed. My phone screen lights up on my lap with another text from Dani:

> They're saying it's a cortina de humo.
> That they might be staging this to distract everyone from the few remaining protests.

I don't know what to text back. That could be it, though it seems like a pretty terrible plan. I mean, she'd have to pretend to be dead forever, right?

My vision goes cloudy. A buzzing noise rings through my mind. I don't notice that I'm picking at the skin around my nails until I see the blood pooling at the cuticle of my pointer finger.

"Do you need a Band-Aid?" Cami asks. Her voice startles me. I realize that she must have left the lunch line to come talk to me—she's not carrying any food.

"No, I'm good," I say, wiping the blood off on my pants.

A few people start shushing everyone else, pointing at the TV.

"O-okay, yes," says the news anchor, holding a hand to his earpiece. "It is now confirmed. Hilda Hernández, the president's sister, was indeed in the helicopter that crashed down forty miles north of Tegucigalpa a few minutes ago, along with another five people, all members of the military police. We're going to the scene with our compañero Eduardo Melgar."

The frame around him becomes smaller, moving across the screen, as a frame with the on-scene reporter pops up next to him.

"That's correct, Renán. I'm right here, just a few kilometers from where the crash took place. You can hear the firefighters' sirens behind me. Only a few seconds ago it was confirmed that, lamentablemente, there were no survivors in this accident. We have yet to learn the cause, but it is presumed that the poor weather conditions played a role."

Someone whistles and yells out, "¡Fuera JOH!"

A bunch of other whistles and yells follow.

I don't know how I feel. A part of me wants to join them. This is the man who's made our lives a living hell the past few years. This is the man at the source of everything—the military takeover, the rigged elections, the night of Maynor's death.

And he just lost his sister. I can't ignore the pain of that, of losing an older sibling. Like I have. The crater of loss that must be swallowing him whole. Us.

I bite down on the meat around my thumb. It's wet and tender between my teeth. Cami touches my shoulder. I think I have to throw up.

"Come on," she says, motioning her head to the front doors. "Let's get out of here."

I look down at my phone. "It's still twenty more minutes before lunch is over."

"Doesn't matter," she say swith a shrug, "come on."

I stand up but stumble, dizzy. Everything's too loud—the TV, the whistling, the rain, the yelling.

"Here," Cami says, extending her hand. I take it.

We run through the rain to the main high school building and head to our next class. Cami throws her drenched backpack over a chair and sits down, gesturing for me to take the desk next to her.

"This is crazy." I shiver, trying to rub warmth back into my arms.

Camila nods. "How are you feeling?"

"I don't know. I—I don't know how I'm supposed to feel," I say.

"However you feel is how you're supposed to feel," she says.

"I just . . . I just want a moment to *breathe*. It's too much." I squeeze my eyes shut, rubbing my hands over my face.

"I know," she whispers.

When I open my eyes, my vision is all blue and purple. I blink fast to clear the spots.

"Something bad is always happening here," I say. "Every time we turn on the TV. And after Maynor . . . I don't know. I think—I think leaving this place might be the only answer. The only way out."

"Libi, I'm not sure it's that simple."

I exhale sharply, louder than I mean to.

"But what if it is?" I glance toward Cami. She purses her lips; something like pain flashes in her eyes.

We fall silent for a moment as a gust of wind shakes the classroom windows. Cami looks down at her desk. I open my mouth to say something else, something not at all related to the helicopter crash, then close it again as I talk myself out of it.

But what's the point of not asking? It's just the two of us in the cold, damp space of this room. And the worst thing that could happen to me already has.

"So . . . you broke up with Pablo?"

Cami's eyes meet me. She looks taken aback, like I interrupted her mid-thought.

"Uh, yeah. Before the elections."

I nod. "What happened?"

"I . . . I don't know. I wasn't feeling it anymore."

"Why?"

I'm thrown by her choice of words, the exact words she used with Pablo.

She raises her eyebrows, and I can tell she wasn't expecting me to insist on an answer. But I can't do this anymore. Just watching things happen around me and not dig any deeper. Not at least try to understand.

"I guess I just never really felt it."

"Then why were you dating him?"

She sighs, though I don't think it's in frustration—her expression looks too soft for it. The light outside shifts, as if a cloud has moved, and a delicate pearl glow frames Camila as she speaks.

"I mean . . . He's funny. We watch some of the same shows, like similar things. And it was nice to have someone around all the time to text and talk to, especially when—well, you know. When you didn't have a phone."

A bitter *What the hell?* springs to mind, ready to burst out of my mouth. But I stop myself, considering her answer for another second, two, before responding.

My mind is on alert, I realize, ready to fill in the gaps of what she's saying. Filling in the gaps means I got to decide for her, for the both of us. It means I can protect myself.

But maybe the truth is better. Even if it's scary. Even if it hurts.

"I don't mean to be judgmental, Cami . . . But that makes it sound like you full-on dated a person who had real feelings for you just because I wasn't able to text you back."

"Wait, what?" Cami's voice rises in panic. "No. That's not what I mean at all."

"Okay." I nod. "Then what do you mean?"

"It's—it's more complicated than that. I'm not saying I didn't like Pablo as a person. Just . . . it took me a while to realize that. That that was all there was."

Cami runs her fingers through her hair, tugging a strand behind her ear. She's nervous. So am I—I can't get my knee to stop bouncing. But I'm also relieved. This isn't going as horribly as I once thought it might. Camila's not angry. She's being honest with me. The least I can do is meet her halfway.

"Cami . . ." My eyes drift up to the speckled ceiling. "I have to tell you something. Just . . . just listen for a second, okay?"

When my gaze falls back to hers, I catch Cami taking a deep breath. She nods at me to continue.

"I . . . I saw your texts. The ones you sent before, months ago, when I didn't have my phone." Cami's eyes widen, and I force myself to keep talking, to say what I need to say before I lose my courage. "I know I told you my phone was wiped clean, but I was lying. I got your texts. All of them."

Cami's face flushes. I wait for it—for her to get mad, to curse me out.

"So . . . that day I went to your house, after your birthday. You'd already—"

"Yeah. I'd seen them. Just the night before, though," I add feebly.

"Why didn't you say something?"

I sigh. "Because I didn't want anything to change between us, Cami. Things were already so awkward. And it seemed . . . Well, a part of me thought, maybe—maybe you regretted sending those texts."

Camila freezes. For a moment, I think that she's going to deny it. That she's going to tell me that she meant every word of those texts. That she's changed her mind yet again, and there is no world, no universe, in which she'd ever want anything other than friendship between us.

But she doesn't. "Yeah," she says simply, in a small, tentative voice. "I did regret it."

"Really?" I can't help it—a grin pulls the sides of my mouth. Cami smiles back at me.

"Wait—wait." I shake my head. "So what does that mean? Like, for us? We never did get to talk after the elections, after . . ." My voice peters out.

"I don't know," Cami says. Her smile falls a little, but her eyes stay soft. "I really do love you, Libertad. You're my best friend. The person I like talking to the most. I just . . . I wish I could've admitted that I had feelings for you—even if just to myself—a long, long time ago. Before everything went down the way it did."

"Same—I feel the exact same way," I confess.

We lock eyes. I don't know what I look like to her in this moment, but I know her face has a shape, a color I recognize. Like looking through a window display at a reality you understand to have been possible, so close you could touch it. But not quite. I know this face, this arrangement of the human mask, because I see it every time my mother goes to call my dead brother's name before remembering there's no one coming.

The bell rings then, startling the both of us. I catch Cami steadying herself with a deep breath. In just a minute or two, we'll be surrounded by thirty other people. Fear snakes through me as I realize that this moment—and the honesty of it—might soon be lost forever.

Camila lays a hand on my thigh and squeezes. Heat shoots up my leg, through my body, at her touch. It's a feeling I didn't know I could feel again. Her gaze is steady on mine, even as other students start filing in around us, buzzing with news about the crash.

Cami doesn't lift her hand from my thigh.

THIRTY FIVE

It's 1:20 a.m. and the game hasn't started, but I'm already fight-ing sleep. Every Tuesday and Thursday and Sunday of the past week, Alberto has made sure we stayed up to watch every single soccer match leading up to the World Cup this summer. Even the ones between teams that don't seem all that important to him. Teams, he informs me, that have never even made it past the first round.

I've kept my promise so far. If it's a game happening at dawn our time, then we're up, sitting in front of the TV, ready to share our predictions and *fuck*s and *come on*s and *dale dale*s. The nights before these games Mami sleeps in my room, so we can take hers. But sometimes, like tonight, she stays with us, drifting in and out of sleep, jerking awake when Alberto raises his voice.

We keep the volume low, since it's after midnight and Abuela is sleeping. I keep trying to remember the last time Alberto and Maynor did this, how they pulled it off. Maybe Alberto was too young for it—the last World Cup was in 2014, after all.

"So. Who do we want to win this game?" I ask him.

"It doesn't matter," he replies, not taking his eyes off the TV. "But whoever wins will play Brazil. I think Brazil will win against either, so it's whatever."

I fight the urge to ask him why we're watching this game at all then. Plus, if Alberto watches it for the same reasons as Maynor, then I already know.

Maynor always liked watching the game for the game itself. He'd comment on the technique of a pass or the strategy of a play. *It must be like watching a dance,* I muse as players run across the screen. Like watching Mami coordinate the setup of a wedding, or Abuela figure out how she'll manage to turn a child's idea into a real costume.

Maybe it's like me, bringing ideas down from the sky, swirling words around my mouth. Writing down lines and scribbling things out until, at last, something clicks. And a poem is born.

Whenever Alberto's not looking, I pull out my phone, texting with one hand by the side of my leg where he can't see it. I've been using my phone a little more lately, mostly to talk to Camila or Daniela or Valeria. I even redownloaded Instagram to look at my poetry account.

Dani and Cami were right: Each poem had over 25k likes. I have more than five hundred unopened messages from people all over the country. It's still too overwhelming for me to go through them, though.

We're supposed to hear back in the next month or so, Valeria texts me now. We've both become obsessed with talking to each other about studying abroad, about leaving Honduras this fall. News of the helicopter accident our first day back only emphasized what my brother's death taught me: This city is not survivable. And if you survive it, you are left mourning and wanting every second of your life.

> I think we got a good chance

I still don't know what I want to do next, if I actually get in. The only thing that comes to me is Maynor, and his incomplete journalism track. Maybe it's not logical, but I want to finish it for him. I had no idea just how close he'd been to graduating.

"Come on, come on, come *on*," Alberto pleads at the tiny men running around the field. His face is blue with the light's reflection, faint purple circles under his eyes.

"I thought you said you didn't care who won," I tease him.

"I just want someone to score," he replies. "So, it gets more interesting."

"Right."

> We should have enough time to figure out all the visa stuff, once we find out.

> As long as protests don't shut down the embassy for weeks again

> That would suck.

Protests against JOH and the elections are still raging across the city. So many others, people who had been holding on to hope for a better life under a new leader, have decided to leave. Two days ago, local news channels reported a caravan of over three thousand people setting out from San Pedro Sula to the US. The majority is not expected to make it.

> We'll see.

> Something always happens.

I lift my eyes from the phone to the TV screen. A midfielder has repossessed the ball from a player of the other team. He's moving fast down the left side, looking for a striker to pass it to.

Alberto and I lean forward—it's a good play. I hold on to the edge of the bed, excited for the possibility of a goal. The screen freezes for a second, then turns black. As does the rest of the house.

"¡Puta!" Alberto yells.

"¿Qué pasó?" Mami asks in a slow, just-woke-up voice.

"The power's out," I say, sighing. "Sorry, Beto."

"Alberto, don't curse," Mami mumbles, turning over. Her rolling shakes the bed under us.

"What now?" Alberto exhales into the darkness.

"I don't know," I say in the direction of his silhouette. "Let's wait for like, ten minutes. If it doesn't come back, then we just . . . go to bed, I guess."

"Ugh, every single day."

It's not, but it is, like, every three days or so.

"Just relax. Maybe it'll come back on in a few minutes."

"Whatever," he grunts, flopping down next to me.

We sit in silence, Mami's soft snores the only noise around us. I think of other times this has happened: The sudden power loss. Being left in the dark for unknown periods of time.

If it happened during the day, Maynor would go to the pulpería and get us plantain chips and Coke, and we would wait and eat and play music on his phone. If it happened during the nighttime, like right now, he'd light a candle and play with the flame, flicking it between his fingers. He'd let the wax harden on his skin and tell us stories that collapsed into other stories. Stories about our dad, or Martha, or something only he can remember.

I'm wrong. The power doesn't come back ten or even twenty minutes later.

"Alberto," I call in a low voice, just in case he's asleep. "Are you awake?"

"Yes," he chirps immediately. "I'm hungry."

"All right. Let's go to the kitchen and see what we can find."

We get up carefully, trying not to wake Mami. I turn my phone's flashlight on and point it toward the floor ahead of us. In the kitchen, I sit and let Beto take my phone to look through the cupboards and inside the fridge. I don't notice the light from the candle approaching until it's right next to us.

"What are you doing up?" Abuela asks.

"Nothing," I blurt, jumping a little in my seat. "We were watching a game, but the power went out," I add. "And now Alberto is hungry."

Abuela walks to the corner cupboard, opens it, and pulls down a jar of peanut butter from the highest shelf. In the glow of her candle, I see Alberto's eyes lighting up. We never get to have peanut butter, 'cause that shit is expensive and Mami hates buying it. She always complains that Alberto eats it way too fast.

"Get some bread," Abuela says to Alberto. "I'll make you a sandwich with peanut butter and some jalea de fresa I made on Saturday."

"Yes!" Alberto cheers.

"Do you want one, Libertad?" Abuela asks me.

"Yes please," I say, even though I'm not really hungry. Abuela pulls four slices from the bag Beto hands her.

The two of us watch as she make us peanut butter and jelly sandwiches in the candlelight. She looks smaller than normal, tired. I wonder if she's actually shrinking, or just slouching.

"Here," she says, placing two plates in front of us. "Don't tell your mom I showed you where the peanut butter is."

Alberto takes a giant bite of his sandwich, and the two of us nod. Abuela starts putting things away, wiping a wrinkled hand over the counter to make sure she's left no crumbs.

She and I haven't talked much since Maynor's funeral. I've avoided her, and it seems like she's avoided all of us. Staying hours and hours in the workshop. Coming home around midnight and leaving, often, before sunrise.

There's no way she has that much work between January and February, especially with all the protests still shutting everything down. What she does during all those hours, I can't imagine. Maybe she rearranges the rolls of fabric. Sweeps a third time, a fourth. Prays.

"How's the workshop?" I ask her.

Abuela pauses as she puts the peanut butter back in its spot, then closes the cupboard door. "Good," she says, brushing her hands over her nightgown. "Slow, but good. Little odd jobs here and there. We'll be okay."

I nod. "Anything fun?'

"No, not really. It's almost time to start thinking about the swimsuits for Semana Santa, though."

"We should go somewhere this year. We never go anywhere," Alberto chimes in, between bites of his sandwich.

"Maybe we find a pool this year," Abuela suggests. "Or we could visit Abuelo in the north coast."

"Maybe," I say. But I don't think we will.

"How's school?" Abuela asks, sitting down with us.

"Boring," Alberto tells her. "Every day is the same."

"Hmm," she says, and I can tell she doesn't love that answer. But she lets it go. "How about you, Libertad? Graduation is coming up."

"It's okay," I reply. "I'm mostly waiting to hear back from the two colleges I applied to abroad."

"When will you know?"

"In the next two months or so."

"En el nombre de Dios, hija."

"Yeah." I sigh. "We'll see."

"Maynor was so happy the day he heard back from that school in Argentina," Abuela says, smiling a little as she brushes a crumb off Alberto's cheek.

"What school in Argentina?" Alberto asks. I'm confused too. I have no idea what she's talking about.

"La Universidad de Buenos Aires, I think," Abuela says. "He

wanted to study communications or journalism, something like that there."

"And he got in?" I ask, astonished. I can't believe that I don't remember any of this.

"He did," Abuela says, nodding. "But then, you know how it is. It was around the time your parents separated, and the coup was the year before. There wasn't any money. Everything was so fragile."

That's right—this would have been about seven years ago, the same time we moved in with Abuela.

"Things are a little better now, though," Abuela continues. "If you get a good scholarship, we'll see how we can help. The government also offers some becas for people studying abroad—"

"I don't want any money from the government."

Abuela stops talking. The annoyance that surges through my body is too sharp, too quick, to be rational, but I can't help it. My plate clinks as I get up and drop it into the sink, throwing away my half-eaten sandwich. Alberto follows me into my bedroom.

"Libi, wait."

"¿Qué pasó?" I snap.

"Oh, come on." Alberto crosses his arms. "You can't be upset all the time about everything."

"I'm not," I snap. He stares me down, and I try again. "I'm not upset about everything, Beto," I say slowly, enunciating every word. "I'm not upset when we watch games together."

"But you're not happy either. You're not excited about it like Maynor."

"Okay, well, I'm not Maynor," I retort, flames of anger scorching the sides of my face.

"Yeah. I know." Alberto rolls his eyes.

"I don't know how to do that, Alberto. I don't know how to just . . . just *be* Maynor for you. Maybe you should find someone else to watch the games with. Someone who cares."

I regret saying it the moment it comes out of my mouth. Hurt flashes across Alberto's face. Still, I'm too mad to call the words back.

I'm trying my best. I'm trying so fucking hard, and I'm tired. I'm done. I lie down in bed, turning to my side, away from him, and pretend to scroll through my phone.

Alberto slams the door behind him as he leaves. I don't fall asleep until the first rays of sunshine begin to paint my room white.

THIRTY SIX

Maynor's nearly empty Coca-Cola bottle, the one he bought while we were in line to vote, still sits in the fridge. I find it late one night while hunting for a snack after God knows how many hours of not eating anything, behind a bunch of other containers and leftovers. After realizing that I can't remember the last time I drank anything either, I take a gulp. The Coke is flat, tasteless. Dull sugar water. I pour it down the sink.

This is what the first couple weeks of February feel like: Months-old bottle of partially drunken Coke. Forgotten, fridge-burnt.

Every school day, I ask Miss Katherine if I have any mail from any universities. Every day she tells me *not yet*, a sympathetic smile lining her glasses-framed eyes.

I walk Alberto to class, and he drags his feet a little less. Things are still off between us, but I make myself watch games at night with him, and he doesn't tell me to go away, which I take as a good sign. I try to pay close attention, to ask questions. He's started to give me more than one-word answers again.

I text Camila, though mostly about Maynor. She remembers so much about him from over the years, supplying me with little facts and memories that I had almost forgotten. One night, after falling asleep watching a soccer game with Alberto, a loud commercial wakes me up around three a.m. I reach for the remote to turn the TV off, glancing down at my phone, and see that Camila's texted.

> Have you tried writing about him?

To this, I don't respond.

The truth is, I have. But I can never get too far before I begin crying so hard it's hard to see anything. Mostly, I end up staring at his handwriting interspersed with mine in the poem we collaborated on.

I text Daniela again too. She reminds me a little of Maynor, sometimes. She knows so much about everything and spends her days where he should still be spending his, at the university. Every once in a while, she sends me a picture of random spots on campus with a flower or tree or vine she likes, and my mind copies and pastes an image of him into it.

The world is not the world without him.

Mami starts wearing makeup again, though she still cries through it most nights. Abuela keeps up her long hours at the workshop. Though I am not any less angry or sad than before, I know what to expect every day now, and that's easier. That's something.

Silence follows the private inauguration of Juan Orlando, as the resistance accepts that there's no way out of it. The protests die down. People get back to work—the work of surviving.

The only thing that keeps me going is the thought of leaving. All

I have to do for the next few months is keep okay grades and move fast if I get an acceptance. It's a waiting game now.

"We deserve a break," Carla declares.

It's twenty minutes before our first Friday class. She, Valeria, and I sit at our usual table outside the cafeteria. A fútbol match is going, and maybe I'm projecting, but even the boys are playing in a lackluster manner. I don't hear them yell at each other even once.

"A break from what?" Valeria asks, tapping her fingers on the table. "Aside from el examen del himno in May and waiting to hear back from colleges, they've barely got us doing anything. It's all prom planning and paperwork at this point."

"Exactly! We deserve a break from the stress of thinking about what comes next. There's a Valentine's party at La Esquina tonight— I think we should all go."

I sigh, louder than I meant to. "I don't know, Carla . . ."

"I mean, of course, if you don't feel ready to . . . I get that," Carla backpedals. "I'm just saying—it'd be for us to unwind a little. Relax."

"There's nothing relaxing about going out drinking with every other eighteen-year-old in Tegucigalpa," Valeria responds, holding back a smirk.

"Well, I think we should do it! We can even leave before midnight if you want. Right, Cami?" Carla says, glancing just over my shoulder.

Before I can turn, Camila sits down on the bench next to me. Her bus is here early, for once. "Right to what?" she asks, setting her backpack down.

"We should go to La Esquina's Valentine's party tonight."

"Ooh." Cami nods. "Yeah—that sounds fun!"

"I don't know," I say again. And I really don't—I don't know if I can handle being anywhere but the same two places I've been for the past month, home and school.

"Come on, Libertad," Cami says gently. "Just for a little while?"

"I just . . ." I throw my head back and spear my fingers through my curls, trying to untangle some of the knots. "I feel like I'm going to say yes right now and then change my mind in a few hours."

"That's okay." Cami shrugs.

"Yeah! Let's just plan on it for now," Carla agrees.

Even Valeria looks convinced. I glance around the table, taking in each of my friends' faces, and something like nostalgia washes over me. *This might be one of the last times we all go out together,* I think.

"Okay, fine. Just for a little while, though."

Later that night, Mami says it's fine. She even seems a little too supportive about it at first—me getting out of the house, doing something with friends. But then the questions start: She asks me about seven times who's going, and how do we know it's safe, and what if something happens?

Finally, after I promise to text her and come home early, she hands me a red leather flower keychain full of keys that I recognize as Maynor's. I have no idea what all the keys are for, though—I only know the one to our house.

I pick up my phone and start texting an invite to Dani. Then I put my phone back down, ultimately deciding against it. I don't think it'd be weird with Cami . . . but it'd be nice for the night to feel like before. Just us from school, like it was a year ago. Instead,

I make plans to hang out with Daniela tomorrow morning.

After hours of lying in bed, staring at the ceiling, I force myself to get up and start getting ready in Mami's bathroom. I can smell her perfume all over the place—she headed out earlier, saying she had a wedding to oversee, looking the most arreglada y bonita she has in a while. It made me happy, to see her like that again. It makes me want to try too, to at least pretend to be normal again, if only for a few hours.

I try on a few things, even some of Mami's clothes, before settling on my own white crop top and ripped jeans. I apply mascara and foundation, the smell of makeup and chemicals on my face after weeks of barely showering unfamiliar, shocking. It's been months since I stared longer than a few seconds in a mirror, and I try not to take too long to complete any single action, just in case I get discouraged halfway through.

Camila texts me to let me know she and Carla are two minutes away from my house. I take another peek at myself in the mirror and decide there's still something missing. Before I can even put my finger on what, though, my feet have carried me to the entrance of Maynor's room, where the door is cracked open a few inches. I take a deep breath and push it open.

The room is dark. Dust motes float in the thin, golden shaft of light that creeps in between the drawn curtains. I still, letting my eyes adjust to the dark. I've only been in here a few times since Maynor's death, and I try not to take in too many details of all his things, left exactly as they were the last night he walked out of the house. I can't break down right now. I can't.

I make myself walk over to his dresser and rummage through the drawers quickly, trying not to breathe in too deeply the scent of him that still lingers over everything, until I find one of his fake gold chains. I clasp it behind the nape of my neck, and stand there, just beyond the light of his window, until a car honk sounds from outside. I blink rapidly, startled, before backing up, shutting the door to my brother's room behind me.

In the back seat of Carla's mom's car, the smells of maybe four different flowery perfumes Carla and Cami have doused on themselves is heady, overwhelming. But I take some long, steadying breaths. I'm glad to be here. This feels right, to be dressed up with my friends in the back of a too-warm car on our way to a club. Like my body knows exactly what to do with this, this distraction, and is grateful for it.

The line of people outside the door snakes around the block. La Esquina is packed. Now that I think of it, Carla did mention that they'd be giving away free shots to the first fifty people who showed up.

"Should we go somewhere else?" I ask nervously.

"No," Camila says firmly, catching my eye in the rearview mirror. "It'll be fine, Libertad. Pablo and Miguel and I think Valeria are already waiting inside. They got us a table."

"Pablo's here? You invited him?" Carla asks, waving for the person behind her to move around us as she starts the parallel parking process.

"No." Cami shakes her head. "He texted me to see if it was okay for him to come with Miguel, and I said yes. I felt bad he even thought he had to ask—he's a good person, and it'd be cool if we could all just hang out."

"I agree," I say, and Carla and Cami raise their eyebrows at me. "I mean, I was just starting to like the guy when . . . well, you know."

Camila rolls her eyes and laughs.

It takes a couple minutes to make our way back to the club, and then a few more to get inside. Thankfully, though the line is long, it moves fast. Inside, the music is loud enough, I can feel the vibrations through the floor. Carla, Camila, and I make short work of finding our friends, who've grabbed a high-top table near the balcony overlooking the street. A giant fishbowl filled with a handful of straws and sour gummy snakes bobbing in the blue liquid sits in front of them.

As we sit, Pablo offers me a straw. I shake my head. He shrugs, lips tinted light blue by the drink, then takes a giant sip. He and Miguel and Valeria all look a little drunk already, rosy cheeks and blinky eyes.

The night moves fast. We see other people from school. We dance a little and try to talk to each other, yelling over the music. When we all sit back down an hour or so later, Pablo puts one arm around Camila and the other around me.

"I love you all so much!" he whoops, and I'm just tipsy enough not to squirm at the feel of his damp armpit against my shoulder. "Even if we graduate and never see each other again. We're all going to go out and do amazing things, I just know it. Seniors 2018!"

Miguel gets up and walks around the table to hug him. "I love you so much bro," he declares, thumping his back. Carla laughs loudly, tosses back another shot.

"Come with me," Cami says into my ear. "I need to go to the bathroom."

Something swoops in my stomach. *Don't assume anything,* I tell myself, before following her wordlessly to the first floor.

The bathroom is just as small as I remember it being a year ago. The floor is sticky, covered with ripped flecks of paper towels. I pull out my phone while Cami pees. To my surprise, Mami hasn't sent me a single text. I try to quash the flutter of panic before it rises into something larger. *How are you?* I text her. *How's the wedding going?*

Before I can pocket my phone, a text comes in from Dani.

> Still on for tomorrow?

I smile.

> Yes

Cami's next to me now, examining her face in the dirty mirror. I catch her eye through the reflection.

"Your mom texting you?" she asks. Her tone is unreadable, and I wonder if she caught Dani's name on my screen. For a second, I consider lying.

"No." I finally say, keeping my voice as casual as I can. "That was Dani."

Cami nods, then busies herself with washing her hands before I can decipher the expression on her face.

"You really all good?" I say, just to break the silence. "Like, with Pablo and stuff?"

Cami shakes her hands off into the sink before reaching for a paper towel. "Yeah. I am. Are you having fun?"

"I think so."

"Good."

"Good," I echo her, swallowing. Then: "Are you thinking about the same thing I am?" The question comes out of me in a rush.

A tangle of both nerves and courage surges through me. Maybe it's the alcohol, though I haven't had that much tonight. More likely it's this place, the ghosts of me and her and who we used to be to one another surrounding us.

"Maybe." The corners of Cami's lips tick up. "What are you thinking about?"

"That we kissed here. Like, a year ago."

"Then yes."

"Thought so," I gloat, beaming. High on the momentum, I add, "I think I'd like to kiss you again. If that's okay, I mean."

"Okay," Camila giggles, stepping closer. "I'd like that."

She tilts her head up to mine. For just a second, I rest my thumb on her lower lip. Then I bring my mouth to hers, running my hands down her arms, resting them around her waist.

We kiss softly, slowly, nothing like a year ago. Her breath is warm, and I can taste a hint of grape flavor in her lip gloss. I cup the back of her neck, pull her closer to me. Something low, achy, burns through me as we press our bodies together.

Despite the rush that zings through my stomach—then lower—our kiss stays sweet, safe. Maybe because, unlike last time, this kiss is full of honesty, everything laid bare between us. Even if there was a knock on the door, it wouldn't brush away the moment into oblivion.

THIRTY SEVEN

Around an hour later, our friends decide to call it a night. Carla is too drunk to drive, so Cami climbs into the driver's seat. I ride passenger while Carla lies down in the back seat, passing out almost immediately.

"Can you find us something to listen to?" Cami asks, nodding her chin toward the radio as she steers the car into the street.

Mami hasn't texted me back, but I try my best not to fixate on that as I shuffle through the stations. *The wedding must be out of control*, I tell myself. *She'll text me when she can.*

I flip through the usuals: 107.7, 102.5, 99.5. Station after station blasts reggaeton—there's not much else on this late at night—which I usually fuck with. But something about the soft night sky has me craving a more mellow sound. The sky glows bright blue—like there's a sheet of white light draped behind the inky darkness. I look for the moon and see that it's almost full, though not quite. It reminds me of the story about Maynor's birth. As we move through Las Minitas, I repeat the story to Cami.

"That's crazy," she laughs. "I hadn't heard of that before—of the full moon rushing births."

"Right? Me neither."

Finally, I find a station playing an old ballad from Shakira, back when her hair wasn't dyed blonde. *That's as good as it gets,* I decide, letting my fingers fall away from the console.

It's not quite midnight, and the city is alive. On every other corner, women are selling baleadas and burritas and meat plates. Most have a line of people in front of them, grabbing a bite to eat before heading home or to the next party. The American chain restaurants are also full, their drive thru lines spilling onto the main street.

A few streets away from my house, I take Cami's free hand in mine. Her fingers are a little cold, but it's nice, holding her hand like this. She squeezes my palm.

"It's wild how close we are to graduating." Cami says, shaking her head.

"Have you decided what you're gonna do yet?"

"Yeah. Probably medicine, like my parents. And probably here."

"Cami—" I start, taking a deep breath. "Do you always want to live here?"

"Yes." Her eyes dart toward me and back again. "I mean, I think so. La UNAH's medicine program is actually pretty good." She sighs. "Also, I have to think about my dad. You know how sick he's been for a long time now. It would suck for my mom to have to take care of him by herself."

Everything she's saying makes sense, of course. Still, I can't help but think about the caravan of immigrants that's probably halfway through Guatemala now, set to reach the American border in just a few weeks. I can't help but think about the poem I wrote about leaving, the one Maynor helped me with.

"I know," I reply. "But there's barely any jobs for doctors here, Cami, and, well, I was thinking. . . . What about everything else?"

"What do you mean?" We've reached my house now, and Cami brings the car to a stop.

"Like," I start slowly, as gently as I can. "What about . . . you know, every other aspect of life? Apart from studying medicine. Are you gonna live with your parents? And, I don't know—are you gonna marry a guy, eventually? I guess I'm a little confused about what your plan is if you stay here. Considering, you know . . ."

I can't bring myself to say it: *Considering you might be gay.* I don't really know, first of all, if that's what Cami would call herself. If she's named it at all.

I also feel weird about Carla sitting in the back, even if she's completely out. Cami lets go of my hand to hug herself. I can't tell if she's cold or if I've upset her.

"I know," she says quietly, after a moment. "For a long time, I didn't really give myself permission to think about it. I thought, maybe, if I ignored it long enough, it would just go away. And then life wouldn't need to be so hard. Does that makes sense?"

It does. I get it, and it blows. Now I feel a little guilty about bringing it up.

"You know . . . it might not all be as impossible as it seems," I try again, lighter this time. "The US legalized gay marriage a couple

355

years ago. That means we're only like, what, fifty years or so away from copying them?"

Camila gives me one of those sad smiles. "Not with this government," she whispers. "And Libertad, I'm just not ready to risk any of this—my family and home and studying medicine here—over something I'm not quite sure of."

For a split second, I'm nauseous, just like the day Mami gave me my phone back, showing me those texts from Camila. I feel both ashamed and pissed. Where the hell does her being "not quite sure" leave me?

But then she picks up my hand again and hugs it to her chest, closing her eyes. As the two of us breathe in and out, slowly, I remind myself that this shit is hard. She has her own process to go through. I asked her a question, and she answered me as honestly as she could.

I want to tell Camila so much, more than I think she can hear right now. I want to tell her that maybe it can be okay. That, maybe, she doesn't need to give up anything. That my brother knew who I was and loved me fiercely, with everything inside him. That there are people like Dani who are determined to live openly but safely here, in whatever capacity is possible.

But I think she already knows all of this. And, at the end of the day, it's not my place to name her queerness for her.

"You have so much time to figure it out," I say instead. "I know you will."

Cami opens her eyes and smiles, for real this time. "We'll see," she responds. It sounds like a promise.

We stare into each other's eyes, still smiling. I think, for a second, that she's going to lean in to kiss me again. But then headlights sweep through the windows as a car pulls in in front of us and parks, distracting both of us.

Nerves rocket through me. I wonder, for a second, if we're about to get mugged, or worse. Then I recognize the car: It's Mami's.

From the driver's seat a man with silver hair gets out, circling around the front to open the passenger-side door. My mom steps out and grasps the man's hand. The two of them walk to the front gate, where the man leans down, and Mami meets his lips with a kiss.

My mouth drops open. After a minute, Mami breaks the kiss and hugs the man, burying her face in his neck. And then it's over—the man smiles tenderly at my mom and lets go of her hand, walks back to her car, and drives off.

Cami turns to me. "Was that—?"

"My mom, yes. And I have no idea who that man is."

THIRTY EIGHT

"Okay," Cami says. "Okay—you have to count from ten to zero really slowly and like, take some deep breaths before you go inside."

My phone lights up in my hand. Text messages from my mother flood the screen:

> Where are you

> It's getting pretty late

> I want you home now, Libertad

I stare blankly at my phone. Of course, the irony is that I've technically been "home" longer than she has.

"Libertad?" Cami asks. "How are you feeling?"

I close my eyes and think about it.

"You don't know?" she probes gently. "It's okay if you don't know how you feel."

"Um, actually . . ." I say, opening my eyes again. "I think I do know this time." I do what Cami says, taking a deep breath in and releasing it slowly. "I think it's okay. It's okay if Mami . . . if she's dating this guy, I mean."

"Okay." Cami nods. "You're not upset, though?"

"No," I say, and I mean it. "I think I'm relieved, you know? She's been sad and alone for so long. Even before Maynor died. So I'm happy that something good is happening to her."

Saying it out loud makes me feel even surer of it.

"Well, that's good!" Cami laughs a little. "I thought you were about to lose it."

I smile. "These days I'm not as hot-headed as you think."

I lean forward in my seat, grabbing the keys from my back pocket. "I'll see you on Monday," I say, and sneak a quick kiss onto her lips.

"Monday," she murmurs, smiling.

It strikes me, as I walk to the front door of my house with the leather keychain full of Maynor's old keys clinking against each other, that this moment is bursting with things I once wanted with all of my body: Kissing Cami with honesty in both of our mouths. Seeing Mami do something, feel something, other than exhaustion. Having plans on the horizon that excite me, like meeting up with Dani tomorrow and maybe hearing back from a college abroad.

It still feels good, just different. Not like these things aren't significant anymore, but like they aren't my whole world. I don't know that my world can ever be whole again in the same way it was before.

Another emotion runs through me now, but I can't put my finger on it. I try to shake it off, sticking the house key into the door.

Inside, Mami has already changed into comfortable clothes. I find her drinking water in the kitchen.

"Thank God," she says, setting her glass down. "I was about to call you."

"Sorry. How long have you been home?"

"Mm, twenty minutes?" she replies casually, crossing her arms as she leans against the counter. It takes everything in me not to make a face; both of us know it's been more like five or ten minutes, tops.

"Where's your car?" I press her, setting my phone and keys down on the table.

Mami raises her eyebrows. "Oh. Um, a friend from work borrowed it. He'll bring it back tomorrow morning."

"Ah, got it. And how was the wedding?" I grab a cup from the cabinet and pour myself some water, sitting down at the table as I take a sip. More than anything, I'm curious to see how long Mami can keep this up.

"It was okay."

"Who is this friend from work?"

"Huh?"

"The friend. Who took your car. Who is he?"

"He's . . . a chef. At the hotel."

"What's his name?"

"Why?" Mami asks, narrowing her eyes.

We stare at each other. The jig is up—I know it, and I think she knows it too. But after five long, seemingly endless seconds tick by, neither of us saying anything, it's me who folds.

"Okay, fine." I sigh. "I saw you kissing that man outside."

Though Mami's expression doesn't change, her body stills.

I know she's dated men, but she's never brought anyone home. Maynor told me once that she was cautious, after our dad, to introduce another guy into our lives before it was a sure thing. While I can't read Mami's face now as she stands there, staring impassively at me, I wonder if she's running through worst-case scenarios in her head. Trying to anticipate whatever I'm thinking, feeling.

I decide it's best to put her out of her misery—I do my best to channel Maynor and what he would say, in this moment.

"Mamá," I start gently. "It's okay—I'm not upset. I just didn't want to, you know, not tell you. And I—all I want is for you to be happy."

Mami slowly walks over then, pulling out the chair across from me. She sits and folds her hands over the table, staring at her fists.

"His name is Walter," Mami finally says, after a moment. "I don't know if I'd call him my boyfriend yet. He works at the hotel; we first started seeing each other in October. But then everything happened, and—well, you know." Mami glances up at me, and I nod for her to keep going.

"After it happened . . ." Mami swallows hard. "I didn't have any space in my heart for anything other than grief and anger. But I didn't even have to tell him that—he just seemed to understand. And he'd check on me still, every single day. Even when I went days without texting him back."

I nod again. It occurs to me, hearing Mami explain all that, what a gift he gave our family. Being there for Mami when the rest of us couldn't.

After everything happened, the world stopped for me—I didn't have to go to school or see anyone. I didn't really have to do anything at all. But Mami had to plan her firstborn son's funeral, and then turn around and go to work. She had to figure out bills and keeping both Alberto and me alive, eating, going to school and getting out of the house.

"He sounds like a really great guy," I say at last.

"He is." The corner of her mouth crooks up. "He's divorced, has one son that's older than Maynor. He's already built his own life and everything."

I reach across the table and squeeze Mami's hand. "That's great. No more little kids for you."

Mami laughs. "Yes—that's what I thought too." She goes quiet again, a pang of something sorrowful moving across her face. "I actually told Maynor about him, right before . . . Anyway. I think he was happy for me, but maybe a little nervous too. I was waiting for the right time to tell you and Alberto."

"Yeah. That makes sense." A twinge of concern laces through me, and I imagine that this is what Maynor must have felt, when Mami told him. He was always keeping everyone's secrets. Mine, Mami's, his own. That's who he was.

I just hope that Walter is a good guy. For Mami, for us. And if he isn't, I hope Mami figures it out sooner rather than later.

"And then I hadn't said anything lately because, well—I guess I just felt so . . ."

"Guilty," I say, suddenly finding the word for the feeling I had walking into the house tonight. "Guilty you were having a good time again."

Mami nods. "He isn't here—" she says, and her voice cracks. I take both her hands in mine.

"He isn't here anymore," she tries again, her chin quivering. "To go out to dinner with the girl he likes. To fall in love. All these things he didn't get to do, Libertad, and we just get to keep living and doing them?"

"I know," I tell her. "I know, Ma. I feel it too." I squeeze her hands, pushing back against the rising lump in my throat. "Whenever I forget, even for a second, and just let myself enjoy something. Then I remember he isn't here, and I feel horrible for forgetting."

"But he'd want us to find as many little pockets of joy as possible," I whisper, my voice going hoarse.

"I know," Mami says. "He was so good."

"The best," I agree. "He had the best heart."

My phone lights up on the table, then, and both our eyes fall to the screen. It's a message from Camila:

Dropped Carla off and made it back safe

"Did you have a good time today?" Mami asks, pulling her hands delicately out of mine.

"I did, yes. It was okay."

"Good, good."

We sit there for another minute in silence, each of us taking turns staring at the table or off into space.

"Libertad?" Mami finally asks me.

"Yes?"

"I wanted to say something else tonight. Te quiero decir algo."

"What's up?" I reply, worry clawing its way up my chest. I force myself to stay seated, to hear her out.

"I know . . . I know that things have been really hard. And that some of those things were hard even before Maynor died," Mami says, splaying her hands flat against the table and leaning forward a little.

"When everything happened with your phone," she continues. "The texts about kissing that girl. I just wanted to tell you that, whoever she was . . . it doesn't matter. I love you. Just the way you are. I'm proud to call each and all of you my children."

I don't know what to say. I nod. Exhale.

It feels like I've been holding my breath since September 15. Gratitude for my mother warms my body all over. But even then, there's still a pang of loss that cuts through my stomach: I'm sad that Maynor isn't here to witness this.

"Thank you," I tell her, my voice trembling. "Yo también te amo and . . . and I'm proud you're my mom too."

"Gracias, hija." As tears travel down her face, I realize that she's probably also been holding her breath since September.

I scoot my chair closer, holding her as she cries. Despite everything, I feel more at peace, right now, than I have in forever.

After a few minutes of crying into my shoulder, Mami pulls away and wipes away the last of her tears away with her hand. "Libertad," she says softly. "I know you probably know this already . . . But Maynor was so proud of you, always. He thought you were just the best thing to ever happen. He just wanted you to be you and do whatever you wanted to with your life."

She reaches out, rubbing a thumb over my chin. "He wasn't as scared as I was."

I feel the tears that I've been trying to hold back break free, making their way down my cheeks.

"Yes," I say. "I do know. I know." And then I hug her again, as hard as I can.

We stay like that, with our arms wrapped around each other, for a long, long time. Outside, the crickets chirp, steady and loud.

"All right," Mami says finally, pulling away. "Time for bed. You said you're going where tomorrow?"

"Lunch with a friend from la UNAH—her name is Dani. She knew Maynor."

Mami squeezes my knee and stands. "Okay. Just keep me posted. And don't ignore my texts," she orders, pointing at me.

"Um, yeah, I'm not the one who wasn't picking up the phone tonight," I tease.

Mami rolls her eyes and smiles. In this moment, she looks so much like Alberto, and like Maynor, when he was younger. It crosses my mind that, perhaps, she also looks like me. But I wouldn't know that.

THIRTY NINE

La UNAH looks exactly like the last time I was here, with Maynor. Despite it being a Saturday morning, it's buzzing with people crossing campus to meet up with friends or work on projects or go grab food. The air feels textured, thick; it's too hot for February, but we're not supposed to be getting any more real rain for a while.

"Slow down," Dani tells me for the third time in the past half hour. "How are you sprinting if you don't even know where we're going?"

"Okay, okay," I laugh. "Sorry."

"You're always moving too fast, Libi."

"It's a city thing." I shrug.

Dani smiles. "Los capitalinos are pretty hotheaded. Rushed."

"Can't help it."

I force myself to walk next to her rather than ahead. It's hard, at first, like it's unnatural for my body to move at this pace. But it gives me time to take her in for the first time since we got here.

Dani's wearing loosely fitted navy pants and a white shirt. She looks like if she put a blazer on she could be heading to a meeting. Something about Dani always feels so adult, even though she's only a year older. Part of it is probably her tranquil demeanor. She moves as if the world can wait, that very little is actually worth sprinting for. Just being around her makes me feel calm.

It's not until the social sciences building is directly in front of us that I realize where Daniela's leading me. I stop walking, my breathing suddenly reduced to short, staccato pants.

"What's up?" Dani turns around to look at me where I've stopped a few steps behind her.

"Are we"—espite the heat, chills race up my arms—"going to the desaparecidos mural?"

"Yeah," Daniela admits, giving me a sympathetic look. "Is that okay?"

"I just—last time I was there was with Maynor. It feels like a lot."

"I know, I know. It will be okay, Libertad, I promise."

Still, I don't move.

Dani walks back to meet me, extending her hand. When I take it, she interlaces our fingers, bringing my hand to her face and kissing the back of it. I take a few deep breaths, then continue moving.

When we make it through the back doors of the social xciences building, I'm blinded by the sunlight. These buildings are both too dark and too hot, like a storage unit. Coming out of them feels like surfacing from underground.

The atrium, like the campus, is just as I remember it: Students huddled in groups everywhere. Little speakers people have brought with them blasting different types of music, clashing with each other in a cacophony of sound. And the walls full of faces—I look over at the bench where Maynor and I sat as he explained to me what they mean. Dani gives me a second to take it all in again before gently pulling me ahead.

"Come on," she says. "We're almost there."

She walks me to the right-side wall, and I realize that this is the closest I've ever been to the faces themselves. They're bigger than they look from the center of the space. I can see the pores of the concrete walls, and where the spray paint from certain drawings is fading. I wonder if the most faded portraits are those that have been here the longest.

I press my palm to the wall. It's cool, despite the heat from the sun. Dani keeps walking until we reach a spot in the middle.

"There." She points.

"There what?" I ask. She could literally be pointing at anything—I feel a little dizzy from all the words and faces and names.

"Do you see that empty space between Antonio Breve and Gerardo Róchez?"

I scan up the wall until I find the faces with those names written under them. Then I spot the white space between them.

"Yeah, I see it."

"It's yours."

I look back at Daniela, blinking. "What do you mean?"

She raises a hand to her forehead, shielding her eyes from the sun. "I secured it. It's yours. I was thinking we could get someone to do a stencil of Maynor's face and just, you know. Paint it there."

I look back at the wall, at the blank space. It's just enough above eye level that it doesn't get lost, but not too high, not unreachable. The space is also wide enough that the face can be big.

Tears pinch the back of my eyes. "It's perfect," I breathe. "He—he would have loved it."

And I know that that's true. Even if I would do anything to never have to see my brother's face on a wall of the dead and the lost. The wall of the taken.

But I can't. There's nothing I can do to change the fact that Maynor is gone. At least here, high on these walls, he doesn't have to be forgotten.

"Good," Dani says, sounding relieved. "I'm so glad. We just need to find a person who can draw his face—"

"Cami," I say immediately. "She's great at drawing and painting. She'd be perfect for this."

Dani smiles. "Great. I'll text her."

Twenty minutes later, Daniela takes me to a crepe restaurant near campus. Despite the emotional morning, my stomach growls at the smells of sugar and pastry and something savory wafting around the dining room. I'm starving.

"So," Dani says, after we've ordered and given our menus back to the waiter. "Have you figured out what you're doing this fall?"

"No." I sigh. "I'm still waiting to hear back from the colleges I've applied to. Any day now."

"But you're set on leaving?"

"I mean . . . yes?" I shrug. "I don't see the point of staying here."

I feel a little guilty about saying it like that because, well, *here* is where she is. But I know it's true. And I don't want to lie about my feelings around this city. This country.

She frowns and nods slowly, like she's thinking hard about how to respond. "Yeah. That's a common sentiment."

I can't tell if she means anything by that. If there's an adjective missing, like that's a common *dumb* sentiment, but I sense disappointment from her tone.

"I'm excited about the mural, though," I tell her. "Maynor would've loved that. He loved it there."

"Mmhm," Dani replies.

We get quiet after that. I feel like I've done something wrong, but I don't know what. Our food comes, and we eat in silence.

At some point, I ask Daniela if her chicken and mushroom crepe is good, and she nods again without making eye contact. I start feeling nervous, claustrophobic even. I don't notice my knee bouncing up and down until I feel her hand touch my thigh.

"What's up with you?" she asks. "You're making the table shake."

"I don't know," I say quickly. "I feel like I said something wrong."

"You didn't."

"Then why are you so quiet?"

Dani purses her lips. "It's—it's hard to explain."

"So, I *did* say something wrong?"

"No, Libertad." Dani glances out the window next to us, overlooking the street. I can see the frustration in her face. Like she's doing the math on something.

"I just—" she starts, grabbing her napkin from the table, wringing it slowly between her fingers. Both our gazes fall to the twist of white in her hands. "I feel like I can't tell you any different. Like . . . like it's your own process to live," Dani says. "And I have to be okay with you not coming out of it the way I hope you do. That's all."

"Tell me any different about what? I'm confused," I tell her, my forehead creasing.

"About how you should feel. You know . . . about leaving Honduras."

Silence falls between us like a veil, like a wall. But before I can even think of replying, the server brings the check. Dani lays some money down and stands—we don't speak again until we're in the car.

"Should I take you home or to the workshop or . . . ?" Daniela asks quietly.

"Home."

She starts driving, and I stare out the front window. I've never felt this way around Dani before. Like there's suddenly something thorny, unspoken, between us.

I hate it.

"Did you see the news, about the caravan?" I finally ask.

"Yeah." She shakes her head. "Pobre gente. Dios los proteja."

"Do you think they're wrong to leave?"

"No." Dani arches an eyebrow, like she knows where I'm going with this. "I don't think anyone is in the wrong for leaving, or for wanting to leave."

"Then what's going on?"

Daniela sighs. We come to a stop at a red light, and she takes my hand.

"My parents tried to leave too, Libertad. Even before it got this bad with food, with jobs. And I never have blamed them for it. I just—" She glances down at where her thumb is spinning a slow, small circle on my hand.

"I worry that you think leaving will make you feel better . . . about Maynor. Which it might. But it might not, you know? And I don't want you to forget how much he believed in this," she says, dropping my hand to gesture around us.

I look out the window again, at the crush of cars and the people weaving between them. At the dirty sidewalks beside us and the hazy afternoon sun above. I take a deep breath and try, as I've tried so many times over the past few months, to see it all through Maynor's eyes, if only for just a second.

All I can see is that this is the place that killed him.

"I don't mean to lecture you about Maynor," Dani continues, hitting the gas as the light turns green. "Obviously I'll never know him like you did, Libi. But from what you described, that seemed to be at the core of him. The belief that where we are right now is worth fighting for. That we live where we live."

This time, I'm the one to turn my gaze away. To purse my lips, stay silent. I feel her eyes looking nervously at me every few seconds as she drives.

"Maynor wanted me to go somewhere else," I say at last. "Somewhere I could be . . ." I swallow, pause. "Out. Gay."

My face burns. I don't think I've ever said those words out loud before—that I'm gay. Of course, Dani would know better than anyone else . . . But still.

"I know," she replies. "Really, I do. But I also want you to know that leaving might not make it easier. And hating it here isn't the only way forward."

"Okay," I say flatly. "That's fine. I don't hate it here, though. I just . . . don't feel any type of way about it."

Dani shakes her head. "That's not what I meant either."

"Okay then, how do you want me to feel?" Despite my best efforts to stay calm, anger sizzles its way up my chest, my throat, my face.

"That's not for me to tell you."

"It seems like it is," I snap.

"I don't think you're listening," she says evenly. And she's right, I'm not. Because I don't think anything she has to say will make me feel differently.

"Then tell me how *you* feel about it," I retort, my voice rising too quickly, too loud in the small space of the car. "How can you just accept that this is how it is? That if you try to do anything about it, you'll probably end up dead? How can you just come to terms with how it was this"—I gesture toward the windshield—"this *country* that made it impossible for your parents to stay. That also, somehow, killed them."

Dani's eyes widen, the echoes of my words ringing like death knells in the space between us.

She doesn't respond, and I don't blame her. I immediately feel shitty for bringing up what happened to her parents. But I'm also too fucking furious and sad and bitter to take any of it back. And it's true, everything I said, isn't it? She and I both know it.

Dani parks wordlessly in front of my house. "Thanks for lunch,"

I mumble, reaching for the door handle, not daring to look at her.

"Wait—I have something for you," she says quietly. "Before you go."

Daniela reaches behind her seat, pulling out a small, brown paper bag. I grab it without opening it, my eyes stinging. Everything in me screams that I need to get out of her car, now, before I start crying again.

"Thank you," I whisper. "Um—feliz día del amor y la amistad."

"Happy Valentine's," Dani says.

I force a smile, still not meeting her eyes, and book it to my house, to my room. I feel so unbelievably guilty. Guilty for everything I didn't get Dani, and guilty for everything she gave me.

FORTY

On the first Thursday of March, we're in the second-to-last period of the day, estudios sociales, when Miss Katherine interrupts Mr. Andino halfway through his retelling of the early years of the cold war.

"Buenas Míster," she says, holding up the envelopes in her hands. "I have mail for some students."

Mr. Andino nods at her briefly, then continues lecturing. This has happened a few times since January. Students around me perk up, as per usual, waiting to see if their name gets called.

I don't move. It hasn't been more than two hours since I last asked Miss Katherine—stopping into her office during my lunch break—if I had any mail. *Not yet*, she told me, yet again.

But to my surprise, between "Luis Pérez" and "Mario Jiménez," there it is: my name. I think I must have misheard her, but when I raise my eyes from my notebook, Miss Katherine is staring right at me. She extends her arm toward me, a medium-sized white envelope in her hand.

I jump out of my chair, nearly tripping over my backpack. Miss Katherine smiles as I grab it. "See," she says in a low, conspiratorial voice, her eyes bright behind her glasses. "I told you it was coming."

I beam at her and run back to my seat, too excited to respond.

I know the smart thing to do is to wait and open it at home with someone sympathetic, in case it's bad news. I've seen it happen often—my classmate's face dropping as soon as they've opened the letter. There were even tears, one time.

But I can't wait. As soon as I'm back to my desk I tear open the envelope, completely oblivious to my classmates' stares. This moment is just about me and the piece of paper in my hands.

I don't have to read past the first sentence. As soon as I spot the *congratulations,* I grip the letter almost hard enough to rip it. I do a quick, silent prayer of relief. It's very dramatic: hands pressed to my chest, eyes to the ceiling and all. I can't help it.

Valeria asks to see the letter, her grin almost as wide as mine. I hand it over to her shakily.

"See, I told you it was a good idea! I told you we had to try," she whispers triumphantly, her eyes scanning the page.

Valeria has received two acceptances and is waiting to hear from a few more places. She seems to be leaning toward a small liberal arts school in Canada, where she wants to study human rights. *It makes perfect sense for her,* I think, as she hands my letter back to me and squeezes my arm.

My acceptance is for a small, private college in the Midwest. It's not a fancy or particularly selective place. In fact, it's a side campus to the main university, which is in a different city. But it's a good school. Known for its generous scholarships to international students.

That still might not be enough, a doubtful voice whispers in my head. But I shove it away. The only thing that matters, right now, is that I have options. I have an option that isn't here.

"How are you feeling?" Valeria asks me, after the bell rings. The two of us stay rooted in our seats as students file out around us, Mr. Andino rushing out after them to take a call.

"Still in shock," I admit, as the classroom suddenly goes quiet. "And grateful—I'm so glad you pushed me to do this."

"Well . . . I miiight have had ulterior motives," Valeria drawls, leaning back a little in her chair.

"What do you mean?" I ask. I can't read her face. Valeria scratches the back of her neck, and nerves flutter in my stomach.

"I've known I have to leave Honduras since I was ten," she says slowly, softly. "Because I've known since then that I was . . . different. And this is no place for people like me. For—for queer people."

I stare at her, shocked, unsure of what to say. Wait—is Valeria queer? How did I not realize . . . ?

"Oh—wow." I gulp. "So, um, you pushed *me* because—?"

"Because you're gay too, right?" Her tone, though kind, is more of a statement than a question.

I bite my lip. My limbs feel like liquid, my head buzzing with thoughts. A few seconds go by, and then I force myself to speak.

"Y-yes," I stammer, hoarsely. I clear my throat, repeating myself a little louder this time. "Yes—I'm gay too."

Valeria smiles at me, and something big, expansive, soars in my chest.

After school, Cami is waiting for me, next to my bus. I tell her about my acceptance as soon as I see her.

"No *way*!" she squeals, hugging me, her arms tight around my back. "That's so amazing, Libertad!"

"Thank you," I whoop, grinning. "I was gonna text you, but I wanted to do it in person."

"You know, I swear I could just *feel* that something exciting had happened," she laughs.

The two of us let go of each other then, leaning against the side of the bus. The metal is cool against our backs. The bus is still off, and the sun doesn't hit this side of it. I'm so excited and jittery it's hard to stand still.

I turn to look at Cami—her nose freckles are multiplying. They always do around this time of the year. All of her arm is touching all of my arm, and it reminds me of all those months ago when we stood here like this, and I didn't have a phone, and hadn't even thought of applying abroad, and we knew each other just as much as we do now but were acting like strangers. And it almost feels like those were different people, those girls who leaned against the bus together like the two of us do now.

Also, I hadn't yet met Dani.

"What's up?" Camila says, shoving my arm lightly with hers.

"What do you mean?"

"You spaced out. Looked like you were kind of sad about something."

"Oh. I was thinking about Daniela," I confess.

Cami frowns. "Did you tell her the news?"

"No. We . . . haven't talked much recently."

"Why?" she asks, dark eyebrows knitted together in the middle.

"I don't know. I mean—I do know . . . but I don't know how to explain it. Or make it right."

"You had a fight?"

I search Cami's face for any trace of bitterness there, but she looks genuinely concerned. Her eyes glow liquid gold in the light coming from behind me.

"Yes. Kind of." I sigh, brushing a strand of hair out of my eyes.

"Oh. I'm sorry."

"How do you feel about Dani?" I ask, fast enough so I can't stop myself. I turn to face her.

"I really like her," Camila says, without missing a beat. "She's great."

"Do you two . . . talk?"

"A little. We got in touch after . . . well, after Maynor. And then we touched base every so often, mostly about you." Cami leans her shoulder against the bus, so the two of us are face-to-face. "Then she reached out to me about the mural. Oh! And I mentioned that I'll be going to la UNAH in the fall, and she said she could show me around, introduce me to people."

"That's nice," I reply, grinning. And it is—both Cami and Dani are so important to me. It's reassuring to know that they're on good terms, that they like each other. That they'll have one another even when I'm nowhere near either of them.

Something drops in my stomach, and I have to push the thought away.

Cami squints her eyes at me and raises an eyebrow. "Do you mean that?"

"I do." I nod. "I just—so what, um . . ."

I swallow. I don't want either one of them to feel lied to, but I also don't know what either of them knows or *should* know. Like, what do you owe people you kiss but aren't dating but aren't just friends with? Are the rules the same as they are for girls dating boys? I'm pretty sure I haven't done anything wrong . . . But maybe there's information I haven't been volunteering that I should've been.

"Well, you weren't a big fan of hers before," I say to Camila. "And I guess I'm wondering what you already know—like, about me and her."

Cami blinks slowly, looking a little uncomfortable for the first time since we started talking. "Um, I know you two were . . . involved. Before everything happened with Maynor. And I know Dani really cares about you, and you about her," she says, digging the toe of her shoe into the ground. After a beat, she raises her eyes to meet mine. "Is there anything else for me to know?"

I don't know why, but I'm nervous all of a sudden. I can practically hear my heartbeat pounding in my ears.

"No, no. I think that's the gist of it. We were involved, like *really* involved, right before Maynor died. And now we aren't. I'm—well, even now . . . I can't imagine having the energy to be someone's . . . you know, girlfriend." I drop my voice at this last word, glancing over my shoulder, making sure no one is listening in to our conversation.

It's easy to forget, sometimes, that just because I've named my secret to most of my friends and family, that doesn't mean the world can just *tell* now. Not that it should. Though a small part of me wonders, sometimes, if it'd be easier that way. If it was an all-at-once thing.

"I figured," Camila says. "Yeah."

A few students file past us, climbing into the bus, and the driver turns it on. I feel the motor's rumble through my skin.

"Did you tell Dani we . . . you know, at La Esquina?" Cami asks tentatively.

"No." I shrug my shoulder. "But I don't have a reason not to. And I don't think she'd be upset or anything, you know?"

Cami nods. I open my mouth, then close it again. I'm so tempted to ask her, *What about you and me?*

But I already said it, didn't I? I don't have it in me to give anything else right now. To be as thoughtful, as loving, as I'd want to be with someone I'm seeing. It also hasn't been more than a few weeks since Cami said she wasn't ready to call herself anything yet, to name her queerness. And as new as I am with all this, I know I'd want at least that much from a girlfriend.

"I love you," I say instead. "So much."

"I love you too," Cami replies, then raises her eyebrows. "Also, you might live somewhere else soon."

"Yes," I agree, my stomach dropping again. The idea of me

actually doing this, of moving away from everything I've ever known, feels so new and unreal and terrifying, now that I have an acceptance. "Maybe. As long as it all works out."

"It will, Libertad. I know it will." Cami pushes herself off the bus and takes a few steps backward, holding onto her backpack straps with both hands. "Just text Dani," she calls to me. "She'll probably be happy to hear from you."

"Cami, wait."

She stops in her tracks. I take a few steps forward, then throw my arms around her, hugging her to me once more. She rests her chin on my shoulder, and I close my eyes.

For a moment, I can't imagine living so far from her that I can't hope for this every day.

FORTY ONE

Alberto doesn't stop asking me questions I don't have answers to all the way home: *So when do you leave? And how many airplanes do you need to get on to get there? When will you come back again? Can I come? What happens to your room here? Is it mine now?*

"I don't know, dude," I tell him over and over. "I have to talk to Mami and Abuela. There's so much to figure out."

"I'll miss you," Alberto says. His face changes suddenly, eyebrows scrunching together. "If you leave, I'll miss you a lot. I . . . I'll go from having two hermanos to being alone." He glances out the window, then down at his hands. "That's gonna suck—even if you don't like watching games with me."

I take a sharp inhale—I don't know what to say to that. And he's right. I might not have been the best big sister to him lately, but I'm still his older sister. And there's a good chance I won't be here with him, in person, for that much longer.

"Beto . . ." I start. "I'm really sorry about the other night, when the power went out. For snapping at you after."

He shrugs. "It's okay."

"No." I shake my head, taking his small hand in mine. "It's not. I like watching games with you. I like doing just about anything with you." The bus lurches over a giant pothole, and Alberto and I slide a little in our seats. He squeezes my hand, and I squeeze back.

"I know both of us lost our best friend," I continue. "But we still have each other. We always will—even if I move to the US." I stare into Alberto's soft, dark eyes, both of us hardly blinking. "I love you so much that sometimes, it feels like if I look at you for too long, I'll pass out. You know?"

Alberto giggles. "I don't feel like I'm gonna pass out when I look at you."

I laugh. "Yeah, yeah. Whatever. One day you'll get it."

"Mmm, no I don't think so." Alberto brightens. "But maybe one day I'll go study somewhere else too."

"Yeah? Like what?"

"Law." He says it so quickly, decisively, that it catches me off guard.

"Oh. Like a lawyer?"

"No. I think I want to be a judge."

"Wait—what? Why? I this still about making money?"

"Well," he says, tugging his hand gently out of mine. "If I was a judge, I'd get to make the final decisions on things. And I'd be fair about it—I wouldn't let politicians pay me off. Like, I would make dads who leave pay for their kids' food . . . And I'd put the police that killed Maynor in jail."

"Wow." I raise my eyebrows. "Um, yeah. I—I think you'd be really good at that, Alberto."

Alberto smiles at me, then turns his gaze out the window. I brush a hand over his hair and lean back against the seat, taking in everything he just said.

Someday, I'll probably tell him that I don't think we can ever win from the inside. But I don't think today is that day.

When we walk into our house, I can tell something is different. It doesn't feel as idle, as lifeless as it usually does every day at four p.m., when it's clear it's been empty since six in the morning.

"Hello?" a voice calls to us from the kitchen, and I freeze.

"¡Abuelo!" Alberto shouts, running past me. Abuelo comes out of the kitchen then, holding his arms out for a hug, and Beto leaps into them.

"What are you doing here?" I grin, wrapping my own arms around the both of them.

"I have some meetings in Tegucigalpa next week, so I thought I'd come a few days before." He kisses my cheek. "Are y'all hungry?" he says as Alberto and I finally let him go.

"Libertad is moving to los Estados—she just got in!" Alberto announces.

"Really?" Abuelo asks, and I nod, swinging my backpack off my back to show him the letter.

Abuelo and I hold the piece of paper together, me translating the English for him. He, like Alberto, also has a million questions

I don't have answers for. The three of us move to the kitchen as we talk, and Abuelo sets down the bowls of rice and beans he's made for us on the table.

"So, have you told your mom yet? Abuela?"

"No, not yet. I just found out a few hours ago—I'll tell them tonight."

Abuelo nods. "We always wanted one of ours to go somewhere else. To try something new. We thought Martha might, and then Maynor . . . but things just didn't work out," he says as Alberto grabs a couple plates and spoons for us. The three of us sit, and Abuelo pats my shoulder as I ladle out the food for me and Beto.

"Abuela and I think of the both of you as our children, you know," Abuelo adds. I shift in my chair. Though I don't mean to, something must flash across my face at the mention of Abuela, because Abuelo gives me a look.

"Yes, she can be stubborn, sensitive," he says. "Sometimes she says the wrong thing, I know. But she really loves you. All of you."

I nod. He's right, of course—I've never questioned whether Abuela loves me or Alberto or even Maynor. But that doesn't change the fact that some of the things she's said over the years, whether about him or the world around us, could be cruel, short-sighted. I know some of it rang in my brother's ears for a long time.

After Alberto and I eat, Abuelo goes to lie down in Abuela's bed. Alberto says he needs to "do homework," but I can hear Mami's TV from my room, where I sit on the floor and reread my acceptance letter over and over again. *We were most impressed by your essay,* it says, just three sentences in.

I haven't thought about that essay in a long time. I stand up and go over to my desk, rifling through the drawers until I find the last draft and smooth it out. It's wrinkled and marked all over, but still legible. *Who is your biggest inspiration?* I had written at the top. Then:

My brothers and I grew up in a sewing workshop, and the only hero we knew was the woman who could make anything come true.

Other kids grow up loving dolls and car toys and dinosaurs. Thanks to my abuela, my brothers and I knew how to pick the right zipper for a dress before we ever heard a superhero's name. We built towers and cities out of her supplies, stacking the naked cones that once held thread rather than Legos. Our hands were always more likely to be full of glitter and sequins than dirt.

I went on to write about the many times we saw Abuela problem solve someone's wedding dress or quinceañera fit in hours, the joy that every single one of her projects brought to her customers. But, even more than that, how I could never wrap my head around it all—how she managed to do this thing in this country. How she managed to start her own small business and keep it afloat. How she managed to raise six children—three of her own and three of her daughter's—off of it. Not to mention growing the business, hiring other women so they too could provide for their families.

Abuela is my biggest inspiration, I wrote, near the end of the essay. *But, as much as she inspires me, I would trade anything for her to have a day off. Because all the American superheroes that my brothers and I grew to idolize for sure take naps and rest and have lives outside of their masks.*

Not Abuela though. And there's nothing honorable about it. Just heartbreaking.

I hug my essay to my chest, and the memory of Maynor sitting on my bed, reading it, comes to mind. At the time, I had been so preoccupied with Daniela, and with Camila's texts, that I thought nothing of handing it over to him. But now I wonder if it had made him uncomfortable at all to read. It was just a few weeks after his fight with Abuela, and they were still acting weird around each other.

For a moment, I wonder if any of it hurt his feelings. He did smile all the way through reading it, though. And, at the end of the day, he loved our grandmother.

I get that unbearable urge that I do from time to time to ask him about it. To ask him if it bothered him at all to read my essay. To ask if he felt the same way I did when I wrote it, the same way I do now. There's so much I didn't get the chance to ask or tell him about.

There's something I can do, at least, with one person. Something I've been meaning to do all afternoon, since Cami's and my talk. I pull out my phone and text Dani, *I got in.*

FORTY TWO

Daniela responds almost immediately.

> Oh my god that's amazing.

I begin to type out a response, but halfway through decide I'd rather hear her voice instead.

"Hello?"

"Can you talk?" I ask.

"Yes, yes. Congratulations, Libertad!"

"Thank you—it's for the college in the Midwest I was telling you about." Dani cheers, and I grin. It feels so good to hear her voice again after the past few days of silence. "I've missed you," I say to her.

"Me too," Dani replies, her voice going soft. "And I'm sorry. I *was* upset. I should've just admitted it."

"You don't have to be sorry." I start pacing around my room. "I was the one who snapped at you. And, you know, brought up your parents . . . I'm really sorry, Dani."

"Yeah." Dani sighs. "I forgive you. I know you're going through a lot right now." I hear shuffling on her end, as if she's gotten up from wherever she was sitting and started walking around. "Also," she adds, "I still don't have an answer for your question."

"What question?" I ask, my forehead crinkling.

"How to be okay. Like, with what this country has done to me, to you. To all of us. How do we keep living here, building a life here. Making things better as we go."

I take a deep breath, exhaling slowly through my nose. I can hear it echoing across the line, onto Dani's end—wherever she is right now.

"Maybe that's okay," I finally respond. "For now, at least, that neither of us knows. Maybe it's enough, that we're both just . . . trying to figure it out." I move back to my desk then, pulling her gift out of the paper bag she gave me a few days ago: It's a thin gold chain with a tiny letter *M* pendant. And it's perfect.

"I really love the necklace, by the way."

"Oh yeah?" Dani says, and I can hear the smile in her voice.

"Yes—I'm putting it on right now." I drape the necklace over my head, squeezing the little *M* in my fist as I remember one last question I wanted to ask Daniela.

"Hey—so, I had a conversation with Camila today."

"Okay . . ." Dani says slowly.

"Well—um," I start. Suddenly, I'm not as brave as I was a second ago. But I push through anyway. "So . . . Camila and I kissed again, at La Esquina. The day before I saw you. And I guess I was just wondering if that's okay with you? Or—well, I don't know. I don't want to lie by omission or—but I can't figure out what the rules are for this. Not like, you and me specifically but like, the universal *this*, like gay 'this'—"

"Libi, Libi," Dani interrupts me, laughing a little. "Stop. You're going too fast. Take a deep breath."

I do, and then I take another. I nod before remembering that she can't see me. "Okay, yes," I say aloud.

"There aren't any."

"Huh?"

"Rules," Dani responds. "I don't think there are any. I mean, there can be . . . but I think you get to make those up with your people. With the people you love, however you love them. I think that's the whole point of it."

I take in her words. They seem so obvious, so simple—but they're not. They don't just feel like a *given*, somehow.

"For whatever reason," Dani continues, after a beat, "we were born or grew up to live outside of the capital *R*-rules of relationships. I mean, we can't even abide by the main one society tries to force on us—that we meet a boy and fall in love and life happily ever after or some other bullshit." Dani snorts, and I chuckle under my breath.

"So I think that means we get to make up the rest. In whatever way works for us, keeps us safe. We get to be creative and imagine worlds for ourselves, ones that maybe haven't even been imagined before."

I flop down on my bed, a few long, drawn-out seconds going by after she's done talking.

"Shit," I finally say. I feel out of breath, even though I'm lying down now. "That's . . . that's amazing, Dani."

"It is."

"And freeing."

"Yeah."

"Scary."

"Also that," she admits.

I blink once, twice. "Thank you," I say.

"You don't have to thank me," Daniela replies. "Someone else told me the same thing a few years ago. I have a feeling you'll tell someone else someday, and on and on."

Outside, the world has grown dark; the crickets just beyond my window chirp a steady note. I think of Camila—maybe I'll be the one to tell her this. Or maybe it'll be Dani. Maybe someone else in a few years in another phone call will, and maybe I won't be the last person she would have kissed by then.

I think of all the people who have said a version of this to each other. Who, in doing so, have drawn themselves a door to a new world they didn't even know was possible. For the first time in my life, I feel happy—ecstatic, even—to be a girl who likes girls.

"Do you ever wonder what it could be like, if you left Honduras?" I ask Dani.

"Sometimes," she admits. "But I think it's important to remember that just because things are better in some countries, it doesn't mean they're all okay. For people like us, I mean. And I don't say that to discourage you or anything. I am so, *so* happy for you."

"Right," I say. "No, I know. I know."

And it's true—I remind myself of different international news I've caught glimpses of through the years. The shooting at the gay club in Orlando not too long ago. On Latin night, no less.

I breathe into the phone. "God, Dani. There's a lot of hate out there."

"Yes," she says in a gentle voice. "But there's also a lot of love, and resistance, and community. More good than bad."

"How do you know that?"

"Because," she says, "people like you and I meet in a country like ours against all odds. And we find ways to take care of each other. Because there's people like your brother. Because I think it is our duty to believe that."

I let her words sit with me. It is our duty to believe that. Maynor would agree.

Daniela and I stay on the phone until I hear Mami and Abuela come home. Until the sky turns dark, and the phone feels hot against my cheek. Before we hang up, I make sure to tell Dani that I love her, that I'm so grateful for her.

"Me too," Dani says, and I feel like myself.

As soon as we hang up, I sprint to the kitchen. Most days the past few weeks, I've stayed in my room until I heard Abuela lock herself in her room, then grab whatever leftovers were in the fridge. But tonight, for the first time in a while, I want to be there, with everyone. With my family.

"Tell them," Abuelo says, the moment he spots me rushing in. "Or Alberto will in about five seconds."

"No I won't!" Alberto covers his mouth with his hands, and I laugh.

"Okay, okay," I announce, looking toward Mami and Abuela. "I um, I got in. To a college in the US."

Mami yelps, and Abuela's mouth drops open. Then they're both cheering, running over to kiss my cheeks, to congratulate me. Sending up small prayers of thanks to God.

"What should we have for dinner to celebrate?" Abuela asks the room. She moves to the fridge to see what we have already, going back and forth with Abuelo until they finally settle on baleadas.

Mami stays by my side, hugging me over and over again. "Mi bebé," she whispers in my ear. "You're so grown. I just can't believe it."

"I know, Mami. I know," I whisper back, holding on to her as tightly as I can.

After a few minutes, when things start to settle down again, Alberto and I set the table. He goes for plates, and I go for the cups and silverware. Abuelo sets a three-liter Coca-Cola bottle he bought for us on the table, and Mami starts telling us about all the quinceañeras and weddings she's got coming up in the next few weeks.

"Abuela," I say, once we're all sitting and eating. "It's almost Semana Santa—are you making swimsuits already?"

"Oh yes," she declares. "We're making extra this year, so we have some on hand for people to buy, not just order."

"Wow—that's a great idea," I reply, impressed as I always am by my abuela's business savvy. "You picked out all the fabrics already?"

"No, not all of them. I'm still choosing some."

"Cool." I clear my throat. "Um, maybe I can come with you? Whenever you go to get more, I mean. I haven't been to the workshop in some time."

"Of course, hija." She squeezes my hand in hers, shakes it a little. Her face lights up like I haven't seen it do in a long, long time.

"So," Mami cuts in suddenly, setting down her fork. "I also have some news, now that everyone's here."

All of us turn to look at her, eyebrows raised. Mami's cheeks flush pink then, tiny drops of nervous sweat beading along her hairline.

"¿Ajá?" Abuelo asks, motioning for her to continue.

"Okay, well, Libertad actually already knows. But the rest of you don't." She takes a deep breath. "A few months ago, I met a man at the hotel. He's the head chef there—his name is Walter."

"Bien," Abuelo says, nodding. "And how long has he been at the hotel?"

"May of last year. We . . . we started seeing each other in October."

Silence descends over us, and I tense up. I have no idea how my grandparents feel about my mom's dating life, I realize—especially Abuela. This could go really poorly really fast.

"Well," Abuela says at last, taking a sip of her Coke. "If he's a chef . . . then you have to bring him over to cook for us some day."

Mami smiles, her shoulders sagging in relief. I catch her eye and grin.

Alberto has a million questions about Walter, and Mami tries to answer as many as she can. He seems just as happy for her as Abuela and Abuelo, which is a relief. Conversation erupts all over again as my family laughs and eats and sips our Cokes. We stay seated at the table together long after our food is gone, long after my brother has wiped la mantequilla from his plate and licked all his fingers.

By the time I climb into bed that night, I feel a way I haven't felt in months: normal. Or, at least, almost normal. I just sat with my family for an extended period of time and smiled and laughed and felt *lucky*.

Which doesn't make me miss Maynor any less, of course. If anything, it only sharpens the pang of sadness that washes through me.

I reach for my phone, opening my Instagram poetry account and going to Maynor's profile. His last post was on the night of the elections, a reshare of "Por fin hemos salido de Honduras" with the caption *lo logramos. We did it.* He must've posted it after the news reported JOH was losing.

My eyes sting. I swipe back to my account's inbox. By now over six hundred people have messaged me. I brace myself, scroll alllll the way down to the first message, open it, and begin to read.

Most of the messages are beautiful, supportive. People from different parts of Honduras telling me who the poems reminded them of, family members or friends or lovers who had to leave to survive. They tell me how angry they are, how ready for a different life. With each one I read, I feel a mix of sorrow and hope.

For some reason, I find myself thinking about Hilda Hernández. I guess, more accurately, I find myself thinking about the president. Once, me and him had nothing in common. Now, we both have a dead sibling. I wonder what his grief looks like. He is the most powerful man in Honduras, but that couldn't keep his sister safe. Accidents happen. There is no respect in my heart for this government, for this man, but I know one thing: I don't wish this pain on anyone. No one should know what this feels like. And he is responsible, directly, or not, for so many people feeling it. This makes me think of someone else with a dead sibling: my uncle. Tío José.

Grief is an impossible thing to make sense of. Some days, I am nothing but anger and blame. Unreasonable and detached. Full of *what ifs.* But today I know the day will come when I might have to allow all the narratives—mine, José's, Abuela's, Mami's—to exist alongside each other. Today isn't that day, though.

I get through twenty more messages before I have to stop. Not out of exhaustion, but because I feel *it* in my stomach. The urge to pick up my journal and pen.

I haven't felt the urge to write since Maynor's murder. But when it hits me, I recognize it immediately. I turn quickly through the pages of my journal, past those filled with my and my brother's words, until I find the next blank page.

I close my eyes and think of Maynor's voice, his face. I can both hear him and see him so clearly. I go back to the night in Alicia's house, when we ran into each other getting water just before la madrugada.

I love simple things. Fútbol. Alicia. My family. Your poems. And anything that makes it easy to believe things will get better for us.

I begin writing a new poem about my brother, and end up with a few lines:

No se le llama muerto,
a quien muere por la libertad.
En su sueño encuentran la eternidad.
Y mientras tu sueño siga vigente,
aquí vas a estar presente.
Tu nombre está en cada protesta,
en cada grito aclamando justicia.
Ninguna fuerza militar te contrarresta.[5]

397

FORTY THREE

Mid-March, the city is a blanket of black smoke over us. We keep praying for rain, something to disperse the smog. But behind the gray, our sun beats on, an oil stain in the sky. Wildfires erupt in the outskirts of Tegucigalpa every other day: some from the accumulation of glass bottles disposed of carelessly in the now fossil-dry hills of grass, most from farmers' controlled burns that get out of control. Airplanes set to land at the Toncontín airport get rerouted to San Pedro Sula and Comayagua. The heat is thick, oppressive; our skin turned saran wrap.

"I can't take it anymore," Alberto complains, for the fifth time in the past hour. "Can't we do this another day?"

"You said that yesterday," I say. "It's not gonna be any less hot, Beto."

He pouts, a real all-lip-out cartoon pout.

"Come on." I wipe the beads of sweat off his upper lip. "Aren't you a little excited to have your own room?"

He shrugs.

After four months, Mami and Abuela have decided it is time to turn Maynor's room into Alberto's room. It makes sense: We can't keep an empty room forever while Alberto sleeps with Mami. His clothes strewn all over the house—some in the hallway closet, some in the laundry room—and his notebooks stacked on different surfaces. Besides, Alberto was always meant to room with Maynor, he just kept choosing to sleep with our mom. Mami even lets him take the TV.

"If you're real smart about it, I bet you could even watch TV all night now."

This gets him, sort of. "Fine," he sighs.

It's Saturday. We're the only ones in the house. This task was commended upon us more than a few days ago, but every day we've found a way to postpone it. I know that if we don't get it done soon, Mami will have to take it upon herself, which I suspect is precisely what she has been avoiding. And I get it. Even with all windows open, the room is impregnated with his smell: a mixture of musk and after-shave and *boy*. How long can a space hold a memory? It's like the air particles didn't get the memo.

We start simple: emptying out the closet. I fill a jumbo-size garbage bag with his clothes—underwear, socks (most of which have a tiny rip where his big toenail would go), basketball shorts. Alberto asks to keep nearly every soccer jersey, despite the fact it'll be more than a few years before they fit him.

"Do you think I'll be as tall as Maynor?" he asks, holding a white Real Madrid shirt over his body.

"Probably," I say. "Maybe even taller if you stop drinking so much Coke."

"That's a myth," he counters. "Maynor told me that."

"He was always just saying things," I say, bagging two pairs of jeans.

"What if I get scared at night?" he mumbles. He doesn't look at me. His fingers fidget with the embroidered emblem on the shirt.

"Why would you get scared?" I say. "Do you mean like—ghosts?"

"I don't know," he sighs. "Maybe."

"You think Maynor's ghost would come mess with you?"

"Not Maynor. Maybe. I don't know. Just like, scary sounds."

"The only scary sound you'll have to worry about is Abuela's snores," I say. "No such thing as ghosts, Beto."

He stays quiet for a minute, throwing more shirts in his to-keep pile. I roll Maynor's one belt up and throw it in the to-give-away bag.

Looking around, I am struck by how little Maynor owned. There are a few textbooks piled on the floor, his gym bag with goal-keeper gloves and socks in a corner, one pair of dress shoes and three pairs of sneakers lined by the wall opposite to the door, two nearly flat soccer balls, three empty cologne bottles. The bulk of it is his clothes, and whatever's in the drawer of his bedside table. I already suspect some of it: weed paraphernalia. Which is part of why I knew that, as much as it sucks, better I did this than Mami or Abuela. I want to get to it without Alberto noticing—older sister and whatnot, but I'm not ready to answer any of his questions about that.

"I'm hungry," Alberto says. He sits on the bed, crosses his arms.

The bed is bare. Abuela stripped the sheets a few days after the funeral, washed them, and put them away without a word. I know she also mops in here every day. The room feels like a dead person's room, but not abandoned.

"What do you want to eat?" I feel more nauseous than anything.

"Plantain chips and Coca-Cola," Alberto says, not missing a beat. Maynor's bed is tall, so Alberto's legs dangle over, not quite reaching the floor.

"I think you finished those last night, man."

"But it's the only thing I want."

I sigh. I have a feeling that more than anything, he just wants a reason to stop doing our task. But we did skip breakfast.

"I can go get some at la pulpería," I offer. At that, he beams.

"Okay." He jumps off the bed. "I have money."

"How?"

"I sold some of my World Cup album stickers," he says, a clear pride in his voice. "Some repeats. Leo Messi alone went for thirty Lempiras."

"All right," I say, stretching, looking at our progress so far, which isn't much. "Hand it over you big hustler."

La pulpería is a five-minute walk, on the corner of our street. Alberto stays in Mami's bedroom, turns the TV on before I'm out the door. The sun hits me straight on; it's half past noon. Our street is not a busy one—we've been neighbors with the same people for years, and everyone knows everyone. I take in the familiarity of it all: the ugly old white dog who barks at everyone that walks by, the old Luis Miguel hits blasting from Doña Sandra's house, the light blue, boxy Toyota Corolla that's been parked in front of the Pineda's home over eight years that no one will try to get fixed.

I get this feeling in my chest—a preemptive missing, a deep longing to be here even though it's where I am. I haven't accepted my university offer yet. It's weird. Before it came, I couldn't wait to sign, to be set, to have a departure date. But once it was a real thing in front of me—something changed. It didn't feel as straightforward as that. I know that this would be a much easier choice to make if Maynor was here. He would know exactly what to say to help me decide, make that leap: one way or another.

And it must be that my longing is particularly strong today, because when I look up from my feet as I get to la pulpería, there he is. Maynor.

FORTY FOUR

He's turned away from me, facing the young woman who works the corner store for her mom on the weekends. But it's him. Black curly hair, white Olimpia jersey with blue neckline, skinny lanky arms. The way he holds his body is unmistakable: a half slouch, like his body grew faster than he could keep up with. Like he is trying to hold himself in.

So much for no such thing as ghosts.

I stop. For a second, I am weightless. No arms, no legs, no body. My vision gets blurry. I think I'm going to lose consciousness.

But then Maynor speaks. "Y me da también unos cigarros. Mentosos."

And his voice is not his voice at all.

Maynor looks over his shoulder then, and I see it. His nose is too small. His eyebrows not thick enough. There's no beard, but there is a mustache. It's all wrong. He's not my brother.

I take a deep breath. Try to regain my balance, blink away the spots in my vision. Despite the heat, the hairs on my arms stand tall.

The girl hands the man his change, and he walks off with his cigarettes and a lottery ticket, nodding as he walks past me.

"¿Qué va llevar?" the woman calls at me, and then I think she must see the terror in my face, because she gasps. But before I can say anything, she composes herself. In a softer voice, "You're Maynor's sister, ¿verdad?"

I nod, walk up closer to the front window. "Yes," I hear myself say. "Maynor was my brother."

"Son igualitos," she says. The corners of her mouth lift, but her eyes remain downcast. "Strong genes, los de su mamá."

I nod again, attempt my own smile I imagine looks more like a fissure.

"I'm so sorry," she goes on. "We—my family—we've been praying for all of you."

"Thank you," I say, because it seems like the right thing to say.

"Nosotros queríamos muchísimo a Maynor," she says, "He was such a good man. Un buen muchacho."

"He was," I echo. I don't know what else to add or how to pivot the conversation. Which happens to me now, a lot. There's hardly anywhere to go after *I'm so sorry* and *we're praying for you*. I try to ground myself—remember that I'm here for plantain chips and Coke. That this can be over in two minutes. But as I'm about to speak, she says, "A bag of spicy plantain chips and a three-liter Coca-Cola?"

"Yes." I nod, avoiding eye contact. "That's right."

"His usual." She turns to grab the soda bottle from the fridge behind her.

I pull the money Alberto gave me from my shorts pocket, set it down on the wooden window lip.

"Don't worry about it," she says, pushing the money back toward me. "I remember the last time Maynor was here like it was yesterday. He read us a poem. Twice. Made sure we knew where our voting center was. He was always checking in on us, asking if any mareros were causing trouble."

"That's just like him," I say, smiling authentically now. "What was he gonna do about it?"

"God knows," the girl laughs. She grabs a bag of Caribas plantain chips from the shelf next to her.

This, I love. Learning new things about Maynor. The different ways people knew him.

"He had a bit of a Superman complex," I add. "Man of the house and all."

She smiles, shaking her head. "Tell me about it. He got in so much trouble with my mom a few years ago with that running tab he opened for the other boys in the neighborhood."

I tilt my head. I don't know what she's talking about.

"He didn't tell you?"

"No, I don't think so. What happened?"

"I think he was still in school. It was right after you all moved in with Doña Mayra. He asked my mom to keep a running tab for him, told a few of the boys he would play fútbol with to get churros y frescos on him if they needed to. Within days, the tab was up to over a thousand Lempiras. You know como es la gente de aprovechada."

I laugh. 'Cause that's just the kind of thing that would happen to Maynor. It reminds me of a different story I've heard, from when he was ten or so and a neighbor tricked him into trading his bike for four firecrackers.

"Your aunt had to help him pay for it, in secret of course. He was scared your grandmother would find out y que lo regañara. After that, my mom told him no more. But Maynor *still* wanted to keep it open, just with a cap. He was all, 'Mire doña Dolores, solo el—"

"Pueblo salva al pueblo," I cut in.

"Yes." She nods, laughing.

"Yeah, that sounds like him." I grab the Coke and Caribas she's bagged up for me. "Gracias," I say, "for this and for the story and for your family's prayers for my family." I add, because it feels important that she knows I mean it.

"Dios los bendiga," she says.

Back home, after Alberto and I have finished the bag of plantain chips and the light in the sky has begun to shift to late afternoon, I am alone in Maynor's room. Alberto, for the first time in his short life, announced he desperately needed to shower. He promises to be quick and come back to help finish setting his new room up, but I don't hold my breath.

The closet is done. It's all Alberto's clothes inside now. We've put on fresh bedsheets and aired the room out. Maynor's old textbooks and balls and soccer gear sit in a box by the door.

I open his bedside table drawer. There's a cloud of old receipts. Underneath those: a Spider-Man Pez with no candy left inside, a half-empty bottle of hair gel, two dirty iPhone chargers. Tucked on a corner, though, there's a little black metal box. I pull it out and shake it—there's a clang of metal inside. The box is locked. The keyhole is small.

From my room, I fetch the leather keychain Mami gave me a few weeks ago. I know the right key immediately; it's small, with a black plastic grip. The box opens easily.

Inside, I find what I expected to: A small metal grinder, two lighters, some rolling paper. But there's more: a passport-size photo of Alicia, which looks like it was taken a few years ago—her hair is long, and she has braces—and a regular size photo of my parents with a much younger Maynor.

My dad, standing on Maynor's left side, wears a suit and blue tie. My mom, in a cream-color dress, stands on the right. They both hold Maynor's hand. Maynor, no older than five or six, wears a graduation gown and cap.

I flip the photo. Scribbled on the back in Maynor's loopy handwriting are the fading words *Kinder Graduation*.

I take the safe with all its contents to my room and lie in bed. I can hear the running water from the shower. We still have to move the TV. But the weight of the day falls on me, and all the zest I've put into Alberto and the room has left me drained. I check my phone: notifications from Daniela, Cami, Mami, and Valeria. I click the screen back off.

I hold the cold metal box to my chest and close my eyes. I'm sweaty in places I didn't know you could sweat. A few months ago, we were praying for the rain to stop. Now we pray for its return.

Tegucigalpa is a city of excess. I used to have two brothers. Now I have one.

Tegucigalpa is a city of loss. There is a man out in the world who, four months ago, shot my brother dead. There is another man out in the world who helped create my brother. Who taught him how to kick a ball and drive a car. Who said to him, *En Tegucigalpa, es la ley del más fuerte.* The law of the strongest.

But my father was wrong. And I think, now, that my brother knew that. Maynor wasn't tough, not in the way our father wanted him to be, anyways. He was quite the opposite; a soft, sentimental boy. Gentle and trusting to a fault. He believed that taking care of neighbors was the way to live where you are, which is here. Which has always been here.

He was also lazy. He let weeks pass him by, smoking weed and laying around. Neglecting schoolwork and following up with job searches.

He was a boyfriend and a son. He was a little clueless at times, but never on the soccer field.

He was an older brother. The best one, at that.

FORTY FIVE

It takes two more weekends for Daniela, Camila, and I to coor-dinate and finish the mural. One of Dani's friends lends her a ladder tall enough to reach the blank space she secured, and we get it to the university by borrowing someone's cousin's truck. Then Dani, Cami, and I all go together to Larach and buy the paint we need.

I feel a little awkward, at first, spending time like this with the two girls that I've kissed and love. The two girls that, if I'm completely honest with myself, I'm a little in love with. But the awkwardness passes as I throw myself into the process of creating the mural with two of my favorite people in the world. We work at it for hours, the three of us, taking constant breaks to stand in the shade, out of the unforgiving late March sun.

"I just want it to be perfect," Cami says over and over again, erasing her own pencil lines and redoing them as Daniela and I take turns painting the parts she's already sketched out. And in the end, it is perfect. I can tell that it's Maynor easily: His curly black hair and itchy stubble. His long, thick eyelashes and perpetually half-parted lips. His inquisitive, soft eyes.

Maynor José Morazán, I paint in black, just under his neck. Then I climb down from the ladder, moving to stand between Camila and Dani. The three of us shield our eyes against the slowly setting sun, staring up in awe at our handiwork.

"I hate to say it," I cut into the hush between us, "but seeing this mural . . . I have one more favor to ask the both of you."

"Yes?" Dani and Cami ask at the same time, turning toward me.

"It'll only take, like, half an hour," I tell Abuela a few days later. "Then you can get back to work, I promise."

"Sí, hija," Abuela replies. "It's just that swimsuit season is the craziest time of the year for us."

"I know, I know," I reassure her, reaching across Abuelo and Alberto to pat her hand—the four of us are squished into the back seat of Mami's car. Just then, Mami pulls into the same parking lot Alicia did when I first came here, which is lucky. I remember the way to the murals perfectly from here.

"Thank you for letting me tag along," Walter tells me again as we all climb out of the car. He came over earlier so Mami could introduce him to all of us, and I invited him along on our trip to la UNAH. So far, I like him. It's obvious from the way he looks at Mami and moves around us that he's a little nervous, that he wants to make a good impression. It's nice, to see a man moving around my mother with caution, and not the other way around.

At the walls, I spot Daniela and Camila standing close to one another, arms nearly touching. Alicia's there too, looking better than she did in January. She's gained some weight back and moves with more easiness than before as she chats with Cami and Dani. The three of them turn around when they hear Alberto shout hello, sprinting toward them.

"Is this where you're bringing us?" Mami asks.

"Qué calor hace aquí," Abuela adds, fanning herself.

"Yes, I know," I say. "It'll be quick."

Camila greets my family. My grandma looks excited to see her, leaning forward to kiss her cheek. Alberto hugs Dani. I see my mom looking confused at that, but if she thinks it's odd he knows her, she doesn't say so.

"This is Daniela," I tell Mami. "She's the friend I've mentioned from la UNAH. She came over with Cami once too, right before school started."

"Un placer," Mami says, smiling, and my grandparents do as well.

"Mucho gusto," Dani replies.

I thought I'd be more nervous to introduce Dani to everyone, but it feels good. Mami squeezes Alicia's shoulder, and we all move to stand in front of the wall.

"¿Entonces?" Abuelo says to me.

I take a deep breath. "Okay," I start, walking a few steps forward and turning around to face everyone. "So—a few months before Maynor died, he brought me here, to these walls. He called this place el muro de los desaparecidos." I swallow, brushing a few sweaty strands of hair off my forehead.

"The faces you see here are people—mostly students and activists—that either went missing or were killed outright, and there was

411

never anything really done about it. Some are from a while ago, like over forty years ago. Some are from the coup . . . And some are from this year."

I move my eyes from person to person as I speak, down the line of my family. Each of them stare back at me, their faces as impassive as the walls around us. I shift in place, wiping my palms on the pockets of my pants.

I'm nervous of saying something that upsets someone, especially Abuela. I'm nervous this is actually a horrible idea that will only hurt them more. I know so little, really, about their process in this grief; we might be in completely different places. But now that I've started, I have to do this—I have to keep going.

"Maynor loved it here. He, um, wished it didn't exist, of course. But he loved that it's a place where we get to remember and honor the people we lost. That the people who were trying to make our lives better won't be forgotten."

I lock eyes with Mami, who's holding Walter's hand. She nods at me. I take it as a confirmation. A *Yes, that's exactly who my son was.*

"So my friends," I say, gesturing to Dani and Cami. "They helped me do this. Cami drew everything and Dani coordinated it, made it all possible. And then the three of us painted it, the portrait."

Finally, I point at Maynor's face. A spike of worry lashes through me, suddenly, as I do. What if they don't even recognize it as Maynor?

"Do you see it?" I ask as my family's eyes dart around, trying to pick out where I'm pointing.

Alberto is the first to spot him. "There!" he shouts. "Next to the guy with the mustache!"

412

Abuela and Mami gasp at the same time. Abuelo takes Abuela's hand.

"I know," I say, quieter this time, "that we would do anything for him to be here with us and not on this wall. That no one's brother or son or friend should be here. . . . But knowing that his face and his name won't just disappear means something. To me, at least."

Abuelo pulls Abuela gently, tugging her closer to the wall so they can get a better look. Abuela raises a hand to cover her mouth.

"Abuela," I say, stepping toward them. "What do you think?"

She doesn't take her eyes off my brother's face. "It's beautiful," she whispers, tearing up. "Looks just like him."

"You don't hate it? The idea of it all?"

"No," she says, shaking her head. "The opposite."

I exhale in relief. "Okay. Okay, good—because I actually have one more face to show you."

My grandparents turn to look at me, confusion in their eyes.

"There," I say, pointing a few feet to the left of Maynor.

And there it is, painted in black ink just under the face of their daughter: Martha Judith Morazán.

"I borrowed the photo of her that we have with all the family pictures, and . . . well, I figured it'd be nice if they were together. Dani got as close a spot as she could to Maynor, and Cami drew her face too, after we were done with Maynor's. I think . . . well, I'd like to think that Tía Martha and Maynor would have liked this. Being commemorated in this way, so close to each other."

Abuela nods, tears streaming down her face now. Abuelo wraps an arm around her. She keeps trying to say something but can't get words to out. I hug her.

"I know," I say. "I know—it's okay, Abuela. I love you."

She shakes and cries. My eyes begin to water too.

"Thank you, hija," Abuelo says for her.

There is a lot I don't know. A lot I don't know if I'll ever get to know, of my own family history even. I don't know if my aunt was queer, if my grandparents would know and tell me about it. I don't know where we go from here—how we heal, how we keep this from happening ever again, to anyone. But I know the first step is to care for each other, like my brother did. What's more revolutionary than that?

Mami walks over and hugs me hard. Alberto joins in, all of us holding each other for a few long seconds. Then Mami lets go, reaching out for Alicia's hand.

"That's our boy," she says to her, pointing her chin toward Maynor. Alicia nods and squeezes Mami's hand, tears pooling in her eyes too.

"Thank you, niñas," Abuela says to Daniela and Camila. "For doing this. I don't know what—" Her voice is lost on a sob, and Dani and Cami nod. Mami takes over, hugging them each in turn. I feel like my heart could burst.

"It was our pleasure," Cami says softly.

We all stay there for a few more minutes, just looking at Maynor and Martha and hugging and crying. The heat is unbearable, but I don't want the moment to end yet.

Dani touches my shoulder. "We'll go get everyone some water," she says, Cami and Alicia by her side. I nod, and the three of them turn back toward the social sciences building.

Abuela and Abuelo make their way around the whole courtyard. I overhear them pointing at faces, at people they recognize. I overhear them say *remember when* over and over and argue over the timeline and details of certain cases. Each of their memories like a wave, the clash against one another inevitable.

I'm struck, as I listen to them talk, by just how much my grandparents have seen. How many different governments and coups and struggles. Abuelo recounts the 1988 protests that ended in the burning of the American embassy, and then the two of them fall silent. I step closer, seizing the moment to ask them a question that's been bothering me for some time now.

"So, it's always been like this here, right? There's always been—I don't know . . . Revolution. Struggle."

Abuelo nods. "Algunos tiempos más que otros," he says.

"But Tía Martha and Maynor both thought there was a way to reach some sort of peace," I press. "If they protested, spoke up about it."

Abuelo shrugs a shoulder. Abuela stares up at the wall again, at the faces of her lost children. Without taking her eyes off them, she says, "No tenemos otra opción. If we stop believing that, we won't survive."

I nod, knowing deep in my bones that she's right.

The girls come back with cold bottles of water then, passing them around. As people hold the bottles against their foreheads and necks, cracking them open and take some gulps, Abuela and I find ourselves on the outside of the group, a few feet away from everyone.

I watch as Abuelo gestures to a face on the bottom-right corner of the nearest wall with his water bottle, and Alicia and Alberto

415

move closer him to hear what he has to say. I watch as Mami rests her head on Walter's shoulder. I watch Cami and Dani sitting on a bench, glancing every so often in my direction and smiling big at one another as they take sips of their water and talk. I overhear Dani tell Camila she just got everything sorted to finally start her own radio show, which she mentioned to me a couple nights ago.

"I'm so scared of losing this," I murmur to Abuela. "You know. If I leave." My stomach swoops like it does nearly every day now at the thought.

"I just . . . I wish I could always feel this much love around me," I continue. "Wherever I go."

"You won't lose this, Libertad. No matter what you decide. This is your home," Abuela says gently. She takes a deep breath. "Look at your mother. There's someone for everyone. And sometimes, it's more complicated than that. From the looks of it . . . you have a lot of love in your life."

Wait. Is she saying . . . ?

"Yeah," I reply slowly, testing the waters. "I have good friends."

Abuela reaches for my hand. "Yes," she replies. "Good friends are important. But it's also good to have people to share our life with in other ways. Different, closer ways."

I follow her eyes to where Dani and Camila sit. Daniela says something that makes Cami giggle, and Cami swats playfully at her knee.

"It looks like you have some very good people to share yourself with, maybe, in those ways. Both of those girls are buena gente."

Though the air feels thin in my lungs, my heart is like an ocean—vast and impossible. I understand. I understand what Abuela's trying to tell me. And it's so surprising but maybe it shouldn't be, since I've never asked Abuela outright what she thinks about queerness, about my queerness. I always just assumed.

There are so many other questions I want to ask her, too many for me to even pick one to start with. My mind races through them faster than I can even process, when Alberto comes bounding over to us.

"Can we go get food now?" he asks. "I'm starving!"

"Yes, let's go eat," Abuelo says from behind him, clapping his palms together. And he's right, I know. He looks sweaty—everyone does. It's time to pack it up and find a place to eat. Tegucigalpa is hot and waiting.

"Actually," I say, taking my phone out of my pocket. "I have one more thing—just one." I placate Beto, who looks like he's about to groan. "I wrote a poem about Maynor a few days ago and copied it into my phone. Would you all like to hear it?"

"Sí, hija. Read your poem," Abuela says, squeezing my shoulder, and I smile at her.

Everyone moves to stand around me, and I drink them in for just one more second. I take in Alberto, who's just begun to shed his baby fat, the soft lines around his cheeks and chin growing sharper—a glint of Maynor's nose in the middle. I take in Mami's wide, expectant eyes and her hair just starting to grey around the temples. I take in my grandparents and Walter and Cami and Dani and Alicia, their hands and faces all in different stages of creasing and tanning and wrinkling under the bright, hot sun. And then I see the faces behind their faces, on the walls. A thousand eyes and ears all around us, waiting.

"Okay," I say, pulling out my phone. "Here goes."

NOTES

1 Do you feel independent?
    Then history is lying to you.

2 Legend has it that when stepping on Honduran soil for the first time,
    Columbus exclaimed to whoever heard,
    "Thank God we have left those deep waves!"

3 "Legend has it
    that when stepping on Honduran land
    for the first time
    Christopher Columbus told anyone who heard him:
    'We have finally escaped those deep waves.'

    "Columbus, of course, meant
    the sea waves from which he came.
    Columbus, of course, was referring to
    the waves crashing against the Santa María.

    "What Columbus didn't know—
    what Columbus, of course, could not imagine
    is that 500 years later,
    his words would be repeated:

    "'We have finally left Honduras.
    We have finally left Honduras,'
    is what my people say
    when they take their children's hands
    and say goodbye to their roots.

"'We have finally left Honduras,'
is what I imagine they say
when they cross themselves
to start a journey of 5,000 kilometers
and ten thousand scars."

4 "'We have finally left Honduras,'
is what my people sing
from the throat,
even with a broken soul
and the raised skin of their feet."

5 Can't call dead,
he who has died for freedom.
In their dream they find eternity.
And as long as your dream continues,
here you will be present.
Your name is in every protest,
in each cry acclaiming justice.
No military force counters you.

Dear Reader,

The hardest part of being the author of *Libertad* are the things I can't tell Libertad herself. Libertad lives in Honduras in 2018. Bessie Flores Zaldívar lives in the United States in 2024. And you, dear reader, are here. Wherever here is. Neither with me nor with her, but also, somehow with both of us. So I ask you to hold with me the things I can't tell Libertad, both the heartbreak and joy of what she doesn't yet get to know.

In Libertad's world, Honduras is under a right-wing government. Honduras has been under a right-wing government since the coup of 2009, which happened when I was twelve years old. Juan Orlando Hernández is the president, through unconstitutional and anti-democratic means that resulted in death and destruction. The idea that the right-wing reign over the country will ever end seems impossible. This is true by the end of Libertad's story. This was also true when I began writing her story in 2019.

But by the time I finished writing the first draft of this novel, in February of 2022, everything about the world Libertad knew had changed. Juan Orlando Hernández was not president anymore. In fact, on February 15 of 2022 (a week before I wrote "THE END" on that first draft) he was captured by US government forces outside his home in Tegucigalpa, put on a plane, and taken to a prison in New York. On March 8, 2024, he was convicted of charges related to drug trafficking.

Months before his capture, in November of 2021, Honduras elected its first woman president, Xiomara Castro, from the left-leaning party Libre. She is the wife of our former president, Manuel Zelaya, who was removed from power in the 2009 coup. The 2021 election was historic for many reasons. The right-wing regime, which I had known for over half of my life—as had Libertad—came to an end. And this was only possible due to the participation of an overwhelming number of young voters that we had never seen before.

Xiomara Castro was democratically elected by the people. The day the results of the election were announced I received countless messages from friends and family saying a variation of *We did it. We won.*

There's a line I use too much—it's not in *Libertad*, but it is in some of my poems and essays. "Tegucigalpa is a crumpled hand-kerchief": I first heard this from my grandmother. She says it when she's telling me a story, about a person who knows a person we know who is maybe, somehow, the cousin of another person who is also a cousin of ours. She usually accompanies this phrase with a hand gesture, bringing all her fingers together, making them kiss.

My grandmother, like Libertad's, is a seamstress who runs her own sewing workshop in Tegus. She has for over forty years. So when I tell you that she knows everything there is to know about Tegucigalpa and handkerchiefs, I mean it.

When my grandmother tells me that Tegucigalpa is like a crumpled handkerchief, I take it to mean that every corner of the city touches, like her fingers. That history, and the things people do within it, is a loop.

Honduras is like a crumpled handkerchief, every corner of its history touching another piece of history. This makes me feel not too far away from Libertad, walking somewhere in Tegucigalpa in 2018, with so much resolve and grief in her heart that things will never change. But also with so much hope, knowing, as I know, that we can't ever stop trying to take care of our people, demanding better from those in power.

The democratic election of a leftist government in Honduras is also not the end of the story. Sometimes, I imagine telling Libertad everything that will happen. Telling her about Juan Orlando's capture and the elections in 2021. Because I know her, I know she would ask me, "So, are things better? Did we win?"

Dear reader, here's where I have to break the news to her—and you—that I don't think I'm the right person to answer this question anymore. I live in the United States. I have for seven years now. I'm openly queer. I write and teach for a living. And while I do return to Tegus for months at a time, I always get to leave. My family does live in Tegus, as do many of my friends. When I ask them if things are better, they all have wildly different, complicated answers.

What I can tell Libertad is this: Our government was democratically elected. This is no small thing. But many of the people in power are still abusing that power. And, as a queer person, you still can't be openly queer and completely safe in Honduras, not really.

The world beyond Honduras is at war. Horrible things are happening to large swaths of people as a direct result of the greed of western powers. And, also, the people who want better for all of us are still fighting for all of us. There is justice in the world, these people believe, as I do, and we must never cease to demand it.

I suspect that Libertad might find this answer winding, unsatisfying. I know I do. But what Libertad, both the character and the novel, has taught me is this: Our queerness allows us to imagine care and justice beyond the ideals of a ruling political party. We are not free until all of us, everywhere, are free.

With gratitude,

Bessie

ACKNOWLEDGMENTS

A mi mamá y a mi papá, gracias por prometerme que soy la hija favorita de Dios. A mi abuela Tesla y mi abuelo César, gracias por luchar por darme el mundo. A Emo, gracias por ser mi compañero de vida, mi primera memoria. A mi Fer, mi princesa, la alegría de la casa, gracias por llamarme hasta que te contesto. Y a mi Santi, gracias por ser el regalo mas grande. Gracias, familia.

Thank you to my editor, Rosie Ahmed, for believing in this novel, for noticing, for asking all the questions, for your gentleness and passion. *Libertad* and I are lucky to have you. I wouldn't have it any other way. And to my agent, Beth Phelan, for believing in me and being so good at what you do. What a gift to have you in my corner.

Thank you to my teachers: Lucinda Roy, who read the earliest version of this novel and nurtured it, and Matthew Vollmer, for every Waffle House breakfast in which you let me tell you my newest writing idea. I wouldn't be the writer or teacher I am today without you.

Thank you to the friends who saw me grow up and become the person I needed to be to write this book: Andrea Aranda, Lia, Aura, Natz. This book is yours. You are my sisters.

Thank you to the friends who found me in this country. Honora and Shaina, for the love and care. Kapreece and Andy, for every ride and game of darts. Devan, for your vision and support. And Acie, for the conversations that live in me.

Thank you to Theo. For every recipe you perfected for me, for Fig, for your commitment to my growth.

Thank you to my queer community—here, and there, and everywhere.